The Confessions of Frannie Langton

ABOUT THE AUTHOR

Sara Collins studied law at the London School of Economics and worked as a lawyer for seventeen years. In 2014 she embarked upon the Creative Writing Masters at Cambridge University, where she won the 2015 Michael Holroyd Prize for Recreative Writing and was shortlisted for the 2016 Lucy Cavendish Prize for a book inspired by her love of gothic fiction. This turned into her first novel, *The Confessions of Frannie Langton*.

The Confessions of Frannie Langton

SARA COLLINS

VIKING
an imprint of
PENGUIN BOOKS

VIKING

UK | USA | Canada | Ireland | Australia
India | New Zealand | South Africa

Viking is part of the Penguin Random House group of companies
whose addresses can be found at global.penguinrandomhouse.com.

Penguin
Random House
UK

First published 2019
001

Copyright © Sara Collins, 2019

The moral right of the author has been asserted

Every effort has been made to trace copyright holders and to obtain their
permission for the use of copyrighted material. The publisher apologizes for any
errors or omissions and would be grateful to be notified of any corrections
that should be incorporated in future editions of this book

Set in 13.08/16.1 pt Dante MT Std
Typeset by Jouve (UK), Milton Keynes
Printed and bound in Great Britain by Clays Ltd, Elcograf S.p.A.

A CIP catalogue record for this book is available from the British Library

HARDBACK ISBN: 978–0–241–34919–9
TRADE PAPERBACK ISBN: 978–0–241–34920–5

www.greenpenguin.co.uk

MIX
Paper from
responsible sources
FSC® C018179

Penguin Random House is committed to a
sustainable future for our business, our readers
and our planet. This book is made from Forest
Stewardship Council® certified paper.

For Iain
And in memory of Melanie, Susan and Joy

'Their past is as little known to them as their future. They are machines that must be rewound whenever one wants to make them move.'

   Charlevoix

'One word
Frees us of all the weight and pain of life:
That word is love.'

   Sophocles

The Old Bailey,
London,
7 April 1826

I never would have done what they say I've done, to Madame, because I loved her. Yet they say I must be put to death for it, and they want me to confess. But how can I confess what I don't believe I've done?

Chapter One

My trial starts the way my life did: a squall of elbows and shoving and spit. From the prisoners' hold they take me through the gallery, down the stairs and past the table crawling with barristers and clerks. Around me a river of faces in flood, their mutters rising, blending with the lawyers' whispers. A noise that hums with all the spite of bees in a bush. Heads turn as I enter. Every eye a skewer.

I duck my head, peer at my boots, grip my hands to stop their awful trembling. It seems all of London is here, but then murder is the story this city likes best. All of them swollen into the same mood, all of them in a stir about the 'sensation excited by these most ferocious murders'. Those were the words of the *Morning Chronicle*, itself in the business of harvesting that very sensation like an ink-black crop. I don't make a habit of reading what the broadsheets say about me, for newspapers are like a mirror I saw once in a fair near the Strand that stretched my reflection like a rack, gave me two heads so I almost didn't know myself. If you've ever had the misfortune to be written about, you know what I mean.

But there are turnkeys at Newgate who read them *at* you for sport, precious little you can do to get away.

When they see I'm not moving, they shove me forward with the flats of their hands and I shiver, despite the heat, fumble my way down the steps.

Murderer! The word follows me. *Murderer!* The Mulatta Murderess.

I'm forced to trot to keep up with the turnkeys so I don't

tumble crown over ankle. Fear skitters up my throat as they push me into the dock. The barristers look up from their table, idle as cattle in their mournful gowns. Even those old hacks who've seen it all want a glimpse of the Mulatta Murderess. Even the judge stares, fat and glossy in his robes, his face soft and blank as an old potato until he screws his eyes on me and nods at his limp-haired clerk to read the indictment.

FRANCES LANGTON, *also known as Ebony Fran or Dusky Fran,*
is indicted for the wilful murder of GEORGE BENHAM *and*
MARGUERITE BENHAM *in that she on the 27th day of January in*
the year of Our Lord 1826 did feloniously and with malice aforethought
assault GEORGE BENHAM *and* MARGUERITE BENHAM,
subjects of our lord the King, in that she did strike and stab them
until they were dead, both about the upper and middle chest, their
bodies having been discovered by EUSTACIA LINUX, *housekeeper,*
of Montfort Street, London.
    MR JESSOP *to conduct the prosecution.*

The gallery is crowded, all manner of quality folk and ordinary folk and rabble squeezed in, the courtroom being one of the few places they'd ever be caught so cheek to jowl. Paduasoy silk next to Kashmir shawls next to kerchiefs. Fidgeting their backsides along the wood, giving off a smell like milk on the turn, like a slab of pork Phibbah forgot once, under the porch. The kind of smell that sticks your tongue to your throat. Some of them suck candied orange peel fished out of their purses, jaws going like paddles. The ones who can't stomach being caught in any sort of honest smell. Ladies. I know the sort.

Jessop hooks his gown with his thumbs, pushes to his feet. His voice laps steady as water against a hull. So *soft*. He could be gabbing with them at his own fireside. Which is how he wants it, for that makes them lean closer, makes them attend.

'Gentlemen, on the evening of the twenty-seventh of January, Mr and Mrs Benham were stabbed to death. Mr Benham in his library, Mrs Benham in her bedchamber. *This* . . . woman . . . the prisoner at the bar, stands accused of those crimes. Earlier that night, she confronted them in their drawing room, and threatened them with murder. Those threats were witnessed by several guests in attendance that evening, at one of Mrs Benham's legendary soirées. You will hear from those guests. And you will hear from the housekeeper, Mrs Linux, who will tell you the prisoner was observed going into Mrs Benham's rooms shortly after she had retired. Mrs Linux went upstairs herself at around one o'clock that morning, where she discovered her master's body in his library. Shortly thereafter, she entered Mrs Benham's bedchamber and discovered her body, and, next to it, the prisoner. In her mistress's bed. Asleep. When the prisoner was woken by the housekeeper, she had blood on her hands, blood drying on her sleeves.

'All through her arrest and incarceration . . . to this *day*, she has refused to speak about what happened that night. The refuge of those who are unable to offer a plain and honest defence. Well, if she can *now* offer an explanation, I am sure you will hear it, gentlemen, I am sure you will hear it. But it seems to me that a satisfactory explanation is impossible when the crime is attended with circumstances such as these.'

I grip the railing, shackles clanking like keys. I can't hold on to what he's saying. My eye swings around the room, catches the sword hung behind the judge, silver as a chink of moon. I read the words hammered in gold beneath. 'A false witness shall not be unpunished, but he that speaketh lies shall perish.' Well. We're all going to perish, liars and truth-tellers alike, though the Old Bailey is meant to speed a liar's progress. But that's not what frightens me. What frightens me is dying believing that it was *me* who killed her.

I see you at the barristers' table. You look up, give me a quick nod that settles on me like a horse blanket. There, laid out like china on a buffet, is the evidence against me: Benham's cravat, his green brocade waistcoat; Madame's lavender silk, her chemise, and her bandeau with the swan feather dyed lavender also, to match her dress. And there is Linux's butchering knife, which, so far as I knew, was in its scabbard in the kitchen the whole time I was in Madame's room.

But it's the thing beside *them* that you're frowning at. When I see it, worry curdles my guts. It's curled inside an apothecary's jar, tight as a fist. The baby. Someone joggles the table and it flattens against the glass, like a cheek. There's a question in your raised brows, but it's one I cannot answer. I didn't expect to see it here. *The baby.* Why is it allowed here? Will they ask me to speak about it?

When I see it, my knees start to quake, and I feel all the terror of that night again. But the mind is its own place, as Milton said, it can make a Hell of Heaven and a Heaven of Hell. How does it do that? By remembering, or forgetting. The only tricks a mind can play.

A wave of memory breaks. She's lying in bed, up on her elbows with her toes pointing into the air, in her hand an apple I'm trying in vain to coax her to eat. 'Listen! Are you listening?' She kicks one of her heels.

'I met a traveller from an antique land,
Who said – "Two vast and trunkless legs of stone
Stand in the desert . . . Near them, on the sand
Half sunk, a shattered visage lies . . ."'

I'm only half listening, because it is impossible, this thing that is happening, my mistress lying with me in her bed and reading me a poem! But also because it was one of those times, when it fell to me to watch what they called the balance of her mind, like a pot I had on the stove. *Is she well?* I'm asking myself. *Is she well?*

She turns to me. 'Do you like it?'

'Who is it?' I ask, stirring her hair with my breath.

'Shelley. Though I like Byron better, don't you? The prince of melodrama.' She turns over suddenly, onto her back, and closes her eyes. 'Byron is proof, if ever it were needed, that a man is merely spoiled by his vices while a woman is soiled by hers. Oh, Frances, *Frances*, don't you think everyone should be prescribed a poem a day? Woman cannot live on novels alone!'

She was right about that. A novel is like a long, warm drink but a poem is a spike through the head.

I told you that story yesterday when we first met. I don't know why, except maybe I wanted you to know something about me and her other than the terrible things that are being said. You lawyers are as squeamish about hearsay as a planter about cane-rats, yet a trial boils a whole character down to that.

'John Pettigrew,' you said, holding out your hand, with your brief still in it so the ribbons dribbled down your wrists. You peered out through all your dark hair. I could see you were even nervier than I was about what lay ahead of us.

Then you said, 'For God's sake, give me something I can save your neck with.'

But how can I give you what I do not have? Remembering is a thing that happens or doesn't, like breathing.

So I told you that story. I suppose I wanted to show you there was love between me and her. Though what good does that do? Whatever she and I were to each other is not a thing you men would care for. At any rate, love is no defence to murder, as you said, though, more often than not, it's an explanation.

But this is a story of love, not just murder, though I know that's not the kind of story you're expecting. In truth, no one expects any kind of story from a woman like me. No doubt you think this will be one of those slave histories, all sugared over with misery and despair. But who'd want to read one of those? No, this is my account of myself and my own life and the happiness that came to it, which was not a thing I thought I'd ever be allowed, the happiness *or* the account.

I have the paper you gave me, and a fresh quill, and your instructions to explain myself.

Any gaol-bird could tell you that for every crime there are two stories, and that an Old Bailey trial is the story of the crime, not the story of the prisoner.

That story is one only I can tell.

Paradise,
Jamaica, 1812–25

Chapter Two

I used to be called Frannie Langton before I was taken from
Paradise to London and given by Langton as maid to Mr
George Benham, who then gave me to his wife. It wasn't my
choice to be brought here, but very little in my life ever was.
I was Langton's creature. If I pleased him I pleased myself.
If he said something was to be, it was. But Langton was a man
who'd named his own house Paradise despite all that went on
there, and named every living thing in Paradise too. What
more do I need to tell you about him?

Where I come from, there's more than one way a man gives
you his name. He marries you or he buys you. In some places
that is the same thing, and they call it a dowry, but it's a truth
everybody must savvy that in some places a man has no need
to marry what he's bought.

This isn't going to be the story of all that was done to me at
Paradise, or of everything I did. But I'll have to include some of it,
I suppose. I've always wanted to tell my story, even though one
person's story is only a raindrop in an ocean. But if you've ever
stood in the sea when rain's coming then you know they're two
different kinds of water. Seawater is nothing like the first cold
drop springing fresh on your face, then another on your tongue,
then another, pat-pat-pat on your closed eyelids until all around
you rainwater's slapping at the sea.

The difficult thing is to know where to start. My life began
with some truly hard things, but my story doesn't have to,
even though nothing draws honesty out of you like suffering.
The receiving of it, but the giving also.

I was born at Paradise and I was still a small girl when they took me from the slave quarters up to the house. For a long time, I thought that was a stroke of luck, but it was nothing more than the liar's habit of trying to make fact better than truth.

Some nights, if Phibbah had left the shutters open and the candles lit, I could creep along the river through damp grass, hide behind the sugar mill, gawp at the house. Yellow light shivered at the windows like church glass, and Miss-bella's shadow stretched grey and tall as she drifted past them. I pictured her inside, getting ready for bed, rolling towards Langton. The syrupy way white women move. Not like the cabin-women, who were quick as hens.

The house was a sight come morning too. Sun shining like Langton's church shoes. Heat already gripping my throat but still a cat's tail of mist. I'd walk the track through the guinea grass up to the front porch. Out in the cane-piece, the men waiting for their bowl of mash. Lime-washed walls, porch wide as shoulders, the logwood shutters Miss-bella made Manso put up to shut out the bad air. I liked the idea that the house was as new as me. Langton used to brag about making Manso and the hired-on stonemasons and carpenters work like clocks for three years getting it plumb.

Then I'd smooth out my brown calico, walk round to the back. Everything, all the way to where the river cut north, black, slow and mud-clogged, belonged to Langton. I'd sit right on one of Miss-bella's campeachy chairs, listen to the floorboards creak, lift my own arms out of the sun the way I'd seen the white ladies do, push my toes down to set the chair rocking. Just close my eyes and wait for the day to crawl towards noon.

Before they took me to live there, I only ever did that in my head.

·

Then one afternoon Miss-bella told Phibbah to fetch me, and Phibbah found me in the lower field with the third gang, where we'd been set with our little baskets of dung to throw into the cane holes. She took me through the cookhouse and washed my feet in the mop bucket, her kerchief fluttering like a yellow moth over her eyes and the heat from her grill slapping at my legs. She spent a long minute grousing how Miss-bella wanted her enemies near, which had given *her* the work of chasing niggerlings all morning, and then a short minute dragging me inside. I asked what Miss-bella wanted me for, but Phibbah was caked in the kind of spite that will not hear.

Miss-bella was in the room that belonged to her, and looked like her also. Both covered in silks and velvets, smooth and cool as lizards. A room so vast I was struck mute when I passed into it, and so wide I felt it was gobbling me whole.

Kiii! This place endless like outside, I thought, *but with a roof over you and windows that decide how much light can come in!*

Miss-bella sat in the middle on her stool, skirts spilling all around her. I might have thought her a spider in a web, but with her small, shining eyes, she put me more in mind of a fly. She had a pitcher of goat's milk set in front of her on a low table, which also had bits of johnnycake strewn across it as if put out for birds, or rat-catching. She picked out a piece of johnnycake. I took a step, which clanged like a bell and frightened me to a halt. There she was, rising towards me on an ocean of black satin. She had to reach for me and pull me all the rest of the way into the room. I remember now there was a looking glass in that room, right behind her. It was the first time I'd seen myself properly – there I was, stamping towards myself, like a wild creature, my own face darting about on the surface, like a fish I couldn't catch. I got another fright so I stopped again, had to be tugged once more.

The johnnycake had cooled and the milk was warm. Both

must have been sitting out for a long time before she sent for me.

'So,' she said. 'You are Frances.'

I made a curtsy.

'It's the name I gave you myself.'

That startled me. I hadn't known Miss-bella to take any interest in me before that very moment. I lost my curtsy and almost slipped and fell. I didn't know how to answer except to thank her. She shook her arm to remind me of the johnnycake she was holding. By then I'd grabbed myself a hunk in each hand from the table, but I took that piece straight from her own hand with my teeth.

She puffed out her cheeks, then plunged her fingers into her mouth as if to lick them clean. 'You *are* a little savage.'

I bit my tongue.

'It is my husband who has decided you should live in this house, Frances.'

'Yes, missus,' I mumbled around the bite I was trying to gulp down before she took any of it away.

'What you and I have in common is that neither of us had any say in the matter.'

'I happy to be here, missus.'

'Well. Seems I must be some sort of mother to you now.'

What to say to that? I never knew my mother but here was the plain fact looking us both in the eye. Miss-bella was white and a very high lady. None such as herself had ever birthed the likes of me in the history of our hot little part of the earth. Brown and thick and strong as a horse I was then, though, being a mulatta, I was paler than any of the other blacks on that estate. With a great frizzled mess on top of my head, not like her own pale hair, which was so feathery the breeze stirred it and lifted it and played with it while it shunned mine.

She said something else, which I fancied was about her own

life and therefore not my concern. She was gazing out the window when she said it too. 'I've lived too many years in a place where the snakes lurk in the house as well as the grass.'

Because she had said she was to be my mother, I chanced a question. 'How long am I to stay?'

She had a high colour on her throat, her hands flittered like a frog's legs, and she looked at me and then away, as if I was the sun and gazing at me too long would hurt her eyes. I thought it strange that she should be so overcome when I was the rough creature brought up to her from the swamp and she the great lady of the house who was giving me pity surely as she was giving me johnnycakes. Miss-bella was frightened of me.

But then she said something that turned my attention sharp in another direction, as if a john crow had just flown into the room. 'However long it is will be too long in the end.'

Chapter Three

That was 1812. Nobody told me why I'd been brought to the house and I was too busy burying my nose in clean cotton and kitchen scraps to puzzle about it. They said I was seven years old, or thereabouts. No one ever stirred themselves enough to be sure. I never had a birthday, or a mother. When I asked her, all Phibbah would say was my mother had run off. 'You won't magic one up by asking,' she said. 'You going learn. We not the ones ask the questions, we the ones answer them. And the answer always yes.'

When I close my eyes now, I see Phibbah swiping her cloth at the cane settee in the receiving room, tilting it to sweep under. I see the campeachy chairs put right in the middle to catch a breeze, the carpets sent to Miss-bella by her sister in Bristol that curled up in our heat like they were trying to rest. The dining room where the porcelain cups and platters and the blue and white teapot rattled in the sideboard. I hear Phibbah hissing, '*Ga-lang*, pickney, just get out of my way. Why you can't just leave me be?'

It was my job to polish the brass and put the flowers out on Miss-bella's breakfast table, fan the flies off her food. But mostly I trailed the house, thinking of ways I could stick to Phibbah, like an apron. She grumbled while she worked, complaining that her old bones were rattling like stones in a calabash, that whoever dreamed up the colour white never had to be somebody's laundress, that white people's furniture never did nothing except breed more furniture. I liked the way her every word was birdsong, through the space in her teeth.

Four of them missing right where my own new ones had just come in.

She'd been the one to pull mine out, so I asked her, 'Phibbah, who pulled *yours*?' Oh, I worried at her like waves on sand. Children are all blindfolds and hammers. Cruel because of what they don't know.

She told me it was none of my business. 'You don' remember it,' she said.

'Why?'

'It happen before you born. Nobody remember a thing from then.'

Most days she did nothing but curse, but in the right mood she fed me scraps of hominy straight from the pot, or a slice of one of her corn cakes. When she sat outside the cook-room in the morning picking peas, and tapped her hand beside her in the dirt, it meant she'd set a few there for me, beside the washbasin. I'd creep over and scoop them into my palm, her arm tickling right beside mine. But she'd never turn, never look at me.

Peas snicking into pewter, Phibbah's smell of coal, and the ley ash and aloe she mixed into soap. If I kept quiet, she might tell a story. But she had to work up to it, like a wave you can see coming from far out. First, she said, she had to find her story breath, which wasn't the same as her living one.

My favourites were the ones about the house.

'Only one reason white man ever build pretty-pretty house like this,' Phibbah said. 'You hooks worms to catch fish. After him come from England and finish him house, Massa send him letter to Bristol. We sabi sure as night going come, white woman going come. Sure *enough* Miss-bella come running – *bragadap!* – same way guinea fowl come running when corn drop.'

Then Phibbah had a new mistress to learn. And she had to watch her the same way sailors watch the sky. *Red sky at morning, sailor's warning; red sky at night, sailor's delight.* Miss-bella came riding high on the driver's bench in the mule-cart, as out of place as a white glove on a drying hedge, a teapot clinking on her lap, the blue and white pattern flocking the rim, like birds on a branch. She'd ripped up the cart cushions to make a little throne. Three nights Phibbah had stayed up sewing those cushions, finishing them off with a brocade leaf pattern good enough for the receiving room. Langton had said he wanted it to be like sitting on a god-damn cloud, the day he went down to get his wife. And here was Miss-bella, using them for her teapot instead of her backside! Oh, but she'd soon learn. This was Jamaica. Things were bound to crack.

Believe it or not, Phibbah said, there was a time Miss-bella and Langton used to ride out together, before she knew Jamaica was a thing she was supposed to be frightened of. Wearing her riding skirt that looked like a cut lemon and her straw hat with the blue feather, grey eyes shining with excitement and Langton mounted up beside her showing her everything he owned. Phibbah was supposed to keep watch, run down to swing the door the very minute they returned. She knew she'd pay if that door stayed closed even a minute longer. But there was a way of knowing when they were coming long before she could see them. 'How?' I'd ask her.

'Same way you track him for any reason. Look out into the fields.'

'Watch the bucks?'

'Mm. Them all do the same thing when him draw near.'

'They look up?'

'Cha! Pickney!' She kissed her teeth, air making its music through her gap. 'Them heads go *down*. Watch. You see it every time, like a wave through grass. Whichever way that wave coming from, is *there* buckra coming from.'

Miss-bella had to be tended like a rose. She had the palest arms I ever saw. Her whole morning's work was keeping them out of the sun. To top it all, she had a waist as narrow as a ching-ching beak, which she made narrower still with a whalebone corset that hooked around her, like ribs. Her bottom billowed under all manner of bustles and hoops her sister sent from the ladies' catalogues. She said life in the colonies could only be survived by prayer and endured with tea, so Phibbah served it every afternoon on the back porch, grumbling: 'Why *we* got the lone white in all of Jamaica mad enough to drink tea outside?'

We set out bowls of sugar water and cobalt poison to catch flies, brought out the orange-bough fan and the porcelain footbath. I hated that I had to wear my calico dress instead of my muslin (soft and white with a lace collar that always made Miss-bella's guests look me up and down). But the muslin was for waiting at table, the calico was my foot-washing dress.

Phibbah stood behind her with the fan. I pushed up the hem of her grey skirt. Her toes flared like little eyelashes. I looked out towards the cane-piece. Scraps of osnaburg and muslin flapping, field-hands moving out of line to dip rags in buckets of water, tie them around their brows. The nigger-drivers high on their horses under the tamarind tree, watching. I wiped the washcloth between Miss-bella's toes. Her feet looked like something dug from a fire after it had died down. Dry, scratched. Not pretty like the rest of her. As the afternoon wore on she grew more and more red-faced. The fan turned a breeze, ship-sail slow. Her words sloshed around us, like the water in the tub. She bent forwards over the cup, and sighed.

'This whole god-forsaken place was *designed* for killing Europeans,' she said.

Phibbah let the fan slap against her hip. '*Kiiii!* If it killing *you*, what it doing to us?'

Miss-bella stopped dead with the cup kissing her bottom lip. Then she laughed. 'Well, it's the Europeans I'm worried about, girl. Me in particular.'

Let me tell you, I saw Phibbah whipped for all manner of petty things: whenever a piece of china-ware went missing, after she let one of Miss-bella's teacups slip and break, once when she was late bringing in the salted cod at breakfast, but never once did I see her whipped for talking back. I asked her about it once. '*That* the only entertainment the woman ever gets,' she replied.

When you look back at anything, time caves into itself, like dirt running into a fresh hole. I see the three of us – the women of Paradise – like figures etched in glass. And it's as if no time has passed, as if that girl knelt at Miss-bella's feet, blinked, then woke up to discover she was the Mulatta Murderess.

From where I crouched, I could see out to the river. Oh, it would be a miracle to feel something soft as that water against my skin again, though I'd settle for lying on fresh-cut grass, or even just the chance to rub my fingers along a fresh-laundered shift. The air was sharp with the smell of cane trash burning out near the river, and the orange oil Phibbah used for polishing. 'Go on in now, girl,' Miss-bella said. 'Fetch some of that pineapple tart you made yesterday. And is there any orangeade?'

Phibbah set the jug by the door. I'd kept my head down all that time, scraping at dirt under Miss-bella's nails with the toe-picker, lifting first one foot, then the other. Heart still hard as a drum, but the rest of me gone soft as butter in a skillet. It was an ivory-handled picker I used, as if that could magic some dainty into Miss-bella's feet. I lifted one out onto the towel beside her chair, to dry, and she and I both leaned back and admired it. Like it was marble in a museum. We used to pretend those feet were pretty as the teacups, same way we pretended the teapot wasn't half full of rum.

She wasn't done complaining. 'I'm so tired of forever staring at these same old no-account hills.'

'We could set out front, sometime,' Phibbah said, 'if you wasn't so stubborn.'

'Oh, no. I couldn't.'

'Get a view of the sea.'

'That's precisely why I could not.' She flicked her a look, sharp, over the shoulder. 'But you'd know about that.'

'About what?'

'Wanting a thing so much you can't bear looking at it.'

Phibbah stabbed and stabbed with the fan, murdering air. 'I thought it was the hills bothering you. Now you say it's the sea.'

Miss-bella laughed into her cup. Then she paused, like she was giving thought. 'Seems I can look neither ahead of me nor behind.'

'Well, then, you can' make no palabber about sitting where you put you-self.'

She waved her hand. 'Do you really think I chose to put myself anywhere on this estate?' We watched her slurp at her tea, set it aside. 'If only my father or my husband would see sense, I'd be down *there*. On the next fast clipper to Bristol.'

Manso swung past us with his tin pail, crying, '*Sook! Sook!*' calling in the cows, lifting his feet across the yard like the mad rooster that had only one rolling eye. Near the shed he shook salt into little mounds. The cows shambled over and licked at it with slow tongues.

To this day, I remember what happened then, because what happened then changed my life, for better and for worse. Miss-bella closed her eyes, rested her book on her knees, creeping her fingers across the leather cover. I saw a *D* nestled into it. A

breeze tussling with the pages. Manso whistling his commands to the cows. *Come in, come in.* The book lay there, just another thing I wanted. Pages white as peeled apples. White as cleaned sheets. There came a wildness in me. How can I explain it? All went quiet, like when an owl flies overhead. Not even the ticking of the fan. I reached up for it, my hand flooding her lap, then realized what I had done, jerked back, snagged myself on Miss-bella's skirt, scrabbled to my feet. She leaped up also. The book tumbled off her lap and into the water. My stomach pitched, like something tossed onto an ocean.

'*Frances!*'

The fan stopped.

'I'm sorry, missus,' I said. 'I'm sorry.' I fished it out and swiped at it with a corner of my frock, fright rattling inside my head. She slapped me. My head like a fish on a line, her hand the hook. Legs flowing to the floor.

That whole island was sun-addled. Heat like biting ants. Light like blades.

I wiped and wiped and wiped. I used my hands, my skirt, shook that book like a mop-head, trying to coax it dry. I wanted to cry but dared not, not while Manso was watching. When I was small he might have given me one of his skewed winks as he passed by, or let me hold the salt on my palm, feel a cow lick, but not any more. House-niggers were the one thing they all hated worse than cane.

I sat by the stables, wiping. I could hear the horses and their whining breaths. Even after the others had gone in from the cane-piece and there was only the mockingbird's *kee-kee-pip* to tell me I wasn't alone, I was still there, wiping. My shadow in the dirt. She'd said I must sit there. 'Make sure you don't try to crawl into any shade. I'll be watching.'

Would she?

She and Phibbah would be in the receiving room, Phibbah setting out the rum. Who knew where on that estate her husband would be?

Early on, in the days when she still rode out, Miss-bella had Phibbah make up the basket with breadfruit and cold turkey and shaddocks and some of the mangoes they'd picked that morning, saying she would take them out for her husband's lunch. It was when she was trying to pour a pint of wine into a flask that Phibbah told her it wasn't a good idea, and when she wouldn't take no for an answer that Phibbah decided to go down with her. She felt sorry for the woman, with her corn-yellow hair and her wrong expectations. They found them under the cocoa-tree, the only place to get good shade that far from the house, Langton sitting like a cocked gun, back to his wife, facing the two girls he had out there. It was lucky he only had them dancing, Phibbah said. They moved easy as water, those two. Dark bodies, bright eyes. Nutmeg nipples waving like streamers. They cut their eyes at the new mistress, and went right on singing:

'Hipsaw! My deaa! You no do like a-me!
You no jig like a-me! You no twist like a-me!
Hipsaw! My deaa! You no shake like a-me!
You no wind like a-me! Go yondaa!'

They'd probably still be right there under that tree, Phibbah said, because for a long time it seemed Miss-bella couldn't move. Except that at last Langton heard the basket drop from her hand and finally turned around.

That had been the end of the riding out, the picnics, and the expectations. Though not the end of the dancing. Miss-bella just had to learn to do what everyone else did. Make sure to look the other way.

•

I glanced up towards the house, where Phibbah would be closing the shutters, lighting the candles with the taper, pulling the mosquito netting from its hook. Miss-bella settling herself on one of her silk stools, putting her feet up.

You will not leave that spot until my book is dry, she'd said. After a time, I gave up, stared down at the letters, small and black and sharp, like little claws. I tilted my head, as if I could *hear* what they were trying to tell me. They seemed trapped, each one shackled to the next one. Line after line. I snapped the book shut, sat back on my haunches. The old carthorse strained up along the sea road, cart loaded high with Indian-corn, the pickneys running beside, yelling and kicking the geese that jostled the wheels.

The back door opened and Miss-bella picked her way through the grass, puffs of dust kissing her feet. She crumpled her face down at me. 'Dry yet?'

I shook my head, twisted my lips. I must have been the very image of misery, sure that now I'd be cast out. No more little head-pats, no more Turkish sweets, no more muslin frock. By then I must have been sun-struck, for I pointed to the *D*, asked what it was. She leaned over me. Her breath was hot and dry as the air. 'That? Dee. Ee . . . *Eff*. This spells *Defoe*.'

Only then did I notice Phibbah had come out too and was standing on the porch, staring.

Miss-bella straightened, gave her a long look. Her voice sweetened to molasses. 'I'll teach you.'

Yes, I thought. *Yes, yes, yes!*

'No!' Phibbah stepped off the porch, looked like falling. 'Miss's . . .'

'Why not?' She nodded, tilted her head.

'Because it's *enough*,' Phibbah said, tripping forward. 'Enough.'

Once, after Miss-bella went in, Phibbah spat a thick stream into the dirt near the rose bush. 'Where would I go? If I left here? Straight up them hills, first thing. First thing. Take me a musket. Then just wait. Wait, wait, wait, for the hottest part of the day, when nobody outside but slaves and lunatics. Then look for that spot of blue.' The blue of a white woman's eyes, the blue they called Wedgwood. 'Then I be aiming straight for her heart.'

Now she just poked her tongue through her gap, stared at Miss-bella.

I stood looking from one to the other, dumb as one of the cows.

'Is a whipping she deserve,' Phibbah said. 'For spoiling you book.'

'A whipping? A *whipping*!' Her eyes sharpened, gleamed wet. 'What an idea. Do you want to be the one to give it to her?'

Now Phibbah took a step back. 'No.'

Kiii, how hate burned through me, then. How it made me wish that I'd never snatched at her dropped peas. Or craved her stupid stories.

Miss-bella looked around, as if deciding where to put a picnic, her eyes squeezing like brass tongs. 'You're quite right. We mustn't spare the rod. After all, we don't want to spoil the child. Tell Manso call the others.'

Phibbah shook and shook. 'What?'

'You heard me. Oh, you'll do it, girl. Or Manso will. Quick. Light's going.' She turned to me, her face dripping sweat. 'Phibbah wants you whipped, so whipped you're going to be.'

I don't know which was worse, that it was Phibbah who gave me my first whipping or that the others gathered to stare at the pair of us. They had to come when called, of course. But most people will take a dose of those things happening to someone else so they know it's not happening to them.

Phibbah waited so long it was almost a shiver of relief when she started. It's always the moment before that's the worst. Your whole body waiting. Then I heard her shift behind me, heard birch whistling. Pain sank into my thigh like a claw. Cut hard grooves deep as nails. Whipped up a thin stream of blood, trapped my breath, buried it deep. Another high whistle. I pressed my forehead into the dirt and grass, tried not to cry, but she gave me ten, one for every one of my supposed years. She whipped until that whip was nothing but an echo in my own head, until, I'm ashamed to say, I screamed and screamed, and first the sky went black, then my mind did.

All through it, Miss-bella stood silent, arms folded, face as smooth as milk. When I looked up it was Phibbah she was watching, not me. Her narrow smile stretched between them, tight as sewn thread. She nodded, made her eyes go small. It was as if some inside part of her travelled across that dirt while she herself stood still, went right out across the yard, and spoke something to Phibbah. In the end, it was Phibbah who cast her eyes to the dirt, looked away first. Swallowing and swallowing, though there was nothing in her mouth. Slowly, the others drifted away. Only Miss-bella still watching.

But it was Phibbah who carried me to the cook-room, set me on my pallet, fetched one of the liniments she made with whiskey stolen from Langton's drinks cabinet. She clattered down a plate of johnnycakes, but I only stared at them, hunger wrestling pride, then pushed the plate away. I'd trapped my anger, like a bird in a cage. She bent forwards over the grill, shoulders going like bellows, held a slab of salted cod spitting into the flame. 'Harder for me than you,' she said. I said nothing. 'She dress you like a doll, now she want train you like a pet. But if Langton catch the two o' you at it, *reading*, it's *you* going feel it. You hear? Listen, Frances.' She spat out my name, like another loosened tooth. 'Listen to me. Not one thing in this world more dangerous than a white woman when she bored. You hear?'

I shrugged. Nothing in my world had been more dangerous than *her* that afternoon. I could see her fingers trembling on the cod's flesh, but she didn't lift them. She was going to blister her hands. Serve her right.

'But you don' –'

I got up.

'Where you going?'

She followed me out. The dogs leaped up, trailed over, their backs curved like ship's skeletons, looking for scraps. 'Go on!' she yelled at them. 'G'weh!'

She gripped my hand. There was a long silence between us while I let her hold me. When I looked up, I saw her cheek beating, like a heart. 'You never stop to think why is *you* get pick. You think is luck? Only you could think is luck.'

'What's wrong with wanting to learn something?'

'Learn to want what you've got.'

'What's that?' I asked. 'What I got?'

She stared and stared and I stared back. A smile cracked her face, she started to shake, and then the shaking crawled slowly over her whole body, like molasses on the boil. She threw her head back and laughed and laughed. And then I laughed too.

Chapter Four

I'm trying to write this story as if it's mine. Yet I look back over what I've set down so far and see how much of my own paper and ink I've spent on Miss-bella. The trouble is nothing ever happened to me except through her. That's just how it was. So many in England have said that must have taught me how to hate. *How you must have hated them, Frannie Langton! The pair of them!* But the truth is not a cloth every man can cut to fit himself. The truth is there was love as well as hate. The truth is, the love hurt worse.

Reading was the only promise Miss-bella ever kept. All that cutting season, I knelt at the table in the receiving room. Happiness soaked sweet as honey while she touched the page, my elbow, her warm breath on my neck. Her hands cool as sponges. If Phibbah happened to pass, she cut her eye, chattered her teeth at me, not caring if Miss-bella heard or saw. She was right, Miss-bella *did* grow bored of teaching, after a time, but I knew enough by then that I could lift out the books in the library when no one was looking, follow along for myself. Even Miss-bella said it: I had miracle-quick learning. Astonished her, and myself.

Phibbah said she didn't like having Langton's name anywhere near her mouth. But she spoke about him all the same. 'First thing I knew about him was when he refused to come when he was called . . . Just like the wayward cur he is.'

His parents sent him to England as a boy, she said, to get his education, same as most of those colonial sons. He'd filled himself up on white people learning, then written them to say he wouldn't be coming back, that he wanted to make a name for himself, to be a man of science. Mistress Sarah's eye-water alone had been plenty enough salt for the porridge when she read that, thinking he must be ashamed: of Jamaica, of their failing estate. Many of those colonial sons got shame too, as well as education, when they got sent to England. Years passed. Then Mistress Sarah sent for him, after his father died, saying now he had no choice: *I beseech you. A white woman cannot be left in Jamaica on her own.*

Letter after letter she sent, and got no answer. Three months later, she too was dead. Yellow fever. Death gave her the measurements of a grill poker, so it hadn't taken long to make the burying dress, but Phibbah had to put it on her too. She found herself alone in the bedroom, with just the body and the washstand and the porcelain basin. She wanted to dash it to the floor. To see how that would feel. A chance like that might never come her way again. Instead, she set about fastening up the plain collar with the jet buttons Mistress Sarah had told her to use, but she was interrupted by the jangle of the old copper bell.

She found Langton scuffing his boots on the mat she'd brushed that morning.

'Why, pray tell, have I been kept waiting?'

'I was tending to your mother.'

'And where is *she*?'

'Passed.'

'I see.' His eyes flicked like flies. 'Then it would have behoved you to attend to the living before the dead.'

'Then him have to come back,' Phibbah said. 'For good. Somebody needed to run the place. Though all *him* do at first was walk. *Walk, walk, walk.*' Trampled around each morning with

a twill-jacketed man, who'd come on the same ship, both dressed too hot. Langton pointed at something, the man nodded; within days it fell like a love rival after a dose of obeah. The old great house, busha's house, the cook-room, the granary, even the sugar mill, one by one. That should have been a sign: Langton was an ill wind. Massa Hurricane. They didn't know where he could have gotten money from. His father hadn't had a half-dollar to spare for as long as they'd known him. One afternoon, Manso dared to ask new Massa his intentions. Langton gave a laugh, roughened by his pipe. Spat. 'Used to be my father's place, boy. I'm making it mine.'

Inside the new house there was a room for every little thing a body could dream of doing in a single day. Eating, sleeping, receiving, tupping. But the library was best of all. *Kii*, your eye could travel all around that room and not run out of books to see.

Reading was the best thing and the worst thing that ever happened to me. I can still see all those spines: Vesalius's *De Humani Corporis Fabrica*, the *Philosophical Transactions*, Newton's *Principia*, the *Encyclopaedia*. But there were novels, too, that Miss-bella ordered, though Langton kept those on the bottom shelves. Those were the books I loved. Holding one was like holding all the things that could happen in the world but just hadn't happened yet. I had to wait until Miss-bella was finished with them, but then I could smuggle them behind the sideboards, read until I heard footsteps. I read with my mouth hanging open, like I could spoon sugar right out of all those books. I hid in the cook-room at night to read by the light of a tallow candle I made myself, beef tallow moulded in an old pewter bowl. Books answer questions with questions, but still I couldn't get enough. And now that I think about it, it was the same all those years later, when I met Madame.

•

One afternoon I found myself blessed with solitude and a book and a view. Langton and Miss-bella had taken the buggy over to the Copes. Phibbah was at her grill. There was nobody watching the porch but the cows, and they were busy nosing the long seep of river. I stole some of Phibbah's rum punch and took myself outside with *Candide*. It was the kind of moment that pinches out happiness like salt into a cake, which meant, of course, that it couldn't last.

I didn't hear the buggy; nor did I notice until I sat up that Langton was upon me, had been waiting for me to look up before he said a word. He squatted to his heels, slow as the river, looking like a thing you were supposed to dread. 'You enjoying yourself?'

The breath sawed into me. I felt something turn in my jaw, like the click of a lock. No right thing to do, other than to let him speak. 'And will you look at my rules,' he said, 'lying broken all around us?'

I almost twisted away, as if to see those poor broken rules, but he held my jaw fast. A pleading noise swam out of me.

'No. I want you to read me a page. Oblige me. I suppose you know a fancy word like *oblige*. Since you're a reading nigger. But what you mightn't know is what'll happen if you don't.'

Wet ran all down the back of my calico. I held myself tight against the urge to flee. He scrubbed his hands. 'I'm going to put you on the horns of a nigger's dilemma, girl. Though I know niggers aren't used to choices. You listening? One. Read me a page, you keep your hands. Or two. Don't read me a page, and then find out what'll happen.'

Words came sweeping out of me the same way I'd seen Miss-bella pray, loud and clipped and beaten. I can't even remember now what I read, but I do remember that when I shunted the book onto the railing, he gestured at it. 'That's yours. To keep.' I didn't know what he meant, until he dragged me sideways like a lady's hem, and said I must start tearing out pages.

Swathes of time go dark on us, but it's not as if we have a say which ones. This whole incident comes back in one long bright line, though I wish I could swallow it down the way he made me swallow *Candide*. Paper mashing to gristle in my throat. Him tapering above, wondering aloud who'd taught one of his niggers to read. As if there weren't only two candidates on that whole estate. I ate until it felt the paper was digging a hole in me, then ate until all I wanted was to crawl into that same hole. But then he stopped short, as if something had pricked him, which he'd have to pull out and look at later.

By the time he did, I'd eaten so many pages of *Candide*, I vomited down my chest. He let me off easy. It was only later I even thought to wonder why.

Chapter Five

Miss-bella was so terrified of sickness she was bound to get sick. On day one, Phibbah had told her the three things she had to do to survive Jamaica. Walk barefooted, so the ground could season her feet; wear cotton instead of wool; and bathe, like it or not. The English hated baths, but no white could survive Jamaica unless they bathed twice a day.

'To survive in nigger territory,' Miss-bella used to say, 'one would be wise to take a nigger's word.' Phibbah burned smoke-pots that made all the rooms hazy with smoke and the smell of orange, to keep the mosquitoes at bay; she rubbed Miss-bella with salves and ointments she made herself, and dragged her kicking into the tin bath morning and night. All those years, she guarded Miss-bella's health as if her own life depended on it.

For Phibbah was a doctoress. She had the knowledge from her mother, old knowledge. So long as you carried it in your head they couldn't take it away, she used to say. Not like weapons, or food, or clothes. Everyone came to her. Yaws to aching feet, she knew what to do for it. How to use capsicum peppers, prickly-yellow wood, guinea rush, John-to-Heal, which Miss-bella called ipecac. Dirt-scratch medicine, the Surgeon called it. Nigger cures. Barks and twigs and leaves. Simply a monkey scratching around in the dirt and finding something by chance to fix his monkey ailments.

The year after I learned to read, a botanist paid a visit to Langton. A Mr Thomson. Hunched, thin, with a wisp of beard like a goat, a black ledger tucked under his arm. He wore a grey wool coat, even at noon, said he was travelling island to island. Someone next door at Mesopotamia had told him about Phibbah so he drove himself up in one of their mule-carts, said he'd come to see the magic Negress for himself. At dinner, he turned the pig ribs over and over in his hands as if he'd never seen the like, sucked seven of them clean to the bone in dead silence, and only after there was no meat left did the talk pour out of him, lips and fingers oiled by grease, about his travels in Cuba and Haiti, the specimens he'd gathered, the pharmaco-poeia he was going to write when he returned to Dorset. 'These Negro Doctors –'

Langton interrupted, sucking in his cheeks. 'Not a one of my niggers is a doctor.'

'No. No. *Bush* doctors, then,' Thomson corrected. 'But they –'

'You know, brutes are not botanists,' Langton spat, folding his arms and sitting back. 'Long said that.'

'Actually, Long said they were botanists by instinct.'

Langton snorted. 'Same thing.'

Phibbah and I watched each other, stuck in our own thoughts, at the sideboard. I could hear frogs clearing their throats, the dogs making piggish little noises outside, giving chase. I was sticky damp under my arms, didn't dare wipe, or squirm. Langton slapped a mosquito into a black speck on the cloth. I peered up at her, wishing she would say something. *Phibbah is not a brute!* I wanted to shout. But she stayed where she was, and said nothing, quiet breaths singing in and out of her, face wide as a black moon.

Langton kept on: 'True, they might blunder now and then onto something useful. But all that voodoo can be a powder keg. At that very estate you've just come from – Mesopotamia – one of the old-timers was reported last year. Her own daughter turned her in. They searched her cabin and found the whole lot, the usual rubbish. Thunder stones, cat's ears, bird-hearts . . .

34

bones. Bones! Imagine! Cope had her transported, and then *bam*! Not a drop of trouble down there since.'

Mr Thomson licked forefinger and thumb, then looked over at us, eyes so dark they almost seemed sorry. And maybe he was. 'Well, yes, but I believe we can harness their brute instincts. We can make adjustments, make something useful of their concoctions. Take the history of chocolate, for example –'

'Chocolate! Let me tell you this, Mr Thomson. My grand-father came to Jamaica to make a fortune, not to turn apothecary.'

'Nevertheless, we must follow the trail. Even if it leads to the Negro –'

Langton cut him off again, with a wave of his hand. 'If my girl knows anything useful, you're welcome to it.'

Next morning, Langton paid a visit to the cook-room, lifted the lid on the hominy, peered in. 'No wonder you getting so fat, girl.' He dipped a finger into the pot, spoke without look-ing up: 'Thomson's a buffoon, but he has something I want. Understand me?'

Phibbah set down her knife, swept up onion skins, tossed them onto the trash pile, smacked the work-table with her hands, and stared down at it, like she was looking for another thing to chop. 'What he have that you want?'

He laughed. 'Publishers. English publishers. Not that you'd know the first thing about it.' He rattled the lid back down, and I jumped. Then he turned to go. 'So you better answer all his fool-fool questions.'

'Or what?'

He turned back, and laughed again, so soft you had to cock your ears to hear it that time. Stared at her. She stared back. 'Or I'll whip that girl right back into the womb.' I scuttled my eyes back down to the napkins I was supposed to be scrubbing.

After Langton left, I drew in a breath, watched Phibbah

wipe the table, and bring down the jug she used for mixing the orangeade, feeling behind the loose brick under her grill for the seasoning herbs. She turned her back while she did, which was always a sign that she wouldn't be in the mood to speak for quite some time, and that I'd better stay quiet until then.

I saw the botanist's book, once. In London. It was in a shop I visited with Madame. *Aloysius Thomson's Pharmacopoeia of the West Indies.* A thick yellow volume, out on display beside the encyclopaedias and the natural dictionaries. Anger tore through me when I flicked through it. Everything Phibbah had told that man about was written in there. The next day I stole down to the same shop with a lead pencil tucked in my palm, hid myself behind the shelves with one of the volumes, and scratched her name on every page.

Despite Phibbah's attentions, Miss-bella took sick. She drooped like young cane and grew too fevered to sit on the porch. Phibbah drew the curtains and put her to bed, while I hid behind the door jamb, watching. Miss-bella's face swelled against the pillows like a ready hog's, all the bloom gone off it. She scraped at the bedclothes, screwed up her face. '*Phibbah!* I think I – need the pot.'

Phibbah helped her off the bed and leaned back on her haunches so she could make railings of her arms and give Miss-bella something to bear herself up with. She puffed out a laugh. 'Least you remember to ask for the pot this time.'

Miss-bella rolled her eyes, dropped her head onto Phibbah's bosom. Into the hot, dark space, she whispered, 'I need wiping.'

Phibbah said, 'Yes.'

Miss-bella's buttocks were saggy as an old man's mouth clawing around a pipe stem, and winked when she flipped herself over. Phibbah swiped a wet cloth into the crack, fluttered it out again, soiled. Her face thickened while she did it, like boiling cane juice after it pulls and pulls on itself until it slows to syrup.

A sick, sour feeling tickled at my throat. *I will never do that,* I thought. *Never! Not for anyone. Not so long as I draw breath.*

The Surgeon was a broad-bellied man, with a large nose that flamed red in the creases, who lived at Mesopotamia, tended the slaves on both estates. He'd made his own fortune selling yaws inoculations, then stayed on because he had nowhere else to go. At the foot of Miss-bella's bed, he sucked his bottom lip, said, 'Yes, thank you,' to a tot of rum for himself, then spooned cocaine drops for her from his medicine chest. He'd bought it off a ship's doctor who'd opened a public house near Montego Bay. There'd been a flood of them setting up shop, old doctors, boatswains, other men with skin tough as saddles. Those who could no longer make their living from the trade since it had been abolished, but nevertheless stuck close to the institution, leeches too bloated to drop off. He pecked a lancet at Miss-bella's arm. Pink flowers of blood bloomed in the basin. Then he leaned forward, screwed his eyes to watch the drops quicken like footsteps. At last, he looked up at Langton, rubbed his hands down his breeches. 'More mercury. That'll do it.'

Miss-bella had been taking mercury for months. Phibbah said she didn't trust it. Too silver, she said. Nothing without colour had any good use.

By nightfall, Miss bella had twisted her sheets into a pile and sat brooding on them, like one of the yellow hens. The room was flanked by dark wood: the dresser, covered with an army of glass bottles and jars, and the night tables, lightened only by doilies Phibbah had crocheted for her. She clawed her fingers into her nightgown and lifted it over her head, her laughter ringing out. It was Phibbah who went over to her and yanked it back down.

Three days later, Miss-bella lost a tooth. It came out yellow as an old pearl. Phibbah took it away, though Miss-bella tried to cling to it. 'Now I'll have a gap, like yours. Ugly.'

Phibbah dropped the tooth into the bowl of water, stepped over a splash of vomit. 'Ugly not the worst thing a body can be.' She lifted a square of damp cotton, and held it as if it had taken her by surprise, like she'd forgotten what she wanted with it in the first place. 'That man's medicine making you sicker than dirt.'

But Miss-bella wasn't listening. She'd spied me. *'Loitering?'* She lifted her head, her face red as beef. 'Don't watch me! Insolent girl!'

Since Miss-bella was ill, Langton said, he'd take his breakfast in the inside dining room instead of out in the fields with his overseers. Keep an eye on things inside. I helped Phibbah serve, platters loaded wrist to elbow. Johnnycakes and butter to start with, and goat's milk she'd got that morning. Langton took his time. Pulled out his chair, settled himself into it, snapped out his napkin, tilted his glass, and pinned his lips around his mouthful of milk. As soon as Phibbah came in, he cleared his throat. 'You know . . . I been puzzling hard about the way things stand upstairs, girl.'

Something about the way he spoke churned my insides. Phibbah must have felt it, too. Her feet hitched, like weeds in a net, and she left it too long before answering. That drumbeat of silence pounded into my own chest.

'Well. Miss's going be happy you thinking on her.'

'No, no.' He raised a brow. 'I don't think she will. You know why? You know what conclusion I came to? I'll be buggered if what ails my wife isn't a case of poisoning.'

Phibbah moved to the table, around it, set down the platter of breadfruit, the bowl of fruit, the gold-rimmed plate that held the salted codfish and his slices of ham and his eggs, too, fried in pork grease the way he liked them. His eyes followed her, shot with blood, as if he'd sat up all night with a bottle of rum, as was sometimes his custom. As if he might in fact still be drunk. She set down the last plate, and turned, unsteady on her feet, said she'd go fetch the coffee.

'Girl!' he shouted. She stopped with her hand on the latch. The way her head whipped up and turned to where I was standing, I knew it was me he was shouting for. My whole body sagged.

'Girl. I said, *come here.*'

'Don't bring her into it,' she said.

The laugh burst out of him. 'It's me who brought her into *all* of it!' He pushed his seat back and reared up over me, brought his face right down close to mine, nostrils flaring wide as the walls.

I stepped away, pasted my ribs to the sideboard.

'You ever see this here girl put something extra in your missy food or drink? Tell the truth.' He brought his face even closer. My heart jumped, but it was the only thing that moved. I didn't even dare pull back. 'Speak or take your chances, girl.'

There was never any call for the truth in a place like that. But it could be there was already obedience bred into me, the same way Langton bred cows for milk and meat.

'Yes,' I blurted. 'Seasoning.'

Phibbah's hand flew from the door handle to her mouth, left the little golden latch shuddering.

Dust crumbled out of the grill and fell away when Manso moved the first loose stone. By the third, all Phibbah's dried herbs came into view, black as biting ants, twisted into oilcloth. And mound after mound of cassava root.

I've had to set this manuscript down for a time, still my pen, still my breath, shocked at finding myself for several hours quite unable to move my hand. But this is to be a true and honest account, which means I must include such sins as I remember, and can therefore confess. Yet writing it down has swung such a hammer of sadness through my head, forced me to face what was mercifully clouded for so long. Now, when all I want is for memory to betray me, to tell me lies, I scoop into it and find nothing but unvarnished truth.

I face myself, as I was then. Young Frances. Word-struck. Thinking that Phibbah – gap-toothed Phibbah, fat, black – was something she'd outgrown. Thinking that all she'd done was tell the truth, as she was bound to. She had seen the herbs, sprinkled in the orangeade. Her massa asked a question, she answered it. Thinking she had to tell the truth to save herself.

Truth. *Truth, truth, truth.* What was the truth? Oh, by then I knew too much to understand that I knew nothing.

I've since learned that cassava root isn't a slow poison. It kills you in two shakes, unless you can get yourself to some salt of wormwood, quick. If Phibbah *had* been feeding that to Miss-bella, she'd have been dead before she could sit on that pot. But I didn't know it then. Nor did I know why Phibbah didn't speak up for her own self. I never will.

None of this stems the vast, abiding tide of my shame.

Everybody knew the very hour when she was hanged. From the top porch, I watched riders setting out along the road that led up from the harbour, bringing the news to Langton. Miss-bella still hadn't left her bed, hadn't said a word, so no one knew her feelings about any of it, yea or nay. Langton met them at the gates. I stood and watched, blood knocking into the top of my skull. He looked up and saw me, curled his lip, then went back inside, racketing the door back into its jamb so the walls shook. My belly flinched like a struck nail and a sob heaved its way up out of me. I wanted to shout, call him back, tell him there was no hiding place, no herbs. *It was a mistake! It was a mistake!*

But, like all good intentions, that one came too late.

What happened that morning is a dark cloth wiped across my entire existence. All my old sorrows sink into me when I remember it, though now I'm struck by terror as well. Terror that I'll find nothing to persuade the jurors in my own defence. That I might meet the same fate as Phibbah. And that I might deserve it, if I do.

Chapter Six

Some of the anti-slavers visit me here, seeing what stories they can harvest out of me for their pamphlets. What makes them imagine I'd agree? They'd only make it into one of those slave tales. It doesn't cross their minds that I might want to write it myself. Mr Feelon was the last to try it. It was hard enough having him here. He was there that terrible, murderous night, and I don't like to be reminded of any part of it. I gave him my answer even before he had time to ask. 'No, thank you,' I said. 'I think I'd much prefer the rope.'

His lips swam away from each other. 'You must suit yourself, of course, Miss Langton. But bear in mind that if you choose to write it yourself it will be necessary to *season* it. Your readers will need to understand. *Show* them why you had no choice.'

I showed him a raised brow. 'If people don't know already what happens on a West India estate, Mr Feelon, you've wasted your life in the printing of all those pamphlets.'

'But the slave tales we print shed light on *suffering*,' he said, his own face running oil, like a lamp. 'Which is the only way to keep attention on our cause.'

All those good-doers, sniffing at the carcass of slavery, craving always to hear the worst thing. The worst thing isn't that it strips the world to scraps and forces you to fight for them; the worst thing is that one of those scraps is yourself.

Mr Feelon's visit, and his talk of suffering, brought Phibbah to mind – though in truth I'm always thinking of her. It set me wondering how I could write about what happened so you could understand. I can tell you I loved her, and that she was all I had. I was all *she* had. I never wanted to hurt her. That was the least of my intentions. I *had* no intentions – there's no other way I can think to explain it. There was nothing in my mind but that black terror. That quailing. That awful, shrinking, grasping, shaming need. To save myself.

Despite everything that's happened, and the terrible trouble I'm in, if you gave me the choice of one moment to undo, to take back, that would be the one. That moment is the heaviest thing I carry. How I long to set it down.

I write this by tallow light, having now paid sufficient guineas to be moved to a cell of my own. No law says I can't read and write here, but for all I know the turnkeys would throw these pages away if they caught me at it, same as they did with Madame's letter when I was first brought in. One click of a key, one turn of the knob, and I'm ready to shove paper, pen and ink under my skirts. They're always spying, which means I must speed my pen. Now, it's a case of gobbling backwards. As if I spent my whole life putting those words in, and now I'm spitting them back out.

It's *Moll Flanders* that leaps into my head sometimes while I write. But *Moll* has always been a favourite, so it's no surprise I should be thinking of it now. Oh, I know it's the kind of smug nonsense that is always written by men when they write about women. A sermon in sheep's clothing, Madame used to call it.

A man writes to separate himself from the common history. A woman writes to try to join it. What are my own intentions in writing this? The simple answer is that it's my life, and I want to assemble the pieces of it myself. Mr Defoe made a novel and a romance out of the adventures of a felon and a whore, so it must be possible that of my own life I could do the same. Though it's only one part of the world that's taken up with novels and romances, the other part being taken up instead with death and vengeance. It's *that* part which crowds the doors of the Old Bailey at cockcrow waiting to see meat such as me tossed at hungry prosecutors.

Some will ask why I address this manuscript to you. A man I'd never clapped eyes on before I was arrested. But there's a simple answer for that also, which is that I want the same thing Langton wanted. English publishers. And I know enough to know that a white man is the only person on God's green earth who can get me one of those.

Miss-bella's health improved after Phibbah's death, which Langton took as a sure sign he'd been right. She and I were the only ones who knew she'd stopped taking the Surgeon's mercury. It fell to me to empty her pot, with Phibbah gone, and I'd seen her let the silver pearls run into it, and it was then that I put two and two together, made an awful sum. 'You never said anything. You should have said something. He would have listened to you.'

Her eyes shrivelled. 'I was sick as a dog, child. I scarce knew what was happening around me, let alone downstairs.'

You weren't too sick to speak. My mind rocked like a ship. 'Tell him now.'

'What good would that do?'

'They killed her. They took her and you did nothing and now she's dead because you never spoke.'

'Oh, no. Oh, no, no, no, child. She's dead because you did.'

No one ever spoke Phibbah's name again, except me, late at night, when my head went quiet and I whispered it to the wall. I had to do the fan and the footbath by myself. Thoughts of Phibbah jumped into my head every time I did, and whenever I saw the new cook shelling peas. Two years passed in that manner, and then came the day I saw blood on the cotton drawers I'd sewn myself, on my fingers when I touched down there. One more thing to hide, washing rags in a pail behind the cook-room, walking crutch-legged through the house to keep the scraps of cloth from slipping down between my legs. All the small joys of my small life coming to an end. Time has its way with all of us, whether we like it or not.

I was fetching the water one day when a group of the hands who were working near the porch, cutting rails for the front gate, picked that moment to strike up their chatter, their whispers following me across the yard, like dogs on scent: *Massa wait long enough but him soon break her in.* I kept going, head down, tramped up the steps. Miss-bella gave me a curled look. 'Don't you ever think to wag your tail at any man in that yard again.'

Quick as she'd picked me up, she set me back down. Said she would do for herself on the porch, got the new cook to bring her tea. But by then she could do nothing but hate me. 'Tell the yes girl to remove herself from my receiving room, Langton,' she'd say. Or 'Langton, I don't want your yes girl in the house when the Copes are here for dinner Sunday next. I trust you to make sure of it.' She could call me what she liked. A name is nothing but some old thing people use for you, or against.

Miss-bella set me down. But just as quickly as she did, Langton picked me up.

If you stood on the road facing Paradise, you'd see the old coach-house off to the left, beneath the silk-cotton tree. The only part of the estate Langton hadn't rebuilt. Miss-bella never went in there. I'd seen him call the hands into it sometimes, one by one. He'd called Phibbah in to wash the floors and she'd come out afterwards with her skirts tied and her hand-cloth over her nose.

When it comes to charting the course of my life, the

coach-house is the place where the map would show a desert full of wild beasts. *Here are lions*, my mark would say. *Hic sunt leones*. How I wish I'd never entered it. The Surgeon – I never heard him called any other name than that – had been for dinner that night, and the pair of them came to me in the cook-room, where I was sitting staring at the grill. I'd felt the Surgeon's eyes on me the whole time I was putting out their pork, plantains, yams and guinea corn, with their wine and the arrack and the Brazilian rum Langton was so fond of. 'Frances,' he said. 'I'd like you to come with us.'

'She's young,' the Surgeon said. I didn't much like his voice. I heard a trembling in it. The rum bottle glinted like a jewel in his left hand.

There were black rocks inside the coach-house that strained towards each other, cold silver rods, liquids belching in jars. That first time, I was afraid and didn't want to go inside. But they only laughed at me and pushed me in, saying it was not magic but science, more powerful than scattered bones and blood and feathers. Langton said it was a room for experiments.

'What are experiments?'

'A way of proving a thing one suspects to be true.'

'What thing?'

'Any.'

'But why prove it if you already believe it?'

The Surgeon coughed. The tremor had jumped from his voice into his hands. The room stretched around us. Two high arched windows shrouded in old webs, a handful of dead flies spilled into one corner, like rice.

I held up one of the rods.

'Calipers,' Langton said, taking them from me, like a knife from a babe.

He told me they were doing very important work in there,

sponsored by a very important man. 'George Benham,' the Surgeon said.

Langton took the bottle from him, gave a bitter-sounding laugh. 'England's finest mind has taken an interest in our little colonial experiment.'

I'd never heard him talk like this with any other slave. It made me bold. 'Your own experiment? To prove what?'

'That a man's whole potential is seeded in his skull, and one can prove that by examining it closely enough. Europe tries to take the lead in the development of this knowledge – men like Linnaeus, Buffon . . . men like *Benham* – but I believe we can make the real advances here, where we're better placed for once to take the lead on something. We can make our own names. Though we need Benham to attract a publisher.' He glanced at the Surgeon. 'Mind you, he needs *us*, too. He might have the name, but we have the specimens.'

I'd soon learn. It wasn't only bodies did Langton's bidding, it was minds. While I stayed at Paradise he measured mine, watched how it bent, sized it as sure as if he'd gripped it with that cold tool he kept in the cupboard.

'Make a long story short,' said the Surgeon. 'You're going to help us.'

'A great help,' Langton said, lifting the bottle to his lips.

'What must I do?'

There was a short, low laugh from the Surgeon.

I saw things in that coach-house that I can't stop seeing now. But worse than the things I saw are the things I did.

In the early days, I stirred indigo and goat's blood into buckets of piss, to make their dyes, sharpened their nibs, pounced on geese for their quill feathers. I kept my head down to begin with, though I soon lost some of my fear. We were by that time forever cooped up together. And I became something worse than fearful. *Grateful.*

When Langton's quill slipped for the first time, I was twelve or thirteen. He reared his head back, looked at it as if it had bitten him. Weakness started in his hands, went through him quick as water. By the next January, he had a hard time to keep hold of a pen at all. I was stirring at a vat of indigo, lifting my dolly-stick, watching the blue drips fall back into the tin bucket. His hand *tap-tapped* at the table, like someone knocking. His face went dark when he looked down at it, then he threw himself to his feet, as suddenly as if he were casting part of his own body away from him. 'Girl,' he bellowed. 'Come here.'

There was nothing he didn't try. Strychnine, mercury ointments, sweat baths, bleeding. His body a question mark over the pot, his stools snicking into it, small and hard as those long-ago peas. Around that same time, the Surgeon died, leaving me with Langton. And, if an invalid is lucky enough to outstrip his own doctor, that is news that's both good and bad.

What can I tell you about the years that followed? I made them dark for so long, sometimes it's as if I truly can't remember. Langton needed a scribe. I was there, I could be taught, and I cost him nothing, which was all he could afford. For a long time, I thought that was the bargain we'd struck.

His brain; my hands. That's how the work got done.

There were times in that coach-house all I saw was my own hands, floating, when the very floor seemed washed in blood. When I went outside myself. First black, then nothing. It was the same that awful morning, when Linux woke me in Madame's bed. I remember how the constable stared and stared, saying they were *both* dead, Madame too. And me thinking, *I couldn't have done it. I loved her.* But having to hear them telling me I had.

•

Miss-bella asked me about the coach-house only once, the year after I became Langton's scribe.

'I want you to tell me what my husband is doing in that place.'

'You must ask him, please, missus.' I hesitated. 'They only wanting me to clean.'

She looked me up and down, struck her palm flat against the porch railing. She laughed, no mirth in it. 'He does nothing but play God! He's a charlatan. Playing at being a scientist.'

Her face twisted, and I turned mine away so she couldn't see what was printed on it. She looked away, also, and lifted her hip flask. The teapot had smashed, long ago, knocked off the table while she was stumbling out of the chair. She kept one hand on the railing, one on the flask, and I could hear her muttering, under her breath, 'They are monsters, because this place makes monsters.'

I remembered then all the stories Phibbah had told me. About the teapot. About the dancing girls. There must have been a time when Miss-bella dreamed her husband would come to *her*, lift her chemise over her head, bare his teeth like an animal, turn her to face a mirror, take her by surprise. There must have been a time when she hoped he would frighten her, when her heart beat for that very thing.

By then, what she knew about me, and what I knew about her, was hidden deep down where we couldn't find it, in the same place we kept any sympathy we might feel for each other.

It was not until the following year that I started performing my other duties.

I was fourteen or fifteen, then, a woman. My own traitorous body had dragged me fast towards that state, the speed at which such things happen on a West India estate. One night, I carried in a flagon of rum, saw the way he looked up at me, and surprised myself by laughing out loud. He was at his table, sitting on his stool, fingers knotted together like newborn mice. The quake in his hands rattled his dissecting tools. I put the flagon down beside them, moved briskly around the room. My usual tasks. Snicked the latch shut, tidied his papers, lit candles. Light spilled onto the table. I couldn't keep down the bubbles of laughter, like hiccups. Felt my sides cracking, as if I was a peeny-wally knocking against the sides of a jar. I kept him right in the corner of my eye, felt his on me. After he'd drunk some, sloshing rum over the lip of the glass, he looked up. 'What's so funny?'

'Nothing.'

'Then why you laughing?'

'I don't know why I'm laughing.'

'You don't know why you're laughing.' He wiggled his jaw.

My head jerked. Laughs shook out of me hard and fast.

'Stop,' he said. I did. Put my arms around myself, trying to slow my own thoughts. Then I went over to the table, wiped up the spilled rum, the smell of it sweet and rotting as a drunkard's breath. 'I wonder,' he said, eyeing me. 'Must be frightening out there alone at night.'

Let me tell you how I felt then. Relieved. Plain and simple. My head smacked empty by it. I'd known it was coming, I wasn't a fool. There were times I'd tried to hurry it along myself, truth be told. Pulled my dress low, smeared oil to get a glisten on my skin. Like washing stones from a cut knee, or cutting the head off a hen, some things you just have to do without thinking or they'll never be done.

Now it would be done. And you can find ways to shut things out *after* they've happened, but not when you're worrying about whether they will.

He gawped at me. I stood wondering was I to unhook my own dress, pull down my own shift.

'Must be,' he said. And I lifted a hand, reached up to my collar, felt my way to my top button. I wanted him to stop talking and he did. He sat back, watched. I told myself to turn around, to flee. I told myself to close my eyes. *Get on with it.*

All of a sudden he shook his head, lurched forward, and before I could say or do anything he'd spewed all the rum he'd just drunk onto the floor.

I started, nearly jumped out of my skin.

The only clean thing in the cupboard was packing straw, so I threw some onto the floor, wiped his mouth and chin with the rest of it. 'Was it the rum?' I asked. A curdled smell rose off him.

I didn't know the whole of it then. After I did, I knew it was his *own* self that had frightened him, coming face to face with just how far he'd go, and how low, which might not have been a thing he'd known until he put his toe across the border. No one knows the worst thing they're capable of until they do it.

That night is just one of the things that leaps to mind when I think of all the reasons they'd be right to hang me now, and when I think of all the reasons why I should have cut Langton's throat with a dull blade and a cold heart. But, looking back now, I see that your own life can be a story you tell yourself, that you can be both the person reading and the thing being read.

That was the sum of my luck. That he'd waited so long. That nobody else had dared. That he allowed us both to think I had a choice, that it was a bargain we made.

And that health doesn't last for anybody, not even for men who own the world. And Langton's health was turning for the worse.

I know what's said now about what he and I were to each other. *The Times* called it an unnatural suit. No one in their right mind could have described it as a suit, but some of what they've printed is true. Which is rare for newspapers, for we both know they travel some distance to the rear of truth. I lived then in a dark place, and maybe it *was* trying to kill all of us. Maybe you had to have some of the savage about you to survive it. And when Miss-bella threw me away, maybe I *would* have thought to make him drink rum, and lie with him, if he hadn't thought to do it first.

Chapter Seven

Fire on a West India estate means conch shells bellow, shock you out of sleep.

I stumbled out of my little room, the smell of barbecue clogging my throat, so thick in the air for a moment it seemed Phibbah might be back, working her grill. I heard Miss-bella, coughing, screaming for Manso, but smoke was pouring in from outside, coming in through the windows black and thick. I felt for her along the wall, but she slapped my hands off, her voice puffed up and quivering. 'Don't touch me! Don't *touch* me. Get *away*!' I left her, and got myself out, down the stairs and out into a night so black it looked like something stuck in a throat, spitting silver. Cattle screaming, turning to beef in their shed. Flecks of light bobbed beside the cane-piece as fire wheezed and tore through the stalks, smoke running behind it.

The field bucks had come down, carrying torches, to fill buckets at the river and the well. Some of them gripped their skulls and moaned. *'Oh, Lawd, Massa, now what to do?'* No way to tell which was real alarm and which was feigned. Bells ringing and conches blowing all over the place by then. Too late.

First thing I did was look for Langton. I spied him some distance away, over by the boundary wall, and staggered over, coughing. I stood at his side without speaking for several minutes, working what I should say to him through my stomach and my throat. 'Fire in the cane,' he said, at last, before I thought of anything. It hardly needed saying, since the fields were burning gold all around us, black clouds billowing.

'Everybody accounted for,' Langton muttered. I knew what he meant. If the fire-starter had run, it would have been easier to pick him out, hunt him down. Now, he'd have to scatter his wrath rather than aim it. Worse for all, except the guilty ones. No one knew who had started it. But it was plain to see *where*. The coach-house stood testament, blackened and destroyed. With the soil dry as tinder and heaps of cane trash blowing, the fire had started in the coach-house, leaped across dry grass left to grow too high, tripped over to the first field, then the next. Now it scrambled in terrible, crashing waves, outrun by cane-rats. The only mystery was why the house had been spared.

The way he whispered beside me made me feel it was a shared problem, and I was on the right side of it. I felt his fist worrying at my thigh, through my shift, then he grabbed my hand, clutched it to still the trembling in his own, and I let him, thinking no one would be staring at us, not then, with them all so busy with the fire. Fighting it, or staring at it. What did it matter anyway, if they saw? They'd stared all my life. Because I was the only mulatta on the estate, and a house-nigger. Because of the coach-house. Because they all thought they knew what I was to him.

Miss-bella had made her way out onto the road, and stood on her own. Our eyes met over the wall, hers small and dark and hard as peppercorns. There was such a smile on her face, you'd have thought she started that fire herself. To flush me out of her house, like one of those cane-rats. I turned back to Langton.

'Can any of it be saved?' I asked, careful, as I always was, to polish out each word. I was eighteen by then, and had cast off many things. The old slave talk had been the first to go.

He shrugged. 'Might burn off the green, could still save the stalks.'

I nodded. 'Get it under control?'

Out at the cane-piece, field gangs sloshed river water from their pails, keeping along the boundary, limping across hot earth. But I saw that Langton had turned away from them, towards the coach-house, or what was left of it. He gave a hoarse cough. 'Idiot,' he said, narrowing his eyes. 'Not a single thing on this fucking estate is under control now.'

Cane gone, coach-house gone, but the house still standing. Ash and smoke blew through for weeks, streaking faces, walls, clothes. Salting the food, leaving a bitter taste, grit on the tongue. Miss-bella ordered Manso to shutter the windows, steeping all the rooms in a dark, perishing heat.

In the end, the fire cleared the whole of Langton's expected harvest. It wasn't even possible to save the stalks. No crop meant no guineas. Jamaica was a sum: men, cane, guineas. One part missing meant the rest would no longer add up, and a man would no longer be a man. Langton wrote Miss-bella's father, who, it later became clear, had given him the loans that paid for all of it, and who still held the notes. The great house, the windmills, the barns, the new stone bridge: all of it had been funded by him. The sum Langton owed him was vast. He asked for forgiveness of debts: *I know, sir, that your wishes will match my own, chief among those being your daughter's welfare.*

But what he got instead was a letter from her father's secretary, informing him the man himself was dead: *Struck by apoplexy, I'm afraid, at the very moment when your letter must have been en route. Mrs Langton informed by separate communication, enclosed herewith.*

Turned out Miss-bella hadn't needed her father to see sense, only to die. Thereafter all the notes he'd held on Langton's Paradise passed to his son, Captain William Adams, who suggested a different bargain from the one Langton had in mind. Langton would leave Paradise, leave them in *peace*, and in return receive a stipend. They'd put it about that Miss-bella was suffering from ill health, having to stay in Jamaica while Langton travelled, with her blessing, to pursue his long-held scientific ambitions.

So it came to pass that Miss-bella managed to lose her husband but keep his assets. And chose to stay in the place she hated, with the brother she loved. Langton learned that blood is thicker than marriage, and *I* learned I was the only thing Langton hadn't mortgaged, so no one thought it strange when he fled to England, or that the luggage he took with him included me.

I saw Paradise for the last time on 4 January 1825, twisting in the cart for one more look at the coach-house before it vanished, a thick slump of bricks and foundation stones atop the ash and mud.

John Langton and his mulatta were a common enough sight in Montego Bay that no one looked twice, even when we took a room at an inn near the shore. We were an old story. All that night the sea churned with the same boiling energy I felt inside, and whisked itself into the pale rocks. Langton leaned against the sill while I cleaned travel dust from his hands with a damp cloth, and squinted at me, as if simply to look at me made him sour as lemons. Through the window came the sound of the sea, making me wish I could go out and walk beside it, see if that would calm my nerves. I could feel that his hands shook, could see that, in his head, he ran over the same old tally. Short, now. The sum of what he owned: *Crania*, his manuscript that he'd been working on for five years, which was worth nothing; and Frances Langton, who the law had told him was worth the same.

The next morning, we sailed for London.

•

There are those in London – even though I was a housemaid here too, and had lost one buckra massa only to gain an English mister in his place – who say to me, *Frances Langton, you were stripped of your free choice by all that happened to you on that plantation*, but I don't know how to answer. Freedom can't be bought with anything a woman like me has to spend, but there are numberless choices between lying down or putting up a fight.

Miss-bella and I had that in common, too, save that I never let myself forget and she seldom let herself remember.

London,
February 1825

Chapter Eight

Somewhere through the Gulf of Florida, sea air tasting like salt-fish and clouds white as bolls of cotton, I'd dared to ask, 'Will I be free there?'

'Where?' He pretended impatience but he knew full well. Every nigger in Jamaica, whether driver, carpenter, seamstress, cook or buck, could tell you. It's why I asked.

Soon as any man breathe English air, he free.

'London.' First time I'd let myself say the word out loud.

He'd sniggered. 'You will be under my jurisdiction. There, as anywhere. That's all you need to know.'

Jamaica was a sum, a calculation. His life, and mine, had been built on the same. What is the yield in guineas of a tally of Africans, plus cane seeds plus overseers, added to God-given dirt and water and sun? Freedom was a sum, too, one that yields as many answers as men who've set their minds to it. I puzzled over it. I went sick to my stomach thinking about it. I'll confess it.

By the time ropes swarmed the decks, and the order came to drop anchor, freedom was my biggest fear.

How well I remember stepping off the ship at the West India docks, like the shock of stepping into a river, cold water coming over your head.

I'd never seen my own breath before. Hanging off my lips, thick and white as the clouds. Just one of many things I could hardly credit. The rain on my face, for instance, light as feathers. English rain weighs nothing. It's the air that's heavy, and always has the seep of water in it. The streets were wet, and seemed to be tumbling under some giant peggy-stick. I stood there amid the dizzying clatter of hammers and scaffolds and barrows moving piles of bricks that were either crumbling out of buildings or being plastered into them, so it seemed to be a city building itself and eating itself at the same time. Waiting carriages lined up along the high wall, horses shying under the dark bulk of warehouses. A crossing-sweeper was knocked down and the line of foot passengers just curved around him, like a river around a rock.

Everything seemed within reach. I lifted one gloved hand, held it out, palm forward. Then jerked it back in. *Stupid.* There I was, queasy and ship-stale, lost in my own thoughts, the wind slicing my ankles. But inside I felt warm as coals, and my heart swelled like a sail. For I'd done what no other house-girl at Paradise had ever done. I'd improved myself.

Arms and elbows crashed into me, swaying me off my feet.

'You new come?' said a gruff voice close to my ear. I spun around, straight into an old seaman. Swollen, wishbone knees, and a greasy, sun-blackened nose. It was plain to see what he thought I was, rubbing one hand down the placket of his breeches. I almost dropped my eyes, but lifted my chin instead. Gave him a cold shoulder. A white man! Such a peculiar feeling brewed up in my chest, then. Unease and happiness, mixed into one.

Then we were clattering along in our own hired carriage. Sweat-stains ran dark against the leather, the stink of all the bodies who'd been there before. On the bench opposite, Langton fretted his fingers along the neck-cloth I'd smoothed on for him that morning, asked for the third time: 'You have it?'

'I have it.' I patted the papers next to my hip. 'All seven copies.'

My own little portmanteau lay alongside. Two twill dresses, my own copies of *Moll* and *Robinson Crusoe*, the black shawl around my shoulders, with Vandyke edging and a pattern of vines and hummingbirds in bright mustard. Everything I owned.

'Good,' he said, staring out. His own hands danced across his lap, shivering the loose fabric of his breeches. I bit down the urge to reach out, press them still. 'Good.'

The sky was thickening, empty save for a peppering of birds. 'Could it really still be daytime?' I said. 'And yet so dark?'

By way of answer, he kissed his tongue against his teeth. In his bad spells, the words fumbled out of him, so he refused to speak, but I knew what he wanted before he wanted it. Now that we were off the ship, he wanted me cowed, quiet. I folded my arms, like clean towels, felt my spit rise, clogging and sharp. I looked down at them, twisted and twisted at the grey cloth I held in my hand. I'd told myself I would forget Paradise, and everything that had happened there. Scrape it off and cast it aside, gone – like slave speech, like slave manners. Make myself new.

I couldn't keep still. My hands smoothed my dress, serge slick as cat fur, and I sat forward, looked up at Langton, looked out. Daring him to tell me not to. My new skirts sighed against the leather. The distance between poor cloth and fancy is all in how it speaks, and it's the same for people, Miss-bella used to say. But rich people's noises are as rough as anyone's, except that they can buy thicker walls.

I pulled aside the small drape at the window. When Langton said nothing, I pulled it back the rest of the way. It was raining, the streets thick with water and filth. Muddy drops speckled the glass.

I hadn't expected London to be crumbling like a stale loaf. Or the streets to be crowded with people in their hundreds! Faces pale enough to vanish into fog, then float up like curds in milk. Langton was *brown* here, his skin cracked, like ageing leather. And so many of them were poor. Whites toothless and dirty; whites fluttering, like sorrowful little flags, as they pissed into the street. Whites with skin grated raw, and pocked as orange peel. Hard, hungry faces. The children were the worst. Hands quick, eyes slow. The first tingles of fear drained through me when I saw those children. I knew only too well that eyes have only two choices. Open or shut. When they go too wide, too black, it's because they can't make space for all they've seen. The sight of those children sparked a memory, the one other thing I carried that I couldn't set down, though it wasn't in my portmanteau. It slammed into me then, whether I liked it or not, made my stomach jump.

In a world of his own making, any man can be God. Langton had made his own world, and then he'd brought me with him when he fled it. I thought it was because he was a member of that race of men who cannot be men without their slaves.

A copy of his letter to George Benham lay across my lap. I'd been the one to copy it twice onto vellum, one copy to send and one to keep, but then I'd been the one to write every word Langton had put in ink for years.

My dear G,

I enclose the amended manuscript. Crania. It saddens me that the work became the wedge between us. But I'll admit that you were right, about one thing at least. A good scientist merely searches for the answer to the question posed, but the one whose name history will record reaches for the question no one has even thought to ask. There couldn't be a better moment for proof that the differences between the varieties of men are not mere flukes of nature but purposeful design. It is even more important than ever, now that England seems hell-bent on destroying the colonies with the prospect of emancipation, so soon after abolishing the trade.

Her politicians need reminding. A mother doesn't eat her young. Not a tender mother at any rate.

I thought that was where we started. How did our paths diverge?
Be that as it may, I still believe a careful reading of the final
corrected version will lead you to reconsider your stance. With your
name attached again, the work would grow wings. There must be
publishers in England (though I know they can seldom be counted on
to see beyond their own noses) who will recognize the commercial
and scientific merit in this.

Pressing matters will keep me here for some time, and it seems
that it will take me longer to reach you than even the infernal
post. Therefore, this must be entrusted for now to the impersonal
medium of paper and ink.

I will follow it as soon as I can.

Yours &c.,
John

George Benham. The important man. The one who'd started
the work on *Crania*, then written to say he'd changed his mind.
The thought that my path was likely to cross his sent a shudder
through me. *Crania* itself nudged my leg, lying beside me on the
bench. Langton's *magnum opus*. I'd written that too, in my best
copperplate. Yet I had to fight the urge to haul it out into the
muck.

'You're as eager to try your new London manners as you
were to put on that dress.' Langton's lips peeled into a grimace,
his words choked to a halt. His illness sometimes stopped
them entirely.

I sprang out of my seat, pressed his hand in mine. 'Cramp?'
'I need rum.'
'No. You don't.'
'What the devil do you know about anything?' He jerked
his hand away, knuckled it to my breastbone, pushed me back.
But then the trembling came over him again, fingers, wrists,

shoulders. 'This isn't Paradise, girl. You can't just . . . clatter out things that have been . . . private between us . . .'

'There are so many things private between us. I won't be able to say a word.'

He looked away, mouth narrowed. His hands, curled in his lap, twitched like sleeping dogs and his shoulders curled too.

Dying men don't just dwell on the past: they invent it.

'I never touched you,' he said.

I moved back to my own seat, rested my head against the cushion, held myself stiff as the leather, taking care not to look at him. When he told me not to get too snug, I paid him no mind.

'This blasted traffic,' he said, peering out. 'That's London for you. Everything moves fast, until you see it's moving in circles. Not a single thing has taken a forward step in two hundred years.'

He decided we'd get out near London Bridge, find a waterman, elbowing through the crowd. I had to trot so I didn't get swallowed in it, nerves stirred raw, thinking of all the things that could go wrong. He might fall, lose his footing, suffer an attack, or simply turn a corner without me, and vanish. There were a hundred ways I could lose sight of him. And then what would become of me?

The cold seemed to carry its own smell, like raw meat, and came on me sudden as a cutpurse. London air, wet as a kiss. I shivered and reached up to tug on my shawl. 'Only way to get used to it is to be out in it,' Langton shouted back. Heads turned. They stared here, same way the sailors had stared on the *Pride*, when there was no risk of being caught. I felt watched as a clock. To be black in a sea of whites is to wish to be invisible.

I kept my eyes fastened to Langton's back, his new black coat stretched tight as a cheek, lifted my feet between mounds of dung, and fat, slithering puddles. Each time I came too close, forgetting to slow my pace to his, he snapped his teeth. 'Keep some space between us, girl.' As if there was any distance that could magic the two of us into gentleman and maid, instead of what they thought they saw: a slow Creole, his mulatta whore.

I didn't have my land legs back, stopped to lean against a wall and let the wave in my head build up and die down. Then I had to run to catch up with Langton again. Three times I chased, not once did he look back. A heavy feeling poured into me.

But it lifted when we reached the river, and my heart took flight. I felt a wind inside me gathering speed.

The *Pride*'s captain had had a map tacked up in the galley; many a morning I'd traced the crooked seam of the Thames along to its bucket-shaped dip, reading the names aloud. Southwark, Bermondsey, Wapping. On paper, it looked like a meandering curve stitched through the city's chest. But maps never tell the whole truth. For London is a river with a city around it. People milled along the bank, leaning over the railing to watch the ships and the building works, which Langton said were for the new bridge. I forgot about the awful smell, found myself wishing I could linger. Across the water, I could see the arches of the old bridge, the clawing spires and rooflines. The wooden hulls clacked against each other like oyster shells in a bucket. The watermen reminded me of nigger-drivers, the way they rode high on their rowboats, spat out from under their hats. Langton said he'd go down to haggle a ride, told me I'd better stay right where he left me. Fragments flew back to me: '. . . to the Strand . . . me and my . . . my *wife*'s serving girl.'

I was black as a fly in butter, and had no choice but to stand out – and stand there too, pinned to the street, as if my own legs were stuck. Spittle flew at the back of my neck. When I turned I saw one of the barrow-women duck her head and fidget a potato back onto the pile, counting on her fingers, like they were an abacus. I lifted a gloved hand to wipe my neck. Told myself my dress was serge. She was the one who looked slovenly, and low, dressed in linsey with a dirty kerchief. I told myself I looked like a lady. At the very least a higher class of maid. Even if Langton only let me dress as such so no one would see what I was, while I travelled with him.

I told myself it was my head that was filled with learning. I'd read Mr Defoe's *Essay on Literature* the week before, settled under the skylight with water tapping at the hull and night creeping above, thinking how confident a man must be to write down his own musings, expecting anybody else to be interested in reading them.

Sometimes I picture all that reading and writing as something packed inside me. Dangerous as gunpowder. Where has it got me, in the end?

I brushed my skirts down again, set my shoulders back, glanced towards Langton. A pair of girls climbed off the back of a cart, slowed to a stop when they saw me, gawping, looking as if they'd reach out and tug at me. The river shook itself out like a sheet. Dark as pewter. Everything in the whole world seemed to be on its way in or on its way out of London, the water waltzing cargo. For a moment, I wondered what it would be like to plunge, skirts flying, heart in full sail, flow myself through all that silvered water. Let it take me somewhere.

A thread of wind shivered through the ships' flags.

One small step. Another. Forward, forward. I stared down at my feet. How much time passed, while I stood there? Then noise came flooding back. Birds' cries. Scuffling breaths of carriage horses. Slowly, the world fell back into place. You can knock the world down, smash its teeth, kick it to pieces, and still it will click back into its remembered habits, like any seasoned slave.

When I looked up, the girls were clambering away, down a street that twisted into darkness. I wanted to follow. A picture came into my head. Me, flying down the blind street, finding a stone cottage, like a coin tucked up a sleeve. Shelves of books, a crackling fire. Nothing else inside it but time. And a woman, though I couldn't see her face. I'd live there. And I'd write. There'd be no law against it. I'd write a novel. The house would be sturdy around us. Plain and clean and warm.

But no one like me has ever written a novel in the history of the world.

'Get!' Langton said suddenly, crept up against my ear. 'Girl, get!' I felt a squeeze at my temples, cold as Langton's calipers, and looked up and saw that a boat was waiting. I leaned forward, sucked in the breath that hammered back into me, and followed him into it.

Chapter Nine

The anti-slavers are always asking me, what was done to you, Frances? How did you suffer? They don't believe any of it could have been done to you unless you were forced. I remember a thing Phibbah used to say: *Only two types of white people in this world, chile, the ones doing shit to you and the ones wanting you to tell them 'bout the shit them other ones did.*

What would they say if I told them I pinned my own self to Langton, even after we came here? That I was the one who followed him? Oh, how they'd leap away! Uncommon, unlikely. But true. They only concern themselves with flesh and bone, as if those are the only things that suffer. As if minds don't.

I glowered at Langton's back from the bench behind. The river lumbered beneath us, the boat's slow rocking reminding me of a mule-cart. I felt each pull of the oars tugging me backwards, felt the anger pour into me hot as gin. London sped past me as if I was losing it.

We got off near the Strand, walked the rest of the way to Covent Garden, where Langton was meeting the man called Pomfrey at a public house. We found him leaning back in his chair, cheeks bristling with pale whiskers, hands locked together above his gut. Ale foamed like fresh cow's milk above his lip. The room was dim and crowded, each table lit by a greasy candle. Crowded with tobacco and the smells of men. Exactly the kind of place you'd expect to find a creature like Pomfrey. When he saw Langton, he looked up, face leathery as a lung. 'My God, man, what happened to you?'

'Twenty years.' Langton braced his wrists, eased himself into a seat.

'That long, eh?' A slow whistle. 'And who's this?'

'My house-girl.'

'Oho. I heard about this one!' Pomfrey gave a wet chuckle. 'Heard you've been squeezing more out of her than the usual tricks. Can't leave home without her, eh? You colonials! You do things the way a man *should*.'

I'd heard about Pomfrey, too. He was a skull-chaser. The abolition law had spawned men like him. Whatever he'd made as a slaver he'd doubled, dodging the English navy across the Atlantic, slippery as butter on hot bread, still using the same fleet of old Guineamen. 'Bastards only managed to scupper me once, but they found us clean as a whistle, didn't they? A very well-scrubbed brig they said to me, at pains to point it out. "Aye, well, I run a tight one, and surely one navy man won't fault another for that," I told them.'

The skulls he'd shipped to Paradise had arrived in wooden crates, packed in straw, labels tied through the eyeholes with pink ribbons. There'd been a man from Madagascar, bullet hole through the jaw. A female Hottentot with a perfect set of teeth strung like pearls. I can still see them, set out in their rows. In death, as in life, each man cohabited only with the same type. Caucasian with Caucasian, Mongolians side by side, Malays, Americans. Negroes on the bottom. One of my jobs was to measure volume, fill them with white mustard seed, which I then poured back into marked cylinders.

Six hundred and twenty-seven skulls. I'd counted them, written down each new crate in Langton's ledger. Six hundred and twenty-seven. A sum so simple, yet so terrible. One plus one plus one, until there were multitudes, all of them now ash, grated fine as sand.

Pomfrey was still eyeing me. 'Man's got the right idea, I'd

say, when he settles someplace that allows him to warehouse his bobtail right under his own roof.' He gave me a feeling like the hair being pulled tight on my scalp. I looked around. Broad backs, yellowy faces, waving arms. No other women, just the two serving-girls. I'd never sat at a table in a public house before. If any of the slaves had thought to gather in such numbers, Langton would have stamped on it at once, scattered them like cockroaches.

I was expected to be quiet, when it wasn't just the two of us, mind my own business and stay out of Langton's way. But I was in a new place: I wanted something new from myself. I sat up, pricked up my ears.

'What's the latest out of Parliament?' Langton asked.

'Nothing new. Coven of wastrels and do-nothings and *castrati*.'

'Just what you said in '06 –'

'Well –'

'– and then they cut the trade with France, which was the first sally before they choked us off altogether.'

Pomfrey waved a hand. 'The emancipationists want to feel they've had their say. *Et cetera*. A lot of hot air. One thing to stop the blasted trade, quite another to cut a man off at his knees. They can't just take a man's property.'

'We need to make scientific arguments uppermost in the debate, Pom, and we need to be quick about it. Any luck finding another specimen?'

'Oh, there are always specimens, boyo. This fair world of ours is stocked to its rafters with specimens. But you want a white nigger, you want one of them albinos, that is going to take time. And it is surely going to take money.'

'I've been in touch with George Benham, who acted as sponsor.'

That name thudded into me. I looked away, down at the

copy letter, resting in the bag at my feet. Pomfrey tipped his chair onto its hind legs. 'Oho. *George* Benham.'

'Old friend.'

'Ha. I know all about your *old* friendship. Know he cut you loose. Cut you off.'

'I've rewritten the manuscript. To every single one of his specifications.' Langton clenched his jaw, looked at me. 'Not to mention I come bearing gifts.'

Pomfrey laughed. 'Mahomet going to the mountain, eh?'

Langton tilted forward. 'The albino is the part of all this that doesn't have to concern him. I want to try for another study – I heard there was one on display in Paris.'

'And?'

'Maybe start there.'

'*Paree?* Paree? Start in Paree? Start *again*, you mean. I still haven't been paid for your last white-nigger chase.'

'Truth be told, Pom, my pockets are let. I was hoping you'd see your way to –'

He scoffed. 'Credit? It's credit you're after? Ha! You know credit's the one thing I don't do. Not unless you're putting *her* on the table?'

Langton blinked. 'Her?' He turned to me. 'Go get some rum,' he said, shaking me off. Four words from him and I was a serving-girl again. But I was glad for the reason to flee the table, had been looking for one as soon as their talk turned to albinos. And to George Benham. I fumbled a handful of coins from his waistcoat, hoping it was enough. I'd done many things for Langton, but counting money hadn't been one of them.

'A guinea for a Guinea,' Pomfrey said, chuckling, watching me go.

When I returned, his words were tumbling downhill, oiled by drink. 'Course getting yourself on a nigger doesn't mean a thing, they do anything and let *you* do anything . . . it means as much to them as sneezing, doesn't it? But don't it make us animals?' He looked up, sorrowful.

'No more than administering a whipping to a dog makes you a dog,' said Langton.

They looked at each other, then at me. Langton's laugh scraped like rust.

I saw how it would be. Langton was nothing in London, and I would be nothing to him. His maid, that was all.

I swallowed, set down his glass of rum, eyed the candle. Would he stop me if I pulled out my worn copy of *Moll*? I wanted the comfort of it then, more than anything. But the sight of a nigger reading gets some men's blood up, I knew. Both white *and* black. There'd been a kind of freedom in knowing the rules where I'd come from, where I could read, when. I didn't know them here.

Without thinking, I reached over to lift the glass, hold it to Langton's lips, to save him having to use his own hands. He reared backwards, shoved at me. 'Where do you think you are?'

'This one –' Pomfrey whistled, letting his chair drop '– ain't like any nigger I've come across before.'

Quod erat demonstrandum, I thought. *Thus it has been shown.* I let the heavy Latin words tumble around my head, same way I did around most white men. Reminding myself I knew things that he did not. *I'm not a house-girl, not just a house-girl.* The same old thing I always told myself.

'Tell you what,' Pomfrey said, stood abruptly, jostled the table. 'I'll do you even better than credit, old cove.' He squirmed his hand onto my shoulder. 'There's a new academy down Marylebone. The School-house. God, is there *any* lass on *any* corner of this earth who knows how to wind a tongue around a cock like a nigger giggler? Let's take your little wench there. Shame *she* doesn't seem to have a tongue.'

I stood too, lifted his hand, like I'd seen Phibbah do once with a grass snake she caught in the grain shed.

'*Quod erat demonstrandum,*' I said.

But Langton left Pomfrey nursing his tankards, saying he had more pressing matters. He got a boy to fetch a carriage: he wanted to go to Montfort Street.

'What's in Montfort Street?' I asked.

'Benham.'

An awful twisting in my gut. It had been there since Langton had said the name out loud. George Benham. We were going to come face to face. *What would I say to him? How would I be able to hold my tongue? Could I beg to be left at the inn instead?* Those were my thoughts as we arrived at Levenhall, which shows you how little I knew of what lay in store.

Houses lined up like new ponies, holding their heads high like they could just prance right out into the street. Langton struck the knocker, a big brass lion's head. The more swell those great houses think themselves, the more they collect jungle shapes to remember the beasts at the door. The walls around us threaded themselves into the shadows until the only solid thing left on the street was a single gas lamp with its yellowy yawning halo. The door swung half open, so I could see only a row of buttons, the corner of a mob cap, then an entire servant, a solemn-looking woman, with a face like a melting candle, the rest of her very stretched and thin, as was her voice.

She introduced herself to him as Mrs Linux, then looked me up and down. 'This her?'

Langton coughed. She turned back to him. 'We just lost a footman, you know. One of our pair. Married and . . . off! To his wife's family. One of *those* is what we need.' She gave me a sharp look, as if the loss had been my fault.

A strange way to answer the door, I thought. If I'd only caught her meaning then, I'd have run a mile, and I wouldn't be where I am now.

Langton said it was quite all right, she mustn't worry, and la-la-la. It was nothing like the way he talked to Phibbah or any other house-girl. Some kind of English music sneaking into his voice.

There was a tang of vinegar at the front door. The house stretched above us, a marble stair leading to a landing on the third floor. Portraits lined the wall, like captured thieves. As she led us to the back of the house I spied plainer wood stairs going up there. For the servants, I assumed. All quiet down below, windows covered with heavy damask drapes, but whispers through one of the closed doors, like scratches on wood. She left Langton in what she called the drawing room. He said I should follow her below, to the kitchen, which I did. It was inside, at least, unlike the cook-room at Paradise. There was a turnspit at one side of it, a maid cross-legged beside the fire with a bit of cheese. Linux lifted the kettle on the hob while I stood at a loss.

'The first thing you'll do is scrub your hands.'

I drew myself up. 'I won't be spoken to in that manner.'

'I will not be spoken to in *that* manner,' she said.

'Is this how your guests are treated?'

She drew in her lips, leaned forward. This is always the way of it. First I'm not seen, then I'm stared at too closely. 'I suppose you'll soon learn how our guests are treated,' she said, at last. 'But for now you'd better learn how our hands are treated, and the first thing you'll do is scrub yours well.'

She knew the way, but I was angry as lightning and just as quick. I got there first, pulled Langton over to the window, while she hovered at the door. 'Langton,' I said. 'She treats me like a servant here.'

He busied himself with the sash. 'Frances.' He looked up at me and there was something in his face that I had never seen there in all the years. I swear it looked like pity. I almost slipped and fell. 'You *are* a servant here.'

It was then it came clear. I was to be Langton's gift.

For a moment, I stood there, rooted to the spot, with that knowledge hammering inside, and his words flying away so I could catch only the tail end of them: '. . . important . . . girl, do not embarrass me.'

I nodded. 'But you're coming back?'

'That's none of your business.'

'Since when are your doings none of my business? Langton?' I reached out.

'Behave yourself.' He pulled back, slapped me. Even Linux gasped. It was the shock of it that thundered into me, more than the strength, considering the state of his hands, how for years I'd thought he couldn't muster anything out of them. You could have lit a spill off the force of my fury, then. But it knocked those words out of me all the same. Those two words I never used: *Massa. Please.*

But Linux pulled me away, by the arm, and Langton watched, and kept himself by the window, and said nothing.

Once we were in the passage, Linux called out, 'Pru!' and the kitchen maid appeared and I tugged and tugged, then gave in, knowing I had no choice but to follow her upstairs, feeling all the dread with which I'd have entered the house had I known what was waiting for me. Pru's fuzzy braid batted at her hips, red as paint, and she looked behind, motioned me to shush. Only then did I hear the noise that was still pouring out of me, which had started downstairs, the terrible moaning. I put my hand over my mouth, stuttered out quaking breaths.

All around us a wavering dark. The carpets gave way to lime-washed wood and then a naked little room. Eaves hunkering over a small bed. A washstand and a pallet in the corner, right under the window.

Pru put a bowl, which smelt of sheep fat, on the bed. 'That's for my hands,' she said. 'But help yourself, if you want.' The rushlight gobbled itself up and the room stood dark and still. I could see only snatches of her. One white arm, one foot rubbing against the other, the neck of her gown winking open as she lifted a nightgown from the nail above the bed. She gestured towards the pallet. 'I've given you one of the blankets and you can take the warming pan. Only for tonight, mind.' She pulled off her dress and stockings, leaned over and pinched her big toe. 'I've never seen a blue-skin this close before.'

'A *blue*-skin?'

'A darky. Like you.'

I could've told her I'd never seen a slaving white girl, but unlike her I could keep my thoughts to myself. I stared down at the pallet. If I lay on it, I'd be stuck. I'd be a maid again. But where could I go? A branch struck the window and cold air brushed at my neck, though it was shut. Outside lay the river, the bone-rattling cold, the dark, twisting streets. *Where could I go?* I felt a sagging disappointment, the nasty twin of all the hope I'd shouldered at the docks. I thought of Langton, wondered if he was still downstairs, if I could run down there, plead with him again. I drew in a breath. Even my skin felt tight.

Pru reached under her bed and pulled out a bottle. 'Don't mind too much about Mrs Linux. She's out of sorts at being caught short a footman – well, truth be told, she's none too happy about *you* either. Blacky servants might be all the rage with some houses. They used to have one here, though I never met him, but Mrs Linux says that ended in nothing but bother, so she'd rather not have another. She says it's all savagery where you're from . . .'

I cried out again. She gawped at me. When I sank to the pallet, her eyes followed, as if she feared I'd howl, bare my teeth, rip into her, like a dog into a hen.

I wanted to do all three.

Have *you* tallied the vertebrae in the warehouse of a man's back? I wanted to ask. Read the *Encyclopédie*? Pulled a heart out of its cage, thick and slippery?

No doubt she couldn't even read, signed herself with an X.

She took a seat on the bed, still watching me. 'Any house can be strange,' she said. 'But you just get used to it, don't you? Though, mind you, I've only been in this one, and the one Ma birthed me in. But people are strange, and people live in houses, and make them strange . . .'

My thoughts scattered and drifted above her chatter. Ran like marbles. Smashed like glass. I cried out again.

'Oi! None of that up here,' she said. 'You should just try to settle. It won't be as bad as that.'

But I wouldn't settle. Couldn't. I pressed a palm out in front of me, felt along the cold stone. It seemed that in England the ground also could become air, slip right out from under you with no warning. Langton had made me disappear. *That* was some magic, to take a body thick with meat and blood and dreaming and turn it into air.

I cringed, then, remembering how I'd shamed myself. *No, Massa. Please. Don't leave me. No, Massa, please.* Remembering the housekeeper, arms crossed like swords, face bleached in anger: 'Was she not informed, sir, about these arrangements?'

Massa. Please.

It was the whine of my own voice, needling into me, that had finally driven me quiet. Not his hands, batting me away, or his own sharp words: 'You're embarrassing yourself, girl, you're embarrassing me. Making a spectacle.'

For some things, there's the same shame in fighting them as accepting them.

'You should consider yourself lucky, you know,' Pru said. She took a sip. 'Being maid to George Benham. Many would give their eye-teeth, instead of howling about it.'

I huffed a breath. 'One master's as bad as another.'

'True. Mr Benham's no *worse* than the next one.' Her eyes scuttled away and back. 'But Mrs Linux says they call him the finest mind in England and we should be proud to work here. And he pays fair, and he stays out of your way, which is more than you can say for many of them. And he dotes on her. Madame. Though she doesn't return it.' She lowered her voice. '*He* can never be exciting enough for her – but nor can she ever be tame enough for him.' Another sip. 'You'd think ten years would be long enough married for her to settle into it. But I shouldn't be tattling, for Mrs Linux don't like us to be familiar.' She set the bottle on the floor. 'It *is* queer, you just being left here. Did you really not know anything about it?'

Not a thing.

I had pictured myself starting a new life in London. Even if it meant having to play maid to Langton. Instead I'd been left with a man I hated before we'd even met, and now had to play maid for *him*. I couldn't think why Langton had done it. But I was always the last to know about a thing, before it happened to me.

Fear sent the walls tilted and black. Would the same work be required of me here that I'd done at Paradise? Was that *why* Langton had brought me? If anyone asked me, I decided – *anyone* – I'd do what I'd never done before: I'd refuse.

I gritted my teeth, sat upright, refusing to lie down, refusing to keep still. My mind skated and skated. A mind can always roam the possibilities, even when nothing else can. That's the awful terror of it. Mine pushed its snout through the front door, into the streets. 'How far are we from the river?'

'What do you want with the river?' She slanted her eyes at me.

'Nothing,' I said. 'Just to know.'

'Aye, well. Couldn't be anything good, this time of night.'

When I could sit no longer, when my lids shuddered, I lay back, staring up at the ceiling. Pru turned over, sneezed, spoke to herself, 'God bless me!'

I lifted my grey rag to my nose. Phibbah's kerchief. The colour bleached out of it by the long ocean. The moon fingered the sill, trembled on the pane and along the wall. My thoughts trailed. Forward was all black, nowhere for them to go but into the past. Which was when I felt the pinch of memory, sharp as salt. I wrenched upright, breathing hard, stared down at the cold floor, at the long night.

After I closed my eyes it was the coach-house I saw behind the lids.

Chapter Ten

Next morning Linux was in the kitchen before us, frying kippers, calling out over the hissing of the oil, 'Prudence. What time do you call this? Porridge is under the fire-cover. Fetch the bowls down.' She turned. Eyes narrow as keyholes. I saw a scattering of scars across her cheeks. Smallpox, Pru was to tell me later. 'As for *you*. You've taken this place with your elbow, haven't you? Lifted the bread right out the mouth of so many English lasses, who'd have been perfectly good for it. Well. You're here now.' She squinted as if weighing me on a set of baker's scales. I lifted my chin.

'No shirking,' she said. 'No skirt-twitching. No thieving. None of the kind of fuss you made last night. A new girl's disturbance enough, the least you can do is be a quiet one. Understood?' She snapped her tongs in the air. 'Understood?'

'She *can* speak,' Pru muttered, clanking down the bowls from the dresser. 'Cat's got her tongue.'

Linux nodded. 'Quiet is good. Last thing we want's a vain bit of baggage. You'd do well to pipe down too, Prudence.'

She spoke to Pru, but kept her eyes on me. I lifted my chin. 'No shirking. No disturbance. I understand.'

'*Ma'am.*'

'Ma'am.'

'You'll be given a rushlight when you need it, soap once a fortnight. I won't abide strange smells.'

I won't make them, I thought. She motioned for me to follow her to the table.

'Do you use spoons?' The question almost choked a laugh

out of me. She held one up, tapped it against one of the clay bowls, which was yellow as a yolk. She leaned over, close, face like a palm-reader. 'Bowls? *Do you know how?*'

I stuffed my voice full of English vowels. 'I am well acquainted with all the customs and habits of English dining,' I said. '*Ma'am.*'

'Your speech is good, at least.'

'Yes. I read. I write, too.'

'Do you?'

That was a mistake. I should have remembered that there are many who find an educated black more threatening than a savage one.

Linux made me sweep the hearth and refill the kettle for the hob and scrub the flags on the kitchen floor with sand while we waited for the water to boil, then sent me with a broom and shovel to light the fires up in the drawing room. The man-servant, Charles, showed me how to shovel up the coal, strike the steel and flint together, holding both away from me and over the tinderbox, then blow on the tinder, which was grudging and limp until it caught in a thin blue flame, and how to push in the taper. After the first flame caught, he showed me how to pump the bellows over it, and then I was on my own with the fireplaces in the dining room and the library to see to, and coal scuttles to fill from the box beside the kitchen, down to the basement and back up, over and over. I worked as quickly as I could, feeling the prickle of sweat at my armpits.

In my head, it was still yesterday. All my humiliation of the night before washed over me again. Those last few minutes that Langton had doled out to me, like mash. The click of his nails against the window.

Massa. Please.

I stared down at my hands. Their new work was simple, numbing, requiring nothing but brute force or mute endurance.

Work that had to be done without thinking. A red rash had crept across my palms, and I tucked my thumbs in, to scratch at them. When I felt the quick, sour crumple of tears, I swiped at them angrily.

I'd belonged to Langton, you must remember, grown as if from a mango pit he'd tossed out of a window, and therefore still thought I was *his* to give, strange as that may seem to you, reading this manuscript of mine in the comfort of your own chambers. This is what I was trying to tell you, when you asked, 'Why didn't you just *run*?'

'I kept forgetting,' I told you.

'Forgetting what?'

'That I was no longer owned.'

That first day was one long putting-away, though memory was a spike buried as deep as Langton's long-ago words: 'The limits of a man's achievements lie at the limits of his desire. You know what that means, girl? Niggers don't want. Therefore, niggers don't do.' Reminds me of a thing one of the turnkeys read out to me yesterday, from *The Times*: *'Take freedom away from any man and you'll make him a brute who doesn't deserve it. That this might be true of blacks, especially of the Mulatta Murderess, proves only that which is already self-evident; namely, that so many of them have had their freedom taken away.'*

Hunger drove me downstairs, but I stopped short on the bottom step. Oh, there was the usual kitchen song and clatter. Pots clanking, water mumbling on the stove. The smell of frying onions. But I heard them chatting among themselves: that was what stopped me. Everything that morning seemed a mountain to climb. I sat, and set the bucket down beside me, listened at the door. I heard Pru asking permission to brew more tea, then Linux murmuring about the carpets, that were Turkey carpets and very dear and possibly beyond saving, since

84

Madame had spilled ink on them, but were to be scrubbed and laid out anyway against the hawthorn. 'Herself's been nothing but trouble this week,' she said.

'The new lass looks like trouble too,' Pru called out. 'She *stared* all night. Gave me such a terrific fright.'

I heard Charles laughing. 'Could be she planned to sharpen her teeth on you.'

'Oh, no! She's all airs and graces. You should hear her speak! Can you credit it? A *black*! We got one who's got a princess shoved up her pin-cushion.'

The scrape of a chair sent me clambering to my feet and I threw myself back upstairs, heart clattering in my chest, feet landing hard as bullets.

It so happened that I was to light fires in Benham's library next. I tried to shake off the angry thoughts that wanted to crack me, like an egg, as well as my dread that I might soon encounter him. But the room was empty, and to find myself alone among books just then was a needful comfort. I stopped at the doorway. Cherry-dark wood from floor to ceiling, black-and-white tiles. On one wall, a pair of tall windows overlooked the street and on the opposite one the bookshelves were divided by marble columns, and a pair of naked statues with eyes like peeled oranges. I leaned over, read some of the names. Hazlitt. Buffon's *Histoire Naturelle*. Benezet. *The Political History of the Devil*.

Candide. I set down my bucket, plucked it out. Its spine creaked like an old woman's knees.

I was on the porch again, swallowing pages. *Imagine the situation of a Pope's daughter, aged fifteen, who in three months had undergone poverty and slavery, had been raped nearly every day, had seen her mother cut into four pieces, had undergone hunger and war, and was now dying of the plague in Algiers.*

A laugh shook itself up out of me, thin as dust. Ha! *Imagine.* Then the tears did come, hot, ungovernable. I swiped at my eyes. I didn't dare read further, shoved the book back onto the shelf. But in doing so I caught sight of my hands, bloated as pork. This was how it would be. Hands in lye, hands in vinegar, hands in soap. I leaned my weight against the bookcase. I'd be the darky maid, underfoot. Another nigger. I staggered blindly across the room. On his desk stood a glass paperweight in the shape of a triangle, and a china plate smeared with egg. Nothing else, save Paley's *Natural Theology*, and his own *Encyclopaedia of the Natural World*. A document beside it, headed *Notes for new edn*. Behind it, an onyx globe tipped over on its stand. Curved gilt arms gripped it around the middle like calipers, and the ocean had been shrunk so small I could have lapped it up with my tongue, continents bright as smashed crockery. Some men want to shrink the world to fit themselves. I could see my new master was one of those.

I lifted a red snuff box shaped like a cat, with jade-green jewels for eyes, set it down, and picked up each of the others in turn. Leather, ivory, bone, tortoiseshell. I ran my fingers over them. And over jars of snuff, all marked with names I'd never read before. I sounded them out. Macouba, Bolongaro, Masulipatam. I lifted one of the jars, opened it. A burst of tobacco and oranges and violets. The smell of men and bright fields and faraway lands. I spied a single sheet of paper, glanced at the door, picked it up.

John,

> *I know that you are an admirer of* le sage *Locke. Let me therefore use his words in the hope they may drill where others have been too blunt to reach: 'Whatever I write, as soon as I discover it not to be true, my hand shall be forwardest to throw it into the fire.'*
>
> *Is that clear enough? I will take the girl, but nothing more. Nor will I correspond any further on these matters.*
>
> *G.*

I dropped the letter as if it had sprung teeth and bitten me. I almost cried out. I looked around me.

How to explain what I did next? A blink of madness. I bent and snatched at my hem, picking at the seam until it loosened, reached once more for *Candide*, pulled at its threading with my thumbnail, and slipped page after page into the safe, dark tunnel of my hem. It would be nothing to Benham, I reasoned, one book out of multitudes, and all of them cleaner than fresh-baked bread.

You mightn't believe me when I tell you I soon forgot those pages were there, but that is just what happened. Nor was there malice in what I did, though there are so many now trying to find malice in *everything* I did. If it was a crime, then I am guilty of it, and I confess it here. But I just wanted to keep that book as close as I could get it to my skin. Not to remind myself happiness was still possible, but to remind myself that *anger* was.

From the hallway, the tick of footsteps. I barely had time to scramble upright, swipe up my bucket and rag, and stumble over to the hearth.

A man appeared. He drew back when he saw me. 'Langton's girl,' he said.

The finest mind in all of England. But he was a man, not a mind. And a large one at that. Wearing a black, well-starched suit, white cravat, shoes polished to blinding. Long nose, sandy hair pulled smooth, tied with a black ribbon at the nape. He looked as old as Langton, but his eyes were bright, his hands steady. He had the gift of health.

But then I disappointed myself. Because it was terror, not anger, that I felt. I drew back. 'Mr Benham? I was . . . I was . . . lighting your fires. Sir.'

He frowned at me, walked over to his desk. Blocked the

globe, like a cloud over the sun. He leaned over and lifted his letter.

I flapped my hands, sure that he'd seen me take those pages. 'I'll sew them back in, if I can, if you'll –'

'Sew what?'

'What is it worth? A few pages out of *Candide*?' I let my arms hang, a sick feeling in my stomach.

'*Candide*?' He glanced behind him. 'Oh. *Ha!* Quite right, quite right. What's any page worth? Of any book? Words as commodities.' He tapped his forefinger to his lips. His hands were pale and girlish, like those of any man who works only in his head. 'Langton said you had some wit.'

In those days, I had a dog's nose for praise, though what I was thinking was that Langton would never have said any such thing. 'He did?'

'He also said you were a machine and he could wind you up and make you move.'

'That sounds more like him.'

He laughed to himself. 'Marguerite will find you droll.'

I stepped back, still in the grip of my terror, but knowing I had to steady myself. The only thing a maid can do with a new master is to study him. 'Sir.'

Along the top of the bookcase, I could see a telescope with a gilt-edged eyepiece, a marble statuette of a horse bucking onto its hind legs, a rocking cow made of plain old wood. I couldn't see what one thing had to do with the next or why they were hidden up there out of reach. They looked like toys he might have found it difficult to part with, as if he was ashamed for the world and his mother to know that the finest mind in England still hadn't put away his childish things. He flipped the tail of his jacket, lowered himself into the chair. 'Stay. I want a word with you.'

'Sir,' I blurted. 'I was not expecting to be left here . . . not like this – that is, I have not been a maid, sir . . . for many years. I –'

'Yes. Oh, yes. I know what you've been.'

'What I've been?' I wanted to flee, not stand there discussing things I'd crossed an ocean to leave behind. *Oh, yes, you know*, I thought. *You're responsible for it.*

But a maid waits to be dismissed; she doesn't ask. Nor had I lit his fires yet.

He made a long study of me before finally speaking again. 'Have you heard of Francis Williams?'

'No, sir.'

He rustled some papers, glanced from them to the top of my head. Lifted his quill. 'Take your hair down.'

'*What?*'

No. No, no, no. My head whipped up, and a memory whipped into it. There'd been a woman at Paradise, named Sukey, who'd lost her hands in the crusher. I'd seen her sometimes, squatting behind the cow-shed, a coin between her teeth. It was charity, Langton said, allowing her to stay on, share the old women's cabin. 'One grateful nigger pays a thousand dividends.' Hitched breeches, a sly grin.

There was only one kind of work Sukey could do, with no hands. When she saw me watching her, my face so sour, she hawked and spat, and the coin flew loose. 'You wait. Massa soon show you what all nigger women born for.'

I answered Benham, spoke the word out loud. '*No.*'

But just then a fist galloped across his door, and Linux pushed through it, carrying a tray. 'Oh! Begging your pardon, sir. I didn't know you weren't alone.'

'As you can see, I am not.'

'No. No. Well –' She stood for a minute, at a loss, darted her eyes at me. 'I thought to clear your breakfast plates.' She scooted forward, came up with the egg-streaked saucer in one hand, the tray in the other. 'I've just admitted Lady Catherine downstairs, sir.'

'Surely that's for you to tell Meg.'

'Very well, sir.' She looked from him to me, chest quivering.

He waited for the door to close behind her. 'I didn't mean it like *that*, girl, I meant only to make a . . . study of your hair. But . . . no matter . . . There is a time to every purpose under the Heaven . . . Where was I? Oh, yes, Williams. Williams! Williams was a Jamaican black, like you.' He dipped into the cat's head for a pinch of snuff. 'It's an interesting tale, you know. The Duke of Montagu wagered that Williams could swallow down an education as well as your average Englishman. Found a tutor to stuff him to the gills with the whole lot – Latin, Greek, multiplication, philosophy. No doubt the flogging and the fagging too. And young Williams proved himself a marvel, by some accounts. Genius where you'd least expect it, like getting oranges from Richmond . . . And –' He flinched the powder up his nose. Snuff drifted onto the table. '– and, after all that, he couldn't *do* anything with himself, though not for want of trying. Ended up going back to Jamaica, I believe, running some little school there, for piccaninnies. Wrote a few awful poems. *Truly* terrible. Let me see . . . I think I remember one . . .' He leaned his head back.

I hesitated. 'A gentleman's education can't magic up a gentleman's life. No more than a poet's education can magic up a poet's talent.'

He jerked his head down again. 'Indeed! Indeed, *Frances*.' He nodded, patted himself on the chest. Some men, if you say something clever to them, always believe it is their *own* trick. He turned to his paper, lifted his quill again. Behind him, books hunkered shoulder to shoulder, like cannons. 'He went out for the Royal Society, you know – young Williams – and they knocked him back because of his race. You do *know* what the Society is?'

'The scientists. *Nullius in verba*. Take nobody's word.'

Another trick, the Latin. He gobbled it up. 'Bravo! Bravo! *Nullius in verba*.'

'You and Langton corresponded,' I blurted. 'About *Crania* –'

'Ah. Yes. I gather *you*'re the one who wrote me back. It was my idea for you to be educated, you know. A sort of wager.'

'A *wager*?' The word shattered in my head like glass.

'So you could say you've come full circle, haven't you, Langton leaving you with me?' A dry laugh. 'The Lord moves in mysterious ways.' He turned to write something else down. 'What do you make of young Williams's tale?'

I quailed, thinking of Paradise. The coach-house. The things that had been done there. I *had* been a machine. Their machine. An automaton. *Wind them up and make them move.* Because I'd been up on my high horse, and had a bit of learning. Because Langton permitted me the books. Because of a scheme they'd cooked up between them. Was that any better than whoring myself for coins or scraps of bread?

I made my next words slow. Made sure nothing showed in my face. 'What I think, sir, is that Mr Williams learned that the price of an education is different depending on who you are.'

'Yes. *Yes, yes*. And *you*'ve been a veritable English schoolboy yourself –'

'I have, and I have not.'

He narrowed his eyes. 'Meaning?'

'I learned whatever would be useful to *Langton*, sir, whereas I'm sure the object of educating a schoolboy is to teach him something that would be useful to *him*.'

'You were an apprentice. Of sorts.'

'More of a scribe.'

'Caliban to his Prospero!' He needled his eyes through me. 'If thy right hand offend thee, cut it off?'

'Pardon?'

'If thy right eye offend thee, pluck it out? But you and I know a thing or two about man's imperfections, don't we, gel? Man's nastiest sins? We know a thing or two about atonement as well.'

With only myself for company in this cell, I'm driven always to think about what they say I've done. To wonder whether that strange encounter with Benham might have been the start of it, a straight path from there to that awful night. For this is where my anger started. Learning that the pair of them had toyed with me, like small boys pulling the wings off moths. Wondering if Benham was the same as Langton. Wondering what he might want from me. For so many years I had told myself that if my path ever crossed his I'd make sure he felt it. And then my courage had failed me when I'd had my chance.

That anger would have been reason enough to kill him, I can't deny it. Tear off *his* wings. Even now, thinking about it, there's that hot quiver of rage again, the same quiver that was there that morning, after Linux woke me up. My head charred and black.

There's no shortage of people who believe I was savage enough to have done it. But some people look at a black and see only a savage, the same way some people will look at arsenic and see only poison. That's how they see me here, too. They even take their time about permitting me to empty my bucket, and some days I'm so lonely I even miss watching the old birds in the communal cell. Maud, holding her hand over the mark where her husband branded her with a poker, or Miss Priss, the wards-woman who used to be a procuress but who makes a better racket in here than she ever did outside, and Margaret and Jane Whimple, sisters, and therefore always at each other's throats.

Now I sit on my own, and the turnkeys try to make an animal of me. Though not even an animal can tolerate keeping company with its own pot. It's them who are animals: 'We could help you plead your belly, you know, even a filthy murderess like yourself.' But they're afraid, for all their talk. I see it in their eyes, and the way they give me a wide berth. I know what they're thinking. *Who else would have murdered the master of Levenhall, but the black he harboured under his roof?*

They might see me as the savage, but didn't Benham and Langton pull me into their own dark corners? Wasn't it them who tried to make an animal of me first?

EUSTACIA LINUX, sworn.

Mr Jessop: Mrs Linux, you were the housekeeper at Levenhall?
A. Yes, for seven years. Before that for Sir Percy. And under-maid for Sir William, the father, before that. I don't know what's to become of all of us now, though a good servant won't want for offers. The Lord provides. Some of the staff are kept on for the time being, to pack up the house, until Sir Percy, the master's brother, gives us word. I am here to tell you that Levenhall suffers now, and so do those of us left within it. There was a newspaperman in the hedge last week, they're as bad as vultures. We had to run him off. Thank God Mr Benham isn't here to see this.

Q. You were housekeeper to Mr Benham, when the prisoner joined his household?
A. I was not happy about it. He didn't even tell me why it was being done. Only I gathered it might have something to do with his own work, given that he was revising his Encyclopaedia, but I never enquired too much into that as he preferred to be left alone with it. What we needed was a footman, but we got her instead. I asked him would he really have us break bread with her? All we knew about her was that she came from that barbarous place. Savagery is a cruel nursemaid, I said to him, and cruel nursemaids rear cruel infants.

Q. How many others were there in the house?
A. Three servants, in addition to the prisoner. Mr Casterwick, the butler-valet; Prudence Rattray, the under-maid; Charles Pruitt, the manservant. Together with the master and mistress, that made seven of us.

Q. How were relations between you?
A. We got along as necessary for getting on with the work. Servants shouldn't be too familiar. Neither among themselves nor with their masters. There was no trouble at all before the prisoner arrived.

Q. And what about the master and mistress? How did they get along?
A. Theirs was a happy marriage. It's disgraceful that anyone would now imply otherwise.

Q. Forgive me, Mrs Linux, but I must speak plain: what about the suggestion of a love affair between the prisoner and her mistress?
A. I hope you don't expect me to dignify that with an answer, sir. All I'll say is that she's the only one who claims it, which tells you every-thing. Nothing but the lunatic invention of a lunatic mind.

Chapter Eleven

Montfort Street ran cobbled and straight. Like a spine. Houses huddled on either side of it, neat behind their little gold knockers. Linux sent me outside with Pru to wash the steps, and Pru went ahead, clumsy with the bucket, glancing back now and again as if to make sure I wasn't going to stop, or cry out, like the night before. I kicked my heels out against my hems, and then, there being no other choice, I went to my knees and dipped my brush. For a time, there was only the scratching of brushes against stone, like mice in a cupboard. Sweat crawled at the backs of my knees and between my shoulder blades. Beside me, Pru's arms moved steady as oars. Soot peeled away in waves under her brush, leaving the stones pale as sand, and I tried to copy her.

My hair broke out of its plait and swung in brown clouds across my face. It was the kind of work that leaves too much room for thought. My meeting with Benham that morning swilled around my head, like linens in a copper. And there was anger, too. The first cold spurt had come from thinking he wanted the same work out of me as Langton had. Then it had come from thinking he wanted what they all want, first my hair down, then my dress. But he'd wanted *worse*. 'You're going to tell me what happened there. Every last thing. Exactly what Langton did.'

No. My head swelled full of that single word. *No.*

I could hear our brushes loud on the steps. All else was black. Only a sliver of memory. The silk-cotton tree. The warm, squirming bundle, the milky smell. *No!* I thought. *Never.*

I squeezed my eyes shut, feeling the bile rise, until Pru poked an elbow into me, sharp as a hook, and motioned for me to get on with it. I pushed down harder on my brush, water darkening the flags. My breath rasped like the bristles – in, out, in, out – clawing at my chest until, after a time, my head hummed, empty and dark. Then the doors swung apart, pushing us backwards, and two women came out. One stout, dressed in a long pink gown that ended in a frill at her ankles. The other taller, slimmer, walking behind with her eyes cast downwards and a black book clutched to her chest. She was the kind of frog-belly pale that is coveted by Creoles of a certain class, that lamp-bright skin they all blister themselves with cashew oil to get, and her hair was scraped into a navy turban. A plume of feathers trailed against her cheek, dyed blue to match, and her walking gown was green, with an empire line. Her mouth wide and red like something in bloom, and neck-bones like the handles on a dresser. Pretty like the Devil. *Anybody who pretty like the Devil bound to be just as sweet,* Phibbah would have said.

I held my brush up, let the suds drip.

She stopped suddenly, on the bottom step, swung her eyes back to where we stood. Blue as those long-ago pails of indigo. Shocking, bright. Little puckers at the corners made her seem sad. 'You are . . . ?'

'She's the new girl, Madame,' Pru called out. 'From the Indies.'

She squinted, little creases pulling like thread around her eyes.

'I'm Frances,' I said, trying to hold my hands over my skirts, where soap had scummed snail-tracks into the blue. The likes of her expect nothing but curtsies from the likes of me, I thought, so I lifted my chin, puffed the hair off my brow.

'I see. *Frances.* How are you finding us?'

'A shock.'

It sprang out, before I could think better of it. But she only laughed. Like coins jangling, copper chiming copper. 'I suppose we are . . .' she said '. . . or *this* place is.' She motioned at the door behind me, where I imagined the lion knocker must still be making its awful grimace.

'Meg!' Pink-frock called out, from the pavement. 'Will you *come*?'

She cocked her head and looked me up and down. Studied me the way the Surgeon used to study a body before cutting, a little stitch of worry between her brows. Suddenly she lifted her skirts and clicked her heels and nodded, the kind of bow a gentleman would make to a lady. *How strange she is!* I thought. Charles opened the carriage doors and helped them inside, leaving us to gape as it pulled away, all quiet again, except for the *plink-plink-plink* of water from our brushes. There being no help for it, I went back to my hands and knees, and Pru did the same, swiped at her forehead with the back of a wrist.

'Madame must be feeling herself again,' she said. Her voice had brightened – the women had lit her up. 'And didn't she take a shine to *you*!'

I made no reply, rubbed my finger into a crack that was already damp with moss, for all the house was new. Green as a stale crust. She pursed her lips. 'Friendliness makes the day go faster.'

She hadn't sounded friendly in the kitchen, but I'd have to swallow my anger, I knew, just as I'd been doing all day. I squatted back on my heels. Thoughts of my new mistress had mercifully crowded Benham out of my head. She'd spoken to me as if we were being presented, one lady to another. I'd felt a tug. Quiet had slipped into me, like water into sand. Like those times when Phibbah pointed at a chicken hawk, or a pair of parrots, whatever she could find streaking across the sky, then dabbed whiskey on my cuts and bruises. Of all London's surprises, I thought, she was the only pleasant one. I dropped my eyes, scraped my brush across the stone.

'That was the mistress?' I asked, though I knew full well.

'Herself, yes. The one in green. With Lady Catherine, who's married to the master's brother.'

'Are ladies so familiar with their servants, here?'

She snickered. 'You want to know what *Madame* will do? Think of what's expected, then imagine the opposite.'

'She's been unwell?'

Pru puffed her cheeks, poked at one with her tongue. 'It's one of *those* complaints that only ladies ever suffer from. Ones like her.' She shrugged, sweeping her brush wide. I watched her hands move. Raw and chapped, shoulders broad as ships' masts. I could hear her clogged breaths. 'The poor are sad every day, and no one sends out to a doctor about it. *She* – well, she's *lonely*, if you ask me. That's the trouble with *ton* marriages, though. Too much space. When you've got only the one room to share, you either kill each other or you make peace.'

I let out a laugh, surprising myself, but she fell quiet again, as if reminding herself that she shouldn't speak so freely.

I stared over my shoulder at the dark cobbles and the tall houses. 'True,' I said, turning the brush over, poking a finger between the damp bristles. 'But we are, each of us, sad in our own peculiar ways.'

'Don't *you* sound like one of them!' She sank into a fit of giggles. 'Airs and graces don't carry buckets, you know.'

'Suits me,' I said, 'since I don't want to be carrying buckets.'

More of Langton's long-ago words came back to me: *The Negro is happy to serve. Born for it. They've never produced a genius, and to expect genius from them would only cause distress. They're as different from us as dogs from cows. Let the Negro therefore do what he is happy doing, for freeing him would do nothing but put the Devil in his head.*

But Pru was poking me, good-naturedly this time. 'No buckets in Jamaica, then?'

I laughed, and she laughed too. 'I've been in service since I was twelve,' she said. 'I swear I see buckets in my sleep. And I'm nothing but thankful for it. I was a skelf of a girl. Didn't have the pair of arms on me that I have now. We went so hungry some nights I'd have eaten my elbow. Ma despaired of me ever getting a place. Mrs Linux said she'd take me on precisely because she knew no one else would, which is how I know she's got a soft side, though she does keep it well hid.' She looked at me. 'But a good servant must know her place, to be content in it.'

That's always been my trouble. Never knowing my place or being content in it.

She turned back to the scrubbing. But my mind swung like wind, so many new things rattled through it. London's sour, clotted streets. Levenhall's narrow hallways, its smells of wool and cold hearths. My new master, tossing questions, eyes big and black as ackee seeds. My new mistress – who had bowed to *me*! *Strange woman.* A queer feeling came over me, like a hand tightening around my chest, tiny hammers knocking at my breastbone. It felt like fright. A new mistress is a thing to be afraid of, if you're a maid and have any wits. But now I know how small the space can be, between being afraid of a thing and wanting it.

MORNING POST, 21 MARCH 1827

Madame Marguerite Benham, as she was widely known – no doubt as a nod to her French *racine* – was notorious as much for her eccentric behaviour as for her ravishing good looks. Indeed, she was once heard to declare that life without adventure was death, and no London season was ever in full swing until Mischief Meg had stormed the gates of Almack's wearing her own buff breeches, and a man's jacket with gold buttons topped by her crowning glory, a swan-feathered turban rumoured to have come all the way from a modiste in Istanbul. Not only pretty but interesting! And that in an age when so many women seem capable of being only one or the other.

No wonder a frenzy attended her wherever she went; no wonder so many described her as beyond compare. The latter a sentiment which, some say, was shared by none other than the Negro boxer known as Laddie Lightning, or Olaudah Cambridge, the African genius, if you prefer his nom-de-plume.

Though we give no credence in this newspaper to vexatious rumour, might it not be said that the ravishing Mrs Benham was prone to adventure as some people are prone to accidents?

Chapter Twelve

There'd been a moment down at the West India Docks, after I'd just stepped off the ship, when I stood stock still and looked around me. Another stroke of good fortune, I thought. Another I didn't deserve. The tall-masted ships and barrel-hulled barges. The tablecloth of fog laid over everything. In the drowned light, the dark shapes of porters dashed between the warehouses, crooked under weighty puncheons of sugar and rum, their shouts knocking against the glass. It had been so different that, for the span of one moment, I'd thought I could be different too.

But now Levenhall's four walls were all my world, and it felt small again, narrow as the inside of a stocking.

That's what I was thinking, next morning, as I watched Pru slide a bowl of broth onto a pewter tray, a cup and saucer beside it, pour in chocolate. She fetched the kettle to water it down. Linux looked up from where she was refilling the coal boxes for the charcoal irons.

'Again?' she said.

'Did you not hear her bell, ma'am?'

'High time she brought herself downstairs.' Linux sprinkled the tablecloth, passed the iron down the length of it, made it hiss. There was a smothering heat. The smells of salt, lime, coal-ash.

Pru shrugged. 'She *is* down. Said she'd have breakfast in the parlour, since the master's out. And she was down yesterday. She went out with Lady Catherine.'

Be that as it may, Linux said, she'd have to speak to the

master about stopping the trays. Madame shouldn't be encouraged to eat wherever and whenever the mood took her. Let things become regular, for a change, and see how long it took her, then, to consult Linux about the many matters that were going stale, to take an interest in her own household, for once.

It sounded very like a plan to starve her out.

Linux said I was to black the grates that morning, before lighting any fires. I was to spend more hours than I'd care to write about at Levenhall making sheets white, and grates black. Those are the two marks of a well-tended English house. And that was my so-called freedom.

There'd been little to no need for inside fires in Montego Bay, so I was going through in my head how Pru had told me to tackle the grates, carrying my cloth, and a tarry paste of lead-black and water, when I stepped into the parlour, and saw that Madame was already in it. Curled small, folded into an armchair before the hearth, holding the same black book she'd had the day before. An apple lay beside her on the chair, and wine glinted from a glass set on a table beside her elbow. She must have finished her chocolate, I thought. A lit candle stood beside the glass in a silver holder, and more of them along the mantel, for they always wanted extra light in those lower rooms, even at the height of morning. I saw I'd have to pass right by her to reach the hearth. My feet hooked on the jamb. She seemed nothing like the woman from yesterday. Quiet, stiff. Wet ribbons of hair hung over her shoulders, leaking dark circles onto her dress. The room was so yellow it could have been planted in good soil, bouquets of lavender and myrtle studded in vases on the mantel and the sill and all the tables. It had the feeling of sunshine trapped in it. Some men are rich enough to make their own weather, I thought.

A gold-framed mirror hung on one wall, a portrait on the one opposite. I jumped when I saw what it was. Madame glistened from the canvas, throat long and white as church columns, one small hand resting on the head of a black boy kneeling at her feet. He was holding up a wooden bowl scattered with corals and petals and shells, his face in shadow. I wondered if this was the blacky servant Pru had mentioned, who'd caused the 'bother'. I looked from her to the painting, back again. The light fell across a dark bruise on her cheek. She reached for her glass, took a sip. Picked up the apple, bit into it.

'Are you just going to stand there?' she said, without looking up.

I flinched, coughed out apologies. 'Beg pardon, ma'am.' When I set down the bucket, tin clanged against the hearth-stones, making me jump and jerking her head up, insect-quick, down again just as fast. I folded over my cloth, knelt to wipe loose dust and ash from the grate, as Pru had instructed, before dipping up the blacking. I saw that she was thin as rope, beneath her bunched grey sleeves. Nothing but silk and bone. I moved my cloth down to the tiles, rubbed one, then the next. My heart picked up a beat as I came closer.

'Oh!' I cried out.

She looked up.

'It's just – I've read that.' I pointed at the book.

'Milton?'

'Yes. Ma'am.'

'Madame. Ma'am is so English.'

I swallowed, lifted my cloth, took some of the paste onto it. She lowered the book, and I could see then that it was ink on her cheek, not a bruise. Thick as shadow. Black blooms dotted also across her skirt. I felt myself wishing I could unpick that word – ma'am – the way Phibbah would unpick a bad seam. Her eyes flicked to my brow and her mouth twisted. Was she laughing at me? Gawping at my hair? I felt it slipping out of the plait I'd tried to make that morning, growing like a sponge in water.

She smiled. 'English maids are not so well-read.'

'I . . .'

'Something new – at *last*. Nothing is ever new in this old bone-yard.' She sloped her head in my direction. Along the margin of the page, a scrawl of words had been pressed in, nicked like a badly shaved neck: *Non. NON. NON!*

'You are writing your own notes in it?'

She followed my gaze. 'Well, if you choose to make one thing happen in a book, a thousand other things do not. When I read, it's those thousand other things that I wonder about.'

'You're a writer?'

'La! A writer!' She shook her head. '*Non*. Not a writer. I am a *wife*. And my own husband would say that is occupation enough for any wife of *his*. Mr Benham is a friend to blue-stockings, but he prefers them in the wild rather than domesticated . . . When Wollstonecraft said that a woman will be crucified for aiming at respect instead of love, she must have meant at the hands of the very man who is supposed to love her . . .' She laughed, and I heard bitter notes in it. Then she picked up the book again. 'Well. Did you like it?'

'You must like it, to scribble so much in it.'

'On the contrary, I think I dislike it intensely. But I have just read *Mathilda* – do you know it?'

'No.'

'Well, I thought to write some notes on its themes, purely for my own entertainment, on the topic of the relationship between father and daughter – there is that kind of love between them, you see, in *Mathilda*, that makes for controversy. Then *this* sprang to mind and I thought I would reread it –'

'The mind is its own place . . . ?'

'Indeed! You *have* read it!'

I had. Hidden behind the grill, stomach flipping with each page. I looked away, towards the cold grate. She sat forward. From the glint in her eye I could see that I'd amused her. 'You are *very* well-spoken, for a –'

'Black?'

'A *maid*!' She smiled. 'For a maid.'

'Oh.' My face flamed. There I was. Kneeling like prayer or begging. Stone poking my shins. I tried to get up. 'Well, I –'

Linux's voice snapped behind me, like a lead pencil. 'What do you think you're doing?' I jumped, turned around. 'Didn't I instruct you yesterday?'

'*Instruct* me?'

'Not to address the master or mistress unless they address you first.'

'La! Mrs Linux.' Madame cut her off, rose to her feet, shaking out her skirts. 'Frances has been answering *my* questions. Is there really any need to stand on such ceremony?'

'I see.' Her face hardened. She looked from her to me, wavered a moment, like someone who'd lost her way. Then she stepped between us, her skirts spreading across my face, like potted beef on bread. 'Since you've decided to come downstairs this morning, Madame, may I take this opportunity to speak to you about the menu for next week's dinner with Sir Percy?'

I felt erased, blotted. My face flared hot. I bent my head to the task that was supposed to have brought me there, rubbed and rubbed with the cloth, watched black creeping into the cracks in my nails, staining my fingertips, crawling across the grate and making it clean.

'Oh, Mrs Linux cannot forgive Madame for being French,' Pru mumbled later, as she bedded herself down, punching her pillow. She snorted. 'That's part of it, anyway. And no house can serve two mistresses. They are always at odds.'

The window-glass hung above the bed, silvered, flat as a mirror, reflecting the bright moon. You had to be this high up to see it at all, I thought. I pressed my back against the hard floor, remembering how I'd gone over to the chair after Madame had followed Linux out of the parlour, how I'd stood staring at her book, then lifted it and smelt it, and how, holding it thus, I'd thought that, no matter the gully between us, here was one thing that had been laid across it, like the first flagstone set into a floor. All while we'd been speaking, it had felt as if she'd forgotten who she was, and who *I* was and, for that span of time, I'd felt like a dog fresh off its leash, sniffing earth. Perhaps that had been freedom, or some measure of it, though it had only been in my head.

I'd noticed a cloying smell, like apples simmering on a stovetop. When I looked down, I saw that it was coming from the apple core, which had fallen to the carpet and lay damp with juice and spit. Already as sweet as any rotting thing. For a long moment, I stood and stared at it, the weight of the book like a brick in my palm.

I fell asleep wishing Madame could see me as I'd been. Not the maid, not the house-girl, but Frannie the scribe. White cambric sleeves rolled up and marked with my own ink-stains, crow-feather pens, trimmed the way I liked them. Feet planted under a table, scribbling until my wrists cried out all their aches and pains. The Frannie who read Milton and Mr Defoe. *Reading, thinking, writing.*

Oh! But I had nothing to mourn, and certainly no business mourning whatever it was I thought I'd had. I squeezed my eyes shut, made my thoughts go black, waiting for sleep.

If she had seen those things, I told myself, she'd have seen my terrible shame, for they went hand in hand. She'd have borne witness to the very things I wanted to hide.

From the journals of George Benham
(Marked by George Benham as:
NOT INTENDED FOR PUBLICATION)

Langton's mulatta. Her eyes have the green cast of ageing metal. A feline slant. She is tall for a woman. Forehead high, and nose sharp. Features (and a cranium) that would not be misplaced on a European. Her skin is not black as such, but burnished to copper. There is a cat's stillness about her also, disturbed only when she clutches her hands suddenly together, as if staying herself from some dread impulse.

That she's comely is no surprise. Some men herald the beauty of the mulatto race and I can see why there might be something of a fashion for them, in certain circles. But it is her mind that surprises! Or should I say excites?

Langton contended that it's not intelligence. Nothing more than a facility for following instructions. 'Black will not become white,' he wrote, 'no more than white will become black. The purification of the Negro is not an object that can be attained.' Though he conceded, when challenged, the possibility of a higher intellect resulting from the *mixing* of white into black; the kind of racial bleaching first described by de Pauw. Whites being the stem of all men, to quote Bomare, but also the stern.

White lymph mixing with black, like a cow's milk into coffee!

What he seems blind to is that the girl's very existence contradicts his two principal arguments: firstly, that blacks are a separate species, and secondly, that the purification of the Negro is impossible. When I pointed this out, he asserted that black is purified only by *becoming* white, and never pure itself.

He is as pig-headed as most colonists, and stores each of his thoughts in separate boxes. Trust him, to spawn his own counter-argument!

I've told her I want the whole truth about his experiments. The very mention of his name spins her backwards. Langton won't have spared her. I know him. No friendship can be closer than that of boys who've boarded together at school. Langton's trouble has always been that he forgets the Earth is a divine creation. Nothing in it, above or below, is amenable to man, for man is bound by skin. To him, Ego and all that Ego does is interesting, as Cowper wrote to Lady Hesketh, but it is also *in vain*.

Her response: 'There is no such thing as truth.'

Delightful!

'You'd have it as Plato would,' I replied.

She asked me why I wanted to know about Paradise, and what I proposed to do with her answers. Her lips crimped up at the corners. A glimmer of that mulishness Langton wrote about: *All of a mulatta's lewd charms, but instead of their pallor and weakness, a nigger's stubborn streak*. A deuced strange way for a man to speak about his own by-blow, but John Langton is a strange man.

When he first wrote, he said his starting point was to be a variation on the old Bordeaux question: *What is the physical cause of variety in the species of humankind?*

No one had made a significant attempt at it since the last century, so I was attracted, of course. What subject could be more attractive to a natural philosopher than such an investigation? I was sure God would guide this enquiry into an aspect of His creation. To begin with, Langton and I shared a hypothesis: that the differences between men are rooted in the composition of the body itself, that they are physiological and not, as some would have it, due to the vagaries of climate and other external factors, and therefore can be deciphered by a careful study of anatomy. Langton offered access to an unparalleled collection of skulls, and it was on my advice that he first thought to measure internal cranial capacity, not just the angles and planes every other bump-reader concerns himself with. I suggested he could do it by using mercury, or shot, to gain an accurate reading of internal volume.

I thought his examinations would be organized on the fundamental principles of phrenology, namely that the brain is the organ of the mind, its different parts perform different functions, and one can deduce certain characteristics of a man by its size and form. In this way, we proposed to compile a survey of the natural mental endowments of each race of men, as fashioned by their Creator. Each to match its own geography.

But Langton always resisted even divine attempts at guidance, so I should have seen there was very little chance he'd follow mine.

At the end of the first year, he wrote to inform me that he sought to go further than the original scope; to expand upon Maupertuis by proving that, if man is the product of the mechanical forces of conception, our traits, including race, are passed to us through sperm, and the Negro's blackness is therefore innate, as well as the Negro's other characteristics: inferior intellect and morality and ambition.

I wrote asking him what had happened to the skulls. He was still taking measurements, he replied.

He had done nothing with them! There was no catalogue. He had wasted all that time blistering corpses.

Worse, his project now pulled towards the argument that the origins of man are profane, not profound, that man is fashioned by sperm and not by God. *Heresy, in other words.* I could not be part of it. There was very little left of the phrenological study I thought we'd embarked on (though I believe now that may simply have been a pretext, to draw me in). Good intentions should never attach themselves to bad means.

Knowing that the greater name will always attract the greater tarnish, I told him I'd no longer sign my name to his project. I offered to purchase his skulls, since he had no idea how to examine them properly. I thought the matter would rest there, we'd go our separate ways. But instead he whitewashed his manuscript, excised all references to his doubtful experiments, and sought to persuade me that we could try again.

But he's retained all his misguided focus on skin and colouring agents. In any event, it is too late now for a further attempt. His old stables burned down before he left, and everything inside. The skulls cannot be retrieved. He has nothing that could interest me further.

Except the girl.

He seeks to curry favour by leaving her here, supposing it will amuse me. It does. But it's also convenient for him. What else could he do with her? I saw how his hands trembled. He's ill. He told us (in confidence) that his wife's brother had cast him out. On *her* instructions! Meg showed the expected degrees of sympathy, and made soothing noises. I wanted to say, *There! See what a truly rotten marriage looks like!*

Perhaps Langton didn't think I'd interrogate the girl.

So far, she's told me only what I already knew. Had to twist her arm to get even that much. The first question she asked was whether I'd turn her out if she declined to answer my questions. By suggesting *duress*, she sought to shame me, of course, implying I was no better than *him*. Clever. Told her, yes, she should consider it duress, if that made it easier for her to answer.

There followed a response containing as much emotion as a Latin declension: 'I was only a scrivener, sir.' As if it had been nothing to do with her; as if she'd been but an instrument, calibrated like a set of scales, then put to use.

She said that he followed men like Littré, Meckel, Le Cat. When he could get a cadaver, he blistered the skin with boiling water, and soaked it in spirits of wine for a week. He copied Malpighi's experiments; first, detaching the web of vessels that is the seat of colour in the skin – the Malpighian layer (tinged black in the African) – then examining the brains and pineal glands of a number of Negroes, noting their blue-black, ashy appearance. He extracted the black bile from those same corpses also, concluding that the stain isn't merely skin deep but rather the Negro is black from skin to nerves to brain, and the stain is evident long before a Negro comes into the world, imprinted on the genitalia, fingers and toes and present also in the male sex organs, and in the sperm. He examined the scrota and labia of all the infants born or miscarried at Paradise over a period of three years. I remember well Sir Humphrey reading aloud his letter on the subject, his one and only paper to find its way into the *Philosophical Transactions*.

She said it was she who copied his early papers. *Replication of Quier's investigations into the origin of blackness in the Negro* and *Elements of Phrenology in a study of plantation Negroes*. A man she knew only as the Surgeon served as anatomist. I think she means Will Buckham, never in all his born days sober enough to hold a pen, let alone a scalpel. Most of those plantation quacks are drunks and, knowing Will Buckham, the greatest danger was that he'd sever one of his own bits. Hearing that he was dead didn't surprise me, though I was surprised to learn it had been the smallpox and not the great one: he was always as chaste as he was sober.

•

My series of questions, and the girl's answers, below.

Were you ever blistered yourself?

No answer.

Did Langton experiment on living subjects?

No answer.

(But I know he did, of course. I read his original manuscript. And I knew that in '23 he'd written to the Society asserting that death should not be the limit of knowledge, that a body could tell us much more alive than dead. There was no reason, he wrote, that a man could not be kept alive through his experiments.)

Were there experiments into the capacity to withstand pain?

No answer.

Were there experiments concerning reproduction?

She answered my question with a question and asked what I meant.

That trick. Explained that I wanted to know whether there were any instances of forced mating. In response, she laughed. Asked if I knew nothing about what happened on a West India estate. It is all forced mating, she said.

Longer answer, verbatim:

'I will tell you this, sir, I will tell you what abolishing the trade did. When a man cannot buy stock, he breeds it. Every woman at Paradise was a belly woman then! Lining up on Sundays, waiting at the front porch for their half-dollars and their maccarronis. "See, Massa! Me breed good new neger for Massa. Big, strong neger."'

(I pictured Langton tapping each quickened womb in the way I sometimes imagine those colonials tapping coconuts before scooping out the flesh. It wouldn't have escaped him that, like Daedalus killing two birds with his one stone, he could increase both his stock and his specimens thus.)

Then she would not say more, and looked considerably downcast.

Was an orangutan brought to Paradise for the purposes of the experiments?

A look of mild surprise.

(I know Langton was on the hunt for one. He had Pomfrey scouring the earth, which has never been a thing Pomfrey could do quietly.)

After a long moment spent biting her lip, she told a story Langton had told her. An orangutan had been kept shipboard for eighteen months by a crew of slavers who entertained themselves by teaching the ape to dress himself in knee-high breeches and a cambric shirt, to ask for tea by pointing to his mouth, and to eat a dish the natives called fungee with a spoon and fork. The creature had suffered such distress on being returned to the coast whence he'd been kidnapped that he threw himself into the ocean to try to follow the vessel, and was never seen again.

Asked her what she thought Langton's object was in telling such a story. *She replied that it was simply a thing that had happened.* (Could very well have asked, what was her object in telling *me*?)

Was an albino ever brought to Paradise for the purposes of the experiments?

No answer.

She grew skittish at the mention of albinos. Told her I didn't imagine she'd had any choice about the things they'd made her do. Her eyes flailed, as if she'd been stung by something. Conscience, perhaps. She looked straight at me: 'Of course I had a choice.'

I want truth. She wants silence.

Circumspection is a liar's refuge. Nevertheless both truth and silence smother guilt.

I've been advised by a group of the Fellows, who've asked to remain nameless for the time being, that I may persuade them I don't condone Langton's conduct if I expose it myself. By doing so, I may be assured of their support for putting forward my own proposals. Just like the *Brookes* slave ship: give people that impression of horror, and it will soften them up for compromise. The behaviour of some West India planters is a terrible scourge but, on the other hand, the problem of compensation drags the government's heels. My own model eradicates the former, while avoiding entirely the latter headache. It all coheres, and gives rise to the perfect opportunity to make the case in support of legislation ensuring the protection of our Negroes, and, by extension, our livelihoods. An amelioration plan along Canning's lines, but with the aim of preserving that which others would destroy.

An account of what happened at Paradise would be just the thing for exposing Langton. But so far the girl only plays at co-operating. 'I cannot remember most of it,' she said, and then promptly contradicted herself: 'I don't wish to.'

Chapter Thirteen

Mr Feelon once said to me, 'Frances Langton, your body might have been currency once, but you own yourself now. In England, we know better than to trade men like barley.' Oh, they're fond of telling you things you already know. I swear they'd fish a man out of an ocean just so as they could shout at him, 'Why, sir, I *do* believe that you have been *drowning*!' It's nonsense, but they think it's true because they believe it.

English newspapers had come to Paradise by ship, news of gas-lights at Westminster Bridge, the campaign against Napoleon, King George's funeral. And in them notices, advertisements, and handbills that were so very like the fly-sheets that had been passed around Montego Bay: '*Black boy, twelve years of age, fit to wait on a gentleman. Talks English very well. To be disposed of at Liddell's Coffee House, in Finch Lane, near the Exchange*'; or '*Run away from Mr Thomas Addleson in Richmond last Thursday, his middle-sized Negress, Harriet, about 30, in a grey cotton dress and a brown coat. About five feet two inches.*'

The same catalogue of people here as where I come from – the hunted and the sold – no matter what they say about English air. All my life I'd known that black bodies have no value, but a price above rubies. And here was a puzzle. A puncheon of sugar is still a puncheon of sugar after it crosses the Atlantic, but what had *I* become? How was I supposed to own myself, elbow-deep in soap, rinsing out Benham's small linens?

All I'd done was trade one master for another. And this one wanted to pick my brains, examine them for evidence of Langton's sins. Whenever I asked him why, he said only that his purpose was his own business entirely, but I should make no mistake that I was there to serve both. Nor had he been satisfied with the scraps I'd fed him, my first lie – that I remembered very little of what had happened at Paradise – oiling the way for all the rest. Though I told myself I wasn't lying, but rather telling only half the truth.

On the seventh day, there was a bundle laid at my place at the table, wrapped in twine. When I tore off the paper, it unfurled into two dresses, made of rough linsey. 'One to wear, one to change into,' Linux announced, staring through the window. I could hear the soft crunch of boots, coal tumbling into next door's chute. When she turned, her jaw clicked, like the lid on the pot. 'Jamaican gowns might be flimsy, but English women are more modest.'

I rolled up the fabric and set it back on the table. 'I *have* a dress,' I said.

But she stared and stared until I rose slowly to my feet, and picked up the bundle. Then she followed me into the scullery, laid both dresses across the copper. 'The brown for now,' she said, nodding at it. 'The green will keep for Sundays.'

I'd dressed myself in my navy serge since leaving the *Pride*, when all of London had been spread in front of me like a picnic rug, and I'd just as soon have peeled off my own skin, but I swallowed, brought my fingers up to my chest, rubbed them along the bodice.

'Too slow,' she said, and swooped her fingers onto me quick as crows, unhooking me herself. Cold seeped around us, like the steam from the copper when Pru heated the bathwater in there. There was a smell of pork and caraway on her fingers from the sausages she'd been making that morning, and the usual scullery smells on top of that. The lye and piss we mixed up for the laundry, old sweat, damp. Her fingers crept down my bodice. All the while she kept up a constant chatter, and I heard a *snick-snick-snick* that made me swing my head in search of a clock, or dripping water. 'You dress for the use to which you're put, *here*,' she muttered, pinching my jaw to keep my face still. 'Do you hear? And you will *not* be wiggling your tail all over Mr Benham's house.'

My throat clenched. *You need this place*, I told myself. *You need this place.* When she saw that I'd made no reply she snapped her head up, fingers stilled on my hooks. 'Have you nothing to say for yourself? I saw you. With Charles.'

Charles? It came back to me, then, that the afternoon before, I'd been in the front hall, shining the clock. Charles had crept behind me with no warning. 'I've been wondering about something,' he said. 'Maybe you could settle it for me.'

'Settle what?' I'd asked.

He sniggered. 'How you sleep on white sheets without getting them mucked.'

Anger made hairpin jabs in my skull. I'd set down the polishing cloth, turned to face him. He blinked and rubbed at his jaw, tottering like a new foal. I stepped close. My voice came out rough. I fancied a murderous tone crept into it. 'Is that what you wondered?' He laughed, but backed away, as if he'd heard it too, that killing note. I thought of the preacher, who used to sit in the heat at Paradise, red as a crab in a pot, calling out Bible verses. *The way of an eagle in the sky, the way of a serpent on a rock, and the way of a man with a maid.* '"Maid" is one of those words that can have many different meanings, Frances,' he would say. 'Servant, yes, but also girl, virgin, unmarried woman.' A maid to a man, a serpent to an eagle. Just something to stick his claws into. *Once a house-girl, for ever a whore.*

Linux finished unhooking my bodice and stepped back. A man and a maid. Perhaps it would have looked like seduction, if you were watching it from a distance. But what was the use in protesting? No doubt she would take his side, tell me she had similar questions herself. I stood mute. Didn't say a word. She must have thought me dumb, frightened. Sullen. The noise came again when she looked at me. Snick. *Snick-snick.* She curled her lip, drew her face back, and I realized it was her tongue that made the noise, clacking like a builder's hammer.

Her eyes scuttled away from me, and she dangled my old dress away from her like a caught rat. 'Dress yourself, then. And, lest you mistake me, girl, I don't want to have to admonish you again, regarding heathenish dress.'

'I'm not a heathen,' I said.

The smile curdled on her face. 'That's not for you to judge.'

Back in the kitchen, she took down a bowl of apples and sorted through them for a tart. 'Who would just *tip* a woman onto somebody's doorstep? Hot off the ship. A gift! A havey-cavey business, if you ask me. It might be done, perhaps, in dark places, it might be done in far corners of the earth. I wouldn't know.'

Mr Casterwick looked up from polishing Benham's hessians, wrinkled his brow. ''Tis done here, too, however, Mrs Linux,' he said. 'It's *been* done. I have heard of it.'

'It is a dark practice.'

'Well, but you'll admit there are dark things done in England, too.'

'I'll admit no such thing!'

He shook his head. 'I don't suppose it needs you to be admitting it for it to be taking place.'

I felt like a shaved cat without my serge. The linsey dress smelt like camphor, buttoned all the way up to my chin, closed like a fist around my throat.

But I didn't have time to dwell on it. Charles came downstairs to say there'd been a commotion at the front door, early as it was: that *colonial* had thundered into the hall, demanded to see the master, and told him to bugger his British manners when Charles had said the master was not at home. He'd been ready to toss him onto his backside, but Mr Benham had heard it all and come down anyway. The news that Langton was in the house split me like an axe-blow. My chest pounded. It shames me to say it now, but I thought he'd come back for me.

The library door was closed. I clutched my rag, and pretended to wipe at it, one ear cocked against the wood. Their voices knocked against each other like bricks being laid, low at first, then Langton's came louder: '. . . you tossed me to those fucking lions!'

'. . . the same delusions of martyrdom . . . nothing.'

'You still condescend to me as if we're schoolboys.'

'. . . still . . . behave . . . as if we are!'

Listening brought me back to my last time in there. Swarmed with questions. I'd asked if he would turn me out if I didn't answer.

'Well, you must do what you want, of course.' An amused look had crept onto his face. 'Though sometimes it's easier to do a thing by convincing yourself you're being forced. As you would know.'

Had there been any other path, I wouldn't have gone down the one of appeasing him. But the truth is I was stuck, terrified of being out on the streets alone. I had to tell him something, though my answers were never fast enough or good enough.

'*We have a common object, girl.*'

'*I wouldn't presume to have anything in common with a man such as yourself, sir,*' *I said. They never notice when you give your modesty a double edge.*

I told him he'd find all of Langton's methods easily enough in Langton's book, but he already knew that to be a lie.

He gave me a look. 'He could have produced a beautiful book of skulls instead of all that gallivanting about with skin. As soon as he saw sense he managed to lose all his specimens.'

Oh, Langton never saw sense, I thought. *He was hell-bent on non-sense, right up to the end.*

'Perfectly awful,' he said, 'about that fire.'

'Perfectly awful,' I replied.

Defeat ate at me, soured my stomach. I listened for a long time, yet heard not a single word about me. The tall windows marched away down the long hall, black and silent under their yellow drapes. Those were the soft bars of my prison. My head felt empty and cold. I had already worked the skin off my fingers. Nothing stretched ahead of me but more of the same. And then what? What became of a mulatta maid in London, when her fingers grew too crooked for carrying pails?

A throat cleared behind me, and I spun around, startled. *Madame.*

'Could there be anything going on in there worth spying on?' she said, tipping her head towards the door. She wore a grey morning gown, with lace and seed-pearls stitched across the waistband, hair hanging loose as the drapes. I tugged at the stuff dress, pinching where it was supposed to be loose, hanging where it was supposed to pinch, billowing around my hips, like sheets pinned out to dry.

'Sorry, Madame,' I said, not knowing what else to say.

'I do not believe you are.' She laughed, and that jerked my head up in surprise, almost drew a laugh out of me in return. 'I see your Mr Langton has come back at last,' she said.

He's not mine. I wanted to ask if she knew whether he'd come back for me, or what was to happen to me, where I could go. I wanted to shout, *How could he leave me here?* Too many thoughts crowded my head and smothered each other, so I said nothing. Silence threaded itself between us. At last, she smoothed her palms down over her skirt. 'Well. I must go in there and be presented to him. No choice.'

'No,' I said, shook my rag, turned back to my cleaning. 'Me neither.'

She laughed, and leaned towards me, with such a warm sweetness on her breath, whispered right into my ear: *'Faith, as you say, there's small choice in rotten apples.'*

CHARLES PRUITT, manservant of Mr George Benham, sworn

A. Mrs Benham was always gadding. I said nothing, while she lived. But it can make no difference to her now. Gaming halls. Unsavoury places, you know. She disguised herself. Breeches, jacket, flat cap. No, I wasn't comfortable about it. There were times I wondered should I say something to the master.

Q. Did you?
A. I was caught between the two of them, you could say. I conveyed her, and brought her back, and any more than that was not my business. I –

Q. Yes?
A. It's just – I did once take the pair of them, the prisoner and the mistress, to a gathering of blacks, in some tap-room off Fleet Street. I heard talk that it was Radicals the mistress was mixing with, towards the end, though I can't say yea or nay to it. Also, I did at one time convey her to an address on Gant Street to meet a Mr Cambridge, Laddie Lightning he called himself. The pugilist? I'm only sorry I did not say something to the master after all, seeing how things turned out.

Chapter Fourteen

February weather drove us down to the kitchen like rats to a hole. Two Saturdays after I arrived, Linux made a fruit cake with raisins for Benham and allowed us a small piece each, and then Mr Casterwick said he would bring his fiddle out, and Pru and Charles set a row of lighted candles down the table, which made it seem festive, though we were just as worn from that day's labours as any other, and the room was musty and dim, and still reeked of salt and old mutton fat. The cake made up for it. Golden and sweet, and no matter that I knew only too well how the sugar was made, I couldn't resist it. I'd drawn my own chair near the door, where I could watch Charles and Pru bicker and carry on, and I let a raisin melt sweet on my tongue, rested my head against the wall. I felt that small measure of ease you get from music, the same as from reading, and the flames flickered low under the stove, giving off a good warmth.

Then, Mr Casterwick's bow scuffled, came to a stop. When I looked up, I saw Madame, hands flat on the door frame on either side.

'Mr Casterwick, you play? I didn't know. I didn't know.' The French way she said it sounded like, *No. I didn't no. No, no, no.*

Linux thumped down her sherry. 'Were we disturbing you, Madame?'

'Oh, no! *Non.* Not at all! Not at all! It's . . . My father . . . he plays the violin. Played. Please.'

'I'm sure I won't be playing what you're accustomed to, marm,' said Mr Casterwick.

'It's the *violin*, Mr Casterwick! Whatever you play will be a lament.'

Some of the cheer left the room, for a mistress among her servants is like a fox among hens: no one knew whether to sit or stand, and even the cat slid out from under the table, shook its backside and nosed out through the open door. Mr Casterwick kept glancing up and losing his place, violin clipped between shoulder and jaw. Linux got up, poured another glass of sherry, cut a slice of the cake. She brought both across the room and set them on the table, swooping her hands above the plate like sea-birds.

'Where is Mr Benham, Madame?' she said.

Madame ignored her, gazing about as if she'd never seen the room before, and perhaps she hadn't: the lady of a house like that never has cause to visit her own kitchen.

'The master, Madame?' Linux repeated.

She laughed and shook her head. 'That is a very good question, Mrs Linux. I suppose you know as well as I do.'

Linux straightened, dusted her hands. 'Well. Here's a bit of cake. Shall I send Pru with it, upstairs?'

Madame crossed the room to where the bellows hung on the wall beside the dresser, bent to peer into the baskets of turnips and onions that Linux lined up below the work-bench, and the locked drawers of knives she kept there. Linux watched her, then went back to her place and clamped her hands together in her lap, all the while casting suspicious looks at the rest of us as if we were the ones responsible for disturbing her peace.

Madame returned to the table, forked up a bite of cake. 'Delicious! But that goes without saying, Mrs Linux.' She spoke brightly, though she appeared unwell, hair clinging to her brow. She didn't look at any of us, but closed her eyes and took up another bite, and we all gawped at her, the music suddenly too slow and too loud in the close room. When it seemed that she would chew for ever, she suddenly clattered fork to plate, and clapped her hands together. 'We should be dancing!' Pru and Charles blinked in confusion, as if she was speaking Turkish, but she waved them onto their feet anyway, swept them into the cleared space, then came towards me and held out her hand. 'Frances? It seems we are a man short. You or I must play the breeches role.'

I jerked backwards.

Kiii, it was like being slapped. First, a moment of nothing, then the lightning inside. I remember worrying about the sticky damp that prickled under my arms from beating rugs out against the hawthorn all afternoon, whether I'd smell sour with it; worrying about my calluses that would no doubt feel rough as sackcloth to her, and about where to put my eyes. But then there wasn't time to puzzle about any of it, for she took my arm and pulled me into the cleared space, and Mr Caster-wick tapped his feet and made his bow sing. There wasn't space for more than a hop and a gallop between table and dresser, and there was nothing in me but held breath. My chest was tight with it. Our knees bounced the table and jostled the chairs. When Pru happened to knock one over she shook with laughter, and that made the rest of them laugh too, and Madame smiled around at everyone and looked pleased.

We latched hands, and I kept my eyes down, watched their feet, copied what they did. It was some English music the rest of them knew, and they stepped together, touched hands, made bow, then curtsy, then bow, like they were speaking some language I didn't understand, and left me always stumbling two steps behind.

Linux sat tall and straight, flicking her eyes over each of us in turn. Now and then she took small, sucking sips from her glass, twisting her face like a squeezed-out rag. Not even that could dampen my mood. I felt my ribs swelling as if they'd split my chest. Music spilled around us, and the floor was loud under our feet, and we laughed and danced. The four of us forgot ourselves, if only for that hour. No one at Paradise had spoken to me much, let alone asked me to dance. So that was a measure of happiness, being part of their dancing. Forgetting time, forgetting the house, empty and silent above us – forgetting all notions of who we were supposed to be to each other. Four people, dancing.

Langton once told me that when the English soldiers rounded up the obeah men in Jamaica, after Tacky's rebellion, they experimented on them. Tied them with shackles, prodded them with electric machines and magic lanterns, gave them all manner of jolts and shocks. It must have felt like thunder going through their bones, or pops of lightning cleaving their skulls. When they could no longer stand it, they were forced to admit that the white man's magic was stronger. *The white man is the measure of all things, and of all things the measure is the white man.*

That was how I felt when we latched arms.

Oh.

No matter what any moment holds, memory makes of it either nothing at all, or unending terror, or ceaseless grief. All I have left of that night are flashes of her diamond ear-bobs, the swells of her moving against me like tides, the feel of her, like a taste I couldn't get out of my mouth.

Chapter Fifteen

English winter is a season of dying things, of long waiting, and wool-thick skies. Underfoot the crunch of gravel, the wet slip of frost turning to mud, a meshwork of rotting leaves and damp grass. It was into such an afternoon that Pru and I were sent out the following day.

Linux had found us at the table, cutting old sheets into tinder to fill the boxes. Madame had flown the coop, she said, tucking chin to neck, like a skewer to a joint of pork. She was likely in the park, and we were to go down ourselves, the pair of us, and see if we could fetch her back in time for Lady Catherine's morning call.

Pru said we should go our separate ways, for many hands made light work, so we separated when we came to a fork in the path. As soon as I was away from her I quickened my feet, heart keeping pace. The park that day was a stew of carriages and foot passengers, boiling in the fog. I soon came to a quieter part of it, a small garden leading down to a stand of elms, where mist hung white as milk, the air as clouded as my thoughts. Winter showed on the trees also, rough peeling aprons of black bark, and curling moss. After I came to the end of the path there, I saw her ahead. Wearing her black spencer, skirts flaring red beneath it, head tilted, dark hair swinging below her waist, hands gripped behind her. Something about her called to mind the image of a bird beating against glass.

I wiped my mouth, made my way towards her. When she heard me, she swung her head. Her eyes bright and wide as the eyes of a doll. Indigo-painted cotton. She smiled. 'Oh!

Frances. I'm so glad it's *you*. I am tired of being hauled back by Charles.'

My own smile stumbled out and I followed a little behind her as we walked, struck so dumb with wanting to amuse her that at first I said nothing at all. Before I could, she was speaking again, saying she couldn't imagine me learning to read in such a dreadful place, and I understood that she'd been talking about Paradise for several minutes.

People always ask the same question, wondering how I could've been so taken up with novels, *there* of all places. They blame me more for reading through it than suffering through it, I think. Novels are heresy, in their opinion; *man* creating man, no need for God. But how could I not read? I always want to ask. How else would I have survived it? What would *you* do, sitting in a dark, locked room, if someone brought in a lighted candle? I'll tell you. You'd read your single copy of *Moll Flanders* over and over until you'd oiled the pages thin from your fingers. 'It was a wager,' I said abruptly. 'Between your husband and my – between Mr Benham and Mr Langton. They wanted to see whether I could be taught.'

'Oh!' The wind shuffled her hair. She crossed her arms and gave a little shiver. 'They made a *wager* of you, and then a *gift*? How perfectly awful of them. But sometimes they can be perfectly awful men.'

I coughed. I couldn't speak about Paradise, but I couldn't be silent either. 'Books were my companions,' I said at last, raising my voice above the wind sweeping the leaves and her skirts. 'And I am grateful I could learn *something*, no matter how I came to do so. It was a way to know that lives could *change*, that they could be filled with adventures. There were times I pretended *I* was a lady in a novel or a romance myself. It might sound foolish. But it made me feel a part of a world that otherwise I could never belong to.'

I stopped. We'd come to the end of the path, I could see the gates that would lead us back to the street, black railings staked into the cobblestones, and Pru standing there waiting for us. I felt I'd made a fool of myself, but I'd also felt weight spilling out of me. My head going light. The memory flying into it of that *other* weight, wriggling in my hands. I'd thought to forget it, blot it like an error on a page. But everything a body does is still there inside it, even under all the time that bleeds over it.

I jumped in my skin. The memory seared my mind, like a kipper held in a hot pan.

When I looked up, she was watching me. 'I know that feeling,' she said. 'Though I think the point of reading is not to feel more a part of the world, but less. To take oneself out of it. On paper, everything can be hammered into shape, though the world is shapeless.' She reached up to hold her hair back. The wind knocked into her, made her seem to be swallowed by skirts and hair. 'The trouble with writers is they spend their lives trying to lie to themselves.'

Mist suffocated trees and sky and grass, made everything so cool and quiet, like we walked under water. Two women passed us, turned and wagged their chins, and suddenly I didn't know how to answer her. My throat closed like a fist. So, I started back, towards the gates, with her following me.

'What did they speak about, in the library, after you went in?' I asked, at last.

'Nothing. Nonsense.' She laughed. '*Themselves*. Nothing of any consequence, in other words.'

Here is another beginning. The moment I realized that the sensation she stirred in me was a feeling of wanting. Unlikely. *Unnatural*. Impossible. Because the thing I wanted was her.

There was a fair just beside the gates, I remember, and the three of us walked through it. Chestnuts and cider spiced the air; boards covered with paper spoke of mermaids, two-headed men, fire-eaters. Tops spun like wind. We stopped to watch a tightrope-walker, a rat frisking across a shorter rope strung beneath him. From a tent to the right of us, a man led an elephant tied with a length of hemp. An elephant! I'd seen a picture of one before, in a book written by a naturalist. But reading about something can never be the same as seeing it. The grey leathery wave rearing up and up, and then the quiet crash, the giant-legged curtsy. The people at the front hopped backwards, made a show of bringing their hands up to their mouths, shrieking laughter. Some people love to be frightened in a crowd, tossing fear around like a hot potato. 'Step up! Step up! Ladies and gentlemen!' the man cried. '*All* creatures, little *or* large, fall under man's dominion!'

I stood on tiptoe to see over the heads in front, everyone jostling. A small boy turned, thin and dirt-smudged and bug-eyed, and tugged on the skirts of the woman beside him, and then *she* swung around, pursed her lips at me. 'Imagine! A great beast like *that* right out in the street!'

Pru gasped. 'Some folk should learn to keep their bone-boxes shut!'

That was when it came back. That gritted hum. Between my eyes, my teeth, my bones. Anger. It had slipped out of me momentarily while I'd walked with her, and I'd felt something like contentment. Now it was back. I gave them both a smile, tight as a well-made bed, let it go wide, to show it didn't bother me. But, mercifully, while we'd been standing there, it had started to drizzle slow drops, and now rain pelted hard as rocks, forcing us to turn and flee. The crowd scattered, too, everyone running off in different directions. When we reached the street again, the fog hung in front of us like a grey cloud, black flakes of soot spiralling through it.

Back at Levenhall, Madame left us to go upstairs, calling for hot water, shaking off her damp skirts as she went, and Pru and I trudged back down, where the silver was waiting to be polished, set out on the table, like rib bones.

That night, I dreamed it was me being paraded through the Strand, the man calling out ahead of me: *Step up, step up, lay-dees, gents! Come see the darky! All the way from the Indies. She'll cook you in her pot! She'll steal your babies, and cook them too!*

MISS PRUDENCE RATTRAY, under-maid of Mr George
Benham, sworn

Mr Pettigrew: Miss Rattray, you come here today to give the prisoner a character?
A. Yes, sir.

Q. Tell these gentlemen, then, in your own words.
A. I don't see how Frances – the prisoner, begging your pardon. Sir, I
don't see how she could have done this thing. I have heard such talk of
how she must have been a savage and that's the reason she did it. It made
me so angry I knew I must come here to tell what I knew of her.

Q. What did you know of her?
A. She had two thumbs, sir, like the rest of us. [Laughter, gallery admon-
ished by the court.] Mrs Linux said she was uppish, but I didn't really see
it. It's true that she was not over-fond of taking advice, unless she got it
in a book. Her own worst enemy, she was. I always told her I knew what
her trouble was. I wanted to be a lady's maid, but she wanted to be the
lady. I'd never known a darky before – you see them in the street, the
soldiers and the beggars mostly, and there'd been a kitchen maid at one
of the houses a few streets over from us, a young lass I sometimes saw in
passing out on the steps pulling on her pipe. What I mean to say is, we
are not accustomed to seeing them and don't know their ways, I suppose.
But with Frances – the prisoner, I mean – I found nothing so strange
about her. She wasn't used to some of the ways of an English house, perhaps, and she had very thin blood, she felt the cold, she did. But after she
started waiting on Madame, a change came on her, her spirits improved.
She was very fond of Madame. Truth is, Madame's spirits improved
also. The way Frances spoke of her. Well. Her feelings were so tender
towards Madame I don't see how she would have done this.

Q. And her feelings towards Mr Benham?
A. Sir. All the world loved Mr Benham except his wife.

Chapter Sixteen

White men dine with each other no matter their differences, and very often because of them. When Benham invited Langton to dinner, perhaps it was for both reasons.

They glared at each other, even as they came in, Madame a few paces behind, Langton's eyes as murked as the dregs in a rum bottle. Seeing him again cut like a cow-hide whip, though I'd braced myself for it. I still felt a bitter snag in my throat. I fancied that he limped, that his shoulders drooped. New wrinkles crawled all over him. He was sweating in his black suit, took his seat without even looking at me. As soon as I laid eyes on him, I saw the old Frances. Skirts trailing like shadows. Thoughts swarming quick and sharp as wasps. Lanterns to be lit, quills to be hardened, books to be fetched down from their perches: Vesalius, Le Cat, Buffon. He'd want buns, buttered and warm; he'd need help to undress; he'd want her to write, scratch out, write again. Always writing. My memory wobbled. I snapped my eyes open, sipped small breaths that scraped through me. The table glowing white under its cloth, nodding yellow flowers, dark plums in silver bowls. Pru on one side, me opposite, so I stared at the back of his head, and his hand, fisted and trembling, around his spoon.

Him not just the devil you know, Phibbah would have said. *You and him the same devil.* I shook it off; shook her off.

He looked across the table at Madame. 'I hope Frances is making herself useful.'

'Frances?' The light made her face all shadows and sharp bones. She raised her glass, so that champagne clouded her from view, stared at him through it, eyes squeezed as if she was trying to remember who I was. 'Oh, yes. I am sure she is.'

Her cold words knocked me like a beaten rug. She picked up her spoon and pecked it at her bowl of soup. She didn't say, 'Frances? She and I have become such friends.' She didn't look at me at all. You'd never have believed she was the same woman who'd twirled in the kitchen hand in hand with her servants. I might as well have been a book-end, for all the attention either of them paid me. Useful. There to serve. Staying where I was put. She was a show pony, glossed by candlelight so her powder-blue dress shone, bright as false coins. I was a mule. My thoughts went roaming out of the room again, to the woman in the park, wind giving her little taps, holding her loose hair back. I began to wonder, had I imagined her?

Ha! Niggers have no imagination. I heard Langton's voice in my head.

Soup, then sweetbreads with caviar. Fried soles and button mushrooms. Tomatoes stuffed with olives. Tongue, glistening pink in its little paper crown. Then beef. The kitchen had smelt of bacon all morning from the white soup simmering on the stove. Each dish was to appear at their elbows, as if they'd conjured it themselves. Dining *à la Russe*, Linux called it. 'Make sure you're neither seen nor heard.' Well, I'd wished to be invisible, hadn't I? There I was, put in my place.

I remember now, writing this, something else Linux had said, when she'd been undressing me in the scullery, stuffing me into the linsey dress. I'd asked why she hated me, and she'd jerked her head up in surprise. '*Hate* you? Oh. No. The Lord made you, girl, just as He made me, just as He made Charles and Prudence and Mr Casterwick. Just as He made Mr Benham. Just as He made the King. God is our superintendent. We are, all of us, and every bird and every flower and every leaf, under His hand. But we are in different ranks! You do not even begin to understand the work Mr Benham does. Nor do I. Nor he ours. There is a natural order and when you know your part in it, and do your work, no matter what it is, in the knowledge that it is God's work, then you will work with all your heart, for you will be working for the Lord and not for human masters.'

Madame lifted her glass again. Watching her, I was ashamed to recognize the stirring of the admiration I'd felt in the park, in spite of my thoughts. The curse of a kicked dog's devotion. 'Have you been enjoying your visit to our little hamlet, Mr Langton?'

'Hardly. I'm here mainly to persuade old friends to behave like friends.'

Benham's forehead shone. He forked up mushrooms, spoke with his mouth full. 'John's had his manuscript knocked back by the Society.'

'Oh?' She cocked her head. 'Is that your skull thing?'

'A trifle more than that.' He set his shoulders back, put his fork aside.

'Is that right?' Her smile spread slow, wide.

'It would only bore you, Mrs Benham, I'm sure,' he said, after a pause.

'Go slowly, Mr Langton.' She peered at him, her voice sharp. 'And let us see whether my womanly brain can keep astride.'

Benham coughed out a brittle laugh. I kept my eyes on the back of Langton's head. I was all anger. Anger a drumbeat. Anger, steady as rain on glass. Anger, like a hot spurt of blood from a wound. For a moment he simply stared up at the dark ribs of the ceiling. I thought he wouldn't speak, and felt cold relief. The sins of Paradise should not be set down on that clean table. I couldn't bear to stand there, while he crowed about *Crania*. But then he turned towards Benham, as if addressing *him*. 'It's a . . . study. We applied the scientific method to studying the anatomy . . . not only identifying the *origin* of skin colour, but examining its effects. We extracted out those parts of the Negro – blood, and brain matter, and skin – that are blackened, you see, reasoned out *why*. Why are they blackened, and how does this account for his excess of fear and stupidity? Your husband and I had agreed to collaborate –'

'We were interested in the same question, that's all,' interrupted Benham, waving his knife. 'And in no time disagreed on everything *but*. You insisted on all that nonsense with skin –'

'What question?'

'Is the Negro a separate species? It's important work, and *should* be published,' he said, staring at Benham.

She cut him off. 'That old polygenist argument. Dogs and cows? That stale old dispute should have been buried long ago.' She frowned. 'You say you experimented on people?'

'*Cadavers*, when we could get them.'

'But . . . you were a grave robber, Mr Langton!'

'Well . . . we can't learn anything about bodies without cutting them –'

'Not the *cutting*. The using people who cannot consent.'

'Dead people –'

'*Slaves*.'

'What would you know about it?'

'The *better* question is whether you were merely seeing what you wanted to see when you opened those bodies.'

'Skin doesn't lie.'

'And hearts?'

'The heart is nothing but a machine –'

She laughed. 'That is an anatomist's answer, if ever I heard one.'

Her husband gave her a sharp look and, for a moment, there was only the quiet spitting of the candles, but then came a strangled noise from Langton, who bowed his neck and swayed as if trying to catch his breath. I almost forgot myself and struck him between the shoulder blades, as I would have done at Paradise. I felt myself tipping forward, my throat clogged with anger, thick and dry as cotton. I let it swell inside. I welcomed it. Into the silence tipped this truth: my anger was aimed at *myself*. I stepped back, and my wrist struck the sideboard and the plates there joggled like loose stones.

He'd set me down. And I'd stayed where he'd put me. A nail in a plank.

I took a step. The words jolted out of me. 'What have you done to me? *What have you done?* Why have you left me?'

I went over to him. I raised my hand, slapped him.

She looked up, Benham too. But Langton did not.

'Will you ever suffer for what you've done?' I asked his bent head. The strangled noise grew louder, became a cawing, choking sound. A spatter of fingers across the cloth, juddering the table, clutching plate, fork, knife. He wagged his lips, but no sound came out. The knife fell from his hands to the floor. 'Oh!' I cried.

I clasped his head to my chest, and the fit passed through us both and hammered his skull to my breastbone. *The same devil. The same devil.* When he went quiet, the room did. I looked up, saw Linux at the door, holding the bowl of compôte and the plate of madeleines. Her eyes flashed, like knitting needles.

In the kitchen, the kettle steamed quietly on the hob. The coal irons were still laid out on the hearth, where Pru and I had left them so we could polish them with beeswax before we put them away. Something sizzled, like hot tongs on hair. Mr Casterwick sat at the table, filling Benham's decanter, and looked up when she dragged me in. I turned. 'I'm sorry. I –' But she slapped me. The floor slipped away, like a tooth from a gum.

Cold stone slammed the back of my head. Her shadow came over me. 'Savage, cunning little chit. You have *disgraced* this house.'

'Mrs Linux –' Mr Casterwick lifted his bottom off his seat, hovered like a fog, thought better of it.

'I'll thank you, Mr Casterwick, to keep out of matters that are not your affair.' She turned around, and I saw a glint of kettle. 'What did you do?' she cried. I said nothing, kept my eyes on the kettle. She tugged at me; I drew back.

'No, *no, no, no!*' I screamed, pulling away, but I'd already been splashed, burned along my wrist. Everything gone bleached and cool and dark. She gripped me by the neck, pulled me to the door. The truth is she wouldn't have got me back upstairs if I'd thought to fight.

Darkness crept across the attic room. I kicked out into it. My wrist stung, the soreness drumming like a heartbeat. A rattle at the door. 'Who's there?' I called out, and then the knob turned, and when I looked up it was Pru, holding her bowl of mutton fat and her rushlight. She knelt beside me, and took up my hand in hers without saying a word, dabbed a scoop of fat onto my wrist.

I looked down at my hand. 'She's going to turn me out.'

'Should have thought of that, shouldn't you?' She laid my hand back in my lap. 'Needs linseed oil, but I haven't got any.'

'Pru.' I looked at her.

'Maybe. What can you do about it? What can any woman do?' she said. 'You get married, or you go into service.' She crossed her hands, gave me a hard look. 'You'd need a character to get a place and you won't get one from her, not now. My ma used to tell us, "Speak when you're spoken to, do what you're bidden, come when you're called and you'll not be chidden."' She shook her head. 'I knew something bad was coming, you know. A coal spat from the grate and landed at my feet after I lit the fire in Madame's bedchamber this morning, and the day before I saw a winding sheet in the tallow candle in Mrs Linux's parlour. And then there they were tonight, three at a table.'

'What does all that mean?'

'Death.' She made wide eyes. I said nothing. A tight thread of silence stretched between us. *Langton* is dying, I thought. I had seen it. There was no hope that he would be coming back for me. At last, she squinted up at the latch, gave out a sigh. 'I'll have to shift, get back down before I'm missed.'

'You risked coming up, for me.'

She shrugged. 'My nan always said mercy is a soothing balm, just as good to give as to receive.' She yawned, held one hand up to her mouth. 'No use greetin' over it now. Whatever it is in the morning, it won't be this.' She patted my arm and then pulled herself to her feet, gathering up her bowl and her light. At the door, she stopped, hand on the knob. 'Frances . . . who *is* Mr Langton to you?'

I slid one hand over the opposite palm, kept them busy with each other. My wrist was numb under the grease, pink as a newborn. I pressed it to a sting, trying to scour the dark thoughts from my head, kept my eyes down so I wouldn't have to look her in the face when I answered.

Pru's still the only person I ever told out loud.

'He's my father.'

Chapter Seventeen

What did that make me? A patchwork monster. A thing sewn from Langton's parts. The sum of his seed, for all I knew: Miss-bella was childless.

It was she who told me, though she waited until it was too late. And, oh, I wanted to kill him, when I learned it, but I wanted to kill *her* also, for that.

It was all quiet in those days. No Phibbah, no snick of peas, no floorboard cracks. The river through the hills, like a long black scar. The sun high as noon. But that's what Jamaica days were like. Either morning sun, noon sun, evening sun, or rain. Never anything different. We stood outside together on the porch. She had stopped me, on my way to the coach-house. 'I want you to tell me what my husband thinks he's doing in there . . .'

'No, Miss-bella.'

'Some brand of wickedness, I just want to know what brand.'

I shook my head, but I couldn't say yes or no. It was some brand of wickedness. I had seen it.

'Girl.' She shook her head, sniffed. 'I speak frankly, and I expect you to do the same unto me.'

'Yes.' I started to say more, then stopped. There was nothing frank about me, not any more.

When she turned her eyes on me, they were windowpanes. 'I want you to consider . . .' She stopped, bent over to set her flask on the doily, her hands slow as tar. 'That man is your father.'

'No.' It slid out quick as a cough.

'Look around, girl. Look around you.'

My voice went small, crawling back to the past, the old talk, my mind scrabbling, clutching on the overseer, the book-keeper, men I had never given any thought to before. 'There are other white men here,' I said. And then I staggered away from her, vomited into her roses. Head swirling like stirred soup. Everything around me stained to the same rust, the colour of the dry dirt, the walls, the bushes, even the dogs.

It was his sickness that had saved me, in the end. His body had long grown too weak to be a burden, to me or anyone else. But not before it had already happened, that first night, the nights that followed it. *I would have killed him, had I known it then.* I let that dark shard in, and had to keep it stored, and hurting, in my chest.

I went down early. Linux was in the kitchen alone, nursing a cup of tea. She was staring down at a pile of coins, and looked up when I came in and said they were for me, so it came to me that she must be turning me out, that they were my wages and, without thinking, I reached out a hand –

'No. When you come back down. You're to go up, now. Madame wants you.'

Her door was open. Books tumbled around the desk in a bramble of cloth and leather. There was a faint smell of fruit, heedless and ripe. A musk of leather and ink. Lilies in a vase on her mantelpiece.

I saw her, crouched among the books. Cleared my throat.

'Frances! Yes. Sit.' She pointed to an armchair, one of a pair, yellow with a winding pattern of blue leaves, pulled close to the fireplace. 'Just a moment, I am . . . looking for something.'

I could map that room now, needing no compass. My

fingers my only tools. Seven steps from the japanned bed to the writing desk, four steps from there to the red cabinet painted with storks. Between them, the portrait of the woman with dark hair and pale cheeks, raised onto her elbows, the field around her dotted yellow, her gown a freshly butchered red. The woman in red. On the mantel, Madame's little wooden box, with her initials carved into it – MD – ringed by bluebells.

A door slammed below and the noise rattled up through brick and plaster and glass. I felt light as ash spat out of a fire. I couldn't think what I would do next, where I would go, if I *was* being turned out. I sat holding my sore wrist with my other hand, watching her. She nudged her books, gave them little smiles and pats. 'Montaigne . . . Johnson . . . Wollstonecraft! Ah! But look at you . . .' She lifted one, flicked it open: '*When I have fears that I may cease to be, before my pen has gleaned my teeming brain.*' She looked up. Her eyes glittered like pins scattered on a floor. Last night's ice had melted and she had decided we'd be friends once more, it seemed, now that there was no one to bear witness to it. 'La! Isn't that just it? Have you read Keats?'

'I haven't.'

'Pity.' She came across and dropped it into my lap. 'I think it *is* true that the best art is driven by fear. The artist swarming with ideas! Like ants, or termites, can you imagine? Eating away. What an image.'

'Am I being turned out?' I asked abruptly.

She laughed. 'What?'

I drew myself up. 'I am not sorry I said what I said.'

'No! Nor should you be. Why, I quite felt like standing up and *clapping*, when you put that awful man in his place. He speaks as if our fate is shot like an arrow into foetal clay. Fixed. Unchange-able. But Locke said we must suppose the mind to be white

143

paper. A *tabula rasa*. One could take any child and make of him a scholar or a thief.' She put out a hand. 'I heard what happened, of course. I am sorry about it. Are you quite all right?' I held my hand away and would not let her look. 'I will have a word with Mrs Linux. It will not happen again. She has *God's* patience. All that smiting and punishing. But I inherited her with marriage, like the dowager's pearls, which never warmed to me either, mind you. Mr Benham will not let me dismiss her. She dotes on *him*. When I first married, I said to myself, a woman with *such* an attachment to a man must be his mistress. Or his bastard. Though she is neither . . . Have I shocked you? I am too frank, I know. Full to the brim with bad habits.'

'Do you know what happened to him?'

'Mr Langton? Mr Benham saw to it. He was returned to his inn. The doctor was called.'

If he died, I thought, *I* would have been the one to kill him. And that thought made me glad.

She pulled back. '*Ah!* There.' She'd spied a volume on the floor near the hearth. 'This is what I was looking for.' She picked it up, read aloud: '*I have spent my life in idle longing, without saying a word, in the presence of those whom I loved most –*'

'Is that a novel?' I interrupted.

'Rousseau's *Confessions*. His autobiography. A book he wrote about himself.'

'I know what an autobiography is.'

'Of course. Do you know, I still remember where I was the first time I read *him*. The friends who had taken us in after we first came here from Paris had a library. We spent many years with them. Oh, *that* was a part of London I could feel welcome in! Someone else's sentences, twisting, turning, moving, as all things must, towards their own ends. Sometimes where they take you is right to your own bewildered heart. One afternoon it was Monsieur Rousseau's voice I heard there . . . Well! I could go on and on about those things. I bore most people to tears. Yet . . . with all that talk of science, last night, I cannot think of anything worse than spending all that time and energy trying to understand the mechanics of life but not the beauty of it.'

'Or the ugliness.'

'Precisely!' She turned suddenly, crossed to the dressing-table, slippers leaving soft prints in the carpet, like tooth-marks in bread. Set the book down and picked up a hairbrush. 'He's a man of words, my husband, but he prefers to chase them. Like some men chase butterflies. And he also pins them under glass.' She turned the brush over and over in her hands, and spoke into the looking-glass. 'We understand each other, I believe.'

'Your husband?'

She laughed. 'You and me.'

'Oh.'

'Is it strange of me to say so?'

A heartbeat, a breath.

'Are you good with a needle?'

'Yes.'

'Hair?'

'You are *not* turning me out?'

'Oh! I haven't said it plain, have I? I want you for my abigail. A *secretary*, I suppose. I *do* want to write, you see. I have decided to, and Mr Benham says I may, and that I might have *you* to help me.'

'*Me?*' I rose to my feet. It came to me that I should not feel pleased. It would only be swapping one kind of maiding for another. An iron cage for a gilded one. But I did. Oh, I did. 'Mrs Linux won't like it.'

'No.' She smiled. 'She won't.'

•

Downstairs, Linux was making hot-water crusts. She smother-ed kettle screams with a clean towel, wrapped the handle, poured water into a copper pot.

'I'm to take up some chocolate,' I said from the door.

She didn't look up, but measured out two scoops of fat, lifted her wooden spoon, beat at the dough. 'For Madame,' I said.

I walked over to the table where the coins had been set.

She stilled. 'You're to take those only if you're leaving.'

'I'm staying.'

Her eyes flitted over to me, boiling black. 'I see. Well, take the chocolate, then. Is anyone stopping you?' She unhooked the keys, threw one at me. 'Isn't she just the sort who'd lap up a darky maid like a cat at a plate of cream?'

I jangled the key in my hand. 'She wants cake rusks as well.'

'Take it. Take it. By all means. And will that be all, Madam Blacky-boots?'

Chapter Eighteen

And what do two women do in a room of their own? Isn't this the question that troubles my accusers most? Such an easy thing to hide in plain sight – a lady and her abigail – all eyes looking the wrong way. There's a turnkey at Newgate who likes to imply it. 'They say the two of you was a nasty pair of flats, under cover of being mistress and dresser.' He's the one who took my letter from me, in the reception, when I first came, not the one who reads the broadsheets out loud. The only letter I ever had from her, now it's gone. They took it to punish me. It makes them want to punish a woman even more, of course, if she stirs up any kind of lewdness in them.

I suppose I must tell you about the first day. I'd never been a lady's maid. She said she'd never bothered with one before. Perhaps nothing we did was as it was normally done. All I can tell you is how it was. Early morning, the watchman still calling out the hour, and the sky hung at the window black as ash. I climbed the stairs carrying her ewer of hot water between two hands. Found her already up and waiting. She was sitting up in bed, legs crossed in front of her, picking at slivers of pineapple Pru had brought up in a little silver bowl. A dress was laid out already, beside her on the bed, a white day dress, with a stiff neck-gauze.

'Oh, Frances!' she said, and went to stand before the mirror, stared at me in the glass. I fancied I saw a slow grin, a flash of red lip, white teeth. Then she cocked her head at herself and let her kimono slip down her shoulders, which took me by surprise, let me tell you. She was nothing like Miss-bella, the only

147

other white body I'd seen. Madame's was naked as a savage, daring me to touch it. Her dark hair swelling full as skirts, her belly, creased like an eyelid. Her small breasts. I swallowed, took a cold, plummeting breath and set the ewer down. She lifted one arm overhead, sniffed. 'A bath this morning, do you think?' I realized she meant for *me* to smell it, too, and shook off memories of Phibbah and Miss-bella, the tin bath, Miss-bella's high, whining complaints. I thought, *How true it is that ugly people have hope while pretty people have expectation.* I'd never seen the use of beauty myself. Nothing but a lucky arrangement of meat and bone. Never dug any holes, or baked any bread. She kept her arm above her head, and I crossed over to her, thinking how each step dragged me backwards, how I didn't dare touch her, because I wanted nothing more, but had to touch her, if I wanted to stay. Touching her was my work, now. My jaw clenched. I leaned forward, fanned by her breaths, and she by mine. Tickling hairs under her arms waved, like babies' legs. I pressed my nose to her. Roses, lemon water, sweat.

'No.'

I turned, brought myself face to face with the dress.

'I am so glad you're here, Frances,' I heard her say behind me.

It was like having a wooden marionette, I told myself, slipping its limp little arms through the sleeves, fastening its buttons. *White women all the same as babies*, I heard Phibbah say. *They just want feeding, dressing, fussing. Then stay out the way o' their shit.* After that, I busied my hands and eyes with the dress, wondering out loud whether I should pass the charcoal iron over it, whether she wanted me to sprinkle it with rose-water, and kept up those gallivantings until the very last hook was fastened in place.

She'd already given me three of her cast-off frocks, which I'd hung on the nail above my pallet. The one I wore that morning was a pink-and-white-striped morning dress with a bow at the collar, gripping at the shoulders and waist and just touching my ankles. I'd put my hair up also, using some pins she gave me, so it crested over my forehead, and I fancied it made me look both serious and sad. When she was dressed, she went over and sat cross-legged on her bed, twisting her fingers into the coverlet and saying we'd make a start on the writing. From the desk rose the smell of orange oil and beeswax. I pictured Pru leaning over it, her polishing cloth swiping at the wood, and pressed my finger to it, leaving a smear like a breath on cold glass.

The snug room, the warm fire, the woman with pale hands and blue eyes. It was so close to my vision that day I arrived in this city that I dared to believe I'd had a stroke of good fortune once more.

A. Some weeks after she first arrived, I noticed that the prisoner had fallen into the habit of going to the mistress's bedchamber late at night. It was just after she started as her abigail; I observed it myself, several times, starting with that very first night. She was crossing the landing which led away from the mistress's bedchamber, the very same place I saw her the night of the murders.

Mr Jessop: What time was this?
A. Just gone midnight.

Q. Where were you when you observed her?
A. Downstairs, in the front hall. From there I could see clearly up to the landing on the third floor. I called out.

Q. Did she show any signs of distress?
A. No.

Q. Did she seem startled?
A. No.

Q. Did she appear to be asleep?
A. No. In fact, she leaned over the balcony, and spoke with me.

Q. What did she say?
A. She'd heard a noise from the mistress's rooms and gone to check, but finding her door locked was going upstairs again. I warned her that she should be in bed and I'd better not find her out of bed again at night. Nevertheless, a few weeks later, the same thing happened again.

Q. And she gave you the same excuse?

Mr Pettigrew: My Lord –
Court: Yes, yes. Mr Jessop, need I remind you to refrain from leading the witness?

Mr Jessop: How did she respond, Mrs Linux, on that occasion?
A. Same as before, sir. Said she'd heard a noise, only that time she said it was a scream. I remember that because it gave me a chill down my spine.

Chapter Nineteen

You want a confession. Or an explanation. *Give me something I can save your neck with.* Well. I am guilty of this. I was a woman who loved a woman, chief among the womanly sins, like barrenness, and thinking. After that, my thoughts were all of her, and coarse and lewd, disturbing as dog-barks. Oh, the shock of it. The wrongness. The dark, surprising glee.

That was the beginning of all my misery and all my joy. So close to what I wanted, yet just as far away. She was writing her own confessions after the manner of Mr Rousseau, who said he wrote his as a portrait. Mr Rousseau also wrote that man was born free but is everywhere in chains. I didn't know what chains he could have been speaking of. Page-gazers like him feel the weight of chains in a feather. When I told her that, she laughed: '*Indeed.* Let one of them try being born a woman.'

She dictated, and I wrote. Her family had fled to England from France when she was a small girl, and soon discovered you can't eat noble titles, though you can suck on bedsheets. Many French starved, she said. Her father had brought his violin and a little chest, in which he kept his eggs. He couldn't bear to be parted from them. Mistle thrushes and wagtails and eagles all came with them, wrapped in cotton in his little box, yet he hadn't thought to bring something his wife and daughter could actually eat. The violin proved useful, however. After a while, he found work tutoring the children of one of the landed families in Wiltshire. It was there that George Benham had found her.

•

Most afternoons, she wanted to sit in the parlour and read.

'Oh, but of course you must come down with me, Frances!' she said. She sat on the blue damask sofa, me at the window. She wanted me to read *Mathilda*, so I would know what she was talking about when I scribed her essay. I read it and didn't like it, and didn't know what I could say to her about it. In the end, I said only that, having had no father or mother, I was nobody's daughter. When I told her I'd never read *Franken-stein*, she said she'd read it to me. We passed three afternoons on that adventure, my heart thudding as I listened with my head resting on the glass behind me. By the time she read, '*I shall die, and what I now feel be no longer felt. Soon these burning miseries will be extinct,*' I burned myself, with the urge to weep. I felt tears creeping behind my eyes and had to turn my face away from her.

She thought it was important for women not just to live in the world, but to think about it. 'Thinking is so much better than living,' she said. 'Montaigne said all the wisdom in the world teaches us not to be afraid of dying.'

Sometimes Benham came in there, too, and they spoke in whispers or not at all. Sometimes her friends came, ladies whose skirts made noises like doves on a branch. But most often, it was just the pair of us. She read to me *The Castle of Otranto* and *Vathek* during the weeks that followed, but neither affected me as *Frankenstein* had.

A month passed. February to March. She said she wanted to open Levenhall before the end of the Season. Soon every day seemed to start with a salon, and end with a soirée, the lower rooms lit bright as stars. I usually took down a book with me, or a bit of sewing, so I could keep my head down and my fingers working, pulling stitches, or following the lines. Perhaps it will impress you that Mr Zachary Macaulay himself called often. Always following behind a group of milk-faced women with tight hair, like a rooster with his hens. He was tall and thin, very pink in the cheeks, white hair waving like rat's whiskers. The first time, he pressed my hands in his. What a grip he had, for someone who looked so weak.

'What a *pleasure* to have you in England, girl.'

I didn't much like his palabber, or his airs of hawkish charity. But I felt the same about all of them. Why is it that every white you'll ever meet either wants to tame you or rescue you? What no one will admit about the anti-slavers is that they've all got a slaver's appetite for misery, even if they want to do different things with it. And, for all their talk of men as brothers, most of them stared at me as if I had two heads.

'She's quite the reader, isn't she, Meg? All those novels?'

Benham had asked the day before whether I'd try my hand at a poem or two, no doubt wondering might he have his own Phillis Wheatley. I suspect *she* led a very sad life, if it was the kind that impressed them. Doing all those parlour tricks. And what they never tell you about her is that she didn't die a poet, she died a maid.

I could never trust someone who'd rather read a slave history than a novel, which was what many of them confessed: '*Surely* novels are a mere frippery, Frances, when you think of the *weight* of suffering in the world. They make such a great fuss out of nothing.'

'Why not?' I answered. 'In the end, life makes nothing out of such a fuss.'

Oh, they all hollered at that. I was as amusing to them as a dog walking on its hind legs.

But misery is certain as a wound clock. There's no need to go chasing after it.

It's hard to tell a remembered story in a straight line.

It pops into my head that I should tell you about the first

time Benham came to the parlour. It was the end of my first week with her. She'd gone down there for the afternoon. I came up from the kitchen with her wine and apple on a tray. When I went in, Benham was there, leaning on the mantel, where he fiddled with a glass of something. Madame was on the blue sofa. I stood rooted, not knowing whether to go forward or back. Neither of them looked up, nor said a word. They were frozen. I wondered what could have been happening that needed to be snuffed out as soon as someone else came in.

I crouched to set down the tray. He swivelled, spoke, voice cold as a blade. Carrying over some argument they'd been having. 'I'm sure I told Linux it must go to storage,' he said.

'Yes. I asked Charles to put it back. Weeks ago. It is funny how seldom you visit most of the rooms in this house.'

'The *only* household matter you've concerned yourself with for weeks. I ask myself why.'

'And I ask myself why you want it removed.'

'Because it's the sort of thing no one should be decking their walls with any more.'

'Or is it because you've given too much credit to nonsense gossip?' She braced her arms beside her on the sofa. She hesitated, then said, 'Let me see if I understand. The *boy* was here, but now his portrait must vanish so you can pretend *he* has. Is that it?'

The portrait. I turned to look at it. The boy. His black jaw a curve of sadness. Pru had told me she hadn't been in service when the boy was there, seeing as she'd been only a child then herself. But she'd had some of the story from Mr Casterwick. He had been brought over by Benham from one of his Antigua estates when he and Madame were first married. *From slave to servant, then*, I thought. *Just like me.* He had been called Olaudah. Madame had bestowed upon him a pet name: Laddie.

'The wee boys were so much more fashionable, once upon a time,' Pru said. I asked her what had happened to him. 'No one will say *exactly*. All I ever heard was that Mr Benham asked him to leave, and afterwards not a soul would even speak of him, save for Mr Casterwick. He says he used to bring the poor mite downstairs to warm himself through, after Madame had him out and about.'

Madame picked up one of the blue brocade sofa cushions, curled her arms around it. He laughed, like something hard tapping his teeth. 'You're far too spoiled, wife.'

She didn't say anything to that. Twisted the cushion in her hands. Some strange look creaked onto her face. A sadness, to match the boy's. He turned away, cracked his knuckles. Still laughing quietly to himself.

I slipped out, closed the door and went back downstairs.

Later that day, when I went to her room, she was tucked into one of the chairs, pages scattered on the floor and on her lap, and I saw that she was feeding them to the fire. Paper burning to black petals and then to ash. Her memoirs. I would soon learn that the work on them started and stopped, depending on her moods. She squinted into the grate after each page, cocking her head. Unblinking.

'What are you doing?'

'Oh. I know, I know. All that writing! Ashes to ashes . . .' Her voice trailed, and she tipped forward with a slow effort. I thought with a stab of confusion she must be drunk. I remembered a conversation we'd had about her papa: *You can always tell, straight away, with drunks. It's the smile. They have cruel smiles.*

She went on until her fingers grappled air, then stared at her empty lap.

I set down the tray. 'Madame?'

When she looked up, she spied the lily I'd plucked out of the vase that stood in the front hall. 'How lovely! I prescribe one such theft every morning. Though they are hot-housed in winter, you know. All the flowers are.'

It was false cheer, thick as a coating of tallow.

'It seems everything is hot-housed here,' I said.

She flicked her face towards me. 'Oh, I have made you cross. I can see that. Destroying your lovely pages. But I read them over this morning and knew they must not be allowed to stand. Everything in the world is *already* more terrifying or beautiful than anything we can put into it. What is the use attempting to add to it?'

Everything in the room, including my time, including me, was hers to do with as she would. What I wanted wouldn't matter. Never had. I swallowed, hoped my thoughts wouldn't show on my face, made myself shrug. 'They are your pages.'

'Oh,' she said. 'Oh.' She gave me a sharp look. 'You needn't feel you must tiptoe around me, Frances. We will be such great friends. I know it.'

'Yes, Madame, thank you,' I said, in a voice smooth as apples.

She pushed suddenly to her feet, went over to her cabinet, and when she straightened, she was holding a vial. Her laudanum, I realized. She'd been careful never to let me see her taking more than Dr Fawkes prescribed. But Dr Fawkes came as often as the tides. Every time, the dose crept like a vine up a wall. Eight grains. Ten. Fifteen. Twenty. I was the one who went down to Apothecary Jones in Knightsbridge to fetch it. How well I came to know his dark little shop, crowded by bottles. Arsenic, prussic acid, laudanum.

She stood for some time staring at the cabinet door. Then she spoke: 'Mr Benham has said I may not publish after all.'

'Oh.'

'Well. I have misunderstood him, it seems. I may write, but that is not the same as saying I may publish.'

She took another swallow, and crossed to the window, still holding her vial. 'First, he tells me to take Laddie off the wall, and then *this*.'

She pinched his name out, as if it would sting to say it. I gave her a hard stare. 'Who is Laddie?'

'Someone who disappeared. That is what they do best here. Pretend not to see a thing, *fermer les yeux* and – *voilà!* – it is not there. The greatest trick in English sleeves. Making things disappear.'

She went back to the window. 'He would only tolerate my little scribbles, anyway, if he could have some guarantee they would be inferior to *his*.' She laughed. 'I was tempted to promise that.'

She always spoke slowly. Because she was foreign, she said. Afraid of making a mistake. She tapped out words the way you tap a walking stick. Cautious. She stood and chewed at her nail. I could hear the small wet sounds of her breath, and moved to stand beside her, not knowing what else to do. This close, her beauty slipped, like a bad wig. Sharp bones, thin mouth. I pressed my hands into the sash.

'What is the *point* of writing for oneself alone?' she said. And then, 'Perhaps clever men should be permitted to marry only women with empty heads.'

'No man can be as clever as the world thinks he is,' I said, and a laugh cracked out of her, took her by surprise.

She looked at me, her face pleated with a smile. 'You *are* amusing,' she said. 'Perhaps I should write about my marriage. About *him*. Publish anonymously. That would serve him right.'

Fat drops of rain slapped the window. Outside, mist clung to hard earth. A cobweb of light hung over the pond, though it was murky and green and had a scum of leaves on it. I could see Pru, beating a rug out over the hawthorn, her shoes slipping in the dew. We stood in silence for a long time. The next thing she said made me whip my head around: 'London is full of so many people, yet all of them so alone.'

The laudanum bottle rested in the crook of her arm, uncapped. The rotten-plum smell of it rose into the air. She took another swig. The closeness of the room, the weather, the quiet made me brave. 'Why *did* you marry?' I asked.

She laughed, sent her tongue out for stray drops. 'It was easy as a wrong sum. I wanted his fortune. He wanted my looks.'

Weeks passed, then a month, taking us into April. Soon they all got used to the sight of me. Meg's black. On her perch at the window bench. I gazed around that room so many times. Now that Benham had had his way, the paintings were all of battle-fields: bayoneted horses with rolling eyes, soldiers dying in blood. I stared through the window at the pond, and the grass, which was bright again, and the birds, which had delighted her by coming back.

There were times I felt light as an empty sack blowing on a pavement.

The ladies spilled in and out like dropped grain, swarmed the table, fiddling counters, biting down on them as they puzzled over their endless games of whist. There was one, Hephzibah Elliot, I noticed most of all. She watched, too. She wore short-sleeved dresses, a veil pinned to her hat by a jet pin that gripped her skull like a tiny hand. I disliked her on sight. Her heavy brow, and her small eyes, and the way they followed Madame above her teacup. She had the shape of a hand-barrow and a voice to match. 'Oh, Hep is not at all handsome,' Madame said once. 'But she does have *very* handsome thoughts.' I had to chew my lip so as not to laugh.

There was something alike about all those ladies. Silk dresses carved to neat little figures, voices fluttering like hand-cloths.

Only Hep Elliot was different, in her shapeless gowns. As I watched them, down would come the feeling that I'd walked up to a window and was peering at them through glass. I knew I'd never belong. And then I saw all of it sharp as knives, and it hurt my eyes.

Every part of me ached with wanting things I could not have. I wanted the courage of the mad. To declare myself. To her. As if mine were the kind of suit that could ever be spoken out loud.

Sometimes I felt a pulse of anger too, I'll confess it.

Relentless as a heart.

Anger was what took me to her door. Anger and want, equal as butter and sugar in a pound cake. I took the rushlight and slipped along the third-floor corridor, laid my ear against the wood. I fancied I heard whispering through it. I listened for the smallest creak to tell me where she was. Was that a footstep at her desk? Was that a cabinet door banging against the wall? Was she leaning on the window sill? Did she lie awake? As restless as me? I wanted to call out to her through the wood. I wanted to say something. I wanted to go through that door. Perhaps she was calling out to me! Perhaps that was the whisper I'd heard: *Frannie! Frannie!* But the thought of knocking, moreover of what she might say if I did, filled me with dread. Terror in my throat thick as meat.

I heard footsteps striking the marble downstairs, and Linux crying out below. I took a deep breath and fumbled my voice down over the railing, telling her I thought I'd heard a disturbance at Madame's door. 'At the *door*?' she repeated, as if it were some African word. 'The only disturbance up there is *you*.'

MISS HEPHZIBAH ELLIOT, sworn

Mr Jessop: Did you know the prisoner?
A. Not really. I usually saw her in company. Sometime in March last year, Meg began to bring her everywhere. She never said much. Her eyes never left her mistress. She watched her, always, wherever she was in any room.

Q. Would you say it was obsessive?
Mr Pettigrew: I object, My Lord.

Q. How would you characterize it, the way she watched her mistress?
A. Observant, I'd say. But then it must have been so new for her. I am trying to be fair.

Q. What of the speculation concerning a love affair between the prisoner and her mistress?
A. I have heard it. I wouldn't want to comment. I believe love affairs are matters that can only be confirmed by the protagonists, though such vast quantities of ink are wasted over them.

Q. But do you believe that was what happened between them?
A. I wouldn't know.

Q. Would it shock you, to hear such a thing said about Mrs Benham?
A. What difference would that make to whether it happened or not?

Q. You were at the soirée at Levenhall on 26 January?
A. I was.

Q. Did you observe the exchange between the prisoner and her mistress in the drawing room that evening?
A. I did.

Q. Tell these gentlemen what you saw.

A. The prisoner came into the drawing room, just after champagne had been passed. We were celebrating a successful lecture series, sponsored by the Society. The soirée was intended to be a commemoration of the last lecture. The prisoner entered the room. She was distressed. Well, she was shaking, she raised her fist. Who can say if it was anger or fear or sorrow? Those things so often look the same. She was shaking, at any rate. You wouldn't have mistaken it for happiness.

Q. Did she say anything?

A. Oh, yes. Oh, yes, she did. She came very close to Meg, right up to her so Meg was forced to take a step back, and she shook her fist again, as I've said, and then she said, 'This is death.'

Q. You're sure that's what you heard?

A. Quite sure. And at such a volume, too, you couldn't help but hear it if you were anywhere in that room.

CROSS-EXAMINED BY MR PETTIGREW

Mr Pettigrew: 'This is death.' That's what you heard?

A. Yes.

Q. You didn't think that strange?

A. That the maid had descended the stair to threaten her mistress's life? Strange, indeed. The evening could barely limp along after that.

Q. Not strange in that sense, Miss Elliot. Strange that the prisoner would make a threat in the present tense. Surely she'd say, 'I will kill you,' or something of that sort? The future tense?

A. I thought perhaps it was due to her poor command of the English language, Mr Pettigrew.

Q. Did she have a poor command of the language?
A. I hardly heard her put three words together before that night.

Q. Then how would you know what her relationship was to the English language?
[Admonition from the court to the gallery for laughing and disturbance.]

Q. She could have been timid? Shy?
A. It's possible. Though she had a forward look about her.

Q. I see. But you would expect a mere dressing maid to be quiet in the company of ladies such as yourselves.
A. I suppose.

Q. Now. Let's come on to Mr Olaudah Cambridge, Miss Elliot. Also known as Laddie Lightning. What did you know of him?

Chapter Twenty

It grows so hot in my cell that the air is thick and damp, and always there is the rattle of bolts, the hammering of boots in the passages, the shrieking from the other cells, worse in the moment just after it stops because then it keeps ringing in my head. When I'm not writing, my head's as empty as any gaol-bird's. The slightest sound rolls around and around in it, and that's when thoughts of her spill in, and cause me at times to doubt my own account. Not just of the murder, but of the love. It's nonsense to say it didn't happen. That it was all in my head. They say so only for *Benham*'s protection. But a dead man's reputation means nothing to a dead man. They took my letter away from me when they first brought me here so that I cannot prove it. And though I have no care about proving it to them, some days I have a powerful need to prove it to myself.

How I wish I still had that folded scrap. Creases oily as fish skin, her handwriting sprawled across the page, the single line that she had copied out herself:

One word frees us of all the weight and pain of life: That word is love.

They say it didn't happen only because they can't believe it could. A woman like her loving a woman like me.

It was all in your head, Frannie Langton.

No. It was there on paper too. Black marks. Necromancing marks, with all the power to bring her from the dead.

It was all in your head, they say. But where else is love if not in your head? And, as Sal used to say, why is it that fucking is always our story, and love is always theirs?

•

It started when she said I should sleep in her room one night, so as not to wake up Pru when we got back.

We'd been to Almack's. She wore her men's costume. Breeches and a cambric shirt. Told me to wear one of the dresses she'd given me, a striped velvet, though I don't know why, for I sat in the maids' room all night.

Maids' room was what they called it, but it was in truth the withdrawing room, where the ladies came to relieve themselves, attended by their own maid. I sat near one of the little screens beside a potted plant. Hands folded in my lap. The ladies had been coming and going, and now it was quiet. Some of the other maids gave tight smiles, nodded hello. But none approached me. I overheard some of them talking and, having nothing better to do, I strained my ears to listen.

'My own mistress says there was talk the poor mite would have been left worrying Meg didn't love him after all, the way he was turned out – bags into the street, and his own arse behind them. The real problem might have been that Mr Benham suspected she loved him too much. That last Season he lived with them, they took up fencing, the two of them together – alone! He hung off her carriage at every party, too, like some shameless baboon. Too big to fit inside by then! She must have known it wouldn't be possible to carry on like that after the boy had grown.'

'How long ago was that?'

'Maybe five years?'

'He's boxing now, I hear,' said another. 'Goes by Laddie Lightning.'

I jerked my head up. They were talking about Madame. The boy in the portrait. I strained to hear more but by then they had moved away.

•

All afternoon I'd been dreading the moment when I'd have to bed down in her room. Dressing her in the mornings was still terrible, but habit had taught me endurance. I knew undressing her would be even worse.

She sat on her bed. I bent to unlace her boots, thudding each one to the carpet. She snapped the buttons on her fall-fronts herself, shrugged off her shirt, and unhooked her bindings. I reached out, carefully, to take the clothes from her, bring her gown. And it wasn't as bad as I'd feared, though my head felt like an empty room, from trying not to look. Not to think. Only a glimpse of dimpled thigh, curve of bone at the hip, the scuttle of dark hair when she shook out the coiled plaits. Then I had this one cold, clear thought. Clear like writing. *This kind of wanting is nothing but begging.*

I rolled out my pallet in front of the fire, thinking I'd never sleep. But I must have, for I dreamed that I woke to find the Surgeon slouched in one of the armchairs, working his knife across the strop. *And one! And-two-and! One-and-two-and* –

He could tell I was awake. I'd gone still as a grass snake. 'Found you,' he said, pausing the blade. He snicked his thumb along it, lifted it to lick off a bead of blood. 'This thing's never sharp enough now, gel. You were the one with the knack for it.' His voice went through me like a bell-strike. *Clang.* I scrabbled to my feet, but he laid a finger on his lips. '*Hush.* She's sleeping'. Only then did I look over at Madame. The top of her skull doffed like a boy's cap, the dusty flower of brain deep in the bowl. 'So little *eggs-han-gwination* when they've been dead a long time,' he said.

Then came an icy gush of terror, so swift I felt I was fainting. It was then that I came awake.

This time, Madame was in the chair. Wearing a shawl over her nightgown. The fire was dying out, but still golden on her face, her loosened hair. Everything they say beauty is supposed to be, she was. She looked up. 'Did I wake you?'

I pushed onto my elbows. Oh, if she knew what I was thinking. *What if I was a gentleman, who'd met you at Almack's? Bent over your gloved hand? Pressed my lips to your knuckles? What then?*

I saw myself giving a tongue flick to soft kid.

Her pulse a hummingbird at her throat.

No one else watching.

I saw *us* fencing in a dimly lit room.

I sat up. 'Should I get fresh coals for your pan?'

'Oh . . . no . . . I never can sleep at this time of day. It is a funny limbo hour, *non*? Neither morning nor night. This is how lonely death must be.'

The candle guttered out and I lit a spill from the fire, reached up to light it again. 'Are you sure I shouldn't fill the pan?'

She crooked her fingers into her hair, then pushed to her feet. 'What I need is a drop more.'

'What's it like?' I asked her, pulling knees to chest.

She paused with her hand on the cabinet. 'What? Laudanum? Have you never . . . ? Well.' She tilted her head. 'I suppose most people think it must be dark and wicked. Pure pleasure. But it is more . . . the absence of pain.' She turned her eyes towards me again. 'Life makes each of us a kettle, boiling up and up and up. Imagine a gentle hand comes along and moves you off the flame. That is opium. It is . . . a gentle rowboat on black water. Sweet dreams.'

She laughed, embarrassed. 'Still. One must be careful not to become like the ones who carry their vials at the theatre and in all the withdrawing rooms. After a time, the drug itself causes agonies nothing can relieve, not *even* the drug . . .' She tipped the bottle back and swallowed. Turned, her eyes all glitter. 'I have been thinking, you know, about the education you received. How fortunate you were. Not just a black, but a woman! You were given a chance many free women will never have.'

'I don't know if it was luck,' I said. 'Langton said he'd only trained me as one would a parrot.'

I heard his voice: *You disgust me.*

'Oh. *Odious* man,' she said, and shivered. She set the bottle back in the cabinet, stretched her arms. I heard the crack of bones. '*Truly.* You are so much better here. With me.'

She nodded, as if something had been decided. I pushed to my feet, needing to turn away. Decided I'd fill the warming pan with the last of the coals. I went to the fire and poked some up, held the pan with one of her towels and crossed to the bed. Her eyes followed me. I knelt to tuck it under the coverlet, and then she came beside me, kneeling also.

She leaned close. 'We are like two playmates in the nursery saying our bedtime prayers together. And now that you are here, I will "lie down and sleep in peace". '

The end of her sleeve whispered against my wrist. She lifted my hand, turned it over. Peered at the lines in my palm. Words rattled to a stop inside my head. It was more terrifying than my dream, and my wrist started to quake, so I pulled my hand away, pretended to tuck the pan deeper under, kept it pinned beneath the coverlet.

My breath clutched at my chest and I didn't dare look up. The drapes were open, navy walls lit by the moon. Many minutes passed in silence. She leaned forward, seemed to catch herself, then came forward again. She turned my face and pressed her lips to mine. So soft. I could hardly feel it. I pressed closer. The longing of iron for a lodestone. I felt a prickle in my hand, like needles in flesh. I lifted it, reached for her face –

She moved away. Put back the bedcovers. 'I – I can manage a little sleep now,' she said.

She turned, as if to hide herself from me, though I wanted

to see every inch of her. She blew out the candle, and the room shivered and then all I could see was black.

I hardly slept. I wanted to wake her, ask her why, press myself along the length of her in the bed. At daybreak, I tidied my pallet and stood for a long time watching the street. Charles came out through the front door, and cut through the mews, off to fetch milk from Piccadilly, no doubt. Shoes loud as hand-claps. Birds fidgeting with song. I went over to the writing table and sat with my hands pressed together, my face warm as a fresh heart. Remembering how she'd caught herself, and wavered like a flame in a draught. How, as if I was something bitter, she had spat me back.

Knowing that a watched face won't long stay sleeping, I drew in a breath, opened the door, slipped out.

I confess that I doubted it. It seemed the whole night had been a dream, from the Surgeon to the kiss. I would doubt it still, if not for what happened next.

Chapter Twenty-One

Longreach was the house of Sir Percy, Benham's brother. Sugar-bought, like everything they own. Madame and Benham were invited there to a party. She wanted to bring her own dresser, she said, since Benham was taking Casterwick. Now she'd no longer have to put up with the long-toothed girl Lady Catherine insisted on giving her, with the cold fingers.

We drove out to Wiltshire in a hired carriage, leaving at dawn and stopping twice to change horses. After a day's travel, Longreach loomed ahead, spread across the landscape. Sprawling and broad-shouldered. A snaking line of elms led to the front door, and inside was all velvet and polished wood and brass. Their rooms looked out onto the lawn. Soft towels had been set out on the washstand, and little pink soaps carved into roses. As soon as we arrived, I unpacked the trunk and her portmanteau, and then she had to be dressed for the fireworks dinner. We were late, and had to rush, and afterwards – wanting to be anywhere but the long corridor where the visiting maids were being kept – I slipped outside and wandered down to the garden, gravel crunching beneath my feet. I kept myself to the side of the path. Hundreds of tiny lanterns swung from the trees. The sky was heavy and purple, and a smell in the air reminded me of the mint Phibbah grew at Paradise. Glasses and laughter tinkled out from the ballroom, where the doors had been left open.

Sir Percy's guests drifted out, and I hid myself behind a stand of trees. Flashes of silk, among the black suits, like oil on water. Ladies in their dresses, gentlemen in their tails. Here were the people the world tells us to admire. I pictured their tinkling laughter choked off by the fear of being whipped, like dogs. Standing in the kind of heat that closes your throat, glancing up at a sun that might kill.

They could not do it, I thought, looking at them. Not even for an hour.

I was angry, yes. So would you have been; so would anyone. The real madness would have been if I had not been angry.

I looked and looked, but could not see her. Then footmen in bright livery came down the pavilion steps to hand out blankets and shawls and I turned away. The dark was split by one crack of light after another, until the whole sky was cleft by light, and the air filled with fireworks, battlefield noises that seemed they'd never end, ribbons of smoke, drifting like ladies in a park. I put my head down and walked quickly towards the lake, keeping myself hidden behind the stand of trees. Some distance away, I sat and curled my hands in the grass, took a slow breath. *We are friends, then we are not. That is her world. I will never belong.* It was what novels and romances had done to me. It was what she had done. The water lay ahead of me, wide and flat and black. I shut my eyes to it.

Footsteps behind me crunched like apples.

'Here you are! I saw you slip away.' She tramped over to me, dragging her skirts. She sat down, following my gaze out to the lake. The long path was lined with hedges. 'In the morning we will see the primroses here,' she said, 'that we cannot see in the dark. There will soon be beds of lavender, by the boat-house, and later geraniums and peonies. You should see them. Well – you *will* see them! English spring is beautiful, you will see – the only thing that makes it worthwhile to live through the winter.' She fell silent and I said nothing. 'Sir Percy's groundskeepers stock the lake with creels of fish to get ready for these parties, you know,' she said. 'Imagine. Pouring fish in just to hook them out! He might as well have them bring out the china service and line the dinner plates up on shore. When I first came to Longreach, I realized I had married into a family who could have anything they wanted. I was just one more thing poured out of a creel.'

She waited, again, for me to say something. I gave a jerk of my head, fumbling with my thoughts.

She lifted a hand to play with one of her diamond ear-bobs. 'You are a woman of few words.'

I raised my eyes, braved the sight of her. 'What did Mr Benham say?'

'What?'

'When you told him you were a fish.'

'Oh,' she said. She laughed. 'I did not tell him *that*! I told him they might as well pour the fish from basket to plate and he said, "Now, Meg, where would be the sport in that?"' She looked out across the water.

'Won't you be missed?' I nodded towards the ballroom.

She leaned closer. 'You are cross?'

'I am nothing.'

'*Non*. You are *something*, Frances.' She reached down, plucked at a blade of grass. 'But . . . you are not happy.'

I shrugged. 'That's a small word.'

I turned my palm over, dug my thumbnail into it, thinking. I looked up, and held her gaze, and did not look away. 'What we did,' I blurted. 'We have not even spoken of it. As if it never happened.'

She blinked.

'And it is sending me mad.'

Oh, I knew I should not have spoken to her in that way. She was my mistress. But I could just as soon stop my own breath as hold the words back. I felt as if my heart was packed tight as gunpowder. I'd had enough of silence, of endless wanting. Of knowing my place, and staying in it.

'I –' She twisted her fingers among the grass stems, plucking and plucking until she pulled one loose and lifted it to bite at it.

At last, she spoke. 'What we did . . . It was wrong of me.'

Behind us, the murmur from the ballroom, like water over rocks. She pointed towards the lake. 'Scoop a thimbleful of that lake under a microscope and you'd see a thousand beings in it. A world in a drop. All *frantic*, dizzied, colliding . . . dying . . .'

My head thumped, like something beaten against a rock. 'So?'

'*So*. There are some things that cannot be brought into the light, Frances.'

'Then let it be done in the dark!' I cried. 'Only let it be done.'

She turned to face me again. 'You are a surprise.'

'I don't want to be a *surprise*.'

She laughed. 'You are so grave . . .'

'You've done it before.'

She hesitated. 'Yes.'

A picture of Hephzibah Elliot. Watching, always watching. But, perhaps, behind that, another picture also. The one of the boy whose mistake had been to become a man.

'With one of those other quality ladies?'

She rested her hand on my arm. '*You* are a quality lady.'

A cry rang out, behind us, and made me jump in my skin.

'Fox,' she said. I let out a breath, and the soft cloth of her voice wrapped around me. *Kerseymere. Jersey. Silk.* 'A thing like this . . . can be *warm* and dark, in the beginning, delicious . . .'

'You make it sound like molasses.'

She laughed again. 'Even *more* delicious.'

Then she pulled me to her, breast to breast, leaned us against the splayed tree trunk, made her thumb a lever on my lip. *'Open.'* My mouth parted wide as the lake, and she kissed me on my lips. Her mouth bitter as almonds. Laudanum. I saw my buttons weave in and out of their hooks, I saw her fingers, working their way down the front of me, I felt air on my breast –

Then she bent her head and took my nipple in her mouth. I jerked like somebody wasp-stung. My back struck tree bark.

'What?' she said. A frown tugged her brow. She pulled back.

I shook my head. The world peeled back to black sky and black branches. Bare and lonely and cold. Stars like chipped ice. Through the open windows, across the grass, came pops of laughter, like the corks from their champagne. Then she caught me and held me fast and kissed me again, and all went quiet.

'Well,' she said. She gave a thin laugh and stepped back and brushed her hands on her skirts. We stared at each other. 'Well . . . I . . .' She looked towards the house.

'Go,' I whispered.

I went in a few minutes behind her. Past the silent trees, down to the long hallway behind the kitchen where the pallets for the visiting maids had been lined up, like dinner plates on a shelf, and I lay on mine, which had been rolled out beside that of a plump girl who smelt like cheese, and who asked me if I'd come down with any of the Londoners.

I felt Madame's narrow hands hot around my waist, and all down the length of my shivering flesh I felt her mouth, though it had only touched me in two places. Lips and breast.

Chapter Twenty-Two

The old heaviness returned, as soon as London lay before me again. Smoky, soot-streaked, hot. The old unease. *What would happen now?* For two days, I'd been back to wondering, thinking the affection between us was a thing I had dreamed. I was her maid again. Nothing more. Benham was always at her side, or one of the other ladies. I'd brought her plates filled with fruit or pastries, which she took without saying a word. I'd fetched her shawl. Carried her picnic basket when she joined Hep Elliot beside the lake.

The horses strained as they pulled towards Levenhall. Benham blinked, turned towards her, took her hand in his. 'You and Frances are quiet with each other, my dear. Have you had a *contretemps*?'

She glanced over at me. 'Not at all. I am sure we are all simply tired.'

He called across the carriage, 'Quite a treat for you, girl, wasn't it?'

I looked at her. The feeling of my nipple in her mouth was like a thorn inside me.

'It was, sir,' I said. 'Quite a treat.'

She gave a small shake of her head, like someone jolted out of sleep.

A cold, sour feeling pressed into me as I watched them, and then I was the one who had to turn away, when he lifted her hands and pressed his lips to her knuckles and called her his dear.

At Longreach, he'd been full of a play-actor's cheer, his smile greasy and slick, his voice loud and self-satisfied. '*Meg!*' he'd shout to her. 'Somebody you must meet.' And she'd go over to him, dutiful, every time, the smile hemmed tight between her cheeks. One afternoon, I'd overheard one of the ladies say: *Open doors will improve any marriage; only truly happy marriages survive closed ones.*

Now he held her hand over his lap and pressed each of her fingers, like piano keys. All the while his eyes sneaked towards me, and I thought he must surely know what had happened between us. The way he fluttered her fingers, like flags. Her face was pale. At finding herself so close to him? Or was it me? With her free hand, she plucked at her skirt. I stared and stared, wondering what she was thinking.

'Do you know, Meg?' He twitched their joined fingers across his lap. 'Some of the westerly farms have been allowed to fall into *such* a state of disrepair . . . I had another word with Percy, told him it's high time he undertook a programme of improvements. Told him the tenants will work much more productively for a benevolent master than a neglectful one.'

There can be no such thing as a benevolent master, I thought. I laced my hands together in my lap, and bit my tongue, thinking perhaps I'd tell him so when he next called me to the library.

She glanced up. 'Is that right, Mr Benham? Well, that is a wonder.'

He gave her a tap on the wrist. 'Not a *wonder*, my love.' He shook his head, laughed. 'You meant to say *wonderful*, of course . . . That's *wonderful*.'

'Yes.' She drew her hand back into her own lap.

Mr Casterwick snored beside me, legs poking out like tent poles.

I watched, and waited. I wanted her to look up at me, but she kept her eyes down.

Benham called her up to his library as soon as we came through the doors, saying he wished to speak to her alone. I stood to watch them go, Charles hefting their bags ahead Then I turned slowly and followed Mr Casterwick downstairs. Cold chicken and boiled potatoes had been left out for us and Mr Casterwick set his portmanteau under the table. Pru asked him about the party and I heard him telling her about the new periwinkle livery Lady Catherine had got from Harper's in March, and the fireworks, and the rows of ham hocks in the basement where the visiting valets had slept, how the smell had given him dreams of being smothered by dirty stockings. Linux busied herself clearing away the tea things, and asked him if he'd noticed whether the Longreach housekeeper used dried fruit in her stuffing. But she watched me all the while.

Mr Casterwick had been given a slice of lemon cake, by the Longreach cook, to give to her, and when he got up to fish for it in his bag, she turned to me, lips small as pin-tuck seams. 'Homer is missing.'

I frowned. 'Who?'

'The cat. The cat. The cat is missing.'

A laugh cracked out of me. It went on and on. I couldn't stop it.

The scrape of my chair made Pru whip up her head.

'Are you accusing me of something to do with the cat, Mrs Linux?' I said. She pinched her lips tighter. 'You think I took him? I have been miles and miles away!'

'How would I know the machinery of heathen business? What I do know is that when you sup with the Devil, you're best to bring a long spoon.'

I stepped back. 'I haven't taken the cat, Mrs Linux. I haven't eaten him. Nor do I have his bones. If you believe I have, you must take that up with Mr Benham.'

She tipped her head. The buttons of her grey dress stared at me, like hard little eyes. 'Going, are you?' she said. 'Upstairs? Yes. Flee. Fly! Flee to her!' Her voice followed me, louder and

louder. 'There's no salvation for you up there! No good thinking there will be.'

Shadows fell across the walls and the bedclothes. It was getting dark, too warm for fires. Books stood sentry in the dim
light. On the shelves around the room, on the mantel, on the
floor. A line of them, leading to her. I stood clumsy at the door,
closed it, and kept my hand behind me on the latch. She was at
her desk, and rose when I came in. All was quiet. How long did
we stand thus? Long enough to see she was herself again. I
watched the little dip in her throat when she swallowed. She
laughed. 'I thought surely you would be frightened of me,
after . . .'

She stopped, curved her hands around her waist, as if she
were cold. My heart thumped against my ribs.

'I have been sitting here for several minutes, *pretending* to
write, wondering all this time –'

Oh! The wild shock when I pulled her to me, like that first
time I tasted ice. The little bird bones in her shoulders and her
neck. I remember how I dipped my head, how we kissed, how
she reached up to cover my hands with hers, pulled her head
back, laughing.

My head felt so hot and so light I had to press my hands to
it. She came against me, solid and warm. I felt her sliding, and
then she was on her knees. I felt my own hands in her hair, her
hands closing around my waist, and there was a cold fire in
every inch of my skin. My eyes flew open, but I saw nothing,
only dark. I felt her still. Her fingers dug sharp into my hips
and I felt her breath, and when she lifted her head and smiled
up at me her lips were shining too.

'Fran.' She whispered it against my thigh. 'Fran.'

When I raised my head, the mirror was before me and I saw
myself in it, clutching her head to my waist. There we were.

My face, the back of her head, her knees. The whole room hung askew; only the glass was centred.

I looked down. 'I suppose I'm your secret now.'

She laughed and pulled me to her.

Later she went over to the door and put her ear against it. Then she fitted the key to the latch and I lit a candle and she took me by the hand and led me to the bed.

'Will we do that again?' I asked.

Her laugh tunnelled under my skin. 'It is all I have wanted since the first day.'

'On the steps?'

'On your knees! In *soap*. Even then. I never saw anybody like you. When we first came here, there were these almond *macarons* my *maman* would buy, when we had money . . . She found a French baker, near Spitalfields. You remind me of those . . . you . . . your skin.' She bent to nip at my ear. 'I wanted to see you. You must have known, surely, when I came to the kitchen that night?'

Her words slowed my thoughts to molasses.

She smoothed a hand over my ribs. 'Just think. You are scribing my confessions, and now my body comes also under your spell. You will know me, body and soul, *n'est-ce pas?* Though self-revelation is never pretty . . . Richelieu said all he needed was six lines in any honest man's hand, and he could find something in them to hang him with . . .'

I felt the blood moving through me. I felt swollen with it. I looked at her. 'I don't believe there's any such thing as an honest man.'

Life is a brief candle but love is a craving for time. Therefore, I was already cursed to want what I couldn't have. What I wanted was to learn her inch by inch. To read her like a book

179

that wouldn't end. I lay beside her, watching the small waves of her breath against the sheet, lashes thick with sleep.

Just before she slept, she'd asked me to move my pallet to her room for good: 'Many ladies do the same with their maids! Had this house been properly designed, there would already be a maid's bedroom over there, where the dressing room is. You could bring your pallet here.'

I turned and turned, and my mind turned also. I lay awake until I heard the first stirrings of the house, the screeches of doors that needed oiling, and Benham's bell from his library below us. He'd be wanting tea, and kippers and coddled eggs, Pru would be up to start the sweeping, Linux would be running her hand along the banisters, making sure Levenhall gleamed, as it always did. The world cannot be kept long at bay.

I had said yes. But had I been answering as lover or maid?

'Where would I sleep?' I'd asked.

Towards the end, Phibbah had slept nights with Miss-bella, at the foot of her bed. *Oh, Phibbah.* What would she say now? I could almost hear her, laughing.

You go on thinking this white woman for you. None of them can be for us. All ducks don't dabble in the same hole.

Chapter Twenty-Three

'There is so much flesh on show in that painting that Mr Benham will not allow it in any other room of this house,' she said.

We were lying across her bed, looking up at the woman in red. It was a painting by her mother, she'd said, and it had been done after they came to England, one of the two things Madame had brought with her when she married Benham, the other being the little egg chest that her father had brought from France, which she'd had carved with her once-upon-a-time initials – *MD*, for Marguerite Delacroix. The violin, like her father, was long gone.

'The only thing I have left of Maman,' she said, nodding towards the portrait. 'Don't you think she looks like a lewd saint?'

I cocked my head, to see her. I was thinking about that other portrait. The little black boy. Thinking how she'd fought to keep *him* on the walls, too, although she'd lost.

Later I answered a knock at the door to discover Linux on the threshold. She screwed her face, of course, at discovering me on the other side of it. But there was a needle of happiness in my chest, such a pain I thought it would kill me, my mind still aflame with what Madame and I had been doing, moments before. Linux could do me no harm. Nothing could. A brothy scent of onions and vinegar followed her in, and she looked around at the tea tray, at the papers scattered on the desk, Madame in her kimono, outstretched on the bed. She took a step forward, stopped. Blinked as if it was the sight of Madame herself that had stopped her. 'Pardon me, Madame, you are . . . working?' She clasped her hands together. 'I'm sure you should be resting.'

'Oh, *Linux.*' She tilted her head. 'First you want me up and about, then you want me resting. There is no pleasing you, is there?'

'Did Frances sleep here? Pru says she never came up last night.'

'Frances is to be my own abigail, now, Mrs Linux. And I will thank you to leave her alone.'

'It's irregular —'

She waved a hand. 'Frances will sleep here from now on. It is decided. And do stop turning and turning like a lighthouse beacon! You are making *me* dizzy.'

Linux had come to a stop at the writing desk. Her hand crept towards the pile of pages. For a time, she said nothing, just went on stroking the wood. 'Well. You must stir yourself, for the time being. You must stir yourself. Mr Benham expects you in the breakfast room.'

Madame sat up. 'I had no intention of being expected.'

'Nevertheless.' Her smile darted out. 'You are. There's a first time for everything, I suppose.' Then she lowered her head, bent to touch a finger to the skirting board. '*Dust.* Pru must do better.'

She had to go down, of course. When Benham called, everyone in that house went running.

After they left, I went through to the dressing room, which was little more than a closet, with a copper tub in the middle, racks for gowns and hooks for towels. Silence stoppered my ears. I sat on the rim of the tub and dipped my hand into the water, cooled to a scum. That needs emptying, I thought, but then remembered Pru would see to it.

The sum of all my duties was to see to *her*.

Hours before, I'd poured water over her hair from the little china ewer she kept beside the tub, watched it make waves down her spine. Like all white women's hair, hers obeyed the known laws of beauty and gravity. Water smoothed it into dark, slippery threads.

What does he want with her? The thought swelled thick in my throat.

I lifted the soap out of its china dish, stepped out of my own skirts. Welcomed the slap of water against my thighs. My shift lay slick and dark just as her hair had done, and I leaned forward, looked down the waking-up length of myself. And then – I'll confess it – I brought the soap under my nose, between my legs, where it felt small and sharp as a fingernail.

I think that was when it came upon me. The madness that has lain upon me since. I lifted her towel from the floor, went back into her bedchamber, sat on her bed, and waited.

From the journals of George Benham
(Marked by George Benham as:
NOT INTENDED FOR PUBLICATION)

Latest conversation with Langton's girl, recorded verbatim.

'Tell me about Mrs Benham.'

   'Madame? What do you want to know about her? Sir.'

   'Stop playing coy, girl. How much does she take?'

   'The drug?'

   'The drug.'

   'I wouldn't know.'

   'More than usual?'

   'I don't know what's usual.'

   'Fifteen drops? Twenty? More than that?'

   A laugh. 'I don't keep count.'

   'Not a laughing matter, girl. I want you to note how much she takes. She is delicate. You must have seen that for yourself. All I want is to know if she shows any signs of becoming unwell. Just tell me what she does, where she goes. I can be the judge of what it means.'

Chapter Twenty-Four

My pallet stayed in her room.

'She wants you in there now?' said Pru, watching from her bed as I lifted my dresses from the hook in the attic room. I left my blue serge, *Candide* still tucked in its hem, forgotten, with my grey rag. I took my time rolling my pallet. My nerves were tuning forks. I feared she'd see the change in me, seared across my face.

But she only smiled at me, shook her head. 'It's a bad idea,' she said.

'Why?'

'She'll get bored. Never let your lady get bored. Courtesans always turf the fellows out afterwards, don't they?'

Always a courtesan, never a bride, Frances.

'What's so funny?'

'What would you know about being a courtesan?' I asked.

She grinned. 'Fair.' She tilted her head. 'But I know more than you about being a dressing maid. And, I'm telling you, for both, familiarity breeds boredom. And boredom breeds trouble.'

Pru had been skittish with me since the night in the attic. I fancied I saw pity, when she looked at me. We hadn't spoken again about what I'd told her. Now I see what a friend she was. Steadfast. I should have said so then, but my head was turned, one foot already downstairs.

The next morning Charles brought up a package. Sweetmeats wrapped in parchment, trailing the label of one of those fancy

Piccadilly emporiums, which Madame left in a china dish on her washstand. Gold rings, ear-bobs, pearls: she mixed the sweets with them as if they were the same. I went over and picked one out and held it to my nose. Marzipan. The same smell that glazed her breath.

'He always plays husband after staying out all night,' she said, from the bed. 'The manners of a tomcat. Blow in at daybreak, snarl out complaints, eat, then sleep all morning.'

The gifts kept coming the whole time I stayed with her in that room: sweetmeats; nuts; jewelled pins; once, a kaleidoscope, the kind of gift you'd send a child. But the man himself never did. Which suited me, of course.

I crackled a sweet out of its wrapper. '*Let* him stay out all night.'

I asked her where he went. 'I have never asked,' she replied, 'and he has never said.'

I remembered what she'd said to Linux, that night in the kitchen. How lonely she'd seemed. *No doubt he keeps a mistress*, I thought. There'd have been nothing odd in that: those *ton* marriages make a wife of one woman and a courtesan of the next. But I didn't like to think about the times when she might be required to play wife to *him*, so I selected a little marzipan heart, just as if I was a lady in a shop, crossed the carpet to stand over her.

My hand skimming her thigh, lifting her gown. Her eyes flying open. A dart of shock. A smile. I snapped the heart between my teeth, and then put my tongue to hers. She pulled me to the bed. Came over me. A soft rain of hair falling against my face.

The other thing I didn't like to think about. That now she was keeping a mistress of her own.

Then we had to go down for breakfast, though neither of us could bear to face him. But he wanted them to be *seen* taking meals together, she said. And if she had to, so did I. He was already at the table, lining up the cutlery beside his plate, even though Casterwick would have had the inch-rule to them twice that morning. I stopped at the sideboard, slid an egg into a cup, for her, poured her chocolate. There was a hush when we took our seats, but some men see silence as a net, to toss their own words into. 'Good to see that you're fit again, Meg. A man expects a sighting of his wife from time to time.'

'I am lucky you have such low expectations.'

He made a noise like a laugh. 'All the better for you to meet them, then, my dear.'

She sent a smile across to me, as if to say, *Patience. The quicker we endure this, the quicker we go upstairs.*

I leaned back into the pinch of my dress, kept my gaze to the window. The weather had turned, and there was a smell of grass, and coming rain, the garden littered with curling blooms that frisked across it, like mice, when the wind lifted. Birds crying out.

I lifted my cup, marzipan sticking on my tongue. Even my coffee tasted like her.

I sent her a look. *Just know I'll come apart if we don't go now.*

I tried to watch her without looking as if I was watching, wondering what he'd do to us if he knew what we did upstairs. Mr Casterwick came in to bring the newspapers and lift away Benham's plate, smeared with kipper bones as fine as hair. I scarcely knew where to put my eyes, so kept them on Caster-wick, thinking idle thoughts. How *his* wages would've been paid for by cane and that was where mine would come from too, if I ever got any.

He was still watching her. Taking narrow little bites of her bread and butter.

'Oh, for God's sake. *Eat!*'

When she jerked up in surprise, the egg tumbled to the floor and cracked, yolk spreading, like a slow breath. Spoon tinkling porcelain. We all turned to stare down at it. He rocked forward in his chair.

She took a small sipping breath, and I saw Casterwick slip out, as quietly as he'd come in.

Benham heaved out of his chair and wavered there a moment, like a man consulting a map, speared the dribbling yolk with his spoon. She saw his hand lifting towards her and recoiled. 'It has been on the *floor*.' The spoon jumped in his hand.

I wanted to jump too. Leap at him, yell, 'All this over an *egg*?' But I held my tongue, though the words strained against it. I kept my eyes down, on the tiles, where yolk was drying, and screwed my thumbs into my palms. The thought came screaming. *Don't*.

He lifted the spoon again, cleared his throat. 'We can wait all morning, Meg. Choice is yours.'

At that, she leaned forward. After she'd taken one quick bite, then another, and another, he stepped back, shuddering his chair away from the table and the spoon onto it. I felt the wood shake. She drew in a breath, which shook too. He gave a little nod. 'I suppose . . .' he said, looking around him almost in confusion '. . . I suppose . . . it's high time I got on with my day.'

She twisted her napkin up to her lips, coughed into it. Then it was *me* she was shrinking from, just as she'd shrunk from him. Because I'd been witness to the whole terrible scene.

'Does he hurt you?'

The idea of her under his thumb sat in my stomach like soured milk. The thought of her eating that mangled egg. Of him pushing away from the table as if she was the one who disgusted him.

The rain had come. Branches close and dark and specked with drizzle. She slipped off her shoes, took her hair out of its coils, saying she'd have some brandy, and as I unlatched the cabinet the thoughts whispering at me sounded very like Phibbah: *Drinking brandy for breakfast? And all that hair hanging loose, like her idle hands.* But I tamped them back, like tobacco into a pipe. She picked up the hairbrush, beckoned me over to the bed.

'You haven't answered.'

A noise of frustration. She pressed the brush between her palms. 'I am not sure *how* to answer you,' she said. 'He does not hurt me with his fists. He does not hurt me now.'

'That could mean a hundred different things.'

'It means he hurt me once upon a time . . .'

'And?'

She dropped the brush on her lap. 'Frannie. You have a choice. I will tell you. But *telling* you will hurt.'

She was steering me away, of course, and I was letting myself be steered, letting myself be pulled onto her lap while she whispered, 'Will you let me brush your hair?'

My little smothered laugh swept away our conversation, like cobwebs. I touched the bristles, soft as her own hair. 'That brush has met its match.'

Knowing a person's story, and how they tell it, and where the lies are in it, is part of love. But I told myself there was no point knowing a thing you couldn't change, though worry pinched at me all the same.

There was no use asking why she wouldn't speak about it. I'd closed my own mind too, after all, to so many things. I gave myself over to her hands and the brush, letting my head go where she turned it, letting it tick from side to side. A tingle through my skull. I leaned into her, enjoying the tug-of-war between brush and scalp. I wanted to walk out of that house with her. If we *were* to leave, what could we take? The money was his. The dresses. The portmanteau. The drawers and all their contents. To all intents and purposes, so were we. The portrait and the egg-keeper were the only two things she owned.

She was in a writing mood afterwards. I remember this line: *We go from birth to death. We go from love to marriage. Of each we may claim an equal understanding, which is to say none at all.*

When Benham called me down to the library that afternoon, the piece of my mind I wanted to give him lay stuck in my throat. Hate can be as strong a draw as love, but it was love that drew me then, a strong rope pulling me back upstairs. I had to hold my own feet fast to the floor.

He was sipping his usual brew of gunpowder tea, toying with his snuff. The same fingers that had put the egg to her mouth. When I came in, he handed me a paper. *The Case for Reform: Black River, Antigua.*

'Slavery,' he said. Spat the word as if he couldn't bear to keep it in his mouth. 'Everybody's scratching about for a solution. Either one thing or the next. Deciding which side will win. Forgetting Solomon's wisdom. The best way to solve a conflict is to give both sides what they want.'

'Didn't Solomon offer each woman half an infant,' I said, 'knowing they each preferred it whole?'

He threw back his head, laughed. Oh, he always found me amusing, perhaps because he thought he had created me himself.

But only a man would think splitting a baby in two was a solution rather than a problem, just like only a *white* man would consider slavery a difficult question. Women focus on what they lack, men on what they want. In all those Bible stories, it's always the women who look back, who eat the forbidden fruit, who weep over hollow wombs, and fruitful ones. Yearning is always a woman's sin. The men never turn around, nor ever think twice about taking a knife – or a cross – to their own longed-for sons.

'That is a paper I am writing on the topic,' he said, taking a sip of his tea. 'In support of proposals that will ensure the welfare of West India workers, while assuring planters of their livelihoods.'

He went on to explain that Black River was his own experiment, his family's Antigua estate, which his brother allowed him to run. He ran it like an English tenant farm, he said. His workers received religious instruction, holidays, their own little patches of land to plant. He believed the solution to keeping slaves was legislation that would ensure their fair treatment and guarantee everybody's happiness, including theirs, and that the key was to convince the planters to do it themselves. 'The guiding principle at Black River is virtue, and benevolence, and therefore affection is not only possible but mutual. My Negroes call me Mister, never Master.'

I had to bite my lip, so I wouldn't laugh. 'And you call them your Negroes and not your slaves?'

He flexed his jaw. 'I'm interested in your opinion, girl.'

Anybody who wants a former slave's opinion is looking to find either a happy slave, or a stricken one. The former doesn't exist, and as for the latter, you already know my thoughts. I saw that part of Benham's interest in Paradise was to set his own methods in opposition to Langton's, and that was why he needed me. His object: not to abolish, but to preserve.

I found I could *not* hold my tongue. 'About what happened this morning.'

'This morning?'

'At breakfast.'

Surprise crawled onto his face. 'Nothing happened at breakfast.'

'You were harsh with Madame.'

His hands flew off the desk; he pushed to his feet. 'You speak out of turn, about matters that don't concern you. A piece of advice. In this house, you're better off taking your cues from *me*.'

I looked down at his sheet of paper, thin as a slip between my fingers. Weightless. White as nothing. I felt a springing anger. 'I don't know the first thing about running a West India estate,' I said.

'All I want is the truth.'

Truth had never set a foot between us.

You own me, I thought. *You own her. You own all of us. Where is the virtue in that?*

I decided to be frank. 'It is a waste of time,' I said, handing him back his paper.

His head jerked. 'How so?'

'There's no reforming what's already rotten.'

There's wickedness in all men. The ones we call good are the ones who care to hide it. And George Benham knew that the surest way to hide your sins is to write your own account.

Langton pretended Negroes didn't have the same red blood as his, but Benham turned his blind eye on his own estate. Even the way they'd trained me seemed to have been their same old nonsense science, very little rhyme or reason. I asked Benham about it, once, when I found him in a talking mood. They'd both been curious about the limits of a mulatta's intelligence, Benham convinced Negroes could be taught to some extent, and that a greater capacity for learning might result after the mixing of white lymph with black. Was Langton eager by then to give him whatever he wanted, so long as the money came back? Benham wanted a mulatta to be educated, so that was what Benham got. In any event, Langton had only finished what Miss-bella had started, though it was just like him to cut the truth in half. And the other truth was that I was the *only* mulatta he'd kept on that entire estate.

It was my own sins Benham thought to write about for all that they were tangled up with theirs. Which is why three weeks later, seeing my chance when he'd gone out to his gentleman's club, I stole his journal, tucked it into the lining of my pallet. Those pages are still there for all I know – though it's possible Linux has already scrubbed out every inch of me that was left behind.

I suppose you'll go looking for them, or someone else will. Just remember not to believe everything you read.

I should have stolen Madame's journals too, if I'd thought of it, if I had known our days were numbered. They would have been more useful to me. A way to keep her. Which was what I wanted most of all. The pair of us trapped together, pinned like butterflies under glass.

As soon as I went back up, she drew me close, and the smell of her flooded me. The very bones slid out of me. *La petite mort*, she called it. A little death. Benham forgotten. When she kissed me, I tasted myself. Like the sea, like salt. Like tears. We slipped together into her bath, which she filled herself. That was a sight, more water spilling on the floor than in the tub. She poured water like she knew she wouldn't be the one to mop it up. But for the span of that afternoon, *I* was the one being waited on. *Tended*. She made me feel like a queen. She took my damp hair in her hands and gathered it off my brow and peppered me there with kisses and, after we'd settled in the water, her back to my front, she said, 'Read to me,' and rested her head on her knees to listen. Steam rose in wet curls, and her hair fell likewise. I held the book away from me. The water lapped quietly. Beside us, the candle flickered to a stub. The door stayed safely on its latch.

How can I describe it?

I was a knot, untangled. The weight of all my memories was gone.

•

Night came, to strip another day from whatever tally we had. We blew out the candles, turned over the pillows, and laid our heads together on them, for sleep.

We were happy, no matter what is said about it now, no matter that they're saying it was me who broke her happiness, and broke her. As soon as I write that, as soon as I even think it, my hand trembles. I must stop here. I fear I'll dig this nib through the paper, to keep from turning it on myself.

Chapter Twenty-Five

At a ladies' gaming parlour she went to with Hep Elliot, she and I managed to find ourselves alone in the withdrawing room, behind one of the screens. I'd brought along her little travelling pot, which she called a *bourdaloue*. It was yellow as piss itself, but painted with gay dancing maids in blue bonnets to trick you that a lady might travel with one in case struck by a sudden craving for soup or blancmange wherever she might be. She had stretched herself out on the bench, her body pressed against the window, gazing out at the brick wall of the next-door building. I knelt and fitted myself to her, fingers to ankles, forehead to knees. She looked down and saw my intention, my fingers on her thighs, her skirts wagging like tails, then looked up at the door.

'Do you do this with him?'

'Mr Benham?'

'Who else?'

I could not bear to think of it.

She looked down at me. 'When would I? You are always with me, so you *know* he is not.' She hesitated. 'Besides . . . he does not want children.'

Good, I thought, though I'd never come across a man who didn't want children, especially one as pleased with his own image as Benham was.

But the question nagged at me, drove me to seek out Pru in the scullery next wash-day, to ask what she knew. 'Only bits I picked up here and there,' she said. 'Madame wasn't considered

195

first water when she came out. Pretty, yes. But French. Nothing she could do to change that. And too eccentric as well, I suppose. Came with too much gossip. Most people will say she was lucky to nab him.' She swilled one of Benham's cravats in the rice-water. 'There was a time I didn't know who to be sorrier for, out of the pair of them. I overheard them once, arguing. Her saying he was only wealthy on the surface, *him* saying that must make them a match since that was the only place she was pretty.'

The following week Madame told me part of the story herself. Her mother had said she was lucky to have an offer: eccentric Meg Delacroix, still on the shelf after four Seasons. Benham heard the rumours about her only after they were married, when it was too late. Divorce would have tainted *him* as well as her, which made it out of the question. He blamed her for that, too, as if he'd been the victim of some trick. The worst of it, she said, was how he'd *played* husband all this time, in public or where any of the servants might see. How he made her play wife. The appearance of marriage with none of its effects, save the roof over her head.

The year after her wedding, her mother had died, leaving her truly alone.

Madame announced that she intended to form a committee to plan a debate. For many of those ladies, time trickled through their hands. They might as well make themselves feel pious and useful with it. Though pious is hardly ever useful. Nevertheless, I helped. I copied out the proposed motion into her letters. *What is the purpose of variety in the species of humankind?*

'What do you think?' she said.

I thought she was turning Langton's and Benham's very own question against them, and said the pair of them would find it instructive to hear sensible opinions on it, for a change.

The anti-slaving business lifted her spirits, and when she was happy so was I. Her friends pressed her to join the boycott. Even if she'd had any say at all in that household, which it seemed she didn't, I couldn't see what good it would do to refuse to buy sugar with all that sugar money. In any event, she was too fond of her sweetened chocolate to go that far.

It was a gasp of rebellion, pitting herself against him, and she knew it. She decided she'd *plan* first and ask him later. Put the cart before the horse, so to speak. In the meantime, the meetings would be social affairs. In that way, when she announced her intention, he'd be unable to refuse without it becoming a public spectacle. There was nothing he hated more than that.

One day, she was too low for hosting, or for gadding about in the park, and said we'd have to make do with the garden. It was very hot, coming towards the start of June. The flowers were out at Levenhall, and I decided to fetch a basket from the scullery, and asked Pru if I could borrow her pearl-handled dressmaker's scissors to snip some for Madame's mantelpiece. I found her unpicking silk rosettes from the hem of an evening gown. Poor Pru could have done with a day in the garden herself. Her eyes and cheeks were red and raw, no doubt stung by lye, and her shoulders drooped. 'I'm *fine*, Fran,' she said, when I asked how she was. 'You know how it is, or perhaps you've forgot already. There's enough work to kill an ox.'

In the kitchen, Linux had a goose splayed out on the table for plucking. I went carefully around her, wrapped some slices of bread and cheese and a pat of butter I'd brought from the larder. When I set the basket on the table, she stared hard at the scissors, which were peeking up over the rim. 'What is it you think you want with those?'

I wanted nothing with them, I said, but Madame had asked

me to snip some of the flowers in the garden so that I might fill her vase. My nerves were all over the place in those days, so I am sure my voice shook. I was lying about that one thing, which I fear now made everything I said sound like a lie. She looked at me askance. The truth was that I was full of some of the savage intents she had suspected of me all along. Lust, chief among them. The truth was that by then I was a threat to the master of the house. *I wanted what he had.* There were too many things I wanted. I can hardly confess them all. There isn't paper enough, or time.

Linux folded her arms and tried to bar my way, but I held my ground and asked, did she want to keep Madame waiting?

It would be *me* keeping Madame waiting, she replied, unless I handed those scissors over. Her hands were cloaked with blood and feathers. But then Benham's bell rang, and she had to answer it herself, with Pru busy in the laundry. She cast me a hard look as she went, but said no more about the scissors.

The garden was hemmed in by high walls. The pond lay at the end, and the gate that led to the mews. The sun was high. Light spilled like lamp oil over the new grass, and made the air hazy. I set the blanket out under the ash tree and laid the food atop a piece of oilskin. She arranged herself under the tree, opened her book – a small volume of poetry – and read aloud. Her voice drifted like a bee between the flowers. The scissors shook in my hand as I clicked at the roses. I decided to thread some of them through her fringe, and so came behind her with the scissors still in my hand. She gave a start, and looked up towards the house, nervous. Her hair was damp and had started to curl and I had to smooth it out between my fingers. By the time I'd finished, several of the petals lay around us, smashed into the blanket by my knees, and the smell rose heavy into the air.

She drummed her fingers on the book, sang some tune she

was always singing. 'It's called *Chanson pour Marguerite*,' she would say. 'One of my papa's.' It was the most drear thing you ever heard, the same repeating, whining notes, but she loved it the way a mother loves an ugly child.

A lather of fear came upon me.

There's the same lather of fear upon me now. Not just the terror of any woman in my situation. It's the fear of the teeming brain. That I might cease to be before I can finish setting it down. I find myself scribbling furiously. As if I must finish it, or look up and discover that none of it happened at all. While I write it, I can still believe it did.

I steadied my fingers, kept them brushing through her hair. Before I knew it, I blurted: 'Is this love, between us?'

She tipped her head back into the silence. 'Oh, there are many ways to be mad,' she said. 'Love's the surest one.'

It was so close to my own fears, it made my heart thud.

A thud came from behind us as well. A sudden bang that wrenched my head up. I looked towards the house. A figure in one of the upstairs windows. Linux. Black as a moth, her mouth twisting. She had slapped the window, and stood gurning down at us. Even from so far away I could see her eyes, and the scars that leaped across her cheek and her pale palm smeared across the glass. She shook her head, drew her shoulders back, and moved away down the passage. Madame jerked the basket towards her, shoving in book and food and blanket. Cramming everything atop the flowers. 'We must go in,' she said. She blinked around at the garden as if she'd never seen it before.

I felt again that same pricking of fear, the cold wash of terror, which I couldn't quite explain.

A. Some weeks before the prisoner was turned out, there was the incident with the scissors.

Q. What incident?
A. There was a pair of dressmaker's scissors, kept in the scullery. I found the prisoner attempting to take them outside, hidden in a basket. I challenged her, and she said she'd been asked to fetch them for Madame. When I questioned the mistress later, I discovered that to have been a lie. That same afternoon, I'd seen the prisoner in the garden, holding the scissors very near to Madame Benham's neck. It appeared to me that she was threatening her with them. But when I asked the mistress about that, she said she had not been threatened. I believe by that time she was afraid of the prisoner and did not want to speak of it for that reason. The prisoner had some hold over her by then. And the scissors were not seen again after that afternoon.

Chapter Twenty-Six

Now I come to Olaudah Cambridge. And if anyone has questions to answer, it is him. Though there'll be no way of getting answers, seeing as Olaudah Cambridge has not been seen since the night of her soirée.

This I know for certain. If Madame hadn't seen him again, she'd still be alive. And she wouldn't have seen him again if we hadn't gone to the Cambridge lecture.

She wanted to go. It was her idea. The anti-slavery cause was all her excitement, then, and she'd read about the forthcoming speech in the *Morning Chronicle*, and then talked about nothing else for two whole days. Her little Laddie, all grown up. In the carriage, she twisted and turned and her eyes darted with excitement. She drew the window-shades, though I wanted to lift them and look out at the ash-dark streets, the domes and spires. Feel that I was a small part of it, at last. Maybe not the apple in the bowl, but one of the grapes.

The hall was near Bloomsbury Square, long and wide, panelled in dark, gleaming wood. They crowded the room, some of the women with arms linked, the men talking only with each other. All of them dressed in brown or grey. Anti-slavery people, mainly. Upholstered chairs lined an aisle as neat as a hair parting. It was dim in spite of the sconces flocking the papered walls.

Laddie walked in with the snap of a sail in high wind, and they took their seats. He wore a black jacket, shiny at the elbows, and, when he lifted his hands, he flashed crooked fingers and mashed knuckles.

He brought one hand down on the lectern, kept the other raised, cast his head slowly around. You couldn't help but stare back. He had the body of a prime buck, but the face of a man who'd rather be dead than owned.

He worked his mouth into a grin. 'Gentlemen,' he began, voice hard as rope. 'When Mr Macaulay asked me to speak here tonight, I wondered what I should speak *about*. Something that would make me more than your pet nigger, more than your entertainment. Just some black you managed to get up onto his hind legs to play tricks.'

Titters burst into pops of laughter, and they exchanged nervous looks. His words went inside to my weak spots. I sat up, jolted. Beside me, Madame shifted her hands in her lap.

'Casting about for a topic,' he said, 'I remembered an Igbo tale my mother had told me. The only thing I remember about her. It was about the Asiki.' He paused. 'The Asiki were human children, stolen by witches and taken deep into dark forests, where the witches cut out their tongues, and changed every hair on their heads, from wool to silk. Changed their skin, too, from black to gold. Next morning the Asiki woke without speech or memory, their mothers and their fathers forgotten. Their homes as well. Full of questions they had no way to ask. If you ask one of them, "Who are you?" they cannot answer. They cannot speak at all! They make ugly barking noises, rolling the stubs they have in place of tongues.'

They sat quiet, tugged forward in their seats. 'All speakers,' he continued, 'at the end of the day, speak about *men*. What men want. Or don't.' He shrugged. 'But . . . the Asiki are not men. They are *changelings*. Men who have no memory. Men kidnapped into silence. Men whose value is measured in beads and brass pans and guns. What would they tell us if they did have tongues? What do they want? Would they tell us they love the back-breaking work of gathering in your cotton? And your cane?' He shrugged again. 'Would they tell us it is for their own good?

'Isn't that what the European himself has told us? That the European's pleasure is the African's pleasure? Aren't we supposed to take the European's word for it? Because who would ever dream of asking the African what *he* wants? It's the European who marches across this little globe, measuring everything, writing it down. Adam. God of all creatures, great and small.'

He made his voice quieter. 'Here's the rub. You asking *me* to speak for them. How can I? Why have you asked *me*? Because you look at a single black man and see all black men. As if one black man is a representative of every other member of his race. Allowed neither personality nor passion. Not allowed to love anybody, or anything. It is for this reason there are so many dead men inhabiting the new world, drifting through cotton and cane. *Zombis*. Men who were left enslaved, even *after* the trade had been abolished. *You* abandoned them. Yes, *you*, with your good intentions. Even abolitionists succumbed to the idea that a man couldn't be stripped of his own assets without compensation. By that equation, those men you left behind are *property*. Machines, not men.

'We might as well give you the blade, too. Since you also cut out their tongues.'

When he came down among them, the men pumped his hands, and the women stared. I stood beside Madame, near the door. I had listened in silence. His words had split me, like a cord of wood, though I didn't want to show it. They'd made me think of Phibbah. Madame's eyes roved after him. Hep Elliot appeared at her side. 'No sign whatsoever of the poor little wretch in your portrait, is there?'

'No.'

'A man now. A young black Moses, smashing his tablets of stone.'

'If you say so.' Madame laughed.

The crowd surged around us. 'Thighs like thunder,' I heard a woman saying, behind us. 'And a *face* like thunder, too.'

He moved through the crowd but it was clear he was making his way towards her. He closed one hand around hers, bent to brush it with his lips. 'Madame *Bebbum*,' he said, and she threw back her head and laughed again.

'That was his old name for me,' she said to Hep Elliot. 'No one has called me that in a very long time.' She turned back to him. 'Laddie. How very nice to see you. This is Miss Hephzibah Elliot. And my secretary, Frances Langton.'

He caught me looking at his hands and clenched them into a fist beside his jaw. 'They ugly for true, aren't they, little mulatta? I'm a prizefighter, you know. The next Bill Richmond!'

'Is that right?' Madame said.

I remember how irked I felt. The way he called me 'little mulatta', the way he danced around us, bobbing on his toes. His white teeth, his pomade-slick hair. A man who spends that much time on mirrors and tooth-powders isn't to be trusted. And he was a different man from the one on stage. Rough, coarse. He used the old slave talk only when he spoke to me. With her he would oil up his smile and start to talk white again. Like so many blacks do when whites are around. The ladies looked from him to me. As if this was still part of the entertainment.

'Your lecture left me wondering, Mr Cambridge,' I said, feeling peevish. 'How many years did you spend enslaved?'

She gave me a sharp look. In those days, she liked to have me with her, as her companion, but preferred me quiet, lest I give us away.

'Not a one,' Laddie replied smoothly, 'having been spirited away to England at the age of four. Unless you think it's *enslavement* serving as page boy to Madame Benham . . . As her secretary you would be best placed to say.'

They all sniggered, as if he'd made a good jape.

'In other words,' I said, cutting him off, 'you are full of ideas, not experience. Precisely what I thought.'

'An honest opinion! That's rare. Where have *you* come from, Miss Langton?'

'Jamaica.'

'You *were* a slave?'

'A house-girl.'

He laughed. 'Precisely what I thought.'

Hep Elliot clapped his back. 'Mr Cambridge! That was a triumph! Plenty to chew on. You *are* clever.'

His eyes were fierce above his white cravat. 'Most whites will be impressed with anything that comes out of a black's mouth, Miss Elliot, if it's dressed up in plain English. One can never know if one is being praised for being good, or simply for being good *enough*.' He sliced his eyes towards Madame. 'What did *you* think?'

She grinned. 'Oh, I thought you were magnificent. I really did. A young black Moses, smashing your tablets of stone!'

Hep Elliot coughed, and Laddie threw back his head and laughed. A bark of laughter that showed all his teeth.

It is impossible to be both black *and* a woman. Did you know that? No one was asking me to give any lectures. They allow some blacks to impress them. Men like Sancho, Equiano . . . Yet I fail to see what was so impressive about them. They wrote, yes. But *thousands* could, if someone would bother to teach them. And everything they wrote was written *for* whites. Petitions. Appeals. It's another of this world's laws. Blacks will write only about suffering, and only for white people, as if our purpose here is to change their minds.

All Olaudah Cambridge had done was get himself shipped over when he was too young to be a servant, young enough to be a toy.

Trays of cordial were passed by waiters bearing silver trays. The pair of them stood close together for a long time, in their own private conversation, and I stood in my place near the door, holding my glass, my eyes ticking, like hands on a clock. I was drowning so deeply in my own thoughts that I hardly noticed when Hep Elliot drifted near, looking from me to them. I took a sip of foul-tasting cordial. 'Oh,' she said, in her drumbeat voice. 'Oh. I see. I *see*. I – Well . . .' She needled her brows together. '*Someone* should give you a warning, poor girl. Meg's been spoiled, you see. She'll only return the affections of those who spoil her in return. And only for a time. See that look he's giving her? Like a man in church? It's the way everyone looks at her. That's the trouble with Meg.'

The trouble wasn't the way he looked at her. It was the way she looked at him.

On the way back, all she could talk about was how surprised she'd been, how Laddie had carved his *own* life, made himself his own man, and was to be admired for it. Benham's old words jumped into my head as I listened to her, and I thought, *Where is the sport in chasing something you're bound to catch?*

A hard seed lodged itself in my gut. When she leaned over me at the writing desk later that night, I pulled away.

'As soon as we leave this room, I vanish. That is all *your* trick.' I stood, put us face to face. For the first time I noticed how thin she was becoming. Her head was nothing but a curve of skin over skull, her jaw hard as the air between us. Her eyes had a hot-wax shine. Was it the drug? I'd watched her drink steadily all afternoon. Laudanum might have been one part of her nerves, that evening, but I was worried that the other part had been Laddie himself. I didn't know which shamed me more – that I had the thought or that I couldn't manage to voice it.

I had to clench my hand in my skirts to stop myself reaching for her. I shook my head. 'I am a fool for wanting what you cannot give.'

'What is it that you want?'

To live together in the cottage of stone. To sit hand in hand outside and feel the heat on our faces and to walk together at the seaside, arm in arm. To tend each other, sick or well.

But those words dried inside me, like pressed flowers. She reached for my hands, and I jerked away. 'You're a pot of water. Cold, hot, cold.'

'If I am the water, dear Frances, you must be the stove.' When I made no answer, she pressed her forehead to mine, took hold of my shoulders. 'I am trying to coax up a laugh out of you.'

I didn't reply.

After taking her tray down, I came back to find her waiting for me. There was a letter laid on my pallet. *One word frees us of all the weight and pain of life: That word is love. Forgive me. Ritte.* I folded it over once, then again, and again, kept it small, folded until it was small and hard, and tucked it into my sleeve. And I carried it there until the night I was arrested and brought here, when the turnkeys took it from me, in the reception room.

The Battle between Lightning and Sullivan

On Saturday last, Laddie Lightning fought Tom Sullivan at Fives Court near Leicester Square. Men of all shapes and sizes crowded the ring, some holding bullish-looking dogs on leashes, while hundreds of others had been forced to climb onto the surrounding roofs, or hang out of the windows overlooking the yard.

The name on everyone's lips was that of Laddie Lightning, whom the King himself called 'the best damn pair of blacky fists' since Bill Richmond. The ring rose out of the centre of the courtyard like a roped-off temple. The Negro pugilist's many nicknames followed him as he made his way through the crowd: Mungo, Black Devil, Devil's Fist, Chimney Sweep, and the men, the dogs – even the ropes! – rippled with the excitement stirred up by the greatly anticipated bout.

Set beside the hulking Negro, Sullivan had a prepossessing appearance, his form compact and muscular. But Lightning's first punch, a left-hander, made a noise like the slap of meat under a butcher's fist, and he swiftly blocked the counter-punch. Although his second merely glanced off Sullivan's cheek, it knocked him back onto his heels, and sprayed blood over those who had thought themselves lucky enough to jockey for their ringside perches. Any advantage Sullivan possessed in superior training was dashed to smithereens by Lightning's sheer brutality. In their third set-to, the two men locked arms and foreheads and snorted at each other like bulls, white wrapped in black – Sullivan clenched tight in the Devil's Fist! Lightning's sixth and final punch left Sullivan reeling, penned to the corner, bleeding from his lip and one shut eye, and unable to come up to scratch, whereupon Lightning, on being declared the victor, mounted the ropes with all the energy he had brought into the ring, and entertained the large assembly by roaring out to them, 'Black I may be, but lily-white in victory!'

Chapter Twenty-Seven

Two weeks later, I went to Cheapside on my mistress's command.

Laddie opened the door himself. His flat was three flights above a bakery on Gant Street. The smell of muscovado and burning sugar seeped out as I drew near to it, reminding me of hot cane juice, of Sukey and her stumps. It was a smell that brought the spittle up, let me tell you – most of you wouldn't be as mad as you are on sweets if you'd ever caught the smell of a boiling house.

A woman passed me on the stairs, scratched her thigh through her skirts and gave me a hard stare. 'You looking for Laddie.' It wasn't a question.

His room was bare as a stripped bed. The furniture ragged, but scrubbed clean. A soapy smell rose above the ovens' hot, syrupy breath. A sheet had been pinned over the single window and a thin white candle guttered on top of the table. I saw his black suit slumped off a hook on the door. He narrowed his eyes. 'What do you want?'

When I said nothing, he went back to studying himself in a sliver of glass, poking his swollen eye, his purple jaw. It seemed I'd caught him in the act of cleaning off a fight. Blood gleamed on the floor. One of his cheeks was pasted with it. He wore nothing but a pair of breeches, wiped his face with his shirt, and spat into the washbasin.

'I'm bone-tired, little mulatta. I'll be bedding down in ten minutes, asleep in fifteen. You have five to tell me what you want.'

I made a show of looking around me. 'Mr African Genius. What would they say if they could see *this*?'

He raised a brow. 'Whatever them have to say about it, their concern, not mine.'

I thrust out the letter. 'I was sent to deliver this. From my mistress.'

'Which mistress is yours?' He settled himself on his pallet.

'You know perfectly well which one,' I said, and he laughed. I crossed the room, no more than two steps, and set the letter down on his chest. 'I'm to await your response.'

'Madame *Benham* got no footman to deliver her letters?' He broke the seal, squinted down at the letter and read it aloud.

'Mr Cambridge,

I have been thinking a great deal about your lecture. Antagonism disguised to amuse. It is a rare talent, to hit dead on the mark, killing off your target before they see the arrow coming. You do for your pleasure what they think you do for theirs.

I am chair of a committee that is organizing a debate sponsored by the Society. The motion is as follows: "What is the purpose of variety of the species of humankind?" Might I interest you in taking part?

Please believe I would be delighted to know you again. Indeed, the entire Benham family would be most gratified, I am sure, to hear how well you have fared since you left us.

In the meantime, I remain, yours faithfully,

Mme Marguerite Benham.'

'Not a love letter, then. Pity.' He folded the paper into a kite, sent it tripping across the room. 'That family. They *ever* gratified? By anything?' He laughed again, leaned his head against the

210

wall and closed his eyes. 'That woman as crazy as the rest. And somehow I doubt it was my *lecture* she found fascinating.'

Voices floated in, a woman's, then a man's, and bobbed away downstairs, like ash in the wind. I wanted nothing more than to leave that room, but I found myself stuck fast. It could have been the drug, which often weighted my limbs in those days, and made everything thick and slow, including my thoughts. She had been giving me little sips, from her own vial. Laudanum softens everything to the same grey shapes as an English fog. Any feeling – whether hope, anger, or happiness – becomes just a flicker in the dark. It was why I loved it. It leaves nothing sharp except eyes. His peered at me through the haze. 'No,' he said.

'I beg your pardon?'

'To the Devil with her. Tell your mistress *some* niggers happy to make themselves into a bit of sport for bored bluestockings. But not this one.'

I bristled. It wasn't laudanum that made my feet stick to the floorboards, I thought, but him. Something about him. Watching him was like pricking pins into my own thumb. 'Is that right?' I said. 'There is talk that *you* were sport for her once upon a time.'

'Is there? Oh, she won't like that.' He licked at his lip, brought his hand up to wipe at the blood. 'What do you think happens to page boys when they grow up?'

'You went to Cambridge, that's what I heard.'

'*They toss you out!* With the night-soil. Into the shit bucket. Not even the mercy of a bullet to the head.'

I had a mind to slap him, nick his gut with his little sliver of mirror. 'Very well. Your answer is no.'

'You run around like this for her all the time?'

Blood, like a taper touched to my face. 'I didn't come here to quarrel with you.'

'No. You did what you came for, yet you still here.'

Before I left, I found myself turning, blurting out, 'You not better than anybody else. White men pay you a sovereign a time to hammer your nose in. You monkey up speeches. White ladies paw at you like some cat.'

He shrugged. '*Every* black in London either a maid or a whore or a prizefighter. If you get the chance to do another thing, any different thing, you take it.'

'Any different thing?' I tossed back. The words scraped through my throat. 'Like that doxy who was leaving here when I was coming up? I can sniff out a man who sells women, you know.'

He laughed, loud and long. He sprang to his feet, and gripped my elbows. It was like being banded by a snake. He brought his face close to mine. His skin was still damp, blood-warm. He smelt like meat. His voice came swift and hard.

'I have the same nose, little mulatta . . . but *mine* sniffs out a woman who's sold herself.'

From the journals of George Benham
(Marked by George Benham as:
NOT INTENDED FOR PUBLICATION)

It always suits Meg to have a companion, and what suits Meg always suits everyone else. Her newest one is always at her side. Sitting in my library, attending my wife. For all the acres of difference between them, they are as like as two peas. Stubborn, changeable, quick. Even the girl's challenging, questioning manner is so very like Marguerite's when I first met her. They almost begin to look alike. Perhaps a trick of the light. I surprise them in the hallways, heads bent together, and then they fly apart and both stare. She is a distraction for my wife, at least. One can only hope this will temper Meg's constant need to be a distraction to herself. She blames me for the last one, as she blames me for everything. But what did I do, other than pluck the lad out of his circumstances, give him a life that exceeded them? There's no crime in that. Nor can a man be expected to continue to employ a footman who once cuddled his own wife on his lap.

My wife. My first act as a husband was to disappoint her. I remember how she settled herself on the bed and stopped to take a swallow of laudanum and brandy, a concoction I'd made for her, thinking it would soothe her nerves. 'It is *all* your *brother*'s money?' she said. Yes, I told her, most of it. She'd thought me wealthy because I lived at Longreach. But England's second sons share the elders' blood, not their fortunes. By dint of primogeniture I am Percy's second in every way, and not just the speed of our respective occupation and vacation of dear Mama's womb.

It is for Marguerite's own good that I ask the girl to keep an eye, though no one is less likely to recognize her own good than Marguerite. I married her knowing I made myself more caretaker than husband. That suited me. Marriage as self-flagellation. A perfect irony. The counter-weight on the scale. Marriage as redemption for my sins. *Let marriage stay my hand*, I thought.

I remind myself of Johnson: *A man should be careful never to tell tales of himself to his own disadvantage. People may be amused and laugh at the time, but they will be remembered and brought out against him upon some subsequent occasion.*

Reputation is everything.

I confess only to God.

I reminded the girl I want a record of everything. Who visits and who writes and who is written to. To whom Meg pays calls. How much laudanum, how often. Told her it is on this condition she stays on. When she asked how she'd manage for ink, I told her to dip her pen at my wife's own inkwells, if she had to. Made her startle like a pigeon. She'll do it, of course. No other choice.

 Why do you want it written down? she asked.

 My motives are none of her concern.

 To quote Ovid: *Exitus acta probat*. The result will justify my deeds.

Chapter Twenty-Eight

Love is not love which alters when it alteration finds.

The heat – a slow syrup on my face, her voice dripping Shakespeare straight into my ears. The line should stop after love, she used to say. *Love is not love.* 'Have you read Shakespeare before, Frances?' Fingers hot on my wrists. Her laugh a shop-bell. Then her face shut, and she sat up, remembering. 'Did he really send no reply?'

'He didn't.'

'La! Well, never mind. I will simply write again. He wants to be persuaded. A bit of flattery. Bring him to the cause.'

'Is it not more his cause than yours already?'

She shot me a look.

'Mr Cambridge said you should go to the Devil and he didn't want your sport.' The words tumbled out on a single breath.

'Did he?' She smiled. 'Well. That is to his credit.'

The following day, I came upon her scratching notes onto her walls. She bubbled like something boiling. All nerves and sweat. 'I have to learn to fend for myself,' she said, without turning her head. She laid her hands flat against the wall, her nails shivering like moons. Ink dripped in black beads from her forefinger. Nothing could be made out against the dark paint, so she took up the poker instead, and scored ash across the skirts of the woman in red. She stepped back and nodded. *Become your own WOMAN!* she'd written.

I lifted a napkin from her tray, dampened it, scrubbed at the wall until my arms ached. The wet ash clung stubborn as moss, and the entire wall looked as if there'd been a fire.

Her voice, from behind: 'Are you never tired of cleaning up after me?'

Her words ate at me. Stitched a cruel embroidery on my brain. I set the napkin down on the bed. 'There you are. Fend for yourself, then.'

She was two women. One confident, the other nervous. One bright, the other dark.

I'd seen from the start how her moods swung, but she'd seemed so happy for a time I'd almost forgotten it. Now they grew rickety and black again, hanging like a burned bridge. I continued to note her doses, as instructed, but the gap widened between the amount I wrote and the amount she took. The cabinet doors stayed open, and the bottles uncorked. The room flooded with that sweet slack smell.

'You remember how it was when you got here,' said Pru, when I went down to the kitchen to make up a tray. Watery tea and rusks. Pru cut a slice out of a loaf curved like a jaw, and made me take that also, with some marmalade, to see if she could be tempted. 'She'll keep to her bed for a few days, but then she'll swing around.'

We were closed in her room (which was why none save Linux remarked on it, later, when we were locked in there again). Benham said Dr Fawkes must be fetched, and I heard them whispering: '. . . bleed away a few ounces . . . hysteric . . . increase the paregoric . . .' I heard Fawkes saying it was an imbalance of the humours, an excess of the black bile. From Benham's response, it seemed it wasn't the first time. Benham said I must fetch a soup bowl and sit with her while she was bled.

When I went back in, she'd cast her covers aside. Worrying about what lay in store. Fawkes swore by bleeding, dieting, hot baths and opium, to restore the balance. 'Those are his articles of faith,' she said. 'Only the opium is pleasurable.' I coaxed her with barley broth, teas, mashed carrot. Nursery food. And I poured out her doses. A little for her, a little for me. I washed her blood from the bowl. I cleaned her. I did it gladly. And never allowed myself to think of Phibbah, or of Miss-bella.

Melancholia. Black bile. The very thing that stains black skin, and that I'd scribed about, for Langton. *Even her affliction is the same as mine*, I thought.

It shrank the world to her bed, and blackened the windows. A great hand pressing her down: she felt it in her head, and her aching joints.

The first evening after Fawkes came, she wanted to sit near the window. The sky was just turning pink and she wanted to see it curling like a ribbon around the clouds. That night, this is what she wrote: *Whenever I stand on the edge of a great height – a bridge, a balcony – I am swept by a sudden desire to leap. But melancholia is not the leap, it is the desire. The constant irrepressible agonizing urge.*

Sad for no reason, Pru said, sniffing.

But it seemed to me she had more than one.

Chapter Twenty-Nine

Two days later, Fawkes came again. He told me to warm some tumblers over the stove, and then he cupped blisters high on her back, between her shoulders. When all else failed, he brought in a jar that had *LEECHES* printed on it, holes punched into the lid. There were hundreds of the creatures inside, like little black tongues, blind as earthworms. I propped her against my chest while he fastened them one by one across her shoulders, and then we waited, him at the window with his hands clasped behind his back, her in one of the chairs, the fastenings of her bodice still loose, and her gown slipping off her shoulders. The leeches grew like soap bubbles, until one by one they fell away and we could carry her to bed.

The only good thing about it was that it drained her enough to sleep, curling and withering, like paper in a fire.

I am sorry to say that my own taste for laudanum grew then. It had started with single drops, but now built to a need that shook through my hands as soon as I took out the bottle to prepare her dose. Before it begins to eat your insides, opium is like a flame. It is all energy, and at the same time all rest. It pulls close all the meshwork of your own brain. Joys become raptures. Best of all, it drains the world away. I grew to need it as she did, the only thing that could soothe my cracked heart. Yet that is one of my most bitter regrets. For that evil substance made it impossible to keep my wits about me, and smudged all my remaining days with her.

During one of those weeks, Mr Casterwick came upon me,

as he said at my trial: once in the kitchen, writing upon the table with a pen that wasn't there; the second time, in the garden, searching for a baby in the hawthorn, saying that I'd taken an infant, and needed to return it.

That frightens me, even as I write it. Because I've no memory of it, but it sounds so much like something that could be true.

Laudanum stripped me of memory, as well as shame.

'You hear such stories,' she told me. 'But all that is needed is self-control. According to Paracelsus, it is the *dose* that's the poison.'

She ran her fingers over the lip of the vial. I sucked and sucked, and she did too. Liquid stuck to my lips. My feet glided over the carpet, the furniture thickened to dark shapes. The blighted world passed before my eyes in a sweet numbness. I had opium dreams. I dreamed a field, stretching as far away as the eye can see. I dreamed cane into it, in long, straight rows. The earth was wet and dark. *The cane has had a good rain watering*, I thought, but when I looked down I saw that the wetness was blood. Mud, blood.

When I looked up again, towards the horizon, Miss-bella was there. This is always how it happens. She looks from me to the small boy who kneels in the grass, his head bowed, gripped by calipers. Then I dream Langton. His voice: *Note this, Frances. Write this down. The bones of the head are moulded to the brain. The size of the cranium, the quantity of the cerebrum.* Then Miss-bella raises her hand, points a trembling finger, and shouts, *You are a monster, you are a monster, you are a monster.* And I look around. Who is she talking to? Who does she mean?

Then I realize that the person she is looking at, the person she is pointing at, is me.

•

The next morning I woke in a lather of sweat, drawing the laudanum vial towards me. The more I drank, the more I needed.

The air thickened to wool, soured my armpits. The day wore on. I fetched down a novel, lay beside her trying to read aloud. Laudanum blurred the pages, so I put my finger between them, tilted my head back. The woman in red stared as if she'd spring from the wall. Her skirts still stained. *Become your own WOMAN!* The more I watched, the whiter her face became. The paint washed together until it could have been anything, until it could have been ash and blood and bone.

I sat up, head whirling.

Madame was too restless to pay attention. A panic had come over her, and now it catapulted her into the cabinet for her dose. A few weeks before she'd fallen ill, we'd attended a Blacks' Ball held in a public house near Fleet Street. More blacks there than I'd ever seen in any one place before, skin from tar to coffee to milk. Some so pale only their hair would tell you the truth. She had gone in her boy's disguise, but now she was fretting that we could be found out. The time for worry would have been before we went, I told her. I hadn't written a word about it in the notes I delivered to Benham. I felt a stab of guilt that I'd written anything, though it had been mostly lies and inventions. I did it because I had to give him *something* since he'd commanded it. Same reason as I'd answered his questions about Paradise.

The room had an air of waiting for something to happen, while knowing it never would. I wanted to stop her nail-biting, and her chatter, so I asked, 'What would you take if we could leave?'

'What do you mean?' she said, lowering her hand. 'Leave? Here? What an idea!'

'What if you could take only one thing?'

'It would be hard to leave my books, certainly . . . but I would take . . . my portrait. *La femme en rouge.* No question.

And the egg-chest. La! *Two* things, then! I am a cheat, I know.'
She smiled. 'Maman would just have to roll herself up and consent to be stored inside Papa.'

I looked up at the woman in red. Her dress a stopped heart. Madame didn't ask me what I would take, perhaps because nothing in that room belonged to me.

White doctors are more curse than cure and Fawkes was no exception. Useful for drumming up their trade, I suppose, but not for making anyone better. I told her the energy was draining out of her with her blood, that we needed to leave the room.

Leaves swung heavy as apples, and sunlight cast green shadows across the pond-water, where flies looped like black thread. But the light hurt her eyes, and she found it still too warm, and would not walk far, though she consented to sit in the parlour instead. I arranged her on the window-bench where she could look out, with her white lace shawl across her knees. She asked if I might fetch her the newspapers, usually left on the sideboard in the dining room after breakfast. When I brought them to her I instantly wished I'd told her they'd already been cleared. For there'd been a bout at Five Courts, a 'blood-soaker', and he was in there. Black fists, blacker grin.

'Look.' She pressed a finger to the sketch. 'Laddie.'

'I can see that.'

I drew away, folded myself at the far end of the bench. Looked out towards the garden, snaking away to the pond. But it had the opposite effect on her. It pulled a thread through her spine, and put a singing note through her voice. She turned the page, said perhaps she'd take a cordial, and some fruit, and did I want to see if Charles would set up the card table?

Until that moment, her melancholy had seemed to be a kind of rootless grief. Now I wondered if the source hadn't been the very man whose image had been the first thing to pierce it.

What was it she'd said, the night of his lecture? Laddie Lightning had become his own man, and that was what she admired. Then she had spelled out her *own* misery on her walls: *Become your own WOMAN!*

Suspicion began to eat at me like rats on leather.

Perhaps she'd still be alive if I'd been able to stopper up that jealousy. But instead I let my doubts stick fast, like mud on a heel.

She kept mostly to her bed, though venturing out into the garden more and more. One morning, as far as the park. Two weeks later, Benham insisted she attend a dinner party with him, a feat she managed only with the help of laudanum, bringing back the smells of all those other people on her. Tonics and potions and pomades.

After a time, she opened the house. Her friends dribbled in. She started going out again. When she did, whispers followed her.

Another spell. The black drop, you know.

Perhaps all that whatever-it-was with the boy should have been a warning to him.

She spoiled him, like a little lord. Instead of the servant he was. Cruel, of course, to raise a child in a manner that exceeds his expectations. Especially a black.

They *should have no expectations at all, of course.*

Their gossip wounded me, but also became the only thing that would soothe those wounds. I wanted more and more. Needing to know what had happened between her and him. But she wouldn't speak of it, and Pru, who'd been my only steady source before, chose that moment to clamp her lips. 'It wouldn't be seemly, Fran, gossiping about all that, not when Linux might spring up any minute.'

I would soon learn more than I cared to about all of it.

Chapter Thirty

They weren't her friends. That was merely the label hanging off them, like those Piccadilly sweets.

One afternoon Hep Elliot paid her a visit, bringing Laddie Lightning with her. An act of pure mischief, if you ask me.

She and I had planned to spend the afternoon at the park. Now I had no choice but to smile through my misery, shift along the bench. Just breathe in all my crackling frustration. Keep it locked inside. I had some pastries with me, which I'd brought up from the kitchen. Little currant pastries in the shape of pigs. Hep Elliot spied the plate, and leaped on it, handing them around, and asking if Madame thought Linux could be persuaded to bring up some of her famous elderberry wine.

I tried not to look at Laddie, but of course *he* drew the eye also. The great stampede he made of himself, pulling to a stop at the mantel. He was suited again, and at least had managed to ensure he was clean of blood.

'Took the painting down?' he asked, scratching at one of the bayoneted horses. 'What a shame.'

She flinched. Her eyes flew to mine as if asking for help, knowing full well no help could come. She'd have to sweep him out of there on her own.

'What's the matter?' he said. 'Not happy to see me unless it's you who picks the place?'

'Of course I am happy to see you, Laddie.'

'Olaudah. I prefer Olaudah, unless I'm in the ring. And I

believe your exact words were that the *entire* Benham family would be gratified to know how I had fared.'

Well, what could she say to that? She pinched her mouth shut. I saw her throwing glances towards the door. Oh, she was anxious. He was right: she might have been happy to see him, but she was not happy to see him *there*. Two of her coils slipped their pins, running into little dark pools that hid her face. He grinned, and shrugged his shoulders, eyeing the mantel again and looking as if he would bite it. I saw nothing there to catch his interest, save for a spray of lilies in a vase that Linux had made up that morning, and wondered if he was staring at it simply not to stare at *her*. He had just crossed to the window bench and she was reaching up to tidy her hair when Benham walked in. The silence that unfurled then seemed a solid thing. Went up like a sail. She struck up some stream of nervous chatter but Benham shushed her, looking for all the world as if Laddie simply wasn't there. He just looked around at each of them, and nodded. Though when he sat and swapped words with Hep Elliot, I heard his voice straining behind its leash of teeth.

Later, I went down to the empty parlour and sat on the window-bench to finish up the bit of white-work she wanted to lay on her mantel. It was in a spider's web pattern, and difficult, with that laudanum-quiver in my hands. All that thread, and having to prick white violets onto white cotton. But she'd wanted violets, and I wanted her happy. She'd said Laddie had caught her by surprise, that afternoon; she was worried Benham might object. I pointed out that *she*'d been the one to write him, and seemed to be forever changing her mind.

After a time, I heard her and Benham in the hallway, him saying the boy was not welcome, her saying surely opening their doors to him was the best way to pour water on the rumours, then asking would he come inside and sit with her awhile. Trying to appease him, I thought. When they came together into the room, I looked down again, hoping to stay invisible, and kept on pulling the ant-bite stitches through the cloth. The drawn curtains sieved out some of the heat, left the room dark enough for them to want candles lit, which Pru came in and did for them. When she'd finished, Benham asked would she fetch him a plate of Linux's almond cake, and then he sat sucking marzipan from his fork. His shoulders sloped like hillsides. For a time, it was quiet, but she sidled looks at him, the way you come at a bad dog sideways. She turned a page of her magazine and reached for a sip of brandy. I had a thirst for it too, but no one had offered me any.

Benham raised his head. 'I see you are indulging again, wife?'

'I am *bored* again, husband,' she replied, thudding down her glass. I pricked the needle in and out through the fabric, drew in a breath. When I looked up from my stitching I came face to face with the painted, dying horses, their eyes bone-white and wide, their chests heavy as anvils. I wanted to pull aside the drapes, to the Devil with the hot air. I wanted him to leave, so I could have her to myself once again.

At last, she set aside the magazine. 'Mr Benham,' she said. 'I have been thinking.'

'Oh?'

'What if we sponsored something like the Bordeaux prize? Invited papers on the debate motion? Have those read out?' Her words crept up to him.

He clanked down his fork. 'Didn't we just speak about this? My answer is no. Besides, the Bordeaux prize was a failure.'

'I wish you would reconsider. There is still time for a change of heart.' She'd become brave, I thought. This was not the same woman who'd eaten the egg in silence.

225

'My *heart* is an ever-fixed mark. Have always said the institution can be reformed.' He licked at a crumb pasted above his lip. 'The *trade* is at an end, has been for decades. Since Frances was a babe.' He sniggered at me. I kept my head down, pretended not to hear.

'But the suffering of the thousands still enslaved is no less of an emergency than those who were transported in the ships.'

'Careful, wife. You'll make yourself sound like a Radical. Half the income that keeps your bottom cushioned on all that velvet comes from those same estates. Don't forget that.' He cocked a hand at his ear. 'I don't hear you volunteering to give it up.' He leaned over, set down the plate, dipped a napkin in a glass of water and swiped at his forehead. 'In any event, I am on the brink of sharing my opinions, which will put paid to that very suffering. Design a benevolent framework for the institution. When my essays are published, the vultures can pick them over. They can scoop out the contents of my skull then. Isn't that what vultures do with skulls? Frances?' He swivelled again in his chair. I hated the way he kept calling on me, the way he kept looking at me.

When I think of her, it's with the kind of love that makes murder seem a lie. But I could have killed *him*.

I busied my hands on the hoop. Needles ticking. The drug made it as if my head was sleeping, even if the rest of me was not.

Searing hot in the kitchen as always. Smells of roasting. A rabbit carcass twirling on the spit, grease burning black into the stove. I took myself a plate down from the dresser. China for me, no more tin. I looked around to make sure Linux was watching. Their heads flickered, like candles in a breeze. The room seemed to curl and uncurl before my eyes. I hardly went

226

down there in those days, so busy was I with Madame. But that evening, she'd said she wanted only brandy and laudanum mixed in a tumbler, and for me to give her a few moments' peace. *A few moments' peace.*

The kitchen had been the sum of all my choices.

I felt that same itch of worry I'd felt earlier, in the parlour. *Did* she draw away? Did she no longer want me? That thought had struck such terror in me that my hand shook, and before I knew it I'd pricked my finger.

Linux's voice creaked like a stair. The supper had been laid out on the table. Pork, turnips, tumblers of ale. A Friday supper. She turned her granite eyes on me: 'Those who know pride will surely also know the fall,' she said.

The Bible lay beside her place. I had no appetite for it. The reading made me think of Paradise, of Phibbah. How Missbella would sometimes mutter, 'The Lord gives and the Lord takes away.'

When I'd asked Phibbah what it meant, she'd kissed her teeth. '*Some* would say it mean that just 'cause a woman have everything don't mean she don't know how it feel to lose.'

The Lord gives, and the Lord takes away.

If that's right, there's nothing you can do but sit back and wait, see what you get, see what gets taken away. Thank the giving Lord, or curse the thieving one.

She asked Mr Casterwick to carve, then started on her complaining. 'On Monday, Charles, I was informed you were impertinent with clerks when sent to make the withdr—'

'Why do you do that?' I interrupted, my own impatience boiling hot. Or was it the drug?

'I *beg* your pardon?'

'Week after week you trot out Charles's sins, or Pru's, or mine. You seek only to humiliate.'

A smile carved into her face. 'Oh. I haven't humiliated *you*, girl.' She lifted the knife away from Mr Casterwick, and stabbed the joint. Meat juices ran pink into the wood. 'Yet.'

Later, Pru brought two of Madame's dresses upstairs from the scullery. I took them from her in the hall, the door shut tight behind me.

'Fran. You're altogether too *bold*.'

'Why do we let her treat us that way?'

She let her voice drop. 'You're a dog barking at the wrong bird. You're only *this* bold because you think she's your friend.' She pointed her thumb at the door. 'There never is such a thing as real friendship between the likes of them and the likes of us.'

'I have to go back in, Pru,' I said. I put my hand behind me on the latch. Already my mind was racing back to her, and how might I coax her to eat. The black night crouched, like a watchman, at the glass.

From the journals of George Benham
(Marked by George Benham as:
NOT INTENDED FOR PUBLICATION)

Came upon Marguerite in the parlour yesterday, over-bright as she always is after every bout, the way the grass sparkles brightest after rain. 'Look who's here,' she said.

Who should be on the settee, next to that Elliot woman, but the boy.

'Laddie!' she announced, gesturing towards him. Nervous. As she should have been. Did it in front of Hep Elliot so there'd be no scene. 'Hep brought him. I had no idea!'

I'm sure she didn't.

Lost and found. He didn't seem at all discomfited on coming face to face with me, but then he'd had the advantage of knowing that he was under my roof. He gave me a half-hearted little bow, every desultory gesture towards me communicating – what? His ambivalence? His resentment? His *revenge*?

Ignored him entirely so as not to give them the satisfaction of a public display.

I sat for a while, then left. Elliot followed me into the hall, pronged her nose at me. She made some remark about jealousy being such a common emotion, for someone who believes himself such an uncommon man.

Later, I made it clear to Meg that the boy is not welcome. No. Not a boy. He has become a man.

I've decided to sponsor the debate, but under my sole name. *What is the purpose of variety in the species of humankind?* The motion was, after all, my own design.

Concerning Meg, the girl still delivers only tidy lines, takes far greater care over her penmanship than imparting anything of any use. Laudanum in prescribed doses. Work on her flimsy memoirs. Outings to Gunter's for pistachio ices, Hooke's library (paragraphs and paragraphs about *that*) and to Richmond for turns about the park with that ape-leader, Elliot. Surely there is more to your days than that, I said. In response, she bit her lip. She thinks to rescue Meg, by feeding me these half-truths.

Everyone wants to rescue Meg.

Meanwhile, that very object of our mutual attention grows brighter and brighter now while the girl grows dull, though I suspect both moods have the same root: to wit, Mr Olaudah Cambridge. To test my suspicions, I asked the girl what she thought of him. She replied that she didn't think much of *Laddie* Cambridge at all, but that in any event it is impossible to think more of him than he thinks of himself. I think she has an inkling she's been thrown over for a new favourite. That's Meg. A magpie's zeal for collecting.

Talk turned again to Paradise. I asked whether she knew Boyle believed the existence of albinos proved that Adam and Eve were white, and all the other races descended from them. She shied away at the mention of albinos, as she always does, the flush coming down her face like a shade descending. Fascinating that she is pale enough to blush!

Perhaps it was the boy turning up like a bad penny that agitated me. So, I pressed her. Cruel, yes, but I have very little patience left for her impenetrable silences, or her lies.

'I've had a letter from your old mistress,' I said. 'From Mrs Langton.' *That* sent her scuttling back into her shell, blinking out at me, watching me as one might watch a fire, looking but not seeing. The news had reached Jamaica that Langton's mulatta has ended up under my roof. Mrs Langton advises me to rid myself of her if I know what's good for my household, but at the same time suggests she knows the whole story about the albino infant.

Let me explain.

The Comte de Buffon is credited with the theory of inter-fertility, according to which if a pair produces a child who is itself capable of having children, then both members of that pair are human. In other words, if the child of a black mother and a white father can itself produce children, black and white are members of the same human stock. Otherwise mulattos would be barren as mules. Clearly the mulatto is demonstrably fertile – witness the terceroons and quadroons and octoroons sprouting like mushrooms throughout the new world – and so it is demonstrably false to assert that blacks are not human, and therefore a catastrophic waste of time. This posed a difficulty for Langton, as I've mentioned elsewhere. I suppose he couldn't turn a blind eye to it for long. Instead he proposed a series of 'experimental matings'. I received this news on good authority, from several of the Fellows; thankfully, I could tell them by then that I had already written to him and cut the cord.

A year later, I heard that he had sent Pomfrey on the hunt for a white Negro, an albino infant 'less than four years of age'. I speculated as to what he could want with it. White Negroes are rarer than hen's teeth. They won't be found in the usual course of trade, not even on the blackest of black markets, not even by that black character, Pomfrey. There'd been a craze for albinos in the middle of the last century. A four-year-old white Negro had been exhibited in the Paris expositions in 1744, at the Académie Royale des Sciences. Maupertuis and Voltaire made such a meal of their own examinations on that occasion! (Voltaire's own description, of an animal called a man because it had the gift of speech, memory, a little of what we call reason, and a sort of face – deliciously ironic from the man who wrote *Candide*!) There have been albinos exhibited in this fair city as well, of course: for example, Amelia Newsham, the white Negress, at the Bartholomew Fair at the end of the last century.

I admit to being torn. No naturalist would pass up a chance to examine such a rare creature. Langton might have seen it as his chance to prove that skin colour, and the other national characteristics, are innate rather than superficial. If the albino were like all other blacks, he would be black in the inner parts as well, in the bile and the blood, and would possess all the other Negro traits. I confess to a momentary excitement at the thought of what one could do with access to such a subject, but not even that would persuade me to join forces with Langton again. I knew he'd long been troubled by the argument that the little *blafard* exhibited in Paris was proof of a vestigial link between black and white, and even more by the assertion that humans were *originally* black (for blacks had bred whites but no whites had ever bred blacks). That would smash his polygenetic arguments that the races are in fact two entirely separate species.

Perhaps Langton was simply curious; perhaps he merely wanted one of his own to keep, as Buffon had done with his Geneviève, his 'high-breasted, sugar-breathed' Geneviève. But I don't believe it is possible to be too unfair when it comes to Langton's motives.

The infant is my best chance of killing all of my birds with a single shot, since I suspect it might be the worst example of Langton's behaviour. I asked her: 'About the baby?'

She jumped, her eyes flew up to me.

ADDENDUM

Have been able to glean some additional facts from her. As with all good confessions, it started with one small, mitigating lie. She says it was nothing to do with her, but Langton did obtain an albino, from the Montpelier estate in Antigua. She does not know (said coyly) how this was possible, given abolition of the trade. The infant was already owned, and, she presumed, that was why he could be purchased. Nor did she know what their intentions were. (This last may indeed be true. I don't think those two Bedlamites knew themselves.)

What happened to it? She refused to say more.

Chapter Thirty-One

What did Shakespeare know? Love *must* alter, or it can't survive.

Her appetite had swelled during my early days with her. Walnuts that had to be cracked out of their shells, hard yellow cheeses, Linux's roasted goose with potatoes roasted in fat, French madeleines. I'd taken my meals upstairs with her, on the pewter trays. But now it was back to broths and eggs, and hunger often forced me downstairs. One night, Linux had made a gooseberry tart and the pot of tea was steaming as usual on the table, with all of them sitting around it. She put the knife down and passed her hand over her mouth when she saw me.

'Booted back down, then?' she said.

A knocking on the jamb. Madame. She'd just come in from some ball. I rose to my feet. Earlier, I'd helped her into her long gown, lined at the bosom with gauze thin as smoke. *I will not need you there tonight,* she'd said. *I am sure you will be glad of the rest, no?* Her long white gloves were still pulled up to her elbows.

'Where is it?' she demanded, looking straight at me. A tremble along her jaw.

'Where is what?'

'You *know.*'

'I do not.' My throat went tight, bridled with humiliation. With all the others watching. Pru's eyes on me, her mouth twisting.

'My tincture. It is not in the usual place.'

'Your medicine, Madame?' said Linux, her own lips smoothed into a smile. 'I could come up if you like? Help you look?'

'No, Mrs Linux. I would *not* like. Because Frances knows where it is.' She tilted her chin, tapping a hand against her skirts. I was in those days always at the mercy of her mood.

'But I don't,' I said. 'I haven't seen it.'

Linux's face pulled like a lace through a boot. 'What if I sent you up some nice chamomile, Madame? Would you like that? Or you could sit down here awhile? There's a lovely tart.'

The next day was hot but with a bluster to it. The park was quiet. We walked in silence, passed not another soul. The trees and flowers and the lake wove in and out of my eyes. The leaves were like little green planks floating on an ocean. There'd been no opium for me that day, and pain roared through my head. I felt cornered by the pair of them. And nothing could stop the tear that crawled up my throat. *Never let your lady get bored.* I stopped on the path. Black birds looped high and sometimes circled low to fill my ears with song or to perch on branches and stare.

'I would move up into one of those elms . . .' she said, her head turned to the sky. We were friends again. 'Or I would make myself a little bed close to the Serpentine, sleep under a blue-black sky, make love to stars. La! What would they say about eccentric Meg Benham *then*?' She turned towards me; her eyes glittered. 'I am sorry I accused you . . . last night . . .'

I was too tired to answer her.

I could pull you behind one of those very elms, I thought, *hook my thumbs beneath your bodice* . . . Oh. Inside, I could do what I wanted. Bend her over her writing desk and kiss her breasts to my heart's ease. But outside I was no one, nothing but a maid.

I pictured myself looping a hurting fistful of hair around my hand. She took a step back.

Now I begin to worry that it was me she feared after all.

•

Later that afternoon, not knowing what else to do, I went into the garden in search of roses. The scissors were still nowhere to be found. I twisted with my fingers at the few blooms left on the bush. Petals fell away from me, like ash. I was bringing in those broken stems when Linux came behind me. As always, her mood was sewn into her lips. 'It's you I'm looking for,' she said. 'I've come from speaking with the mistress. She's asked for Pru to take up her tray.'

'What? *Why?*'

'Do you truly believe you're owed any explanations, girl? Occupy yourself *downstairs* for a change.' She smirked, her smile slipping and clawing. I turned away from her, one foot already on the stair, but she reached out and held fast, her fingers tight around my wrist.

'*Down,*' she said.

My mind scrambled and scrambled and scrambled, but got nowhere.

She set me to work scrubbing pots with sand. A pile of them slumped in the basin, coated with grease. Soap spat up onto my sleeves when I plunged my hands in. It felt like a fall from grace. Pru came down, saying she was no longer needed upstairs, as Madame had decided to go out. Again? My heart pumped. I stilled my hands above the basin. Fingers withered and dripping, like leaves. I hated the way my own mood teetered, trying to keep pace with hers. I hurried to finish the pots, thinking only about how to get back upstairs. When Linux had left, I slipped away, to the staircase, the hallway, her room. This time, no one stopped me.

She was gone.

My hands fled away from me of their own accord. Mantel, bedcovers. The dying roses. Her drawers. Her cabinet. The kindness of laudanum. Though it did nothing to stem the awful sour terror rising through me, like a flood. I drank more and more. Then, for the first time since Benham had asked it of me, I became a spy.

They were in her egg-keeper. Of course. I felt a low scrabble of panic in my gut the moment I decided to open it. I put out my hands to grip the lid, tried to steady myself. My hands. How I'd hated all my life to watch them going about their work. I didn't know how long before she'd be coming back. The woman in red watched from the wall, her eyes wide, in warning or in judgement. I opened the box. Lifted out her black brooch. Beside it lay a gold ring, what they called a signet. A man's ring. Then a lock of grey hair tied in a black ribbon; a letter – to Papa – from *Marguerite Delacroix, aged 7*; a single white pearl, lost as a tooth. I lifted them all out. Even the simplest thing was all confusion in those days, my mind and my hands gone slow, my own face a puzzle in the glass. Therefore, when I first saw the scraps of white, I thought, *Here are her father's eggshells. Smashed. Peck-peck-peck.*

The world slid away. The lid slammed shut, and almost took my fingers with it. *Peck.*

Not eggs. Letters. Letter after letter after letter.

Why did I reply 'at last'? It seemed to me someone should take pity on you. Does that satisfy? The more interesting question is why you kept writing. LL

You are as persistent with this question as you were with your unanswered letters. I will be frank. Your first letter I took for a bored woman's self-indulgence. I was not bored enough to answer it. Now I am. But you still haven't answered my question. Why did you keep writing? I will venture a guess. You are lonely. LL

You say your husband is sympathetic. He is not the man you think, though he is the man I remember. Sympathy without action is nothing more than an idea. LL

You already know my story. When I arrived here as a boy, I thought it was a place as bright and shining as Heaven. I'd lived my first four years in a slave cabin with my mother until Mr George Benham, in his wisdom, decided I would serve, and plucked me right off his estate. I remember that my mother turned away from me, before I left. She refused to speak and, indeed, began to behave as if I simply did not exist. It made the parting easier on me, of course. Who can say what would have made it easier on her? I don't remember much else. I've drawn a shade down over the rest of it. Five years, then he married you. I thought you were an angel. Everything you both surround yourselves with is so soft and luminous (even, if I may bring your husband into it again, your ideas). After I was sent down from Cambridge, I decided to take that name for myself. I became Olaudah Cambridge. For a time I was able to disappear. Some among your kind find it droll that I have named myself after that great university. Thumbing my nose at it. While I was there, I was introduced to some frilly baroness who asked me where I learned to speak English so well. I replied that even a parrot might be taught this uncomplicated language. It has served me well. I entertain myself by doing what you found me doing. Taking whites for sport. From the podium, and in the ring.

I won't meet you simply because you command it, nor would you think much of me if I did. LL

From him to her. All of them.

Every mother hates her own babe. That's what Phibbah used to say. The hate is a needful part of mothering, same as love. Always there comes that one moment. Early days, and they're red, thunderous, ugly. Their feet kick, like dogs digging dirt. You're awake knowing you need to be in the fields before the sun and you're going to stay out there long after the sun too. It's in *that* moment you wish it gone. Not a long wishing, just a blink. You feel it like your belly dropping out of you, all the way down to gully-bottom. And as soon as you do, the need boils up in you never to feel it again.

But it going come again. That blink. When it comes time to really let them go. That's when it going come.

What can I say in my own defence? When I closed my eyes, I still saw the letters behind them. Folded small as daggers. They pierced holes in me, and let the intention pour right in. But I pressed myself against the window, flattening my skirts, my cheeks. Fighting it, I forced myself to stare down towards the pond, remembering how she would pluck at the grass whenever we sat there, and scrape through the dirt. Muck her nails. I curled my arms around my waist, holding myself back. A half-hour I stood there, perhaps longer. But she didn't come back. A cloud swung over the sun and showed me my own face darkening the glass. I stepped away from it, turned towards her desk, pulled out a clean page. Lifted the pen.

Chapter Thirty-Two

The world had gone wrong. There were the letters, where eggshells should have been. Madame's sins.

And me, committing them to paper.

Then the door creaked open. There was Linux. *Smiling.*

'You never stay where you're put, do you?' she said. 'Flitting from husband to wife like a bee to honeysuckle.'

'What are you accusing me of now?'

'Not accusation, girl. Facts. Strong enough to swing from.'

One arm peeled away from her chest. It had been so long since I had seen my blue serge that I'd been slow to recognize it. The dress I'd worn to London. The dress I'd left in the attic. Then we raced each other down the halls. It was a strange echo of my first night, the sconces empty, the walls bathed in sunshine. Light cutting into dark.

This time I knew the way as well as she.

She knocked the jamb, shivering the frame. Benham gave a bird-hop, raised his hands to palm his waistcoat, as if we'd caught him dipping them where they didn't belong.

'What in God's name . . . ?'

She leaned over and dropped the bundle onto his table.

'A dress, Mrs Linux?'

'Beg pardon, sir, it's what's inside.'

'She means there's a book sewn there, in the hem,' I said. 'One of your books. Which I took from your library. *Candide.*'

'Stole.' Linux tapped a fingernail on the serge. '*Stole.*'

Benham looked down at the dress, up at me.

I sucked in my cheeks. 'I wanted something to read.'

'It has turned out as I've been saying all along, sir,' said Linux, her voice slipping with glee, 'and I take no pleasure in that, for in keeping with her character the girl has proved herself a thief. Perhaps you will heed me *now*. There is a greater danger in keeping her, though I know you believe it is a mercy. But what is said about them, sir? The African is *sly*, and *lascivious*, and *lazy*. And she is all those things! And a danger to this house besides.'

Were things not so dire, I'd have laughed. She might have been reading out Langton's own words that I had scribed myself.

'Words,' I said. 'Paper and ink. Why should words be commodities? Didn't you say something similar to me yourself? On my first day?'

Before he could answer, the scrape and rustle of skirts and boot-heels coming to a stop. I glanced up and saw Madame, looking at me strangely.

'Oh, yes, Madame,' said Linux. 'This concerns you. Your abigail has been caught, I'm afraid. Caught, yes. Thieving.'

'What?'

Benham gave out a laugh. 'Well, now. That's a strong way to put it, Mrs Linux. Let the girl consider this a warning.' He turned to me. 'Mrs Linux will deduct from your wages a sum which I will calculate and give her due notice of. If we're lucky you'll pay it off before we all cock up our toes.' He puffed himself up. 'Let that be a lesson to us all about the grace of forgiveness.'

Linux's jaw swung open. Her cough stuck in her throat.

I knew why Benham wouldn't turn me out. Nothing whatsoever to do with grace or forgiveness. He spoke out of the side of his mouth, which is where all his words came from. He wanted the truth about that infant. He wanted the truth about her, also. And I hadn't yet given him either one.

But still I wondered. *Could* I leave? Take myself someplace else?

Become your own woman, she'd written. The thought struck me then that perhaps I could.

I turned. Could I ask her to come? It was the drug talking, of course. The courage of the mad. She had betrayed me, I had betrayed her. But what would the world be without her in it?

She stood trembling. All of her seemed made of glass, and I saw, for the first time, her expression – not shock but rage. And it was then that I looked down at her hands. There was the note I'd written, and left upstairs. My heart stuck to my ribs.

'You have been spying on me?'

The School-house
August 1825–January 1826

Chapter Thirty-Three

Out! Out!

Her voice rang in my ears as the door closed behind me. I stood on the step with a hand clapped over my mouth. Then I made my feet move. Across the street, past the rows of houses, along the park gates, on towards Piccadilly. Hour after hour I wandered until, when I raised my head, I saw the river. Westminster Bridge. My footsteps sounded a drumbeat, and I bent my head against the cold thwack of rain. The gas-lamps spanned one end to the other, sitting on top of their little domes. There were only a few stars. I strained to see the tall masts, and listen for the river beneath the creaking ships and the dull, rattling hackneys, wandering like great chained beasts.

I stood, clutched my shawl. *Now you can be your own woman*, I told myself. It was cold comfort. I had seldom been outside without a destination of someone else's choosing. I kept hearing her last words: 'Get out. *Get out.*'

Two days, I stayed close to the river. By day, I watched the ships go in and out. When night snapped my heels, I huddled in quieter spots and fought sleep, back to the wall, head to my knees. I dreamed of shillings clinking in my fist, though a knife would have been more use. I tried an inn. *No working girls*, they said. *No touting your wares here.* I came back to the bridge and looked out across the oily water and the winking lamps. Without laudanum, my mind was awake, and raging. And remembering. Even my teeth hurt. By the second night, my hands shook like leaves. I folded in two, vomited. When I straightened, I lifted my skirts, trying to keep them up out of the filth. A voice came from behind me. 'Looky! Black as the night, yet trying to keep yer skirts up out of it!'

My head had emptied so I could barely move.

'Quiet, aren't you? *Puss?* No use fighting it, love. You're as filthy as that muck and you know it.' A cold hand curled around my elbow. I spun around with my hands up, but ribbons of sweat clogged my eyes.

Silence. My whole body clenched. Head down. Breathing. I could tell that time passed only by the clack of boots striking cobbles. I'd beaten him with my fists, but it was whatever he saw in my eyes that had beaten him off. Dog barks tore through the night. *Finally*, I thought. *Finally. I'm being punished at last.*

Next morning, I kept my eye on a row of houses, set back a few streets from my lair. People came and went. Messenger boys. Deliveries. Maids with packages. Ladies, waiting for their carriages. I went back to my alley, damped my fingers in a puddle, and tried to smooth down my hair. I fluffed my skirts around me, wiped my cheeks with the hem. Then I went back, started with the busiest door.

Most of them threatened to call the watch. The last one did.

A maid with no character, whether turned out or run off, is worse than one of the scraps of rubbish you see blowing along London's streets.

I tried begging. I tried standing up to do it, at first, but soon learned it worked better the dirtier you looked, the lower you crouched, and the further out you stretched your hand. The coves weren't *giving*, you see, they were buying. What they paid for was humiliation. Yours, as an indemnity against theirs. After an hour or so on my knees on the pavement outside a coffee-house, a man approached. He had a watch on a chain under his grey waistcoat, one eye a toad-goggle, the other half shut. 'Money for nothing?' he said. 'Not very enterprising of you.'

He gave off a powerful smell of raw onions. Said he was writing a diary of the streets, and would put me in it. *You and everyone else*, I thought, but what I said was: 'I'd much prefer the black drop, sir, if you have any.'

He scraped out a laugh.

'I mean it,' I said. 'Aren't writers more reliable for drugs than scribbles?'

He said how unexpected I was, like finding a guinea in mud, which he supposed he had, if one stopped to remember that the coins are themselves named after Guineamen. Then he laughed at his own wit, fumbling at his breeches, and said that, as my luck would have it, he had more than one thing that might tickle my fancy, back in his rooms.

I took my skinny earnings back to the coffee-house, tried to buy a drink. I was turned away. For being a woman, they said. But at a table in the corner, nose tucked into a newspaper and a cup, was a face I'd thought never to see again. Pomfrey. He saw me through the window, tapped the glass. When he came out, he remembered me straight away: 'Langton's girl! By the looks of it, that's some tumble *you*'ve taken, since he left you.' I said nothing. There was a long silence while he sized me up. But I was sizing him up, too. Wondering if I could bring myself to sink so low.

'I think I have something useful for you,' he said, at last. 'Remember me mentioning the School-house? My contact there gives me a finder's fee.'

I remembered something. If you're sinking, and someone throws you a log, it can be a weight or a raft. But the quickest way to drown is fighting it.

•

I know what's said about my time in that place, how it counts against me now, shows me as a savage character and unrepentant whore, as Jessop would have it. But the first thing to know about whoring is that it's work. You do it same way you'd empty a chamber pot, head down, nose pinched. Many an English wife must get herself through the same activity in the same fashion.

'Bright-eyed thing, aren't you?' Mrs Slap said. She squinted. 'In the right light, you could play innocent.'

My stomach lurched. 'But I'm not.'

She laughed. 'All you need's a white nightgown and a fresh razor. Though looking at you, you could just as easily go dark.'

'Dark?' I jerked my head up. She was giving me a choice. I didn't yet know what.

She smiled. 'You ever whipped anybody?'

Chapter Thirty-Four

You can't ever get clean enough in a bawdy-house. It's even worse in prison, where the simple act of lying down covers you in the kind of muck you'd find under a cow's straw. But at least at the School-house I had my own bathwater and my own tin tub. And my own Martha to thump upstairs, carrying bathwater to the Scarlet Room, which was mine also. Or, at least, the one I slept in. Though I could see Martha's brown eye rolling at the keyhole while I washed.

Mornings found me stretched in my little tub. Arms and legs hooked over the sides, and the swill of water warm as blood. But my heart was always somewhere behind me. Was *she* in her own bath? Between her sheets? Was it Pru who brought her chocolate up? Did she still see *him*? In my mind's ear, I still heard her, screeching: *Get out! Get out.*

Memory swamped me, and I slapped at the side of the tub to stop it. I sat up. From outside a shout wedged through the window. *'For what shall it profit a man if he gain the whole world but lose his own soul?'*

You could set your clock by those Bible verses. I hated them, but it was one of the things I'd learned to endure in my first two weeks there.

With the diarist I'd fallen into a hole. At the School-house I had to step down into it. That first morning a woman came out to fetch me, took me to an empty bedroom. 'You're to dry out in here,' she said. 'Then the old Slapper will want a word.' That was the first time I blessed my eyes on Sal. A gleam of shaved head and a wink of gold ear-drops. Elbows jutting.

My own breath knifed me into the pillow, coughing.

By the time Sal came back, night had fallen. Nothing showed in the doorframe but the lights of her eyes, her cigar. Black skin through a scarf of smoke.

I've lost her. I turned over, tried to scrabble back into sleep.

'Oh, no. Up you get.'

'I can't. I can't . . .'

'Girl.' Her voice floating above me. 'You thought it was a question?' Even with my eyes closed I could feel her staring. 'You going have to make yourself useful or make yourself scarce.'

But she let me stay put. Through the shakes, the terrible needles pricking my flesh. Laudanum can be pure bliss going in, yet it's nothing but pain to rid yourself of it. I vomited, I sweated, I slept. Each time I woke I barely knew my own name. You wouldn't wish it on a dog you were *trying* to kill. I heard Sal come and go, felt her hands. A week of that and you could say I was weaned, in the sense that the drug made me sick even to think of it. But I couldn't cure myself of the longing to go back. Not even Sal could help with that. Memory was a hook, twisted in my gut.

Now I was well again, and working. Sal came into my room, as was her habit every morning. She perched on the tub, and lifted one of my feet into her hands. But she took one look at my face, clucked her tongue, and dropped it. 'You still fretting about you white woman?'

She hated when I spoke of Madame, so I didn't answer her, but rose instead, flooding the rug, pulled on my dressing-gown. From the window, I could see Mrs Slap. Bible in hand, black-bonneted, fat. Wide everywhere except her eyes, which she narrowed at me, then at the street. '*Whosoever shall be ashamed of me and my words in this adulterous and sinful generation,*' she called out, '*of him also shall the Son of Man be ashamed!*'

To the neighbours, Mrs Slap was Mrs Austen, a widow from Cornwall. We were her darky maids, Sally and Frances. I still thought it a miracle that she'd said I could stay, which made Sal laugh. 'Don't mistake that for charity. You going earn her plenty. White coves go mad for nigger gals! Two things they can't get enough of. Flogging. Them all raised up on it. They get the taste in school and then for ever after either got to be giving a whipping or getting one. And sugar. The browner the better. And you a mulatta to boot!'

After my bath, Sal and I went for a walk. Some days, all the beauty in London is right above your head. We walked from Cleveland Street to Oxford Street to New Bond Street. I made up stories out of the signboards for Sal's amusement. Hemp bags plump with coins swung next to geese laying golden eggs. There were gilt-edged purses, pewter ships rocking on black oceans, clerks with backs curved like quills. Bare-chested mermaids. Greed and gold and lust. The smells of hot chestnuts and ginger and melting butter swelled around us. Sunlight scrubbed everything clean. Our own chatter blended with the jangle of the hawkers and pedestrians. Some heads turned, but we paid them no mind. The day was too beautiful.

I smoothed my hands along the waistline of my new dress, a pink satin with black rosettes. It was the first thing I'd bought for myself. Sal wore her golden ear-bobs, shaped like conch shells, brown kid breeches and a crimson bandeau around her head. We stopped to buy chestnuts and, when we turned around, stepped right into a man waiting in line. Fat, a gut like the prow of a ship, a thin straggle of beard. 'Savages,' he muttered. 'No room in this country for the likes of you.'

Sal stopped, elbows akimbo. '*More* than enough room. Maybe it's *you* taking up too much.'

He spat. 'Nothing but savages and whores.'

'Says a man who only got him own well-larded palm to keep company with.'

By now she'd attracted a crowd, and was drawing laughter out of them, too, and that got him angry. Aflame, beetroot, he pushed his face towards hers. Beak to beak, like fighting cocks. 'I don't have to stand for this from some nigger,' he said, 'come here to eat the bread of idleness.'

'*Sal.*' I pulled at her. 'Sorry,' I said. Held my hands up. I could feel all eyes on us.

Around the corner, she turned on me. Our good mood vanished, like soap suds in a drying sun. 'Why you say sorry to him?'

'You always start trouble.'

'Me? I was walking.' She sucked her teeth. 'And you? You always looking at clouds and tripping over you own damn feet. Just like a house-nigger.'

The words were like a slap. So much like something Phibbah might have said. 'Sal –' I said.

She spat. 'You might be 'shamed of me. But that's 'cause you got white hopes. I got *Negro* expectations.' She turned on her heels. 'And stop following me. I not you mother.'

Sal's words smacked Phibbah's voice right back into my head: *What that gal say only vex you 'cause you know is true. You a house-nigger. You thought that made you better off, and now you not so sure. Tell the truth. All your palabber, only to still end up right here? Right where you already were. You get your precious freedom, and is it any better for you than being a slave?* Her voice was lodged in my throat. Memories scraping at me.

I think that's why I did what I did.

Chapter Thirty-Five

Sometime towards the end of my first week at the School-house, Mrs Slap had sent for me to meet her in the library. Yes, there was a library there, too. Full of books I'd never seen in any other. Boileau's *Histoire des Flagellants*. *A Treatise of the Use of Flogging*. I found her writing up her ledgers. Any time I saw Mrs Slap she was holding the Bible or one of her ledgers. Ten thousand a year, in a good year, the other girls had told me.

She held up a finger for me to wait, and only when she was good and done did she set down her pen, give me a hard stare. Carrying on with her sums in her head, no doubt. Pounds of flesh, my weight in coins.

There was still that sour taste in my mouth, dregs of the drug and the vomit. I licked my lips, and said nothing.

'Here's the most important thing you need to know while you're here. In this trade, and in *this* branch of the trade, there's only one way for a girl to thrive. And that's by learning to judge a man's appetites. Now, some of it's more than enough to turn your stomach, I grant you, but who are we to stop a man's nastiness if it's his own self he wants it done to? No. That's not for you to judge. But! You give them just enough. Let them think they're getting as much as they want. It's up to you to see the line. Save them from their nastier appetites.' She gave the quill feather a long stroke, same way you'd go about trying to raise a man's flag. '*However*. It *is* for us to judge what is appetite and what is thirst. *Appetite* is what we cater to, here. Thirst? No. *Thirst* will make you claw out your own throat. Thirst will get my house shut down.'

I nodded, swaying, the shelves blurred. 'Yes. I understand. His *appetites* are fair game, not his thirsts.'

'His?' She threw back her head and laughed. 'His? But . . . I wasn't talking about his thirst, girl. I was talking about *yours*.'

The coves went by first names only. Henry was one of my regulars. Drooping jowls and a mouth as small as a mustard seed. For all I knew, he could have been the Archbishop of Canterbury.

I did know what he liked. Being birched, whipped, flogged, stung with nettles, swaddled, holly-brushed. Kissing my feet while I lay back on the chaise; being taken over my knee for doing his sums incorrectly; being paraded downstairs in nothing but a corset and kid slippers. Sal said he surely had to be a lawyer or a priest.

Men like him were the ones who wanted scarring, always happier to let themselves loose under the whip hand of a black. That put the white girls' noses out of joint. But we'd already been in the bondage business, no matter that it had been at the other end.

The School-house was brightest after dark. All the sconces lit, all the girls scraping themselves out of bed, or back in from wherever they'd been. The light scattered like water from a pail, shining the drapes, beeswax masking the smell of sweat. Henry was my visitor for the evening. I stripped his clothes, made him wear the frilled apron, stand at the grate where I could keep an eye on him. I made my voice harsh. 'No costume tonight. You going take me as you find me.'

Henry wanted me to sound 'African'. The more African, the better, he always said. I heard his breath catch. 'What're you going to do to me?'

I shrugged.

This is all the freedom there is, I thought. *Take it where you find it, or you don't get it at all.*

The smell coming off him. Salt, sharp. There was a whine in his voice. '*Miss Fran? What are you going to do to me?*'

'What?' I wondered aloud.

I'd taken the birch out of the bucket where it had been soaking. There'd be a sting in it. I tapped it into my opposite palm.

Raised my hand.

And then the clock slid down into some deep hole. Black. Blank. Sticky as coal-tar.

I heard steps running upstairs, down the hall, outside my door. Boots. Keys.

One moment, I raised my hand and next moment Henry was being carted away by Mrs Slap, and there was that hot blister through me all over again. Like the drug.

Then it was me who had to wait. I crossed the red carpet. A churning in my stomach. Not so much that I had shocked myself. No. It was that I'd thought maybe it was coming back. The old violence. The blood on my hands. In my mind's eye, I saw Paradise. I saw the coach-house.

I heard the door open, heard the creak of the bed, and looked behind me. Sal.

I pressed my brow to the glass. A carriage pulled up outside.

'My head hurts,' I said.

Sal gave out her coconut-husk laugh. 'Not as much as his back.'

'It's like they expect us just to pass through like shadows,' she said to me later. We were in her bed. She'd taken my head into her lap and was plaiting my hair into rows. 'Just don't make no fuss. Don't let them know we here. Is *them* bring us here yet still they act like we just come to eat up them little white babies! That's what the real trouble is, you know.' She laughed. 'White babies. No African better get in the milk, not even one drop. Maybe one day this whole place full of mongrels like you.'

Sal had said sorry for calling me a house-nigger, I'd said sorry for being one, made her laugh.

'What do you think Mrs Slap will do?'

'Some questions don't have right answers. Just have to wait and see.'

'Wait and see is the trouble,' I replied. 'We're always waiting and seeing.'

She finished up the last row, palmed her hand down over my brow. My scalp tingled under her hand.

'My old master brought me to England too, you know. I ever told you? Is like them *trying* them damnedest to make sure we all have the same story.' Her face moved like water as she spoke. 'We hardly even reach good when that old bastard cock up him toes. The landlady turn me out, though the rent was paid in advance.'

Before they came, the summer she turned sixteen, he had sold Sal's children out from under her to pay off some card-game debt. Three of them, the smallest only ten months. She dreamed of killing him. She supposed they were *his* children too, though he never saw it that way. Then one day he came to her and said he needed to see a man about a dog, in England – something to do with his no-good grown children – and couldn't do without her.

'So. We come here. Apoplexy give me my free paper. And there I am. Right out on the streets. I ask myself, *What now?* And then I hear the answer, plain as day: *Sally Beckwith, no more buckra massa going pull you out the cane-piece and fuck you for free and then make you take the shame of it and the blame of it.*'

Next morning, I couldn't eat. My own nerves flavoured the bread sour, turned the coffee solid in my throat. The faces of the other girls danced around the table, wild-eyed. 'You'll be all right, Fran,' they said. Their laughs still came easy. But the truth was, no one knew what would happen to me, and the only reason for them being awake so early was because they wanted to find out. I sat tall, drumming my fingers. Sooner or later everybody's luck turns bad. Sal reached under the table, patted my knee. 'You be *all right*,' she mouthed.

Mrs Slap was in her library, having a smoke. She laughed, as soon as I went in, flicked a spear of ash into her tray. 'I see you *have* gone dark,' she said. 'But we've had a request, not a complaint. Seems *your* thirsts quench his. Lucky for you. He wants more of the same, every Saturday, usual time. And try not to kill him.'

She waved a hand; smoke closed around her like fog.

So, far from being turned out, I became *notorious*. As Sal was fond of saying, I had to beat the customers away after that. (Ha!) Everybody wanted Ebony Fran. The African savage.

Her specialities were the ones who wanted scarring.

Chapter Thirty-Six

After a week or two, I was the only one who still fretted about those minutes, like something that had rolled under a bed. That time when my head had gone dark and filled with blood. What terrified me was that the world hadn't so much fallen *away* as fallen into place. That I was the one submitting, even when it was I who wielded the whip. For all those weeks, I lived in terror of closing my eyes. Whenever I did, there was the coach-house, burning to the ground, and me standing inside it, my hands moving, but the rest of me stuck in mud. At Paradise, time began and ended with the scalpel in my hand. In between, it seeped black. And it had been the same blackness with Henry; that very blackness you say I must use *now*, as the cornerstone of my defence. Telling me to say it must have been the drug, since I couldn't have been in my right mind, if I killed them as they say I did.

I don't want to say it, because I am terrified it might be true. I know that memories hide sometimes for the simple reason that we could not bear their weight. That sometimes it's mercy that unwinds the clock.

When night comes now, it's black as a rotted tooth, and I dream her into it. I hear her voice: *Death is the only thing that scares me now.* I see Benham shouting, and hear myself shouting too. Though that part isn't a dream, but shreds of memory, torn from a black cloth.

But, in time, thoughts of what I'd done to Henry faded. I settled to my work. Five months I stayed. I got used to being with the other girls when the house was empty, playing at Loo and cribbage in the corridors, leaning against the walls, or sitting on the velvet settees in the parlour before it filled, watching the fire. Small threads of happiness. Come morning that whole corridor was a dawn chorus. Girls calling down for their ewers of vinegar and their gin. Seven of them, all waiting for Martha. I had a sheaf of paper I'd bought myself at Wickstead's, though all I did was stare at it, spent so long thinking *what* to write I never wrote anything. Eating breakfast with the others, from the same table where someone had been served up for the customers' dinner the night before. It could feel almost like a little family, if you ignored the Berkley horse in the attic, the planks nailed together with leather straps, and the human skeleton in one of the kitchen cupboards that had been bought from resurrectionists.

But that happier part of me strayed back to knit itself to the broken part. Like a cracked but still-living bone. Madame was a door that wouldn't stay closed; I thought of her so often that when one of the other girls said the name 'Benham' one morning, pointing at a newspaper cartoon, I thought for a moment it was I who'd said it, and slung my hand up to my mouth. But it turned out Benham had written a 'biographical sketch of his friend, John Langton', which made the pair of them sound as saintly as chicks just hatched. That made me laugh, and so did the word 'friend'. Then I looked closer and saw the announcement. Langton was dead. The news scrubbed my mind clean, like windows flung wide to let in air. Everything went black. I had to steady myself against the table before I could read on. In spite of their public differences, the celebrated natural philosopher and diarist George Benham would deliver the eulogy. When I read that aloud, the girl laughed too. 'Oh, I know *him*,' she said.

'*Langton?*'

'No, the other one.'

Sometimes, she said, when you whip a cove, pain goes inside them, and hooks their secrets right out.

But it wasn't Benham I was concerned with then. The awful clock of Langton's heart had stopped. He'd outlived his doctor and, now, a twin misfortune: he'd been survived by his own ambitions. *Crania* was to be published after all, in the light of the interest stirred up by the author's death. But I took some small pleasure in knowing he hadn't lived to see it. Later that morning, Sal propped herself on my pillows to listen to the details about the funeral. Miss-bella had been still in Jamaica and unable to attend. It had been a sudden death; the body had tripped a chambermaid bringing fresh sheets. Apoplexy. 'Your old bastard get the same damn death as mine!' Sal cried.

She knew better than to ask me how I felt about any of it. And I knew better than to tell her.

Even now, writing of it, I'm afflicted with some queer feeling that goes right through my spine. I fear to write about it. You will judge me for it. How could you not? The news cast me down, same way thinking about it casts me down now. One part of what I was feeling was regret.

He should have died before now, I thought, *and I should have been the one to kill him.*

The next day, work done for the night, Sal and I went down to Hyde Park Corner, to one of the kitchen stalls. We bought saveloys, and ham sliced right off the pig, took our food to eat in the park. My satin skirts trailed behind us, and so did Sal's laugh, a scurry of fresh mint from the single leaf she chewed after smoking. If Sal had known what I was thinking, she'd have boxed my ears. Because I was wondering if *she* was there. Would I see her? Would I turn a corner on one of the paths, and find her there? It was the thing I wanted most, yet feared even more.

I leaned over for a bite of ham, which was hot and salty and coated my fingers with grease. 'Sal. Do you know anything about George Benham?'

'George Benham.' She swung her head towards me. 'Why you ask?'

'I worked for him. That's where I came from.'

'That's who your old bastard gave you away to?'

'Do you know him?'

She sucked on her cigar. 'And *that*'s who you white woman is.'

Something was hovering on her lips, and I had to wait for it. Her smoke stung my eyes and I fiddled with a button on my boot. 'Don't know much about George Benham,' she said at last, 'except to know if that's where you was, you better off here.'

She ground her cigar out under her heel. 'Saw *her*. Once.'

'*What*? Where?'

She laughed. 'Settle yourself! Not yesterday. I went to the fisticuffs. It was just before you came. Laddie Lightning was fixing to break his knuckles on one a *their* champs. Name slips me. Some big, lardy fellow. Drew all the niggers like flies, a course.'

'I must have been under a bridge at the time,' I said, trying to raise a laugh, drown out his name.

'*Oho*. You missed *something*. He jumped them ropes afterwards, words flying, spit flying. Blood just lashing off him. But then him just stop – *braps* – and bow, like so. Like him lifting a hat . . . but him never have no hat. Him staring at somebody. Everybody turn see who. Was like him put footlights on her. She the only white woman up front. Wearing some head-wrap, like she fooling a soul. She shook her head at him, then she left. But she was all the talk afterwards.' She gave me a look. 'That's how I knew who she was.'

I twisted my hands into the grass. 'Well. What were they saying?'

A pause. 'Nothing kind.'

'What did *he* say?'

'Who? Lightning?'

'Yes. To her.'

She looked up at the sky, dark as her cigar ash, stars simmering through the trees. Then she brushed down her skirts, sucked her teeth. 'I never hear any of it.'

Chapter Thirty-Seven

Though it was Madame I craved news of, I learned more about Benham at the School-house than in all the time I lived under his nose. If I think about him now, I think about all those words he wrote, scrubbing his own history sure as Pru scrubbed his floors. And that eulogy, saying that though he might have differed with his great friend on the *answer* to the slavery question, they were united in seeing it as the cement of England's fortunes. They agreed that the Negro had a natural place, they simply disagreed about how to treat him while he was in it. Benham himself would be quickest to tell you he campaigned for improvements, let *me* sit at his own table, cut the cord with Langton, who was despicable in truth (though he let *him* sit at his table too). But there's a split in the minds of men like him, because it's also true that he once told me he might not want to abuse his Negroes, but neither did he want to marry them, and that this world was built on slavery, from pyramids to plantations, that we're all members of the same human species; nevertheless there is a hierarchy of men.

'At least,' Langton used to say, 'I put my hands right down in that dirt beside a nigger. I walk through that same dirt bare-foot beside him, too. Before I make him cut my cane.'

Who's to say which of them was God, and which the Devil? Or whether they were both devils or both gods. They both owned slaves, and no man can be virtuous who does.

Whenever I write about Benham, I remember something you said about the arsenic, the receipt from Apothecary Jones that Jessop waved at the jurors, how you argued that it was like Cobbett's red herring, drawn across the path to put the hounds off the scent. But the same could be said of Benham and Langton, too. They were savages, yet it's *my* so-called savagery that's being drawn across the path now, leading everyone away from theirs.

Benham's eyes had become as raw-rimmed as my own before I left, as if he, too, had fallen under the spell of some drug. Keeping to those night-time hours of his. The truth is, there was less to George Benham than met the eye. Spying on *her*, asking me to spy too, when all along he was the one who needed watching. Yet nobody was watching him.

I took the newspapers every morning. And Langton wasn't the only ghost to find his way to me by that route. One morning it was raining, so there was no chance of a walk. I took my bread up to my room, with a scoop of jam, and an apricot fancy for Sal. She brought her little mirror, and propped it on my mantel while she shaved her head. I watched her smooth soap across her scalp, crooning some tune under her breath. Then I looked down at the paper and the shock climbed up into my throat.

'What happen?' Sal said. 'You see duppy?'

The nose was wrong. Too harsh, too narrow. She'd curled her hair into those fat swinging sausages they had all wanted that Season. 'It's *her*,' I said. 'Says here she was trying to swim in the fountain. At Almack's. Do you know Almack's? Finally gone and got herself banned.'

But already I was skimming the remaining lines, tripping over my breath. She'd had Laddie, then the drug, then me. What did she have now? The drug again, I thought. Only the drug. She'd sworn she had *not* been trying to swim, that the patronesses were simply looking for scandal, *anything* to give their tedious little Assemblies a thrill. I didn't notice until I straightened that Sal had stilled, razor pinched between two fingers. 'Fran. I done. You hear me? Done, done, done. I done talking about you white woman, and all them white people you left behind. *You* should be too.' I watched her, and swung my jaw shut. 'If you count losses all the time,' she said, turning back to the mirror, 'losses be all you have.'

What had I lost?

Two faces pressed together in the dark. Small embers of breath. The feeling that here was all my happiness at last.

Some things are always better done by someone else, like pulling teeth. I needed someone to thread twine between my heart and the door handle. Two mornings later, I shoved a fist under my pillow and crossed the hall. Sal was still in bed, smoking, a tray propped on her knees. Each morning she made Martha bring her whatever puddings and jellies had been left in the dessert bowls the night before, and a single cigar. She said she felt not an ounce of guilt about the sugar. 'It surely better to eat than make.'

It was always warm in Sal's room. Mrs Slap had put a marble surround in there at the fireplace, with laughing cherubs carved into it, and there was a rose-pink settee in one corner, beside Sal's paddling bench. Even Sal looked softer in there, her face smudged with sleep. I handed her the clipping, folding the page away from me.

'You kep' this?' Her mouth shrank like a thirsty flower. 'You love to pull pain right off the goddamn shelf.'

'Seems so.'

'All right.' She looked up at me. 'What I suppose to do with it?'

'Burn it.'

Five months. Through September, through the drying leaves, then the falling ones. I stayed to watch London moving towards dark winter again.

I'm close now to having to write about all those things I wish I could forget, yet I can *only* write about them, for there are some things I will never be able to say out loud. Now, I must come full circle. Departure to return. But what I haven't told you yet is that Mr Benham sought to turn me out again, the very day he was killed. And that I argued with him, not just with her.

But, first, I must return.

One night, I found someone waiting in the Scarlet Room I'd never have expected. Not in a month of Sundays.

'How'd you –' I reached behind me for the knob. But then I tightened my shoulders. 'Hello, Pru.'

'How are you, Frances?' She cut her eyes around the room. Mantel to bath to bed, and back again. She clutched a reticule to her chest. She'd dressed like it was an afternoon off. A grey muslin with a yellow stripe. *I get every afternoon off now, Pru.*

'Madame sent me.'

'So I see.' And it rattled me like a door on a latch. 'You want to sit?'

'Oh, no, I –' She laughed, looked down at the bed, took a little step back. 'I'd better not, hadn't I?'

'Suit yourself.'

She gave me a thin smile.

'You must take me as you find me, Pru.'

'I know.' She drummed her fingers against the purse.

'Well?'

'Madame's sick.'

'She can cure herself by leaving that vial alone.'

'You *have* turned stony. I thought you cared for her.'

'And *I* thought there's no such thing as friendship for the likes of us.'

'Maybe.' She frowned. 'But there *is* such a thing as decency.'

She set a folded paper on the bed, turned to go. 'She said to give you that.'

The seal. Her initials. MD. And the *fleur-de-lis* pressed into blood-red wax. A letter. From her: *I am unwell. And I fear only you can make me better. And I am sorry. I was mad for you once and ever will be. Will you come back? Please come. Ritte*

'Will there be any answer?'

'No, Pru. No answer.'

But after she left, my hand shook so I could barely hold the page.

And, oh, in spite of myself, I was glad.

Levenhall
January 1826

Chapter Thirty-Eight

I climbed the stairs, snicked the latch, opened the door. There, half shadowed, head tucked onto her hands, just as I had pictured her a thousand times, there she was. My thoughts made flesh.

I crept around the bed. She was asleep, so I gazed my fill. Paced footsteps into the carpet. Bed to mantel to bed. Nerves all pins and needles, and heart pacing in its own cage. Her face was pinched in sleep, fluttering the sheets with hot breath. Drapes closed thick at the windows. The red cabinets were unlatched. No sign of any amber bottles.

I needed to busy myself. I sorted her books into piles on the tea-table and the desk, matched a glove on the mantel to one below the bed. I emptied dead roses from the vase, swept blackening petals into my palm, folded her kimono. I couldn't stop myself searching the writing desk. Nothing from *him*. There was a strange smell, blood-sweet, though I'd cleared out the roses. The air was stale, and heavy on my skin. All the while she drew hitching breaths and did not wake.

I circled the room and couldn't find my bearings. I sat, stood, sat again, until finally I stood and just stared at the woman in red.

When I drew back the drapes, she finally came to. 'Frances! You got my letter? Is it truly you?'

'Are you ill?'

She hesitated. 'Only tired.'

'I came to see how you fare. If you're well, I'll leave.'

'Are we not friends any more?'

'You turned me out.'

'Oh, I *have* wished for you to come back.' She drew herself up against the headboard, rubbed at her mouth. Her hair was knotted like the veins on an old woman's legs. I had to stop myself reaching for the brush. Perhaps the smell was coming from her. She looked fevered, unwashed. She drew the sheet to her chin. 'You are so changed.'

I curled my hands. *You are not.*

I emptied her pot into the night-soil bin, rinsed it outside. The kitchen was empty but there was a loaf set on the counter, warm as a new babe. I took down the breadknife and cut a slice, fetched some cheese from the cold larder, cut an apple in half. I found some cold tongue under a towel and I cut a slice of that as well, set it on a plate with the bread and cheese and some green olives.

Pru came in out of the scullery, carrying a clutch of Madame's evening dresses, and took such a fright on seeing me that she dropped them. But her smile ran out quick as a flag up a pole. 'Frances! You came. I knew you would.'

'What's all this?' I pointed upstairs.

'Told you. Another of her spells. This time, Mr Benham says she mustn't be disturbed. Not even to clean.'

Benham had been the one to open the door, which had jangled me. *I know things about you,* I thought, on coming face to face with him again. I'd gone there armed with my new knowledge, ready to use it if I had to, force him to let me in, but when Linux came up, dusting her hands on her apron, he'd told her sternly that I was to be allowed to stay. Her face shuttered, and she scuttled back downstairs. He blinked at me.

'I'm here to see Madame,' I said, lifting my chin.

He shook his head. 'You will find her changed.'

She vomited as soon as I unwrapped the food, though I couldn't say I blamed her. I held the pot under her chin until she finished.

She slumped her head over it, tapped her thumbs, made it ring like tin.

'This is not the drug,' she blurted, wiping at her lips. 'I am weaning myself.'

'Oh.' I thought back to my nights on the streets, and with Sal. 'You'll need water.'

'I'll need brandy.' She gave a weak laugh.

Her face went dark, and her eyes too, and she turned them to me. She let the sheet fall. 'Oh, Frances, darling Frances,' she whispered. 'Something terrible.'

I turned away.

If she needs me, I cannot stay away. That's what I'd told Sal, and she'd got up and walked out without another word, not even to say goodbye.

A sick feeling tickled at my stomach. '*This* is why you sent for me.'

'I sent for you because you are dear to me, because –' I went to the bedside table and swirled brandy into her glass, swallowed down that drink and poured another. She watched me. Set the basin aside and gripped her hands. '– because you are dear to me. I do not know what to say,' she said.

'You are not ill.' All I could see was the swollen lip of belly under the nightdress.

'*Non.*' She twisted her lips.

Brandy burned the back of my throat. Then the thought struck me. My lips went cold. *Of course.* Whose it was. I turned. 'Does Mr Benham know?'

I helped her into the bath. My nails scraped along her spine, thin as a string of pearls, her shoulder blades pressing the skin of her back. I was shocked at how she'd dwindled. Everywhere except her round belly, she was skin knocking against bone. Clear skin. The truth between two people is a slow poison, though I'd say that love is even worse. The truth dribbled out between us then.

It had been the drug, she said. After I'd left, she took more and more. As many as eighty, ninety, one hundred grains. It's a wonder she hadn't died. A pity, I thought. A blink of hate. It had taken only weeks for her to recognize herself as a true opium-eater. Even then, she couldn't stop herself. She started to eat it raw, and it had made her fevered, and mad. As deranged as any Bedlamite. She remembered hardly any of it. Her memories of that time were all noise and light, shapes and shadows. Several times she'd thought she heard me calling her name, or answering when she cried out to me. Sometimes she'd thought she saw me at the writing desk.

She tried to turn around, look at me, but I pushed her back. I lifted the pitcher, poured water over the hard shell of her belly, over her pink nipples, over her skin in private floods.

'It was only once. I went to see him, because I had no one else. And he was my friend, once.' She went in the carriage, swore Charles to secrecy. She needed help . . . she thought . . . she thought . . . she didn't think. 'Everyone had accused us already . . .'

'*He* didn't notice?'

She looked to the door. 'He only *notices* when my misbehaviour scales the walls and makes news that gets back to him. And you had left me . . .'

'*You* turned me out.'

'Turned you out?' She twisted, still trying to catch my eye, and again I held her at bay, feeling once more all the wretched agony of that afternoon. '*Non! You* said you were leaving, Frances. Remember? You told Mr Benham. I was upset, because of what I found, but I would not have turned you out.'

I sat back on my haunches. My head spun. Remembering the bluster I'd felt, thinking I could just walk out and fend for myself. The echo of her shouts. 'We remember it differently,' I said.

She shook her own head, her back quivering under the washcloth. 'All that time . . .'

'I found your letters, you know. I found them that afternoon.'

'Letters?'

'From him.' His name sticks in my throat. I can't say it. 'You kept them. In your egg-chest. It's the only reason I wrote what I did for Mr Benham. I shouldn't have. I should have torn it up. I would not have given it to him.'

She fell quiet, drew her knees close, and spoke her next words to the water. 'Those were letters between friends. I admired him, yes. But as a *friend*. How can I explain it? He made something so extraordinary of himself –'

I snorted. 'A man. I know, I know. He made a man of himself. Because he *is* a man. And free to make of himself whatever he wants.'

'But – Fran – you know that is not quite true. He was only a child when Mr Benham brought him here. Then he was like a son to me. My greatest shame is not that I proved them right, but that I proved *myself* wrong. You will not forgive me. He will not forgive me either. When I went to see him, it was as if there was something in him that wanted to wound me . . .'

That was all she gave by way of explanation. It was not enough, but I can never hope for more. Loneliness drove her to him. Loneliness drove her always. She hadn't known what to do. She'd called for me. Even in her sleep, she called for me. I was the only true friend she had. Finally, it had been Laddie himself who'd told her what he'd heard on the streets about Ebony Fran, and where to find me.

Sending for me was not friendship, I thought.

She said no more, only sat forward, her back curved as a blade. A blade that should have finished me there and then, had it been merciful.

Look at you, said my own voice, close at my ear. *Look where you are. Back on your knees.*

I pushed away, to my feet. Water splashing. I was picturing it. The rotted-fruit smell of Laddie's rooms. The baby, curled in the dark like a wet fist. 'First thing a baby do is wring you inside out,' Phibbah used to say. 'Then it spend the rest of its life wringing you outside in.' I set down the cloth, left her to dry herself.

Looking at her put a sour taste in my mouth. When she stood at the mirror, one hand curved careless, nails ragged and torn, looking at herself and worrying, I turned away. It was *she* who told me to tell Linux that now I was there she was not to be disturbed. That I would tend her, bring up her trays. She wrung her hands and kept her eyes fixed on the door, as if she thought we were being watched. But Benham never showed his face, the rest of that afternoon. He stayed in his library. Deep in his work, Linux said. 'He's almost there. Pulling the real meat out of his raw material. And you choose *this* time to bring your disturbance to his door.'

If she *was* weaning herself, I saw no signs of it. It was her nerves, she said. Needing the steadying hand of the drug. I needed it too. Craved it. All that night opium fever moved through her and, at times, it clutched at my hand and said all manner of unspeakable things. *I could come back with you, Frances, I could keep it –*

I went cold. In my mind's eye, I saw a little mulatta girl, dandled on my knee.

'No.' I made myself say it quickly, shook my head. Some things are not possible in this world. Some women are born knowing that, some have to learn. Oh, but I should have said yes. I know that now. *Come, my love, come with me, come what may.* Isn't that how they'd have it in a novel or a romance?

Mr Casterwick came up to say Benham wanted her downstairs in the parlour. I followed her down, thinking I'd see about making her some tea. But I crept back, put my ear to the door. Snatches of talk. Loose threads. *Why can I not do it in my own time? . . . Please, let me . . . do it on my own . . . You stifle me with –* And then, only mumbling.

In the kitchen, the heat was stifling. I sat at the table to wait for the kettle and felt it like wet muslin over my face. The room was empty. My head filled with thoughts of what he could want with her. I hadn't been there longer than a few minutes when Linux came in, knocked her boots against the jamb, and unknotted the strings of her bonnet. I coughed to make sure she looked up and saw me. When she did, her scars flared red. 'You.' She glanced at the stove. 'What's the water for?'

'Tea.'

'For her?'

'Who else?'

'What's the matter with her?'

'What do you mean?'

'It's been three weeks now since she left that room. If it's as bad as all that, we must send for Dr Fawkes.'

'She doesn't want the doctor.'

'Then why are her doors locked? It's always when you're in this house that it fills with secrets.'

Before I could answer, Mr Casterwick came to the door. 'Mr Benham requests that you join them upstairs.'

She sat on the blue sofa with her hands crab-clawed in her lap. I tried to catch her eye, but she looked away. I couldn't tell anything from the set of her mouth, but I could from the way she refused to look at me. 'Come in,' he said. His face was tight and he jerked his neck, so it clicked forward; the knob in his throat slid up and down. 'Sit.' I went to the window bench. My old seat. Outside, a liquid earth, wet and green. The light fading. He waited for Mr Casterwick to shut the door. 'I've been speaking with my wife.' Her hands twitched. Laudanum shakes.

I pressed my hands into the bench. 'You told him?'

He laughed. 'Why do you think I allowed you back, *knowing where you've been?*'

Nausea. A vinegar wave from gut to mouth. My mind swung. I had to shake my head to make myself pay attention.

'. . . take the child.'

'*What?*'

'Those are the conditions on which you have been allowed back.' He swivelled his head to her. 'On which Marguerite will be allowed to stay . . .'

I scraped up a laugh. '*She* asked me back.'

Still she would not look at me.

'I've asked my man of affairs to find a house,' he continued. 'It will be . . . discreet. You'll be given a character. A lifetime annuity. Do you know what that means? Enough to set you up somewhere, pay for its upkeep. *More* than you'd need in a lifetime. Afterwards, you'll stay there. She'll come back.'

'You're asking . . . ?'

'You'll take the child and raise it.'

I looked at him. How the world bends to the will of some men. I remembered what Sal had said, on my last day at the School-house: 'You better not be thinking about going back. To *her*? How what she do you any different to what massa do any of the rest of us? I don't care *what* she wants. Couldn't be any good. You know it, too. Don't just go running. *Don't do it.*'

I turned to her. '*You* want me to take it?'

I wanted her to look at me and tell me she was sorry. But she twisted her face and slid her palms up and down on her skirts, and said nothing.

'And do what with it?'

Benham shrugged. 'What do you mean, gel? Whatever you want. It'll be nothing to do with us.'

Every part of me was screaming against it.

Knowing where you've been.

When I looked up, he'd gone to stand behind her at the sofa, and it was as if I stared at a high blue wall behind which stood the pair of them. I felt a pang, a terrible hunger. I felt soiled. *Knowing where you've been.* I shook my head. 'Now you *both* want me to wash away your sins.'

He worked a smile onto his mouth but it did not go there willingly and she kept gulping and gulping, and I turned blindly, straight into a little table. One of the room's numberless crystal vases dropped, and shattered.

When we were alone again in her room, she broke apart, too, like a bundle of firewood. She took my hands. 'Do not worry about the vase,' she said. She brought her face close, raised a hand to my cheek. 'I am sorry, Frances. He said he would divorce me. I had no *choice*. Oh, I hate him.'

I felt a lurch of anger; it flipped inside me like a tail. 'It's the Garden of Eden, then,' I said. 'It is *Paradise Lost*. You will be the fallen angel.' I laughed bitterly. 'And then you'll have to join me in the streets.'

Words kept tumbling out of her like stones. 'Do not be so cruel.'

'You are singing a different tune. *Yesterday* –'

'Yesterday was madness talking.'

'It could only have been madness. What else could it have been?' I raised my voice.

A bow of silence, pulled tight. *She swings back and forth on this, same as with everything else*, I thought.

She let her hand drop. 'Will you do it?'

Before I could answer, before I could *know*, there came a knock at the door. Linux pushed past me when I answered it. She looked ill herself, her face pebbled by the scars. She must know something of what it's like, I thought then, for the mere act of showing your face to the world to make you feel shrunken, and small.

She had a tray in her hands, a single glass. 'Mrs Benham,' she said, 'the parlour has been swept now. You're not to worry.'

'Thank you.'

'If you are not well –'

'You are mistaken, Mrs Linux.'

'I've brought you water.' She swayed. I stood by the mantel, breathing hard, and she flicked her eyes over me too. 'You *do* seem fevered. I can't see why the master won't just send for Dr Fawkes.'

Madame rose from her chair and held her shawl tight around her and made her voice sharp. 'Mrs Linux. I do not want your help or your presence.'

'No.' She blinked, scuttled forward, set down the tray. 'No. No. Very well.'

I heard her shoes clacking away down the hall after she closed the door and wished I could follow her.

Rain shook like a gourd, rattled at the windows. It was damp, again, and grew colder and colder. That night she woke weeping. Bursts of memory, and remorse. 'What have I brought on myself?' She drank more and more laudanum, licked constantly at her dry lips. Her skin felt warm. I drank too. It went back in easy as water. That is a thirst that never goes away. Opium rowed me across black oceans, back to the guinea grass and the cottonwood and the coach-house. I saw the lines of people, waiting. I saw myself, holding a little blade. I saw blood.

As she slept, I lit a candle and went to the shelves and took out her books, one after another, and tried to read, but the fog in my head wouldn't let me. The glass was fogged, too, with rain and cold. I sat beside her. Time was moving away from us as it does for everything, but now it was ticking towards life as well as death.

Chapter Thirty-Nine

Benham's agent came the next morning, and sat for hours with him in the library and, after he'd left, Benham told us both that the man had secured the lease on a cottage on the coast near Cornwall. Isolated enough. They could now start to put it about that he wanted peace and quiet, and would go there to finish his *Encyclopaedia* away from the noise. Madame would go with him, to convalesce, for it was no secret she'd been unwell. They'd take no servants but me. He'd stay to see the thing done.

I let myself picture it.

'How many rooms?' I asked.

'What?'

'How many bedrooms?'

'One. I think.'

'Where would I sleep?'

He turned back to his desk, opened the cat's head and took a pinch of snuff. 'How would I know, girl? There'll be some-thing – a kitchen, I'm sure.'

Something splintered in me. I felt the sharp pain of it in my head, blinding. I blinked. I laughed. The whole time she'd sat without speaking. Now she looked up.

'What?' he said. His eyes slithered to her.

I kept mine on him. 'What about the infant?'

'Would be yours, to do with as you will.'

Her rooms spread measureless. Time did too. Grey dust over everything, twirling in the air. She wouldn't let Pru in to clean.

For a time, she neither spoke nor looked at me. I sat on the bed, she at the desk. Miles between us.

I watched her twist her hair to ropes, jerk out of her chair. A marionette. The drug. Her husband's demands. Her own confusion. Thin as a fly-leaf, with that terrible energy wicking through her.

'One of the mercies of my marriage has been to discover that I would never want *his* children. Now he tells me I must not want *this* one. But it is as if –' she stopped '– as if *this* baby has come with some trick that shows me how to want it.'

Her words went through me, my own pain so large that I hardly had room for hers.

'If my scandals stay quiet, he does not care. But the minute he decides that I am an embarrassment . . . *again*, he requires me to contain myself in my own rooms. Let things blow away. Or – how do you say? – blow *over*. He spies on me so he can know what measures to take, when. If I must go somewhere, during that time, then he sets Lady Catherine as guard dog and gaoler . . .'

I thought back to that first day, on the steps. 'And you oblige him.'

'And I oblige him! What choice do I have? He only agrees I may go out and about again eventually because otherwise the talk would be worse.' She gave a thin smile. 'When he asked you to . . . *watch* me . . . did you think he might be looking for evidence, to have me sent away?' A laugh. 'It would never be the *asylum*, not with him. Too prosaic. Too *public*. He would never want it known that his own wife had sunk so low.'

I held my tongue. She had no idea how low *he*'d sunk. The truth about George Benham would have broken her, then. I could not tell her.

'But *this*,' she continued. 'There would be no way to hide it. If I have a black child in the wake of a divorce – everyone will see *his* shame.' She looked up at me, her face green as a pear. 'Yet if he divorces me, he knows he could not control whether I had it or not. And could not be sure that I would *not*. Therefore, a new marriage pact: he will *let* me stay, but I must give it away to you. Then give *you* away.'

I shrugged. 'Well, then, leave. Have it. Why not?'

She gazed about her. The same four walls they'd always been. The same trap. And she had dragged me back into it. Hurt sometimes puts a person in a hurting mood, and I spoke harsh words, then, which I bitterly regret. But if we could make peace with the dead there'd be no cause to mourn them. I told her she was too selfish to have a child, that she was a coward, that she had brought everything on herself.

Her eyes grew dark. Nothing would calm her. She took more and more laudanum, asking me to forgive her. 'What am I going to do?' she cried. Her body clutched itself, and she went still. I was worried, thinking this might be another of her spells. Her mind travelling someplace else. Her voice grew so thin I had to strain to hear her. Did I remember, she asked, how we'd talked about what she'd take with her if she could leave? I told her we both knew she would never leave. 'You're a pendulum,' I said. Then she started trembling, and said she wanted sleep.

Through the rest of that day he came in and out of her rooms, to tell her all the things she would and wouldn't do. She was to host a soirée, plan it for the night before they left: 'Make a big show of your glowing health, play up the restoration of your spirits. Invite the cuckold-maker. Oh, yes. Invite *him*. Show everyone there's nothing wrong here. Give them Marvellous Meg.' She would be happy, she would shine. Oh, she'd better shine.

A few days later there was a soirée. But there was to be no cottage. And no baby. Only murder. And blood, so much blood.

ROBERT MEEK, sworn

I am a constable. On 27 January 1826 at approximately two o'clock in the morning I was called to Levenhall, the town residence of Mr George Benham. I was shown upstairs to the library by the house-keeper. I examined the landing minutely, and found copious marks of blood there, as well as on the floor in the library. I entered the library and discovered the body of Mr George Benham. I was then taken to Mrs Benham's bedchamber, where there were also marks of blood pres-ent, on the floor outside the door, and on the carpet inside. Mrs Benham's body was discovered in her bed. There was a large quantity of blood also in the centre of the bed. The carpet appeared wet as if attempts had been made to wash it to get out the blood. The prisoner was found asleep beside Mrs Benham's body. I was present when she was woken by the housekeeper and heard her say, 'I can't remember, I can't remember.' She said it over and over and appeared to be in a state of some distress, after which she refused to say any more.

I was told Mr and Mrs Benham had been hosting Mr Feelon and various members of a planning committee of the Anti-Slavery Soci-ety, formed by Mrs Benham to organize a debate which had taken place earlier that day at the Royal Society of Science.

I later retrieved a knife from a cabinet inside the bedchamber, which appeared to have been wiped clean, containing not a trace of blood on it. There were cold ashes in the grate. I was handed other items by the housekeeper: a receipt for arsenic made out in the name of the prisoner; a jar which had been found beside the prisoner's pallet, in the maids' bedroom upstairs, which appeared to contain a human foetus.

I found a book in the cabinet also. Paradise Lost, written by Mr John Milton. I produce the jar, the knife, the book, &c. I took the prisoner to the watch-house that morning before she was transported to Newgate. She said not a word, neither at the watch-house, nor the whole time she was being transported.

The Old Bailey
7 April 1826

Chapter Forty

Here we are, then.

Jessop, prosecuting. Stout, thin-lipped, the kind of face that would look solemn at his own wedding. I shiver. The room so vast, so crowded with the heat and smells of all those bodies, yet cushioned quiet by all the marble and velvet and brass. The sword hanging above the judge's head. The light coming spit-clear and yellow through the arched windows. Jessop swings towards the jurors, who stare like cats. He wags his jowls. He's told them about the School-house, and they've pretended shock, though gaming and whoring are the vices that feed off men like them, which is why there are a hundred prostitutes in London for every wife. He's shown them the jar, the foetus. He's reminded them that I was woken in my mistress's bed, that I had blood on my hands when I was woken, yet claim I can't remember how it got there.

'You will hear from Mrs Linux, the housekeeper at Leven hall. She'll speak to the prisoner's character –'

You leap to your feet. 'My Lord, need I remind my friend that my client's character is not to be entered into? He should know better.'

Jessop grins – small white teeth buried in his fleshy cheeks, like sugar cubes in a bun – and saunters down one end of the barristers' table. 'Of course, My Lord, of course. The rule hasn't shifted for many years, though I see the custom of hesitating to interrupt one's opening is wobbling on its feet.'

The judge chuckles and Jessop spins on his heel as if even his gown is smirking, flying up around his shins. 'The only words the prisoner spoke that night regarding the whole dreadful affair were, "I can't remember." How convenient. It would be a first in my experience – indeed, it would be a first in English *law* – were it to be so easy for a murderess to reach safe harbour simply by scrubbing clean her own devious mind.' He snaps the lapels of his black gown across his chest. 'There's the evidence, gentlemen. I daresay it needs only half of it to make the case. The prisoner was a woman from a god-forsaken place, but Mr Benham took her in anyway, gave her safe harbour. She was turned out for thieving, but she crawled back, bent on revenge, and *murdered* him, and his wife.

'It's never to be entered into lightly – condemning a prisoner to death – but if the case is proved, that will be your duty. And, though it be melancholy, you must do it. Each Englishman's house is his castle, gentlemen. Do your duty, so we may be safe in ours.'

The prisoner knows nothing of the case against her until after her trial starts. You've already told me that you'll be forced to try to cross Jessop's bridges as he's building them, and that it will be a scramble to keep up. It's not fair, of course, but there's very little that's fair about Old Bailey justice.

He calls his first witness. Dr Wilkes, the house surgeon at Westminster Hospital. Swollen chest, short legs. A bullish chin that slops over his neck-cloth. He gives me a fleeting look, turns quickly away. I'm here to be gawped at but no one can brave the sight of me for long, it seems. Turning to the jury, he tells them he's done over twenty autopsies, gives it all the slow weight of a sentence he'll no doubt have engraved on his tomb. I've opened more bodies than that, but it's prudent to keep that to myself, of course. At about four o'clock that morning, he says, he was called to Levenhall, where he examined the bodies. Mr Benham had sustained deep gashes to the upper and middle chest, and Mrs Benham the same.

He instructed the bodies to be taken to the hospital where he conducted the examinations himself, recording the cause of death in both cases as exsanguination.

'Later that day, the constable handed me a butchering knife, which he said had been recovered from a cabinet in the bedchamber. It was the same knife produced in evidence and shown to me here. I matched the blade directly to both victims' wounds.'

'Did you note anything else?'

He hesitates. 'Mrs Benham had recently been with child. There were clear signs. Enlargement of the uterus, general flaccidity, oedema of the bladder. A large corpus luteum in one of the ovaries. An apothecary's jar containing a human foetus had also been delivered to me at the hospital, and I concluded that it was in fact the product of that pregnancy, and about eighteen weeks' gestation.'

Silence follows those words. A single cough comes from high in the gallery. Pews gleam through clouds of smoke. Jessop lifts the jar. 'Is this the . . . ?'

You leap to your feet. 'My Lord! This is outrageous. What is the meaning of bringing that here?'

Jessop turns to the judge. 'I believe that's a matter for legal argument, M'Lord.'

'Which my friend knows full well is not permitted to me. But as a matter of *law*, since there isn't a single word about this on the indictment, it can have no place here. Nor, as a matter of *law*, can a foetus be murdered. That . . . thing is inadmissible.'

The judge shakes his head. 'Mr Pettigrew, you aren't alone in finding it macabre. Mr Jessop?'

'M'Lord?'

'You'd better land quickly on the point of it or I'll have it removed. We don't all have the iron stomachs of medical men.'

'Very well, M'Lord. Dr Wilkes, were you able to reach any

conclusions about how the foetus had been removed from the womb?'

He looks at me. 'It couldn't have been born alive, but that's not to say it couldn't also have fallen victim to whatever caused its mother's death. By God's hand or by a savage one.'

Jessop grimaces. 'Thank you, Dr Wilkes.'

All heads turn as you rise to your feet again. Your question comes quick and sharp. 'You say it could not have been born alive?'

'No.'

'Nor can you say how it came to be still-born?'

'Only by speculating.'

'I see. My Lord, I have no further questions.'

I give you a hard look. Is that all? I'd hoped you'd start with some clever card, some trick hidden beneath your black gown. Isn't that a lawyer's merchandise? How else will you save me? Now I feel a sprinkle of cold doubt. You shuffle through your papers as Dr Wilkes elbows out of the stand, glaring at me again as he goes. Even the judge is squinting at you. Backsides shift. Time moves as slowly as the smoke. The air is thick with noise and heat again, the buzz of discontented whispers from the gallery. This is not the meat they came for.

I have to press my tongue hard against my teeth, so I won't cry out.

But there's no time to dwell on it. Linux is next. The sight of her is like a fist to the gut. The same feeling I had that morning, hearing her cry out, '*Murder!*'

She keeps her head straight, refusing to look at me. Buttoned ankle to neck all in black, a white collar around her throat. But once she's in the stand she's hemmed in by all that wood, which gives her no choice but to face me. Accuser and accused. Her scars are red today, fat as ticks swelling with blood. She slaps her hand atop the black Bible and swears to tell nothing but the truth, *so help her God*. On her lips, it's more command than oath. She straightens her shoulders and the room goes quiet. Dread digs into me. *Now* it will really start. I slow my breaths, lean over the railing. If there's anything here that can help me, I need to find it. Any small crumb.

She says it's a mystery to her, why Benham let me stay after I came back, as well as being his own fatal mistake.

'I used to find her with the master, you know, cooped in his library alone. They would always fall silent, when I entered. Such is the way with those women, isn't it? They learn to set themselves as traps for their masters before they even come up to their knees. She had some hold over *both* of them. After she came back, the mistress kept herself in bed, claiming her head was bad, though now I know it must have been her condition . . . The prisoner wouldn't come away from the door, nor would she let anyone in. The mistress seemed agitated. I believe she was terrified of her!'

You shoot up out of your seat. 'My Lord. I object most strongly. I'm sure I don't need to state it.'

'Yes, yes, Mr Pettigrew. Mrs Linux, you must give evidence of fact. What did you see with your own two eyes?'

'I saw the mistress was afraid, sir! But when I went to the master about what was happening, he said only that the pair of them were to be left alone. That was the day of their soirée.'

'Can you tell us what happened on the night of the soirée?'

'Charles came down to the kitchen to say the prisoner was causing a commotion, so I went up. I was just in time to see her threaten Mrs Benham. She went very close to her and shouted, "This is death."'

'"This is death." You're sure?'

'Quite sure. She said it twice. And some of the ladies were

so overcome they had to withdraw to the smaller parlour, so I told Charles to take her up to the attic, where she couldn't cause any further trouble. We should have sent for the constable straight away, of course. I wish we had. But we still had to see to the guests. We were a long time seeing everybody out, making the house secure. And when I went to speak to the master, he said we *weren't* to send for anyone, that he'd spoken with the prisoner himself.'

She sucks in a breath. 'Just after midnight, I went upstairs to make sure the front door was on the latch. I saw . . . *her* . . . crossing the landing above, up on the third storey, walking towards Madame's bedchamber. It was dark. I saw only the shape of her. But she seemed distressed. She cried out. Though I could not hear what she said.'

'You're sure of the time?'

'The guests had all left by ten, the master and mistress had gone up soon after. I checked the clock at that time, and I checked it again when I saw her. I called out to her, but got no answer. Well, it was so very like those other times when I'd caught her wandering around up there at night . . . that it ate at me. I asked Mr Casterwick what he thought we should do. "Go up," he said, "and speak to the master again." I decided I would, just to make sure. I went up. And that's when I saw blood –'

'Where?'

'Spots of it on the stairs. On the landing just – just outside the library. I –'

She stops, blows into a white kerchief, says she wishes she didn't have to speak of it.

'Yes,' says Jessop. 'Yes.' He puts one hand on his hip, making a bat wing of his gown. All the patience of a terrier at a rat hole. 'Take your time,' he says gently. 'Some things are beyond description, Mrs Linux. Nevertheless, such things are the business of the Old Bailey.'

She gives out a sob. There's a terrible quiet, only the whispery shuffling high in the gallery. They, too, smell blood. This is what they came for.

'I went in. It . . . it was the smell that stopped me. The kind you can feel, sticking to you. I felt my way to the mantel, lit one of the candles there that had guttered out. And saw it. Blood!' she wails. 'The whole floor a black sea, and my poor master lost upon it!

'I – For a moment, I couldn't think what to do. Then I fell to my knees. It was all I could think. I prayed over him for the longest time. I said the Lord's Prayer. A few times, I can't remember how many. I had to breathe in that – that *smell* all the while. I went out to the passage and knelt there. I – cast up my accounts. The constable later found the . . . found the mess.'

She makes a show of putting herself together, patting her bodice.

'I went up to the mistress's room, thinking I had to summon her. I let myself in. You might have thought it was the master and mistress both in there asleep, at first. Bedcovers pulled neat as sails, and –' she lifts a hand to her cheek '– there was the *same* smell there. That terrible smell. Oh, I knew then it would be something I didn't want to see. I put the covers back – and that was when I saw the prisoner and the mistress. The bed covered in blood. That's when I saw the mistress was dead.

"Then I screamed, and that brought Mr Casterwick, who sent for Charles. Charles went to fetch the watch, and it was all such a dreadful shock I didn't mark the time then. That's when we woke the prisoner. We did not want to wake her before the constable came.'

'How was she when you woke her?'

'She wouldn't wake, not at first. I had to pour water over

her, from the pitcher. When she sat up, I saw her hands were covered in blood. The constable asked her what had happened and she said, "I can't remember." That's all she would say. She just kept repeating it.'

She tells them she later found the jar and the receipt for arsenic under my pallet and handed those items over to the constable when she came back down. The constable found the knife in Madame's cabinet, beside the laudanum bottles, and her copy of *Paradise Lost*. It had been wiped clean and laid there beside the bottle and the book with the care a surgeon might take, putting away his instruments.

'Surgeon or *butcher*.' She seems to spit the words straight at me.

Oh, I know only too well. It's butchery when there's no need to keep the animal alive.

'Apart from the blood, there was nothing out of place. As if the room must have been *tidied*. Another odd thing, sir. You see, the mistress had come below that night, just before their guests left. She came down to the kitchen, and – *oh* – she was wringing her hands, her voice so thin and soft you could hardly hear her. She wanted to thank us, to tell us the evening had gone well, and not a one of us was to be downhearted about what had happened. She came round each of us in turn. I'll never forget it. I remember her hands when she clasped mine, so small, so cold. Trembling. She's upset about what happened, I thought. But now I know she must have been frightened. She must have been *terrified*.'

Those words sink me into a terrible black mood. The thought that Madame *could* have been afraid. Of me? It pushes my head down.

When I look up, you're on your feet. You couldn't be more different from Jessop. He took the floor like an actor, all eyebrows, teeth and hands, the better to see him up in the gallery, his gown more up and down than a whore's nightdress. *Yours* is planted firmly on your shoulders. For a moment, all you do is frown at your papers, as if studying them. Thinking. It's a seeping silence, after all of Jessop's bluster, and Linux's sobbing. The room goes quiet too.

Silence can be a chisel. Perhaps you're making her wait in the hopes that you can use it in that fashion on her.

You look up. 'If I understand you correctly, you went straight from your master's dead body to your mistress's bedchamber.'

She purses her lips. 'Is there a question, Mr Pettigrew?'

'You were awake, moving through the house. You were in the library, then the bedchamber. Is it possible that, in order to cover your own tracks, you now seek to lay my client's on top?'

'You're as addled as your client if you truly believe all that. But I suspect it's more a case of her paying you by the word.' She laughs. 'I am not the one who made threats, and who was found covered in blood.'

'Blood that could have been transferred onto my client while she lay beside her mistress.'

'A likely story, sir. Her mistress massacred right next to her and she never woke up?'

There's no answer for that, of course, so you're forced to switch paths. I could tell you there's no shaking Linux off. In any event, she *isn't* the one who had blood on her hands, and no story to account for what she'd done. Nor has anyone come to bear witness against her. No one will ever see her as the monster, if the choice is between me and her.

'Here is another puzzle. Such a savage killing. Then *tidying* up. How would that have been done? Why tidy the bedchamber and not the library? I am having some difficulty with all of this.'

'You seem to be having difficulty with many things. Sir.'

I hear snorts, laughter in the gallery. My stomach sinks. How is it a laughing matter? Would they all be so entertained if I was swinging in front of them? I look around the room. All these people who'll go home tonight to suppers and families, I suspect they would. I dig my nails deeper into the railing.

You flick the tails of your wig behind your neck. 'It was you who said there was nothing out of place in Madame's bedchamber.'

'There was a dead body in that room.'

'Yes, but those were your words, Mrs Linux. I am quoting you. *Nothing out of place*. The room tidied up.'

'Perhaps you should ask your client,' she says, giving the jurors a sharp look. 'I am not an expert in murder.'

'*There* we agree, Mrs Linux. However, it's your speculation about this murder that points the finger at my client.'

'I believe it's for the jurors to say where the finger points.'

'But *you* believed it was the prisoner who had done this dreadful thing?'

'It's His Majesty's government that says so.'

'Doesn't His Majesty say so because that is what you told His Majesty's constable?'

'There had been a *murder*. Two murders! And the master – the master . . .' She breaks off into a sob, raises her kerchief. 'So, when I found *poison* among her possessions, and when I found that . . . thing, I reported them. *Naturally*.'

'Thinking that, since my client had purchased arsenic, she must have been planning to stab someone to death?'

She hesitates.

'Mrs Linux. Why would a woman who'd gone to the trouble of buying and hiding poison stab her victims to death? And this receipt for arsenic you claim to have found, why, it's like Cobbett's red herring, leading the hounds away from the hare! Isn't it a *fact* that arsenic is used frequently by quality ladies for their complexions? Had Mrs Benham had receipts for arsenic from Mr Jones before? Careful now – I will call him here if need be.'

'Your *client* threatened them, that very night. She cannot lie her way out of it now. Twenty people heard her. All the master's guests.'

'You say she lost her temper, flew into a rage, killed one, got upstairs, killed the other, and then in an instant fell into such a deep sleep you had to pour water over her to wake her? How would *that* have been done?'

'That is a question she should be asking her own conscience.'

She stands, and stares. The silence always feels heavy in court. It is a room full of words, perhaps that's why. They echo even when none are being spoken. Words are all your trade, you lawyers. You spoon them in, or knife them in. Flatter, cajole. Dripping with malice or kindness, depending on your purpose. Tricks. Hooks. You nod at her and glance down at your brief. Gentle your voice. 'You see, Mrs Linux . . . there were reasonable explanations . . . yet you and Constable Meek went haring about after the prejudicial ones, ruling out all others without any further enquiry.'

She turns to me. And there's such hatred on her face. She and I are the same. The thought twists like a serpent. *She and I are the same.* Equal in our devotion. Equal in our anger, too.

You wait, but still she says nothing. 'Don't you know your speculation could hang my client, Mrs Linux?' you say quietly. 'Don't you *care*?'

She tucks her lips in.

'You say there'd been a disturbance in the drawing room, during the soirée?'

She breathes out. 'Yes. The prisoner making threats.'

'Did anyone hear a commotion upstairs *after* your master and mistress went up for the night?'

'No.'

'Nothing at all?'

'But that was not unusual. We could not hear the upper

rooms from so far downstairs. We were in the kitchen, the stove going, the noises of the clearing, and cleaning.'

'You did not see the prisoner commit these terrible murders?'

'No.'

'Nor did anyone else?'

'No one has said so.'

'How did you and the prisoner get on?'

Her jaw twitches. 'We got on with things.'

'There was animosity between you?'

Another hesitation. 'No more than the usual. I ran that house, sir, and the servants in it. It would have been impossible, then, for them to be happy with me all the time, or me with them.'

She blinks.

'What kind of master was Mr Benham?'

'What business is it of yours?'

'It is the business of this court.'

'A good master, a fair one.'

'You felt the prisoner was a threat to the household, you tried to warn the master, you wanted her turned out.'

She makes her eyes small. 'I wasn't wrong . . .'

'On one occasion you burned her hand, with the kettle –'

'That was an accident! What has she said?' She whips her head around to me again. 'What has she said? That was the night she attacked one of Mr Benham's guests at dinner. Mr John Langton. The one who'd brought her here, given her to Mr Benham. I took her down to the kitchen. She'd disgraced the master by what she'd done. I expected her to be turned out *then*, though she wasn't. They took pity on her, always, and look how she repaid them. When I tried to make her go upstairs, she rushed at me, nails flying, she was trying to claw at me, and I had the kettle still in my hands. I had yet to make the teas for after dinner. *That*'s how it happened, and that is God's truth. Is she trying to blame me for it? You can say what you like but I *saw* who she was. I saw her exactly. And I was not wrong.'

'Did her race count against her, too, so far as you were concerned?'

'It was her deeds that counted against her, not her skin.'

'You bullied her.'

'No. I did not.'

'You bullied her. You harassed her.'

'No.'

'You set your mind against her from the start. Dark in complexion, dark in nature. Was that what you thought?'

'*No.*'

You stare at each other, only the soft sounds of the courtroom between you.

The silence really is a marvel, here. So different from the gaol. There, the constant shouts and cries and squealing hammer and hammer at you until you spark and bend, like an iron nail, and can never feel straight again. Newgate's noise is a pigyard noise. Now it's all this silence that seems loud.

Her chest is heaving, and yours a mirror to it. The floor heaves too, like the floor of a ship.

I look at the judge, squirming on his bench.

He glances up at the clock.

'Perhaps, Mr Pettigrew, this is a convenient moment.'

Chapter Forty-One

Of all the time-keepers in that courtroom, it's the judge's stomach that will most often have its way. Either that or his bladder.

Lunch.

While the judge goes for his marrow soup, or whatever they're serving up in the judges' dining room today, the turnkeys allow you and Tomkin, the lawyer instructing you on my behalf, a few moments with me. You both stand facing me. It's a dark, nasty little corridor, no gleaming wood, no green velvet. Just cold grey walls, grimy flagstones underfoot, and the smell of prisoners. Feet and fear. The thought sinks into me that this is where I may belong for the rest of my life, if Jessop succeeds in shortening it. The kind of place deemed fit for creatures like me. Prisoners. *Murderers*.

The pair of you puzzle at me, like schoolboys working on the same sum. My head echoes with your words from our first meeting: *Give me something to help you with.*

You tap your papers against your chin. Shake your head. 'Let's start with the foetus –'

'Why? It's nothing but a distraction. You said it yourself.'

'What I say to them and what I say to you are two different matters.'

Tomkin coughs into his hand. 'He holds your brief, Miss Langton, you must take him into your confidence.'

'Jessop's painting a picture of you,' you interject. 'It's an old trick. Getting the jurors to look at something the judge is going to tell them to forget. It's prejudicial nonsense, and shouldn't have been allowed. No point leaping about with objections Makes the jurors think you can't confront the facts, and they never give a toss for lawyerly tricks. But if you don't explain it, they'll think the worst, that you're a –'

Baby-killer. The word claws at me. A pulse of panic.

'I've defended only one other black, Miss Langton. One. In that case, the judge decided the prisoner didn't have the intellect required to understand the nature of the oath. Though he spoke three languages! Do you see? That . . . thing would never have been allowed, in any other case, but in *this* one –'

You stop, as if something has just occurred to you. 'Have you been baptized?'

'How would that help?'

'You can tell them you're a Christian, at least . . .'

My hands crimp into fists. 'I know they'll all think I'm brutish enough to have killed my mistress. But I did not.'

'What about the possibility that you *did*?'

My heart rocks like a ship.

'We could argue it that way, you know. You've been enslaved all your life, you were brought here, given away. It would have been inhuman *not* to fight back in those circumstances. Might not get you acquitted. But I could argue for transportation.'

'No.'

I think back to how she looked, when I found her, guarding that small silent clotted thing.

I promised, I know. Forgive me.

I draw in a breath, and face the two of you. 'It was not her husband's baby. She . . . and Mr Cambridge –'

You look at each other in surprise.

'She didn't want anyone to know. I kept it because she wanted to bury it when she was well.'

'She was unwell?'

'That's the reason I went back. She wrote to me and asked

me to.' I tell you about coming back, how frightened she'd been.

'Frightened? Of what?'

Of her husband, of what he might do, of her own narrowing choices. I tell you about finding her that day, inconsolable. I say that she'd seemed, even before her loss, to have sunk into a well of grief. Tomkin looks surprised, as if wondering how such a thing could ever be considered a loss. I tell you what Benham had proposed. But then I trail off, knowing I'll be wiser to leave certain doors shut.

I tell you how I loved her. How I tried to help her. I don't tell you about my harsh words. I don't tell you that the thing she was frightened of might have been me. When I finish, I'm shaking. I try to hide it by flexing my hands in front of me.

'I loved her,' I say again, because it seems the most important thing to say.

You look at me steadily. 'You loved her. That doesn't change my advice. Even had it been mutual, it is more likely to harm than help your case.' You glance down the hallway, lower your voice. 'What happened afterwards?'

'Afterwards?'

'After you found her, as you've described?'

I pause. *Caution. Careful. Do not say too much.*

'She went to her soirée. Mr Benham required it.'

'And then?'

My mind races. It's my own self I'm trying to outrun. When I reach inside, there's nothing. That trick, somewhere between remembering and forgetting – and the only refuge I have left.

Give me something I can save your neck with.

I can't remember.

From the end of the hallway, a clang of metal. The turnkeys. No time left. You turn to Tomkin. 'What do you think?'

'That we can't do much with any of *that*.'

'No. But –' You stop. 'Something struck me when I was cross-examining the housekeeper. How would it have been done? To kill one, then the other, and to be in such a deep sleep immediately afterwards? She took an excess of laudanum. Might there be something in that? What if we find a medical man who can make a defence out of it?'

Tomkin looks at me. 'I know a doctor in Cheapside. Used him last week on something else. He might have knowledge of such matters. But where do you go with this?'

'If we can get a doctor willing to swear to it, couldn't we argue that she couldn't have had the capacity to form an intention, not in that state? *Therefore*, the indictment, at least for murder, must fail?'

'Lack of malice? Well. This is a first, I think, Mr Pettigrew. Unprecedented, so far as I know –'

'*No.*' You both flicker at me in surprise. 'It makes me look guilty,' I say.

Tomkin shakes his head. 'Miss Langton. It is a defence.'

In the end, having no other, I had no choice.

Chapter Forty-Two

The judge comes back. Jessop calls his remaining witnesses to say their piece.

First, Constable Meek gives his testimony about the blood on my hands, saying I tried to clean myself on the bedclothes: 'I knew it wasn't hers, sir, because she had no wounds herself, save some bruises at her neck, no doubt made by one of the victims trying to defend themselves.' They all look at me when he says that. The pounding in my chest works its way to my throat. No matter how I swallow and swallow I can't swallow it down.

Next comes Mr Casterwick, turning his hat this way and that while he speaks. 'I tried to stay out of matters that were none of my concern. However, it was quite apparent in those latter days that the prisoner was behaving queerly. She'd stop in the middle of doing something and then be quite unable to remember what she was about. Once I came upon her in the garden, near the pond. She said she'd come out in search of an infant, that a child had been lost. There was no infant at Leven-hall. I wondered if I hadn't caught her in her cups, truth be told. Once she was left downstairs, in the kitchen, after everyone else retired. I found her at the table, head resting on the wood, and her hand moved, as if writing something. Only she had no pen. And when I went close to her, she said, "Oh! My head. Such an ache in it, we'll have to open it."

'I regret now that I did not tell Mrs Linux. I felt sorry for the girl, you see, and she begged me not to. Mrs Linux suspected that she was stealing her mistress's medicaments.'

Finally, it's Charles's moment. He says that when he managed to get me upstairs on that dreadful night, I jittered on my sleeping pallet like a loose wheel and he could see mischief upon me, that he should have seen then that I would 'come off' and, if he had, he would never have left me, and his master and mistress never would have been killed. To everyone's shock, not least his own, he begins to cry.

The afternoon wears smooth. All this makeweight evidence, tipping the scales against me. Slowly, slowly. But none of it has helped to fill that gap. The light stretches thin, glints off the sword above the judge and the mirror above me in the prisoner's dock. An old gaol-bird told me it's put there so judge and jurors can better see the prisoner's face. English justice. The mirror and the sword. First, they force you to face yourself, then they force you to face death. Fear gnaws deep in my guts. I long to run. To flee. How could anyone bear to stand still for so long and hear what other people have to say about them? But the prisoner is forced to watch, to listen. And I know that, if I move a muscle, the keys will push me to the floor, drag me away.

And then, at last, with the light nearly gone, the judge smacks his bench, making the white edges of his papers curl up like fingers, and says he's surprised that we've reached the end of the day before the end of this trial. 'I'll give you one more day.' But, in the light of his crowded docket, the pair of you had better come prepared to finish on Monday.

And there ends the first day.

Because it's Friday, I face two days in Newgate before we come back. They stretch ahead of me. Minutes will flick lazy as dogs in sun, hours will gallop. The clock's either as orderly as a multiplication table or as unruly as a fart. But this whole rigmarole *should* take longer than it takes to clean windows, shouldn't it? Why should you beg permission to take your time fighting for a woman's life? Nevertheless, we must set our clocks by the judge, for he's the sun who rises and sets over the Old Bailey. And he says it's taking too long.

Chapter Forty-Three

Monday morning. The second day. After I'm brought in, you lean over the prisoner's dock, bounce on your toes. I try to still my hands, to quiet the clanking of my shackles.

'I have a surprise,' you say. A small grin. There's no time to say more than that, for the judge is coming in.

I'd welcome a surprise. The events of last Friday, and the week-end at Newgate, have worn me out. There was a riot last night: a group of the old girls hacking at the cell with stones chipped out of the wall. It's how they say goodbye to the stone jug when they've been sentenced to the hulks. Transportation is a fate worse than the gibbet, some say. Though I'd welcome it now. It's no wonder they behave so in there, for a corset drawn too tight is bound to split, and even more so if you squirm against it. Newgate's that sort of corset. They squeeze us from there to the Old Bailey to the Dead Man's Walk to the gallows. Like they're making sausages. The thought makes me clutch at my own stomach, and I'm taken aback for a moment to feel silk there. I look down. A new dress. I'd almost forgotten. One of the good-doers brought it on Saturday. *Something for court. You can't wear that rough thing you had on yesterday. They'll convict you on the strength of that alone.* I do feel the power of this new dress. A kind of dignity coming back. A greater confidence. Held up by that, and your promise of good news, I hold my skirts, and lean forward so I can pay attention.

When you tell the judge you'd like to recall Dr Wilkes, Jessop sits up, frowns.

'I know he was here on Friday, My Lord,' you say smoothly.

'I noted Your Lordship's observations about time on that occasion. However, a few questions have arisen and I'd beg Your Lordship's indulgence. I won't need to trouble him long.'

You lift one of your papers, and peer at the doctor over the edge of it. 'Dr Wilkes. The science of pathology enables our bodies to speak, when we can no longer speak for ourselves.'

'In the sense that the body itself can tell how it died, that is correct.'

You nod, as if to flatter him with your approval. 'But there's an art to it?'

'Art?'

'Knowing what to look for. An understanding of human nature . . .'

He smiles. 'Knowing what to look for separates scientists from charlatans. And I dare say *actually* finding it separates them from artists.'

There are a few chuckles. The doctor lifts his hand to stroke his chin and I fix my eyes on his fingers. Thick as sausages. *How does he work with those?* In my mind's eye, they root in blood, pull flesh apart, spoon out livers and brains and hearts. I sway on my feet, close my eyes, and see the Surgeon, waggling his own paws.

'Did you note Madame Benham's stomach contents, Doctor?'

'I applied a stomach pump, yes.'

'What did you find?'

'Only the remains of the ordinary food she had taken.'

'Nothing unusual?'

He gives a shrug. 'Carrots.'

'Anything else?'

'What are you getting at?'

'You've been in court before, Doctor?'

'More often than you, by the look of things.' Laughter

billows out across the gallery. The doctor lets the wind take his chest, smiles up at them.

'Many times, then?'

'I believe my curriculum vitae was established on Friday last, when you declined to ask me any questions.'

'Yes. Very well. Let's come to it.' You fiddle with one of the inkwells, bend over it as a woman might, to smooth an iron over a cloth. I'd have liked a trade like yours, I think. Selling words.

'You see, it's been said many times, here in this very court, that only God sees a man's heart. But I wonder . . . *We* must try, mustn't we, to see to each other's hearts?'

'Is that what lawyers do now, Mr Pettigrew?' He smirks.

'Even surgeons must try.'

'There's no room for sentiment in a surgeon.'

'Or an anatomist?'

'There's not much call for it. Corpses being incapable of emotion.'

'But you've built your profession on the fact that they speak! *People* come to you, Dr Wilkes, no matter the condition you receive them in. People, who were . . . partial to figs! Or the smell of their babies, the joy of walking beside the ocean, the prick of the sun on one's nose, and –' You stop, as if embarrassed. 'Well . . . any of those small joys that may come a man's way while he has the breath for them.'

Dr Wilkes smirks up at the judge. 'A pretty speech, My Lord, but I wonder, what is the relevance of these questions concerning a woman who's been stabbed? It's like blaming soured milk for a drowned cat.'

The judge, caught picking at his teeth with a finger, lowers it. 'Yes, I agree. Mr Pettigrew, I'm afraid you've lost me as well.'

'I *am* going somewhere, My Lord.' You turn back to the doctor. 'Did you make any enquiries about Madame Benham? Her habits? How often she took opium, for example?'

The judge taps a hand on his bench. 'Mr Pettigrew. At some point if a man hasn't got anything on his hook, he might assume the problem is his bait.'

'My Lord, I've been led to wonder whether Dr Wilkes overlooked the presence of opium in the stomach contents. I'm instructed that Mrs Benham was a laudanum addict –'

The doctor juts out his chin. 'I'd been informed that Mrs Benham had been taking laudanum for some months, on advice of a physician. I can't now remember his name. Folke? Falk?'

You glance at your paper. 'Fawkes?'

'Fawkes. Yes. I think that was it. The presence of the drug would have been entirely consistent with that medical history. Mrs Benham had attended her soirée earlier that evening, and appeared in perfectly good spirits. Testing for opium, even if such a thing could be done, would have been nothing but a wild-goose chase.'

'Did you perform any tests?'

'Mr Pettigrew,' interrupts the judge. 'Set yourself down a different path.'

'My Lord.' You take a step back. 'Something else is troubling me, Doctor. Do you see here the clothes worn that evening by the victims?'

'Yes.'

'Well, then, *look*. His clothes are soaked. Bow to stern, as they say. Do you see? As if he bled and bled again. Like the old superstition which held that a corpse's wounds would bleed when the killer approached – "open their congealed mouths and bleed afresh", as Shakespeare wrote. Yet hers are stained only *lightly*.' The lavender-grey silk clings as you hold it up, a woman holding fast her lover's ankles. Splashes of dark dried blood on the bodice. 'How would you account for it?'

He pauses, folds his arms. 'Simple, Mr Pettigrew. He had

numerous wounds. Stabbed over and over, and stabbed deep On the other hand, hers were not so deep.'

'*Not* so deep?'

'No.' His voice blunt as granite. But he hesitates. A heartbeat. Or is that only the spinning in my head?

'Yet you still swear positively that exsanguination was the cause of her death?'

I can't look at Dr Wilkes. I can't look anywhere. Velvet, brass and polished wood are all stripped away, until all I can see is *her*. The whole dread scene. The meat-slab of her laid out on a cold table. The black blood puddling through her lungs and heart. Her body nothing more than a sack for organs, a pop of eyes and tongue. I stumble forward. I cry out. Heads turn. One of the turnkeys takes a step towards me and I shake my head, to show them I'll be good. I must try to compose myself. But now I can't *un-see* it. What a mess they would have made of her! And I'd done the same. To so many. *So many!* I sway on my feet, close my eyes, fall into the darkness inside.

The turnkey steps forward, grips my wrist, yanks me back into place. 'Sorry,' I whisper. 'Sorry.' I look up meekly, snatch for breath. The judge nods, and he releases me and steps back, but I've lost the thread of what the doctor was saying, have to lean forward to pick it up again.

'. . . it was obvious from the bodice, Mr Pettigrew, just as it was obvious from the body.' But he blusters when he says it, and looks unsure.

As you take your seat, Jessop gives an annoyed little toss of his head, and I see that, for the first time, there's a ruffle to his crow-black feathers. He darts a look behind him. '*I* have no further questions for this witness, M'Lud, and, quite frankly, I'm surprised he had to be troubled to come back here for such a damp probing as that.'

But both Jessop and the doctor look up, towards each other,

when you say you wish to call Dr John Pears. The courtroom falls silent. All eyes turn to me in the dock, as they do whenever we must stop and wait. Dr Wilkes stops, going up the steps, wipes his hand along his breeches. The room waits. After a few minutes, Tomkin scurries out, comes back in. Shakes his head, then goes out again. You narrow your eyes up at the gallery before turning back to your papers. 'My Lord, I – ah, might I request a brief adjournment, to take instructions?'

When you come back, you give a twitch of your gown, which hangs flattened and black. It has slipped, and your smile has slipped, too.

'My Lord, it seems it will be Dr Lushing this morning, *not* Dr Pears. I wonder if we might adjourn again until the half-hour, to allow him time to arrive.'

'Very well, Mr Pettigrew. Let's hope Dr Lushing hasn't also disap*peared*,' says the judge, snickering at his own joke.

Dr Wilkes, arms hooked over the gallery railing, gives a single blunt nod. When I look up again he's gone, and you are too. Leaving me to wonder what it's all about.

Doctors all seem to have skittering hands and skin under their eyes that sags like purses. As if it's a profession that draws men unable to sleep or sit still. Dr Lushing tugs at his side-whiskers while he waits for you to start. You have been shaken by something, I can see it. By what? You draw a deep breath, tap the papers in front of you. You're composing yourself. You fiddle your gown up, then remind him of my claim to have taken laudanum on the night of the murders, which rendered me unable to remember anything thereafter.

He leans forward. 'Oh, yes, I was very interested in your client's claim, Mr Pettigrew. Most interested. It has the hallmarks of a classic stupor. There's been a great deal of scientific debate recently covering these states. Somnambulism, animal magnetism, mesmerism.' He ticks them off on his fingers. 'All of those states seem to involve consciousness and unconsciousness to the same degree and at the same time. A split down the middle, one could say. The person affected can still have the will to act – people have indeed been known to perform very complicated actions – but the moral nature is entirely wanting, because they have lost the regulating power of their own minds. In other words, they are not responsible, not in a moral sense anyway. Somnambulism is more common than the man on the street, or even the man on the jury benches, might think. Alfred the Great was a sufferer, as was La Fontaine. Condillac.

'It *is* a kind of insanity, in the sense that it is also a kind of dreaming awake, a *link*, if you will, between dreaming and insanity. It causes the sufferer to act on false impressions as if they are real.'

'I see.' You glance at the jurors. 'For example, a woman might believe an infant to be hidden under a hedge and set about looking for it, though there is no such thing?'

'Yes! Exactly that. In such a state, one of my patients wrote an entire symphony yet next morning remembered not a single note. Another walked the lanes around his own estate all night, shot a fox and dragged the body back all the way through his own top field. Next morning, he swore he'd been in bed the whole time and he'd still believe that, too, except the whole thing had been witnessed by the local priest.'

'Those were somnambulistic trances? *Sleepwalking*, in colloquial terms?'

'Correct.'

'Could the same state be produced by an excessive consumption of opium?'

'That's what excited me about your case, Mr Pettigrew. I believe, quite strongly indeed from what you've told me, that what your client experienced was akin to a somnambulistic trance, except of course we're talking not about a sleeping state but a *soporific* one. Under an excess of opium, as in a dream, a user might also act under false impressions. The delirium in this instance created by the drug itself. But the *memory* of those actions could then be obliterated by the stupefying effect, resulting in the same split in consciousness.' He hooks his fingers on his own lapels, as if he's the prosecutor, rolling out his argument like a tailor's cloth. 'These matters, gentlemen, are as exciting, as *reliable*, as any of the century's scientific advances. You may have faith in that.'

You look pleased with yourself again, reaching up to finger your wig.

But frustration knots my guts. This might be a good lawyer's trick, but it siphons up all my own doubts, all my own fears. As if my own defence will be the very thing that seals my guilt.

This is planting someone else's idea like a cuckoo in my head. *If* you killed her, Frances, this is how. *Twin shapes, shadows moving in the dark, until one goes cold*. But is that real? I know that blackness all too well. My heart staggers behind my ribs. It would have been unknowing. Of all Lushing's paid-for words, I cling to that.

When it's his turn, Jessop tosses his papers onto the barristers' table. 'Insanity! That is indeed an accurate assessment of this entire defence.'

'Well, no, that's not what I –'

'Do you mean to suggest that the prisoner could have killed Mr Benham, taken herself upstairs, killed his wife, cleaned the carpet *and* the knife, and then – *presto!* – got into bed, all in this alleged somnambulistic state?'

'Oh, yes, very possible and I should say –'

'The *savagery* to butcher them both, yet the presence of

mind for all that . . . tidying up.' He huffs out a laugh. 'It's hardly likely, Doctor. Those are not involuntary actions. Not some pitiable automaton, but a person making decisions, acting with care and deliberation, even self-interest.'

'As I've said, Mr Jessop, there is the will to act, yes, but there is this form of mental derangement laid over it. Think of the moment between sleep and waking, when it is difficult for the mind to be conscious of its own condition or even the condition or location of the body. It is a form of derangement close to that, save that it can last for hours.'

'Sleepwalking!' Jessop throws up his hands, spins around to the jury benches. 'My friend makes a circus of this court.'

You jump up, palms flat on the table. 'My *Lord*, were I permitted, I'd argue that my client's state amounted as a matter of law to non-insane automatism. It might be novel, but isn't that how the law develops? By looking for advances, by building on foundations –'

'Mr Pettigrew.' The judge pinches his lips together. 'You are sneaking *argument* in through the back door again.'

'Nor can he cut his cake both ways, My Lord,' Jessop cries out. 'Does the prisoner say she *didn't* do this terrible thing? Or that she did it while sleepwalking? The sleepwalking defence kills her denial dead.' He wags his lip, pleased as a cat with the warm squirm of feathers on his tongue.

Chapter Forty-Four

After Dr Lushing, Pru, dear Pru, comes and gives me a character. But it seems too little, too late, my head now teeming with the same dreadful image that's no doubt filling all their heads. The butchering maid, the mistress dying in her bed. But I try for a smile, for Pru has been a friend, and a true blessing. This may be all the thanks I can ever give her. Her own smile thins, like something mixed in water, no doubt thinking of Madame, as I am. She says her kind words about me, a soothing balm, and then I lose her to the crowd. The second morning draws to a close, the judge breaks for lunch, and then the afternoon is upon us. And I am next to speak.

The prisoner is never permitted to take the oath, which is one of the many ways they tell us what we're worth. But I find myself thinking it's a good thing I'm not permitted to swear to it. I stare around the courtroom. Faces on top of faces, pressing as if against glass, layered like a grim cake. Sucked cheeks and slanted brows. A shot of panic, hot and swift as laudanum. *How can I speak here? Who will listen? Who will believe me?* I lean forward. 'Sirs.' My own voice booms back at me off the sounding board.

'I was faithful to my lady, and happy to serve her. When I came back to Levenhall, it was because she sent for me herself. She was not well . . . and I . . . came back to *nurse* her. I loved my mistress. I couldn't have done what you say I've done *because* I loved her.'

My thoughts crowd each other like frightened cattle and I

see you give a small shake of your head. *This will harm your case, not help it.* I find myself wishing for the drug again. To wet everything and make it slide easily, whether in or out. I must tiptoe around my first days back, picking out what I can and cannot say. 'It has been said that I am an opium-eater, that I have been a whore.' I pause. 'Those things are true. I *did* fall into the habit of taking opium, but it was my mistress who gave it to me, saying it was to help me sleep.'

I press my hands together. *Steady. Steady.* 'And for a time last autumn I . . . did live at the School-house. That was the work I could get. I had to eat, and it was a more moral course than thieving. Mr Benham forgave me for it, and I'd beg your forgiveness, too, if I need it. I'd remind you –' I lift my chin '– if *bawdry* alone was cause to convict of murder, there'd only be a handful of women left in all of London.'

High up in the gallery, a flurry of fans. Bright as butterflies. Sniggers. Even Jessop coughs up from his papers in surprise.

I'm a puzzle. They expected a sly African. Or a bent-double maid. A mulatta whore. The Black Murderess.

Which one will save me?

My next words are as much of a shock to me as to them.

'Sirs, I wonder . . . in the whole sum of history, by what order have you white men been wrong more than you've been right?' An uproar. From the whole crowd of them, there rises a squabble like hens quarrelling over corn. Judge, jurors, clerks, turnkeys, barristers *and* gallery. One of the jurors shakes his head. I'll have put them off me, as so often happens when you speak the truth. It's the reason so many do not.

But I press on. 'Whatever it is . . .' I raise my voice '. . . *whatever* it is, *that* must be the whole scale of human suffering.'

I come to a stop, needing to draw in both breath and courage to go on. Swarmed by the cries, the heat, the gold letters hammering into my head: *A false witness shall not be unpunished.* The

319

unbearable smell, so very like the reek of this city when I first came to it. Perfume on top, but down below, where rotting always starts, a stench. There's not much you can do to get rid of an honest smell, which you'd know if you'd ever been a maid, or the sort who can't pay another to maid for you. I lift my head, and try to fix my eyes on the stone columns at the very back of the gallery, so I don't have to look at the jurors, or the other snarling faces, so I can compose myself and speak again. But what I see up there makes me cower. *It can't be.*

A row of bodies, *black* bodies. Where there were no bodies at all before. They straggle against the columns, some leaning, some straight. They march down the stairs, jut elbows on the wooden railing, press chins on fists. There are so many of them. They slide onto the benches, nudging people down with their hips. They gawp. Same as everyone else. But their hands are still, their faces are ashen as the marble, and their eyes are all white, blank as paper. Unmoving. They stare and stare. I feel a blink of confusion. But then I see precisely what to scoop out of the stew of my thoughts, like a candle brought into the dark room inside my head, and I tilt my head back, the better to see them. I take in the sight of them. There's the new-bought Coromantee. I never thought to see him again! He lost his leg under the plough, and his will to live under the Surgeon's knife. The carpenter. Whittled to bone by yaws, and despair. The milk-toothed boy, hair springing like burrs in grass, mother-smoothed with palm oil. The man who seemed to be all belly, broad and hairy, with curling yellow toenails. Gullah, of the rum-dark eyes. I see them. I see the coach-house. The small arched windows just below the roof. The night like black oil tipped against the glass. Wind muttering against the loose pane. The cadaver, under wetted muslin. The lectern, on which stood Vesalius. *De Humani Corporis Fabrica.* Me, coughing. Always coughing. The thick flags of smoke from the tobacco burning

320

in pans. And gunpowder in vinegar. The sting of the arsenic solution pumped through the corpse.

I find I can speak, after all. I raise my voice again. 'You think I am a monster.' The bodies nod. Heads flying every which way like cotton dolls shaken by a child.

Gullah squints her eyes. Go *on*.

Confess. Confess. I look down at my hands.

'Mr John Langton, my old master, brought me to London.'

Go on.

'He gave me as a gift to Mr Benham.'

Tell them. Tell them what you are. I glance over at the jurors on their benches, and cough. What happens to me won't have a thing to do with what you *or* Jessop say, but whether these men like the look of me or not, which is a thing that is already decided: it was decided in an instant, when I was first brought into the room. The rest is only drawn out to make a show for them. And the jurors, the judge, all of you, are men, made loose by balls and bragging, with no earthly notion how tight it can get inside a woman's skin.

Then the words pour out. 'Mr Langton owned the Paradise estate, in Jamaica. He owned me. He and Mr Benham made a wager. They'd find a black and train him up. Discover the limits of his intelligence. That's how Mr Benham explained it.'

One hand twists over the other. 'Why did they choose me? Neither is here to answer. But Mr Benham once told me Langton wanted a mulatto, not a black. That was part of it. And it could also have been because I was that bastard's *own* daughter. His own flesh.'

I press my tongue against my teeth. Look up. The bodies nod. *Go on.*

'Just to have the pages of a book beneath my fingers. Fresh air. Early mornings. A view. A mirror. And a bed. People want to see something unusual in what I did there. There was nothing strange about it. That's what slavery is. *Their* minds, our hands.'

The judge creaks forward, taps his quill. 'Mr John Langton is not on trial here, girl!'

'You might think it was just a matter of one cut after another, like slicing a loaf, but you need all manner of tools to open a man. Scalpels, yes, but also bone-saws and scissors and double-blunt hooks. Forceps and blowpipes and needles. Knives for brains and knives for cartilages and knives for bones. Kept in a wooden chest the Surgeon bought from a ship's doctor, fastened with two brass clasps and lined in velvet, like a rich man's coffin. Like a set of dinner forks. Ivory handles.' The judge is still banging, and I let the words tumble out, racing to finish.

'I'm the one who wrote out Langton's manuscript. *Crania*. He used his own slaves for his experiments. Only the dead ones, at first, for he said the dead can't complain. But neither can slaves. Soon he decided there was more to learn about living men from living skin. He used fire, pierced their skin with small knives, even the soles of their feet, had vices fastened to their skulls, cut them open awake, sewed them up *after* they'd fainted. He chose who would be put to bed with whom, so he could write it down, and their offspring would be written down also.

'He supposed that blacks would breed, not only with other blacks, but also with the orangutan. The two are close kin, he said, and other planters had tried it.

'Well. He had me write letters for him. Most to skull-hunters, for there are men who will scavenge across the globe for any single thing you want or can imagine you want. He had me write to Mr Leforth Pomfrey, asking him to find one of those creatures, send it to Paradise by ship. That was the worst of it. When that creature came . . . that was the worst of it . . .' Panic strokes my throat loose. 'I was his scribe, but I was worse. I did worse. I opened bodies. Many of them. I confess it! *I confess.*'

I look up. 'George Benham was just as bad –'

'*Enough!*' the judge shouts, his face knitted into the expression of a man straining over his pot. He looks at me, aghast.

Gripping the railing, I pause. 'Sometimes . . . sometimes I think the whole aim of this entire universe is to force us to admit the white man has stronger magic.'

'Prisoner at the bar!' cries the judge. His jaws snap shut. The whole gallery is in an uproar now, benches quaking, some of the men leaping to their feet, waving broadsheets curled into batons.

The turnkeys step towards me, hands in fists. The darkness is in my head again, same as it was that night. The sharp pain of my fingers digging into wood is the only thing keeping me in the room. I look up into the gallery. Every eye staring. The bodies nodding, all blood and teeth.

Then the turnkeys are behind me, pinning my hands. My shackles clank and rattle at my back. But I'm not done yet.

'Even being the offspring of debauchery and vice,' I cry out, 'I am sure I did not do this thing!'

Jessop leaps to his feet, leans over the table, his hands either side of his brief.

'That was quite a . . . tale.' Looking at him, I feel nothing but fatigue. I rest my hands on the railing. 'You are a monster. You say it yourself. *I* say you are the monster who killed Mr and Mrs Benham.'

I shake my head. 'That is not true.'

'It was an act of savagery, what was done to them.' It isn't a question, so I don't answer. He sways forward, gaze sharp as a wasp-sting. 'Will you tell us what services you performed, at the brothel where you worked?'

I hesitate. 'The School-house was a spanking parlour.'

'Where you administered whippings?'

I flick my head.

'Is that a yes?' He lifts one of his papers, glances down. 'You spoke of John Langton. John Langton's estate. John Langton's experiments. A large part of the Paradise estate was burned to the ground, I understand, in 'twenty-five, just before you came here. Following a slave rebellion. Is that true?'

'There was no rebellion,' I say.

'It was a savage place.'

'There are savage goings-on *here*, also.'

'You've been made bitter by those experiences. You've been made savage yourself.' He speaks almost gently now, needle rather than blade. 'Be that as it may. Mr Benham took you in, showed you a kindness. Which you repaid by thieving –'

'No.'

'By seeking to address yourself to his wife.'

I draw stale air into my lungs. He *wants* to terrify me, to make me doubt myself. But I have held this one true thing, from that day to this: 'I loved her. She loved me.'

But, in the vast courtroom, the words come out hollow as quill barrels, even to my own ears. I hear the shuffling, the whispers. I can imagine what they all must think. I can imagine what *you* must think, that I'm sinking my own ship. But no matter. There *was* love.

'Your *mistress* loved you?' He scoffs and shrugs his gown, gives me a long stare, makes sure I'm the first to look away. 'So that was why you argued with your master.'

'No.'

'Why you killed him.'

'*No.*'

'You threatened them with death,' he rattles on, as if I haven't spoken at all, 'and then you made good on that threat.'

I see the gold light shining against the drapes. I see all their shocked faces, weapons formed against me. *Meg's darky maid! How she follows her! How she torments her! A strange one, I've always thought it. Something in the eyes . . . How dare she? How dare she?* I see *him*. Olaudah Cambridge. Madame, wavering, pulling away from me.

'*This is death.*'

He swings his head. 'I beg your pardon?'

'*This is death.* That's what I said.'

Please will you stay upstairs, Frances? Please sleep in the attic. I cannot see your face, now. I cannot bear it. It reminds me . . . it reminds me . . . And then I had called her a coward. I'd *wanted* to hurt her, as she had hurt me.

Jessop paces like a bull behind a fence. '"This is death." What did you mean by *that*?'

'I was upset.'

He sucks his teeth. 'Upset enough to kill?'

'*No.*'

'Was it the end of this imagined love affair with your own mistress that had you so upset?'

'It was not a love affair.'

'No? What was it?'

'It was love.'

There's an outcry at that. He shakes his head. When it dies down he snaps his teeth, and makes a quick meal of me. 'You say you came back to nurse her. Did anyone call a doctor?'

Those words echo like a shout down a well. *Call a doctor. Call a doctor.*

'No.'

'No, what?'

'No one called a doctor.'

'Why not?'

'A doctor wasn't needed.'

'You hesitate because you are *lying*.'

My heart slaps, to hear him echo my own thoughts. 'My mistress was often unwell, sir. She was an opium-eater.'

'You are a fantasist. Your entire testimony has been either a deliberate distraction or plainly fictitious. You'd stop at nothing. Not even blackening her name to clear your own.' He's sneering now, each word rattling at me through the dock.

'*No.*' But my own voice has shrivelled.

'It suited you to prey on her in her time of weakness.'

No.

He stands, waits. As if I haven't spoken. *Have I?* I can no longer tell if my words have fallen inside the room, or just inside me. I lick my lips. 'No.'

'What about this?' He taps the jar. 'Are you responsible for this also?'

You uncurl to my rescue, *at last*, and leap to your feet.

'My Lord! I must object. We've argued this. That jar . . . there's not one word about it on the indictment. My client is *not* charged with infanticide. It is prejudicial. What is the meaning of it? He must withdraw it.'

The judge blinks up slowly. 'Yes, I . . . agree. Mr Jessop, perhaps you should remind yourself that it is your duty to extract only those facts relevant to the charge on the indictment. To what charge does this evidence relate?'

Jessop rocks back on his heels, pats his papers, scratches his wig, and bumps the table in his confusion. The thing inside the jar swills quietly. I stare at it, thinking that when all this is over, it's possible that I'll get the right punishment for the wrong thing. Time may have caught me at last. The room fills with hushed whispers and the slow smoke that smells like burning grass.

Your hands go to your hips, taken aback by your small victory.

I look from Jessop, up to the gallery. Gone. They're gone. They got what they came for.

'Have you done this sleepwalking trick before?' Jessop asks, forced to swerve away from the foetus, and trying to pick up speed again.

'I wouldn't remember.'

'Anyone ever *told* you that you have?'

'Well, Mr Casterwick –'

But his voice skims right over mine. 'Mrs Linux testified that on several occasions she discovered you late at night, outside your mistress's rooms.'

'I –'

'You weren't sleepwalking then?'

'No. I was going to see Madame. I –'

What can I say? *I was going down to her rooms. Because I wanted her. A longing so powerful it picked my feet up, drove them down the passage to her door. Made me think I was mad.*

'You were awake,' he says, teeth gleaming. His mouth a trap. 'Perfectly awake. All those other times. As you were at midnight on the night of these murders when you walked towards your mistress's rooms. And when, shortly after that, you stabbed her to death.'

'I was asleep,' I say in my shrunken voice.

He gives a shrug of a smile, like a jacket he's trying on. 'But everything you say is a fiction. The invention of a mind scrambling to save itself. Why should these gentlemen believe a word of it?'

Oh. Then my knees melt. I remember Linux shaking me awake into the cloud of her breath in the cold room. Her face a puddle in the half-dark. I remember she cried, *Murderer! Murderer!* and the constable said, 'Dress now, we must have you downstairs at once,' and his voice swam to me, but I couldn't lift my arms or my legs. He was a heavy man with a raw-looking face, black in the door frame. Black eyes, black-hatted. I saw a shadow taking shape beside me, which I then saw was

Linux. There was blood on my hands, and the bedcovers too. She pinched me, hissed, 'You're to come downstairs!'

Jessop's questions hammer and hammer at me, drive me like a nail inside myself. I'm in the prisoner's dock, but also in her room, in her bed. The covers, the nightstand, the woman in red. And I can't bear to look at her, can't bear to hear that she is dead. I try to cover my ears.

Sleep, Frances. Sleep.

Jessop swivels to look at the jurors before his next question, his face lit with satisfaction. 'Mrs Linux also testified that you locked your mistress in her rooms, on occasion. What do you say to that?'

'I did not.'

'You *terrorized* her, during the days leading to these murders. Didn't you?'

I laugh, though I know I'll seem like a Bedlamite. '*How?*' My mind gone syrup-slow. 'How? How would I have done that?'

No, I want to say. I want to laugh, to scream, to shout it out. *She* terrorized *me*.

Chapter Forty-Five

It ends as it began. With Jessop's snapping gown, his ship's horn of a voice.

'Gentlemen, I've never seen a more straightforward case. Not in all my years.'

I'm too tired now to hold myself upright. But I have to. I must listen, until the end.

'My friend, Mr Pettigrew – more a learned friend than a sensible one – has done his best.' He smiles down at you, where you sit fidgeting with the pink ribbon on your brief. 'He has tried to harangue you with all kinds of nonsense. But when you blow his puffery away, what is left? Nothing. Sleepwalking! Sleepwalking and amnesia!' He snorts. 'Perhaps he should take up the pen, gentlemen . . . One might well say he's as much of a fantasist as his client! Perhaps he, too, has been taken in by her. Like Mr Benham was.' He shakes his head. 'But, gentlemen, in this court, we trade in fact.

'The notion that sleepwalking could explain these crimes, let alone excuse them, that would be a murderer's charter!'

It speeds up now. All eyes turn to the judge. His quill drips over his papers as he speaks, ink crawls across them, and his clerk reaches up to move them to the side, just as he's been serving him, tenderly, quietly, attentively, the whole way through.

The judge turns to the jurors. 'Gentlemen, you are now charged with considering what you have seen and heard and delivering your verdict. It is true that, as a matter of English law, murder must always have that constituent part, malice aforethought and that, in our law, malice aforethought requires consciousness. If you believe the prisoner did in fact commit these crimes, but without that requisite degree of consciousness, because she laboured under a state of mind that was so disordered as to deprive her of responsibility, then that would be akin to automatism, which Mr Pettigrew mischievously suggests must have the same effect as the defence of insanity. To wit, the essential element of malice aforethought would not be there and the charge would not be made out. It is a novel argument, but it is one which it is your misfortune to have to trouble yourselves with.'

You look up, give a small shake of your head. You'll fume later about his choice of words – *mischievous*, *misfortune* – but you make no objections while they're being said.

'I know it has been a long trial,' he continues. 'I leave it to you to put an end to it.'

Then, time bearing down on me, catching me at last. The past, the present, the future, all at once.

Newgate Prison

Chapter Forty-Six

There's one more story left to tell.

21 October 1824
Male infant of Paradise plantation, 10 months old or thereabouts.
Length of body: 26 inches
Circumference of skull: 17 in
Weight: 16 lbs
Born to Calliope, 20, Negress, bought off Montpelier estate, Antigua, from Mr Buxton Hardy, together with her infant, by Mr John Langton, Paradise estate, Jamaica.

Head and skin covered in a pale down fuzz. Skin dry and firm. Suet-like complexion but normal colour in the gums. Nose, flat. Hair, woolly. Broad, flat features of the Negro. Eyes disproportionately placed, asquint. But complete lack of pigmentation in skin and eyes defies racial origins. An albino. Intend to conduct examination, as Buffon did with his white négresse, Geneviève. Believe it will be possible to contradict his supposition that the condition is a degenerative fluke. To begin with, examination of skin specimens is proposed. Thereafter the child will be kept for further extensive study.

Chapter Forty-Seven

The baby was asleep on the table. I could hear its mother outside, scratching at the door. As if that would tell him she was there. It was a relief when it stopped, but it always started again.

Langton had sent for her as soon as the pair of them arrived. Bought in from Antigua, thanks to Pomfrey. 'Bring me that pickney tomorrow. You hear?' Switching to Creole talk, same way he always did with his slaves. 'I'll let you sabi when you can come get him back.'

She wrung her hands. 'How *long*, Massa?'

Three full days, so far. But I'd seen the papers in his skull-cupboard. He was selling the mother on. Cart was coming for her in the morning, she just didn't know it yet. He was going to keep the child. For observation, he said.

'What for?' I'd asked.

'To note the limits of its intelligence, identify its capacity for learning.'

Same thing that pair of demons had been doing with me.

He only made me take the usual measurements, to start with, watched me snapping the calipers open, fixing them in place, slapped at them when I didn't work fast enough. I curved my palm over the span of the baby's head, the pale frizz of its hair. Protecting it. From him, from *me*. Startled when he spoke again.

'Skin,' he said. 'Let's get on with it.'

With the Surgeon dead, I'd had to learn dissection, whether I liked it or not. What would Benham have written about any of this, if I had told him? Certainly not how I quailed, looking down at that child. How I felt my stomach curl. How panic thickened my breath. Ahead of me lay the same two choices as always. Do what Langton wanted, or do what I wanted.

Not this, not this. Please not this.

I lifted the scalpel, set it down again, knotted my hands together.

I would never be able to confess it to anyone. But it wouldn't matter whether I confessed or not because *I* would know.

Oh, I stated my objections. The child was too young, should not be separated from his mother; the coach-house wasn't a place to keep an infant; how did he think he could raise one in there? And on and on. But to no avail. 'This is the worst thing you've asked of me,' I said.

'Pickney going hardly feel it,' he replied.

My head crowded with things he'd said over the years.

Blacks don't feel pain. It's what makes them so well suited to the work.

God doesn't waste good souls in black bodies.

George Benham is forced to come to me, for a change. All this data flowing from colonial laboratories.

Look at you. Even you. Proving that the principal thing you're made for is following my instructions.

Only God knew what else lay in store for that child, but I didn't want to find out.

The scalpel had slipped. Plunged into my own hand. Hardly a surprise, the way they shook.

The baby cried and cried, and could not be consoled. Langton leaped to his feet. 'Careful! *Careful.* Idiot girl! Can't afford to lose him.' Not for the first time, I knew he'd gone mad, and felt I'd gone mad with him. I looked him dead in the eye, holding my injured hand.

335

'I cannot do this.'

In response, he kissed his teeth. It had never been about what I could do, just what I *would*.

But, mercifully, the accident convinced him to pause. Give me time. 'Put yourself back together,' he said, nodding at the cut on my hand.

Water. Bandages. A tincture, to calm the child. Nothing could calm *me*.

Afterwards, Langton had spent the afternoon studying Helvetius and Voltaire. Their notes on their own examinations of white Negroes, Helvetius's speech concerning 'the little white born to black parents, who displayed a limited intelligence'.

Now he was pulling the infant's toes apart to squint between them. I'd never seen anything whiter than that baby. Whiter than a frog's belly. Whiter than a bucket of skimmed milk. Eyelashes pink as gums.

I went over to the basin, scooped some water up to scrub across my cheeks, let it seep through my fingers, numb my face. Stared at him down the long length of the room.

The space was heavy with the smells of lime and gunpowder, the syrupy light of the candles on the table, darkness spilling like water into the space around them. Silence rang loud as church bells in my head. The baby twitched its foot out of Langton's quivering hand.

I hated his hands. His work-starved fingers. His nails, which I was required to cut. Hated that I'd once stood in that same spot undoing my own buttons yet he'd said not one word about why I should not. How I had hated him for that.

I hated him with my whole soul, but I was stitched to him. Therefore, worst of all, I hated myself.

How he made me look inside all those bodies.

I hated the man named Benham, who had given him the idea.

●

Now that I look back on it I realize Miss-bella had taught me for spite, but he had finished it for the same reason. That day he made me swallow those pages, he must have known he'd found the very thing he needed, to tempt Benham's interest.

I went over and lifted the child away. He woke with a startle. I could hear his mother, through the door, trying not to sound angry, trying to sound like she was begging, instead. 'You took my baby. Thought you supposed to give him back? What you doing to him?'

Hate twisted in my chest. And dread, too. Of the next day, and what would be expected of me. And of the day after that.

Langton said he was going back to the house, told me to keep an eye on the child. I had to grind my teeth not to answer him.

The baby was warm as a chick, staring up at me, sucking on the heel of its hand.

Dundus. That's what the others would call it. Nothing but bad luck. They thought I was bad luck too – another mal-formed creature. *Coo 'pon her! Drifting 'tween that porch and that coach-house. Like she own the place! That passel of dried-out old goosetail feathers in the crook of her arm, like firewood. Like she for-get she a slave. She a neger, for all she might talk white.*

I listened to the scratching at the door.

Then I crouched next to it, and spoke. That silenced her. 'Tomorrow. Wait for the house to go dark. Then wait an hour. Find a clock. Beg one, thief one. Go get him from down next to the bridge. Get him quick. Don't know where you can go after that. That's going to be your problem. Whatever you do, don't bring him back.'

Next night, down to the coach-house, Langton and Miss-bella asleep. Started with the cabinet, stood back to let the torch press against the window sashes. I had to take myself back to the house quick, after that, but I stopped on the path, just for a moment, and let myself look. The smoke came in small fists, then slackened out into the night air. The wood burning clean. The sight of it froze me where I stood, struck such a queer chime in my heart. Swarms of ash spooled up out of it, like small black birds.

Intention had flown in, when I'd held that baby. I knew I was going to set that fire. Spring myself from that trap.

Chapter Forty-Eight

I feel as if I've been struck a blow. The judge droops the black cloth over his wig. He glances across at me. I grip the railing tight, because otherwise my hands will fly away. All my limbs will fly away, all parts of me. I can't look at you, couldn't bear to see one of your careful smiles, or, worse, nothing at all. I can hardly hear the judge's words. I must keep my eyes on his face. There's still hope, until a thing happens, that it could happen a different way. But then it happens and it is nothing but memory.

The jurors' verdict echoes while we wait. I allow myself to look at you. You sit, and stare straight ahead, like a man at a tomb. I follow your gaze and see that you're staring at the stone columns behind the judge's bench, at the sword, at the gold letters.

The truth is that I am a murderer.

'Frances Langton,' says the judge. 'The scriptures say that whoever spills a man's blood, his blood shall also be spilled. I have no choice but to give you the sentence of the law. I hope you will make use of your short time remaining on this earth and repent, and I pray that the example you are about to set by your suffering might have a good effect on others and deter them from committing the same grievous sins. In saying so, there is nothing left for me to do but to pass on you the dreadful sentence which the law requires and direct that you, Frances Langton, be taken from here to the place whence you came and thence to the place of execution where you will be hanged from the neck until you are dead.'

There is a spinning in my head, and a mewling, and then nothing but the quiet, desperate beating of my own blood.

I'm sorry.

I realize I've said it out loud. I've shouted. I've yelled.

I'm sorry, I'm sorry, I'm sorry.

Chapter Forty-Nine

Then, night squeezing in. Gaol-birds calling. The rattle of hearts in all those cages. Worst of all the way I shake and shake, like laughing, and cannot stop. Asking for laudanum. Begging. Give me just a thimble. A lick. The turnkey, laughing, shifting his breeches with his hand. Oh, they can get you anything, if you give them a mind to do it. But there's a price. There always is.

If he leaves me alone, if he leaves me with nothing, I will see them. Snipping roses down to their blunt red heads. Pearl handles winking.

Morning comes, whether you want it to or not. The keys tell me you're here. 'You slaughterhouse hens, nothing but callers.'

I straighten my bedding, though there's that awful quake in my hands. But maybe you've brought me something, some wisp of hope.

What you've brought is a man. A long sleeve of bones, twisting in his woollen jacket. He looks even more downcast than you. I see his eyes darting around, taking in the little pallet, the green mould curling up the walls. He wrinkles his nose. It's a salt box, for God's sake, I want to tell him, a cell for the condemned. It's not supposed to be fresh.

'This is John Pears,' you say. 'Who was to have been yesterday's surprise.'

He rakes his hair off his head, grips it in his fist. 'I've come here to tell you in person how sorry I am . . . Miss . . . Langton.'

'Dr Pears was until recently assistant to Dr Wilkes,' you say. The doctor keeps his head down. You give him a sharp look. 'You've come to say something, Dr Pears. Say it.'

He sinks onto the mattress, hooks his hands on the great pegs of his knees. 'I was present during the post-mortem of your mistress, Miss Langton. I told Mr Tomkin, last Friday – I – I don't know how to say this.'

You snort. 'Best way to say something is to say it.'

Pears heaves the words out. 'I don't think she had any wounds to speak of when she was brought in.'

A stumbling doubt shakes through me. 'She *wasn't* cut?'

'She was. But I think it was after the fact. When I came to examine her there were clear signs that those injuries had been inflicted post-mortem.'

'I don't understand.'

'I think her wounds were inflicted sometime between the time of death and the time of autopsy. I conducted a very careful examination. I'm sure of it. The incisions were too neat, pale around the edges . . . such a small quantity of blood . . .

'And when we opened her, there was a distinct odour in her stomach contents. A smell like bitter almonds –'

Yes. I know it. All too well. I take a step back, straight into the table. The moment snags, and snags me with it.

'– an indicator of opium. Her lungs and sinuses were congested, her heart also. There was cyanosis of many of the organs, including the skin. Signs of poisoning. Taken together with my suspicion about the nature of the wounds –' he shrugs '– I told Wilkes we should test. *Argued* for it. But he refused. The laudanum had been prescribed, he said, and therefore was not a matter to concern ourselves with.'

You interrupt, impatient: 'Wilkes swore on cross-examination that there was no reliable test.'

Pears hinges backwards, against the wall. 'No test for *opium*. But there are ways to detect morphia, which is its active principle. Dr Wilkes would have been correct to say other evidence would be necessary before any sound conclusion can be reached. But, considering what I suspected, about her wounds –'

'Sound conclusion about what?' I say, the words dredged up from my throat, slow, dry as cotton.

'About whether it could have been a case of death by poisoning.'

There's a whip of anger in your voice. 'All we needed, *Dr Pears*, was a grain of doubt. A *grain*. The only thing that determines whether the prisoner's shown the rope or the door.'

What you mean is something that would have had the jurors looking in another direction: some other murderer, some trickster excuse. But *this*? This has shaken loose the thought that's been there all along, one I haven't looked at, because I didn't want to see it.

I put my hands over my ears, blocking out Pears's noise. But nothing ever blocks Phibbah. *Men got their hands full with the big deaths, we make do with the small ones.* I thought about how she'd always mutter to herself while she was fixing up her potions, that list she tapped out through her teeth. Boiled gully-root to flush a womb, or crushed peacock-flower steeped in river water. If those failed, tinctures in the milk, a needle through the fontanelle. Ground cassava root if it was the mother not the baby you wanted to kill.

The mother, not the baby. The mother and the baby. The baby, then the mother.

A cold moment of truth.

Here, at last, was a terrible certainty, which had come matched with an equally terrible doubt.

Pears unfolds himself with a click. I want to sweep him off the bed, so that I may lie in it. 'But who would have cut her? Why did Wilkes lie?'

'Same reason I didn't testify, I'm sure.'

You scoff. 'Because you're cowards?'

He reaches up to tug on his cravat, turns to me. 'It was *I* who searched out your lawyers. Said I'd attest to my findings and let Wilkes swear to his. Giving him the benefit of the doubt, I thought it could be a difference of opinion. Some surgeons search only for what they expect to find.' He drops his chin. 'I thought we'd simply let the jurors decide.'

He works his mouth, as if getting ready to spit, or cry.

'I thought – *foolishly* – But I received a letter. From the hospital. I was told only that the family had made their wishes plain. Concerned about any hint that she'd been an addict, let alone any suggestion of . . . *self-murder*. Though it could have been pure accident, of course. It happens. Ladies exceed their doses, having built up a tolerance, over time.' He looks up. 'I wonder whether – Wilkes might have been pressured to make those wounds *himself*. But, regardless of who made them, they were made post-mortem. I'm sure of it.'

For the first time since that terrible night, my heart is still. But always that stabbing grief. And now rage as well. At Pears. At the Benham family. At Wilkes. *Reputation is everything.* I can see just how Sir Percy would have done it. Threats. Guineas. Sweet-talking. Thinking there had been one murder, what harm in making it two?

'I'm very sorry,' Pears repeats.

Oh, if he says that one more time, I'll stopper up his throat.

You jerk your hat back onto your head. 'Cut this long tale of yours short, Pears. The tests were never carried out. You've repented, you're *now* prepared to swear, have assured me you won't go clucking off this time, *et cetera*, and we hope – *you*'d better hope – that it isn't too little, too late.'

Then you tell me, more gently, that Tomkin is submitting a letter to the judge as we speak, including a transcript of what I've just been told. 'I don't suppose it needs me to tell you we don't have much time.'

Pears looks at me. 'There was one more thing. I didn't believe the wounds sustained by Mr Benham were consistent with the knife that had been produced. That knife was double-edged, and the gashes were too narrow. I suggested that another search should be made, for some instrument that could cause the skin to *contract* around it after it had been pulled out.'

This I do not want to hear. I take a step back. There's a rattle from the street. A cart overturning. Rocks pelted at the walls. I hope you'll think that's why I jump.

'Are you all right? Miss Langton?' I hear you, from far away: 'She's overcome, and no wonder. There has been an egregious miscarriage of justice, and *you* had no small part in it . . .'

I put my hand to my throat. I'll tell Pears. I'll tell him. No search would have found that weapon. Here it is. Memory, clear, cold. Where it has always been. Benham's face. He's shouting. I'm shouting too. His face twists in front of me. The scissors twist. My hands.

But you're already preparing to leave, which I tell myself gives me permission to say nothing. Before you do, you ask me to focus on the events of that night. You say it will help my case to remember as much detail as I can. *Anything* I can think of, which you will put together with Pears's word. 'Best as you can remember.' *Give me something I can save your neck with.* My best hope now is to throw myself on the court's mercy, you say. No hope for a pardon, but leniency, perhaps.

Chapter Fifty

I've heard nothing from you since. But Sal came and found me this morning. How it made my heart leap to see her. I tried to give her my attention, push other thoughts aside. She hadn't been at the trial, she said, because the old bastard's children had come for her. They'd just appeared on the doorstep one day, bailiffs in tow. Apparently, there's been no end of trouble for her since my trial. Everyone in London knows where the School-house is now. The old bastard's children claimed Sal was their property, left to them in his will. Mrs Slap said she had to go, not to bring any more trouble. For six weeks she'd been a maid. Sal, a maid! I tried to picture her with bucket and soap and rags. Oh, she made me laugh, with her tales of seasoning their tea with their own piss! She'd been able to buy herself back, with all her savings from the School-house. All her lovely coins, poured out in a golden stream, right into their grasping hands.

She grinned. 'I suppose I rather pay them than pay some lawyer to fight them. And I got my free paper now.'

She told me the broadsheets are saying that the Devil was in me and put it in my head, that I wanted to carve the Benhams and boil their bones into soup and that I do not repent of it, save that I didn't get that chance. I didn't want to talk to her about any of it. I asked her about Laddie, but she knew nothing. Laddie's made himself a loose thread. I suspect he didn't want to face their questions, or their English justice.

We held hands, we watched the candles dwindle and burn.

She'd brought me food, a blanket, some paper and a pen
Added to the sheaf you had already left.

Best of all, a copy of *Moll*.

I won't say more about Sal's visit. It was like that elephant, so long ago. No matter what I write, you won't know what it was like. She did bring one last thing, which I saved until she left. A letter. I opened it, pulled one of the candles closer. It was from Miss-bella, addressed to: '*Frances, former housemaid and latter-day whore*', care of *THE SCHOOL-HOUSE*. I suppose she must have read the papers too. Perhaps it amused her to write me at the brothel rather than the gaol.

Frances,

I do hope this reaches you.

My husband is long gone and Phibbah even longer. Therefore I must write you.

I heard he gave you away as soon as you got to England, which must mean he knew how close death was for him. I believe it is also close for you.

It has outraged my brother that I am writing to you. His sister, penning a letter to her husband's bastard! I think he saw it as the last sign, if he needed one, of how this place has rotted me like a thrown-away apple.

My husband's bastard. Those are my words. My brother's were not as delicate, though I don't intend to spare your feelings in this. In fact, I intend to be as cruel as I can.

My husband's bastard. And now my confessor.

I was the one who told you. I did that to be cruel as well. As long as I live, which will now be mercifully brief, I will be cursed to go over and over back to that porch, to your mulish answer when I asked you what you were doing in that coach-house with my husband. Cleaning, you said. Cleaning! As if anyone inside or outside that house was fooled by then into thinking you a maid. I told you he was your father. His bone and his flesh. Oh, I could see the horror on your face. You said you were going to be sick. You vomited on my rose bushes – do you remember that?

The things the two of you did were abominations, even in a place awash in abominations.

But I am not writing you about that. I am writing about your mother. You used to ask about her. Over and over. I used to hear her, when you asked, telling you to leave her alone. She was the reason he brought you to live in the Great House, you know. She is, I suppose, the reason I was kind to you at the start. I wanted to hurt her. I even made sure I was the one to name you, that she'd have not even that small serving of a mother's joy. He was fond enough of her, in his own way. (These things are very seldom black and white, are they?) Fond enough to promise that you would never be sold away, that you could come up out of the quarters, that you would not be put in the fields. You were never to know the truth. But she'd have told you, just as I did, had she still been here. I'm sure of it. Anything to stop what the two of you were doing.

I suspect there were others before you. Babies, I mean. If there was one person on that whole estate who knew how a woman could go about saving herself from children she didn't want, it was your mother. Before you came, Langton used to say the pair of us – she and I, I mean – were barren as a pair of shipboard hens. Ha! You proved him wrong, and then it was only me. The idiot. He was as blind as all men to anything that would suggest his own inadequacy, or a woman's choice. Those herbs she gave me. I made a joke of it. Give me this day, my daily orangeade. The thing that saved me from having to bear his children. And for that, I am grateful to her.

I don't understand how you slipped through your mother's cracks. Perhaps she was tired, by then, or perhaps her usual tricks just

didn't work. However it happened, you were Langton's only child,
and I take pleasure in that.

You were born, she ran away, and then he hunted her down and
dragged her back and he ordered Manso to take his chisel to her
teeth. But he cut off his own nose to spite his face, as they say. She
didn't hold the same appeal after that. Oh, but he was fond of her.
He made her those promises, after all, about you.

I learned the hard way that this is a place where a man keeps his
concubines and his bastards in plain sight. The very woman who'd
spit in your porridge in the morning could be fornicating with your
husband that night.

How it destroys all of us.

I am tired. I will finish this. Where was I?

Your mother.

In the Bible, Laban gave to his daughter Rachel his handmaid
Bilhah, to be her handmaid. And Rachel's sons were the sons of
Bilhah, her handmaid.

We were Rachel and Bilhah, she and I.

My husband no doubt believed that in the next life she and I will
still be out on that porch, surrounded by dying English roses, me
with the tea, her with the fan.

I think he is wrong.

Mrs A. Langton

My stomach clenches. I'm back in the dining room, telling
Langton about the orangeade, telling myself I was only speaking the truth, forgetting how many sides the truth has. I can't
see how terrible it will be, because all I'm thinking about is
me. Fear makes my mouth dry as salt. I'd seen it, of course,
during the years that followed, who she was to me; there was,
after all, only one woman it could have been. All those times
I'd asked her, perhaps I was just waiting for her to tell me. She
hated me sometimes. But I believe there was love, too.

So many things to tell her. How guilt has run through me, all this time, keeping time with my blood. How, even now, to think of it, to write of it, makes both leap in my chest. How sorry I am.

A child's understanding is dark. Sometimes light is blinding. I shake the letter out on my lap and read it again. And then I'm on the porch. I watch Miss-bella's slow hands reaching for the glass. Phibbah behind her with the fan. The orangeade. That's how they managed it. Not poison, those herbs in Miss-bella's glass, but her daily dose. Make sure she stayed barren. But in Jamaica there were two truths. One, all bush medicine is obeah if they say it is. And two, white women never take the blame.

Chapter Fifty-One

Light skims the bars. I feel the mattress shift. Madame sits next to me. She has her little black book, her quill. She's making her notes. Any minute, she'll take off her boots and pull me into her lap, and kiss me, and I will never want to open my eyes and let her go. Nothing between us but a tendon of breath and this fresh morning, rinsing everything with light. I've even managed a little sleep. Then I huddle my knees in, to watch her walking away, lavender silk brushing her ankles. She looks over her shoulder, tears in her eyes, shining like ice. *What can I say to make her stay?*

And then the sudden knowledge. A flare of light.

What would you take with you if you could leave?

I claw my way to my feet, bang my fists across the door, cry out for the keys. No answer. No one comes. For the first time in this god-forsaken place, all is wretchedly quiet. Not a shuffle. Not a whisper. I knock until my hands are numb, until I feel my own frustration beating through my skin, like a second heart. Then I stop, listen to the walls creaking around me. I serve other masters now, and nothing will happen until they come.

At last, I'm permitted to send word out, and then follows the agony of waiting.

That single silent nod of yours slams into my throat. Prickles salt into my eyes.

I had hoped to be wrong.

'It *was* behind that portrait,' you say. You give me a sharp look. 'Tucked in against the frame. How did you know? More to the point, why could *this* not have occurred to you during your trial? Tomkin found Meek and asked him to go back to the house. They went together. He noted the contents, if you're interested? This is a copy. The document itself has gone off to the judge.' You hold it up, gingerly, like something that might leave a stain.

And I snatch it, so I can read it myself.

Death is the only thing that scares me now, and yet the only thing that can take away my fears.

   I am sorry.

It strikes me that these may be the last words I will ever read, these last words she ever wrote, and I read them greedy as a calf at a teat. Delivered by the woman in red, tucked behind her frame.

I am sorry.

'It bears her signature. Here.' I point. 'Ritte Delacroix.'

'Yes,' you say. 'Self-murder. There can be no doubt.'

The long dark days following my trial, it seems even the skies have turned black with spite. Fits of lightning at the window, so the light seems to slice the walls. I pace my cell. A felon should never dwell on her own verdict. It's a waste of time, when time is all she has left. Yet I'm sad to say that's precisely what I do. I think about my trial, about you, about that defence you concocted. You're all the talk here, even though you lost. That Sleepwalking Defence. Lushing called it science, but it seemed closer to magic if you ask me: a black shade drawn down – by sleep or intoxication – then a kind of dreaming madness in its wake. That was your own spell, to make them think me an automaton, a *zombi*. Then I stop dead in my tracks, struck by the thought that it was the very spell some would say Langton cast, the minute I set foot in that coach-house. *Stripped of my free will.* But death can be a choice too, the dark link between dreaming and madness. Her *melancholia* that same black link, opium the shade she drew down on herself. All those rotten branches, growing from the same black root.

Chapter Fifty-Two

Even now memory sieves those hard stones of grief. But I must draw back the shade. Hold a mirror up to that night. Her truth now forces me to set mine down also, to face myself and what I've done. Forcing me to bleed, and bleed again. I feel sure I can come close to the truth of it, which is as certain as we can ever be about the truth.

A breath.

And here it is.

I couldn't sit still, I went downstairs in search of her. Through cold rooms, through narrow passages, through the darkened hall. The windows shrouded in fog. I couldn't hold onto anything, tried to grasp the table, but I stumbled. Fell. The grandfather clock shuddered. The hall was empty and dim, but there was light and life in the drawing room, and it drew me. The very same longing that had driven me to her rooms in the dead of night. Polished wood gleamed like eyes, the doors gaped. Dark shapes twisted against the walls: people circling, talking. Most of them turned and gawped at me. A crush of skirts and perfumes and hair. Violin music coming from somewhere far away. I stopped, stared.

Benham took a step, raised his hand. *Stay back.* I saw Hep Elliot. Laddie.

Her.

She was beside the long window, at the heart of a small crowd. Head tilted, glass raised. *Laughing.* When I saw that it split my heart like a cord of wood. She moved from one guest

354

to another, then the next. When she saw me, she came to a stop. The room went still. Their murmurings fell upon me like rain. *Meg's strange, darky maid.*

When I reached her, I lifted my chin, gathered my breath.

'Sssh. Frances.' Her nails pressed into my arm. 'Sssh.' I tried to shake her loose, but she wouldn't let go.

This is death.

Linux shouldering through the crowd, Charles in tow. Forgetting her manners. Her wide jar of a mouth, her eyes sour as plums. But it was Madame who told me to leave. 'Please. Do not make a fuss.' Her eyes black. I saw fear in them, and the coil of some darker thing.

The room breathed again as I turned on my heel.

Charles took me to the attic. But I went back down, to her room, sat on the bed. I kicked my feet against it. Books slumped in piles, like dark stones in a well, and the walls pressed in. I felt the same sick clutch at my stomach that had taken hold of me when I saw her. I got up, lit a candle, remembered how they'd all been congratulating themselves. Congratulating *him*.

What a debate! What a speaker! What a man!

While *I* had been forsaken. I was being turned out again.

Earlier that day, I'd come up from the kitchen to find her in bed, drapes of blood on her legs, the gown bunched up around them. Not her own blood. The baby had finally let go, and she lay curled around it. A little beached thing on the sheet. A little mulatta. Like me. All babies are pale, did you know that? You can only tell how dark they're going to be by the fingers and the toes. This one slipped into my palm; a little girl; a tiny blood-dark head; feet small as nails.

Her face crumpled when I shook her awake. 'Let me sleep . . .' Her eyes rolled, her breath too. But, at last, she let me take it. I worked on the living body first, then the dead one. This was work I knew. I kept my hands busy. Washed her, changed her gown. I felt the fire move out of the grate and into my bones. Watched the ash cool white. 'I'll have to get fresh sheets,' I said. 'And we'll need to burn these.' She didn't even look up. I drew an almighty breath. 'I'll have to burn it, too.'

That roused her. She sat up, slid her hands across the bed. 'No.'

The bottle was on the bedside table, and I could see the tooth-marks of the drug upon her. Only a dark swirl left, mere dregs. My hand quaked with wanting it myself. I'd have licked the rim.

'How much did you take?' I asked.

She frowned. 'I have not slept since you were here.'

A tiny flame. *She needs me. Still.*

'How much?' I repeated.

'I didn't know what you would decide. And I have been all agony, waiting. I wanted –' She gave a sharp cry. She wouldn't look at me. 'But when I *saw* it – And now. I –' She broke off. 'I only wanted –'

'You wanted what you got,' I interrupted. 'You wanted it gone.' It was cruel of me. All she'd done was make sure she wanted no more than she was allowed.

She trembled, under the bedcovers, made me promise we'd bury it, and begged me never to breathe a word. A promise you already know I've been forced to break.

I nodded towards the basin. 'Are you going to tell him?'

'No.'

'He'll find out.'

'He will. But not today.' Her mouth flickered. 'I swear I *will* wean myself.'

'He will be glad of it.'

'The loss? Or the weaning?'

'Both.'

She needed it, then, she said. She had to look well, fool them. Fool *him*. *Give him Marvellous Meg*. What was needed was a resurrection. Laudanum, she said, was the only way she could survive the night. We'd have to smooth her skin with powders and her nerves with the syrup. She'd wear breeches, under her skirts, padded with towels. It would take a small miracle to get her downstairs, and get her sparkling. I lifted the second bottle from the cabinet. 'Some brandy, too,' she said, so I got that as well. She opened for it, the spoon tipping to her mouth.

I told her I'd bring fresh sheets. But, first, I brought the little creature up with me to the attic, wrapped in a bedsheet. I thought no one had seen me. I went out. Bought the jar, bought the arsenic.

A body can be embalmed in arsenic. Did you know that? Useful knowledge for your trade, no doubt. It was useful for the one I'd practised at Paradise. Most of my learning has been a burden, but that was one of the only fruitful things I learned: arsenic and water, four ounces to a gallon.

After I'd done it, I couldn't stay in the little room. I covered it over with my pallet and went downstairs, onto the basement steps, tried gulping at fresh air to calm myself, to go back up and face her. I was still there with my head against the railings when Benham sent Charles to tell me he wanted to see me, in his library.

'I've been upstairs,' he said, 'taking an opportunity to remind my wife of her obligations for this evening. Quite a voyage of discovery. Her bed looked like it had been the scene of some fresh carnage.'

The sheets. I had left the sheets. My stomach clutched.

'Perfect timing, of course.'

The thought stretched, curled. Struck me still as a stopped clock. He was going to send me away again. Then he said it: 'I have no further use for you.'

'You needed me when you were trying to spoon what I knew out of me, and when you wanted me to take her child –'

'What else could have been done with it?' He snorted. 'Only man in all of London she had to steer clear of had to be the one she fucked.'

I'd stayed quiet about what I knew. But now my anger rose to meet his. Like strangers being introduced. 'You only know where I've been because they know *you* there. They know you bought girls. Fresh off the stage-coaches. Didn't you wonder if I'd find out? You keep apartments in Marylebone, or Sir Percy does . . . You're both members of that club. What do you call yourselves? The Devilish Gentlemen?'

He hissed, drew back as if I'd slapped him. But with anger, not surprise. As if he might have been expecting it. 'Those girls were prostitutes, and sold themselves.'

'What did they sell? Their bruises? Their split skin? You kept them months against their will. One of those Devilish Gentlemen crippled a girl. But I'm sure you know that. 'Cause the talk is that it was you who did it.'

His mouth twitched but every other part of him stayed still. 'That girl has been looked after –'

'Even *now* you try to excuse yourself.' I closed my eyes, felt the pop of anger. Though I didn't know it then, it was the only thing I had left. 'The finest mind in England? But it's not always the mind that makes the man, is it? In some parts, they know the man.'

Then his hands started flying, fast as cards out of a deck. He shouted. Called me a thief, a savage. Said this was blackmail, added to the tally of my other crimes. How could I think I had any power over him? But he was wavering. Unsure now where

I could do the most damage with what I knew about him – there, or on the streets. Which is why he said I was to stay until he'd decided what was to be done, already pulling his papers towards him. But the whole time he kept his eyes on me.

'That's where you're wrong,' I said. 'This time I'm staying to suit myself.'

The night stretched before me deep as a well. I was a stone he wanted to cast into it. I found her door locked. I roamed the halls, went outside, stood beneath black trees once more picked clean as bones. In the kitchen, wine-glasses had been laid out, and silver platters for canapés. Everyone else upstairs, cleaning. It smelt of salt and meat. I watched the clock. Paced and waited. I knocked into the table, and the glasses jumped.

When, at last, she let me in, I had a question burning through me that I was afraid to ask. The truth is she frightened me. I didn't ask because I didn't want the answer. Same reason I'd turned my eyes away from the tiny swaddled bundle earlier in the day.

She wanted to wear her lavender silk, so I took it down. Did she shrink from *me*? Did she avoid my eyes? When I lifted the dress, she raised her arms. The shadow of the silk darkened across her neck like a blush. How delicate she was, and had always been. She had never had the courage this world requires. I told myself to speak.

'He said I'm to leave. Do you agree with it?'

'I do not.'

'But you will do nothing about it?'

The white gleam of her in the glass. I wanted to walk out of there, then, and ask her to come. But what could I offer her? A bedroom in a bawdy-house, if I was lucky.

It would be death, for a woman like her.

Speak, Frances. Say it. Just say it.

But that was when she turned, twisting her hands. 'Please stay upstairs tonight? It will cause too much trouble with him. And – I . . . cannot bear –'

'Cannot bear?'

'To be reminded.'

I told her she was a coward, then. I said other horrible things.

This time, as you know, I did not obey.

After Charles left me in the attic, I crept back down to her room. It gaped around me and I gaped back. It was so like a room in a novel, for hiding treasure, or lunatics. Yet it was the place where I'd had my own romance, my own measure of happiness, fleeting as it was. Inside as well as out, there was nothing but smothering black. I went to the cabinet, took out the bottle, touched my lip to the rim, and felt the drug, cold then warm. *More.* I sat. Waited. *More.* I knew she'd come. Arranged my hair and skirts as prettily as I could.

She pushed open the door. 'No one knows I'm here. I must go back down soon.' I sat up.

She went straight for the bottle and tipped it to her lips. The thought shuddered through me that it was the drug she'd come back for, not me. She held the bottle out. Her eyes shone like poisoned fruit. 'Shush.'

'*Did* you ever love me?'

'I am all in agony, Frances,' she said. 'And you wonder about love.' She touched cold fingers to my cheek. Her eyes looked flat, dead already. I thought of her small affections. How I'd sucked it all down like a child's ration of sweets. How she'd sucked me down, too, as greedily as she drank her tinctures. She took a dose, gave me one too. And another and another. I try to think what it was I saw on her face. Pity? Fear? Now it was my hands plucking at the sheets as I sat and watched. She drained the glass and turned to leave. But she stopped at the door, her back quivering.

'I think it – it has broken me,' she said. I didn't need to ask what she meant. Then, 'He *can* divorce me now,' as if she had just thought of it, clutching her own sleeves.

'Then come. Let him divorce you. *Come.*'

She shook her head. 'I did not agree with him about you, Frances. I am sorry. But if it is the only way . . . Please. Go back upstairs. Go back.'

I called her name.

She spoke her wounding words, and left.

I took more laudanum, took the bottle upstairs with me. No chance of rest. I listened to the carriages, their guests departing, and tried to slow my breaths. A minute passed. An hour? Time wriggled away. I couldn't measure it.

When I crept back down, she was in bed. Dark hair pooled to her waist. A single candle burning. It seemed that her eyes were fixed on the woman in red. For a strange moment, I thought each of them was about to speak. Then I saw she was asleep. I felt the heavy crawl of the drug. Slowing me down. I felt rooted. I tried to take a step. Her head felt hot.

Then I was in Benham's library, swaying over the jamb. 'I think we should call a doctor. She's not well.'

He looked up, laughed. 'I'm quite sure she isn't well.'

'Send for Fawkes, then. She might need help, for the bleeding.'

'It's the drug, as you well know,' he said. 'Her constant solace. Tomorrow she'll be the same thorn in my side she always is.'

'But it could –'

His laugh as bitter as the laudanum on my lip. 'It's nothing. And even if she *is* ill . . .' His head wove. 'I think it was de Sade who said he'd prefer a dead mistress to an unfaithful one. One could well ask how one prefers one's wife.'

'You're *drunk*.'

'It was a party, girl. Everybody's drunk.'

The room was shrinking like wet cotton.

'All those nasty little gossips . . . right . . . about that nigger cuckolding me.'

Oh, but so did I. My throat felt gritted. The blood rose in me, like flame through a wick. Rage welling hot. 'You pretend you're without sin. Sit here casting stones at the rest of us. You pretend your hands are clean. But all of it is your doing. *Crania*. Langton. Me. You brought Laddie here. How is that any better than what Langton did to me? And *her*. Forcing her into your small spaces . . .' I brushed my face with my hands. 'What if the world knew what kind of man you really are?'

I saw it. I saw it. He was even more afraid of the truth than I was.

I took a step back. The drug skimmed everything soft, made my pulse beat like wings. 'Maybe I should put all that education you force-fed me to some good use,' I said. 'That would be quite an *exposé*.'

The old darkness was slipping into my head. His heels clicked through it. He raised his hand and slapped me. The room sagged, tore. I gripped him, but he slapped me again. The tails of his black jacket scuttled around us, and the drug made a strange, slow dance of it, thickened the air, prickled sour under my arms. I twisted my fingers at his cravat. He raised his hands. Scraped at my throat.

Find your backbone, Frannie.

I shook him off, reached down to my skirts.

It was quick. It's a wonder they didn't hear it downstairs.

That afternoon in the garden, the summer before. In Madame's room, while she'd slept, I'd cut a hole in my pallet.

Because Linux accused me of stealing them: that was why I'd done it. And they had stayed there all that time.

But now I had them in my hand.

I clasped them high above us. It felt like flying. The room torn open to the black underneath.

I was defending myself. That is what I choose to write here. If I was still the prisoner in court, some silver-tongued Jessop would ask why I had those scissors with me, when I went down to the library.

Did you bring the scissors downstairs?

Wasn't your pallet upstairs?

You armed yourself, didn't you, before coming down?

But I don't have to answer any further questions.

Afterwards, I went upstairs. What choice did I have? I should have run, of course, taken myself back into the streets. But I went upstairs to lie down next to her. The sight of her dragged my heart, like an anchor on rocks. How would I explain myself to her? To anyone? I passed my hands over the books on the table, the mantel, trying not to look at her. Blood had trailed along behind me, so I wetted a towel and wiped the carpet. I took the brush and pan up from the hearth, swept at the cold ashes there, kindled up a fire, then stood back to watch the flames coming. There was some of the drug left in the bottle I'd brought with me. I drained it. I wanted my mind blank. *Tabula rasa.* Inside all soft and black like soil. The only sound was the crackle of the fire. More laudanum. More and more until the bottle was drained. I felt my hands go cold, let the bottle drop. Let the towel fall into the fire. All my own blood left me, then. I heard her voice. I swear it. I am sure of it. *'Sleep, dear Frannie. Sleep.'*

Then, just as I told you, I slept.

•

They woke me, in her bed. They told me she was dead. It must have been *his* blood, around us in the bed, and on her, carried there on my own hands. There are things that cannot be written down. A terrible privacy. Like death, like love. Those things I felt then. I felt a pulling, a tearing, felt my heart dangling like a severed and torn and muddied root.

Before I went down to ask Benham to fetch the doctor, I'd thought she was sick, sleeping. Now I see that she must have been dying, even then.

I'm coming to the end. As I write, all I see is her. Opening the cabinet, laying her book inside, taking out one of the amber bottles. All that care she took. Lined up like instruments, isn't that what Linux said? Like laying out the dead. The last time she ever opened that cabinet. The last time she ever took out the bottle. The last time she crossed her room, towards the portrait, her letter in her hand . . . Was she as terrified as I am now? *The dose is the poison.* Oh, and she was the poisoner herself.

I have wondered about the knife. The one Constable Meek said he took from her cabinet. Why was it there? When she went to the kitchen that night – or at some other time, even earlier than that – could she have brought it up without them seeing? It pains me to think of it. But Pears swears she didn't use it, that it was laudanum she chose, in the end.

It's possible that Meek put that knife inside the cabinet *himself,* or that he never found it upstairs at all, but only said he had to make sure I took the blame. They'd have needed to produce *some* weapon, after all, since they'd never found the scissors, hidden in the skirts I was arrested in. I doubt they even kept those, seeing how filthy they were.

•

I know I should have told you during our very first meeting about what happened with Benham. That one burden, at least, I can finally set down. Like all those times in the coach-house. Like that time with Henry. The world went black, and black things were done in it.

But would you have understood?

I knew I had to tell you my story first.

Chapter Fifty-Three

I have received your letter. I am to be pardoned for the murder that wasn't a murder. As for the other, I will hang.

Chapter Fifty-Four

Across the flagstones, through the chapel yard, thirty-five steps to the chapel door. I counted. That's the real miracle, the time they let us spend outside.

I turned my face up. The clear sky, and the arched windows gleaming, like iced buns on a baker's shelf. I breathed in, slow and deep, almost expecting the smell of sugar. Too soon inside, we were herded into the condemned pew, no choice but to sit with our knees poking the coffin they keep in there. You pray there's nothing inside it, though no one will say. They make us stare at death before we face it.

We were there to be stared at, too. It's instructive for the other gaol-birds to see us on our final night. The service for the condemned. Some of them reach for us, try to touch us on our smocks. *Put in a word for us*, they say, *where you're going.*

The windows here are lined with greased paper, just like the rest of the gaol. Every room dim as mist. Still, the light dribbles in. Pale, but enough to watch the heads around you go from black to ash to white. Like coals burning down in a fire. The same high windows as the courtroom, and the same green velvet, come to think of it. The room is laid out much the same as well. I suppose it's so you know they're both about the same business. The King's chapel, and the King's court. Though it's the Ordinary who's in charge here, not a judge, and he wears white robes, not red. For we're washed clean of blood, now. We are judged. Condemned.

When they came for us, for the service, I told them I didn't want to go. But you're to have God in your last days, here, whether you like it or not. Like swallowing a purgative. I'd rather have laudanum, given a choice, but Newgate is a clockwork universe, and everything in it works towards a single end. Mine.

Hanging's an efficient business.

There we sat. Knees twittering, like birds on stumps, heels clanking like bell-clappers. Who could be more restless than a group of the condemned at forced prayers? There are six of us for tomorrow. I sat next to a thin woman with a jaw like a shovel, legs scabbed with sores big as coins. She kept lifting her skirt to pick at them. 'What will happen to us?' she said, fishing up one of her plaits and sucking it. I told her not to look too far ahead, because when you can see what's coming it makes pain more like pain, and pleasure less like pleasure. Then we fell silent, though she began to cry. I didn't say more, not wishing to bring her spirits down further, for they'd have nowhere to land but on me. We don't speak much among ourselves, as a rule. Or with anyone else for that matter. There's no point.

The Ordinary, stout, white-frocked, waved his arms and spoke to us about the wages of sin. The only wages I'll ever earn, it seems. I tried to lean around him to read the plaques on the wall. I could see they were writings from Exodus, but not what they said. I'm so hungry to read I'd read anything, though the Bible would not be my first choice. But he blocked them with his waving arms and his sour face. He's to write an account of each of us, as you know, before we're hanged, and publish them in his Ordinary's Accounts. Another thing they don't give you any say in. He'll try to make us sound pious and repentant, no matter how nasty we are at our rotted-apple cores. Full confessions and cautionary tales. I plan to say nothing, when it comes to my turn.

An hour outside with the sun on our faces would have been

a mercy, far kinder, and God knows I need that more than Him. Besides, He'll have all the words soon enough if they're right. Why does He need the last one?

Everybody I've wronged is long gone. But I fell to my knees anyway, in the condemned pew. Oh, it caused some disturbance. Flocked all around with hands and robes. 'Get up! Get up!' they said. They tried to batter me back into my seat, but I held fast. My hands dragged like claws along the wooden bench. I'm no longer afraid of them. Oh, the things we do on our knees: confess, beg, pray. Love.

I beg your pardon, Phibbah. Calliope. I beg your pardon, baby. Both babies. Every last headless body left behind at Paradise. I beg your pardon, Madame.

In the end, hearing only silence, I rose.

What would you want to be remembered for? If you had one last page and one last hour, what would you write? In the end, this is what I choose. My account of myself. The only thing I'll be able to leave behind. That there were two things I loved: all those books I read, and all the people who wrote them. Because life boils down to nothing, in spite of all the fuss, yet novels make it possible to believe it is something, after all.

But now I must set down my pen, and face what is coming to me, though it is more than I deserve. I must thank you, before I do. You gave me the reason to write, as well as the means. I've asked Sal to bring this to you. There'll be money enclosed. It should be enough to pay a scribe to make copies you could send out. I'm not fool enough to think my story would sell. But the Mulatta Murderess's might. Perhaps there's enough of her in these pages to tempt a publisher. It isn't lost on me that I am ending my life the same way Langton ended his, in the hope that my mutterings will find their way into ink. Some of us are the hewers of words, while the rest are merely the hewers of wood. Perhaps someone will be interested in all of this. Though I won't hold the few breaths left to me. As Langton said once, most publishers can't see past their noses. Probably not far enough to see a woman like me. I've left everything else to Sal, such as it is. I saved a little money at the School-house, and there's my grey dress, and my copy of *Moll Flanders*, though she'll have to get someone else to read it to her. I imagine Sal one day, watching some dusky little mulatta girl hanging off her mother's hand. She smiles, as she does every time she sees a mongrel who reminds her of me. 'Look 'pon dat, Fran, look 'pon dat. We still here! We fruitful! We multiplying!' She laughs her big, wide-open laugh.

But these pages are for you.

12 May 1826

I close my eyes.

A murk of people and smoke stretching back to the sharp church steeples. Pie-sellers, carts, broadsheet-sellers. Babies being passed overhead. Pikemen at the corners, pressing them all back. A scrap of cloth blows across the platform to the hangman's boot. He doesn't notice. If he does, he doesn't look down. His mouth as serious as a knife. Nothing to me but the great hammer of my heart, my feet. But, kiii, the air's fresh! Sweet. Cold. I drink it in, drink it down like milk, I feel the great choking feeling of breathing rising to fill my chest. I slow my breaths. I'm afraid. I'm afraid. The morning is pink as flames. I raise my head and let the sky touch my face, and I see her. I feel a tug. I say her name. Marguerite. A whisper.

A whisper becomes a shout. How I loved you.

I am afraid. I am afraid.

But the mind is a different place, and there, soon, we will have days together.

And time.

Author's Note

Francis Barber was a young Jamaican boy brought to London in the eighteenth century and sent into service in the household of Samuel Johnson; Johnson wrote that he'd been 'given me by a Friend'. The idea of being 'given' in England, where all men were supposed to be free, was the springboard for this novel. Barber's story was chronicled by Michael Bundock in *The Fortunes of Francis Barber*.

For the scientific aspects of the plot I drew on several useful texts, in particular Andrew S. Curran's *The Anatomy of Blackness*, Richard Sheridan's *Doctors and Slaves* and two articles by Lorna Schiebinger: 'Medical Experimentation and Race in the Atlantic World' and 'Scientific Exchange in the Eighteenth-Century Atlantic World'. Langton's *Crania* was modelled on *Crania Americana*, a book published by Samuel Morton in 1839 (I have taken a novelist's liberties with the chronology).

I am indebted to several books about early black immigrants to London, including *Black London* by Gretchen Holbrook Gerzina, *Reconstructing the Black Past* by Norma Myers, and *Staying Power* by Peter Fryer. Laddie's story was inspired by the relationship between Julius Soubise and the Duchess of Queensberry.

I read testimonies of American slaves in *Before Freedom: When I Just Can Remember*, edited by Belinda Hurmence.

Barbara Hodgson's *In the Arms of Morpheus* was a useful and fascinating exploration of the use and effects of laudanum among the upper classes.

I also consulted records of actual legal proceedings, among

them the early nineteenth-century case of Jane Rider, the Springfield somnambulist, and Rufus Choate's 1846 defence of Albert Tirrell in Boston, USA, as well as the Old Bailey online archive.

Other helpful sources included Kirstin Olsen, *Daily Life in 18ᵗʰ Century England*; Catharine Arnold, *City of Sin*; Peter Ackroyd, *London*; Dan Cruickshank, *The Secret History of Georgian London*; Jennifer Kloester, *Georgette Heyer's Regency World*; Venetia Murray, *An Elegant Madness: High Society in Regency England*.

In May 1823, George Canning introduced a series of resolutions for the amelioration of conditions for West Indian slaves, including religious instruction, leading to the imposition of an amelioration plan by Order-in-Council in Trinidad and Tobago the following year. I have given George Benham ideas in keeping with those proposals, save that his aim was to preserve slavery rather than abolish it.

Some of the remarks attributed to Langton and Benham were written by real West India planters, including Matthew Lewis and Edward Long. Matthew Lewis's *Journal of Life on a West India Estate*, including its references to 'belly women' and 'shipboard hens', and Thomas Thistlewood's journals provide two vastly different first-hand accounts of life in Jamaica by West India planters. Both diaries reflect the opposite extremes of the white man's reaction to Jamaica during the period, which swung between cruelty and condescension.

Acknowledgements

Not a page would have made it into print without my husband, Iain.

My love and thanks to him, and to our children, Ashani, Christiana, Marianne, Nyah and Lewis, who made me feel how proud they were of Mom at every stage. I am equally proud of them.

Just over two years ago, I walked into Nelle Andrew's office with fragments of a novel. She saw a future for it and made sure I did too. I couldn't imagine a better agent, or a more phenomenal woman.

I'd also like to thank Alexandra Cliff for her help and advice *en route* to publication, as well as the entire team at Peters, Fraser & Dunlop.

I was lucky that this book passed through the hands of three incredible editors: Katy Loftus (UK), who seemed to read my mind from our first phone call to the last line edit, Emily Griffin (USA) and Iris Tupholme (Canada), for their wisdom and insight. They made this a better book.

My thanks to the entire team at Viking, including Rosanna Forte, Anna Ridley, Jane Gentle, Hannah Ludbrook, Lindsay Terrell, Emma Brown, John Hamilton, Gill Heeley and Scott Heron. And to Hazel Orme, an eagle-eyed and patient copyeditor. My thanks in advance to the teams at Harper Collins in New York and Toronto.

I owe a huge debt to the English teachers and librarians who entertained my endless requests for more war poems and more Jane Austen. The debt I owe to Mrs Mountcastle can never be repaid.

My thanks to everyone involved with the MSt programme at Cambridge University, in particular Jem Poster, who supervised early drafts; Sarah Burton, who sent me a book of oral histories; Midge Gillies, who planted the seed; and my fellow students, Jo Sadler and David Prosser. My thanks also to the judges of the Lucy Cavendish Fiction Prize, as well as the team at Lucy Cavendish College.

My friends kept me sane, laughing and, in some cases, fed: Jo Sadler, Emma Wiseman, Sasha Beattie, Dalia Akar, Cassie Wallis, Hana Akram, Helena Reynolds, Magda Embury, Penny Brandon, Rosalie Wain.

Finally, thank you to my parents, for encouraging my love of Jamaica even after we'd left it. And to my Jamaican grandparents: Florence and Theodore Grant, and Henry Duckworth Collins, whose sacrifices and achievements made my life possible.